Twelve
Days
in May

Niamh Hargan was born in Derry, Northern Ireland. She is an entertainment lawyer, and a regular attendee at the Cannes Film Festival. Whilst there, she always focuses resolutely on the work at hand, and does not get at all distracted by the sunshine or the celebrities. She doesn't even really care about that stuff.

Twelve Days in May is her first novel.

Twelve Days

Days

in May

NIAMH HARGAN

HarperCollins*Publishers*

HarperCollins*Publishers* Ltd
1 London Bridge Street,
London SE1 9GF
www.harpercollins.co.uk

HarperCollins*Publishers*
1st Floor, Watermarque Building, Ringsend Road
Dublin 4, Ireland

First published by HarperCollins*Publishers* 2022
1

A catalogue record for this book is
available from the British Library

ISBN: 978-0-00-851888-2

This novel is entirely a work of fiction.
The names, characters and incidents portrayed in it are
the work of the author's imagination. Any resemblance to
actual persons, living or dead, events or localities is
entirely coincidental.

Set in Sabon by Palimpsest Book Production Ltd,
Falkirk, Stirlingshire

Printed and bound in the UK using 100% Renewable
Electricity by CPI Group (UK) Ltd

MIX
Paper from
responsible sources
FSC™ C007454

This book is produced from independently certified FSC™ paper
to ensure responsible forest management.

For more information visit: www.harpercollins.co.uk/green

Mostly because of my mother, Roisin, whose belief in me is steadfast, and often hilarious, and has made everything feel possible.

And because of my grandmother, Isabell, who knew how to tell a story.

Chapter One

To say that Ciaran Flynn ruins Lizzy's first day in Cannes seems a little pathetic, and maybe hyperbolic, and certainly like it gives him a degree of power he does not deserve. But the fact of the matter is, he somewhat ruins her first day in Cannes.

She checks into her Airbnb – a cramped little apartment that is really more like an en-suite bedroom – and she thinks about him.

She sits on a bench by the *pétanque* court, eating an ice cream cone, and she thinks about him.

She goes out to dinner with all her co-workers from the Scottish Film Board, and still, she thinks about him.

Of course, had Lizzy simply gone elsewhere for lunch that afternoon, she knows that the whole thing might easily have been avoided. As it was, she had been in town no more than an hour, just off a sticky-sweaty bus from Nice, and she'd chosen the little place on Rue Saint-Antoine entirely at random. It had felt, in the short term, like a very good decision. The sun was shining out on the patio and, up by the hostess station, a man was engaged in a small-scale battle of wills with a café employee. This, frankly, was the sort of thing Lizzy lived for, in people-watching terms.

'I asked your colleague here for the ham and cheese sandwich,' the customer had been insisting, his frustration ever more apparent. He spoke in the sort of Estuary-English that, in Lizzy's estimation, sounded a little affected somehow; as though it may have materialised *after* the receipt of a two-hundred-and-fifty-grand education. 'But just with chicken instead of the ham. She said that wasn't possible, so I said I'd take the ham and cheese to go then. Now apparently there's some kind of issue with that, too.'

'Yes,' the waiter had replied. '*Sur place* only. We do not offer our dishes . . . *to go.*'

He'd said this so disdainfully, in English so heavily accented, that Lizzy had been sure he must've been having a little fun with the situation, play-acting somewhat. She'd felt a frisson of delight dart through her. It was just good to be back.

The thing about this town was that – at least during the festival – it could often seem like an entity all of its own; like a sort of large film set or holiday resort. European-ish, sure, but essentially untethered to any particular nation or sense of normality.

Then, every so often, the true situation was made clear: Cannes was in *France*.

And Lizzy herself happened to love France. She loved the French, even. Nonetheless, the fact remained that in France, at least according to her experience, there could quite often be a gap between the way things were, and the way you might ideally like them to be. This was not a gap that could be closed by sheer force of personality.

The customer before Lizzy in the cafe had been very far from the first uninitiated visitor whom she'd seen mistakenly think otherwise.

'Alright then mate,' he had conceded wearily. 'I have to say, though, it's just a bit like . . . y'know. You got all these people coming into town for the film festival, they wanna spend money . . . I don't really understand why you can't just take the thing you were gonna put on a plate and put it in a box, d'you know what I mean?'

A long pause had followed.

'I see what you mean,' the waiter had said then, primly.

The other man's whole posture had shifted. 'Oh! Well . . . great! Fantastic. I'll just take—'

''Owever, it is 2.45,' the waiter had interrupted. 'Unfortunately, the lunch service completed at 2.30. You can sit outside only for drinks now.'

At this, Lizzy had almost laughed aloud, which was very unkind because, over the years, she had been thwarted so many times in exactly this way herself, and doubtless she would be again. She hadn't quite been able to restrain a little splutter into her coffee cup, though, and when it threatened to draw attention her way, she had rushed to avert her gaze, reaching reflexively for her cell phone. Moments later, out of the corner of her eye, she'd become vaguely aware of another person approaching, clapping the English man on the shoulder.

'What kept you? Are they killing your chicken out the back?' this new arrival had asked. It wasn't so much *what* he had said that struck Lizzy, but the *way* he had said it. That voice.

3

Her eyes had flickered back upwards from her phone, and there he was.

Of course, she'd seen Ciaran occasionally, over the past twelve years – in silhouettes on the street sometimes; staring out at her from the TimeHop photos that periodically popped up unbidden on her phone; once, on the front cover of the Culture section of the *Sunday fucking Times*.

The real thing, however, had turned out to be quite a different experience.

And by some force that was probably no force at all, just coincidence, his eyes had landed right on hers.

Lizzy had just about managed a mute raise of her hand before he'd looked away sharply, turning instead to meet his friend's curious expression.

'Who, her?' she'd heard him mutter. 'Nobody. Just . . . somebody I used to know.'

He'd rushed to chivvy the other man along – with some further complaint, no doubt, about the unwashed public, or their tiresome over-eagerness – and then he was gone. Without so much as another glance in her direction, he'd walked straight past her.

That's the thing that gets Lizzy the most, now.

Does she want to be Ciaran Flynn's friend? Absolutely not.

Does she want anything from him whatsoever? Also no.

That he had outright ignored her, though? That had been too much. The *hubris* of it.

Probably, she thinks to herself, with some perverse little bit of relish, she should not be surprised. Success doesn't always change people, but when it does, it is not known to be for the better. How embarrassing for him, really, to have believed his own hype like that.

Of course, the other option, a tiny voice inside of Lizzy whispers, is that Ciaran is still perfectly down to earth with other people, but that he had simply found himself unable to stand the sight of *her*.

The prospect smarts in a way that she would never, ever, admit out loud. But, to herself? Yeah. To herself, she can acknowledge that the thought gnaws at her when she might otherwise be, for example, trying to figure out the rules of *pétanque*, or paying attention to her boss over *moules marinière*. It makes her feel sad and angry and confused, and of that particular buffet, she knows the anger is probably the least healthy thing, but it turns out to be by far the easiest to metabolise.

*

The next morning, Lizzy throws open the shutters to let the day in, and she decides: she is *done* with thinking about him. *Fuck him!* she thinks blithely, feeling high on Vitamin D. One day was fine – maybe she could fairly legitimately claim that he stole that from her. But any more than that, she suspects she might just be giving away. And this is the Cannes Film Festival. Over the course of the next twelve days, forty thousand film-makers and adjacent 'creatives' will circulate in and out of town to do business, drink rosé, and talk about the need for strong female characters. It's important for Lizzy to be on her game work-wise. Maybe this year more than any other.

In her teeny-tiny bedroom, the process of getting ready is a delicate balancing exercise. She'll be meeting lots of new people, or reuniting with those she hasn't seen since last year's festival, and therefore she definitely wants to look better than she usually does. But, not *so* much better that the co-workers who see her every day will think she's tried pathetically hard. She settles for a new mustard-coloured sundress that, if asked, she might tell people is old, a jacket that actually *is* old, and an attempt at some minor improvement to her hair with the curling wand. Then, she's out the door. It's a perfect 23°C as she ambles along the main road in town – the Croisette – stopping along the way to pick up coffee and a croissant for breakfast.

There are many versions of this festival, and in comparison with helicoptering into a luxury hotel in Cap d'Antibes and being chauffeured down to Cannes for the premieres and yacht parties, Lizzy knows that her particular version is decidedly low-rent. It's holding on to expense receipts, and going to the pharmacy for blister plasters, and sometimes, shoving a Steak 'n' Shake burger in her mouth in between meetings because she has time for nothing else. Nonetheless, looking around her now, she can't help but feel pretty satisfied with her lot. These twelve days are still more energising than the entire remainder of her year back in Edinburgh; still more glamorous than anything she ever would have imagined growing up in Ferndale, California.

This early in the morning, the streets are quiet. In fact, as festival attendees collect their passes and ease into the swing of things, the whole opening day is typically fairly calm. There is just a pleasant hum of activity, a sense of anticipation in the air, as Lizzy makes her way past all the designer stores and down towards the International Village.

Running parallel to the beach, the International Village is a sectioned-off chunk of road, guarded at each end by an airport-style security scanner and some Frenchmen avoiding eye contact. Within it, a red carpet has been laid, and a row of temporary white 'pavilions' erected; marquees, essentially – the fancy kind, with walls and carpets, and back decks that lead directly out onto the beach. Each is rented by the national film commission of a different country, twenty thousand euros the minimum price-tag on having some little corner of Cannes to call your own. Meetings and panel events throughout the daytime give way to cocktail receptions and showcases in the evening, and over the course of the festival, delegates could more or less make their way around the world, culinarily-speaking. Word would get around: *there's sushi and sake over in the Japanese Pavilion tonight; are you going for margaritas in the Spanish Pavilion?* Yes, it was true that having finagled your way into such events, you were then required to at least feign some interest in the cinematic output of a particular country or producer. But that is no great hardship for Lizzy. So far as she sees it, she has to do quite a lot of that in the context of her job anyway, and oftentimes *without* any free food or drink into the mix.

By the time she gets into the Scottish Pavilion, some of her colleagues have arrived already. There is that same palpable buzz of excitement that she'd felt outside, and she greets everyone with much more enthusiasm than she might on an average Thursday morning.

Only half a dozen of the Board's regular staff members get to come from Edinburgh to Cannes, and their festival-time duties fall into three basic categories.

The first is to meet with those delegates who haven't made very much, if indeed anything at all – people who thus might well be quite bad at making films, but who nonetheless are extremely keen to explain why the Scottish Film Board should provide them with some cash in order to do just that.

The second – and more important – job, conversely, is to meet with (or, make best efforts to *get* a meeting with) those who have made *lots* of films already. People whom the Film Board is desperately keen to lure to Scotland's many and varied filming locations with the promise of tax incentives or support packages or the sacrificial gift of a firstborn child, if only said filmmakers could be persuaded to accept.

It can be sort of discombobulating, Lizzy always finds, bouncing from being the woo-ee to the woo-er a dozen times inside a day. But, the third thing required of staff goes at least some way toward combatting that whiplash. It is to 'be available'.

The theory, presumably, is that if Steven Spielberg should by chance wander into the Scottish Pavilion, see the sweeping still shots of the Highlands that adorn mounted screens everywhere, and be struck by a sudden compulsion to ship in his next hundred-million-dollar production, there should be someone immediately on hand to discuss that with him.

In practice, being available, for Lizzy, mostly means wandering around wearing a lanyard with a saltire on it and answering emails on her phone. Or, alternatively

– and, in fact, far preferably – sitting up at the welcome desk, shooting the shit with whoever else is around. She's taken the executive decision to dedicate more or less the entire first day to 'being available'.

'Seems pretty mental to be getting paid for this, doesn't it?' Shauna says, as Lizzy sidles up next to her on the deck, and the two of them look out over blue sky and blue sea. Shauna is the Film Board's graduate marketing assistant. She has a thick Glaswegian accent, bright red hair from a bottle, and a level of confidence that not everyone in the office seems to find appealing in such a young person. Lizzy mostly admires it. Sometimes, she catches herself thinking of the two of them as being roughly the same age, and then she realises – no. She *had* been roughly Shauna's age, back when she'd started at the Film Board herself, at twenty-three. Now, she's thirty-two. Which isn't old. Of course Lizzy doesn't think that's *old*. But neither does it seem to correspond quite so comfortably to the thing she'd definitely been for such a long time before – namely, *young*. The notion that perhaps her life might have taken its basic shape by now – that certain things, if they were going to happen at all, maybe would have happened already – has begun to creep into her consciousness in a way that has felt a little like loss. And the crazy thing is, she doesn't know why, because she has a good life – an incredibly lucky, good life. It's just thirty-two, she thinks. The liminality of it. Occasionally – and especially when combined with four or more cocktails – it has proven to be somewhat of a petri dish for panic.

Shauna, wide-eyed and on her first trip to Cannes, is years away from such concerns. 'I don't really know what to do with myself,' she continues, looking around giddily.

Inside, several rows of seats are neatly set out in front of the little stage and podium, all ready for the afternoon's programme of events – and at the tables and chairs on the deck, there are already a couple of early birds working on laptops. But all is serene. There are more staff members in the Scottish Pavilion than anyone else.

'This place'll be packed by tomorrow morning,' Lizzy says. 'You should just enjoy it while it lasts. Go take a walk around the other pavilions. Pick up some free pens.'

'Can we just walk into all of them?'

'All of them except the American Pavilion. You have to pay extra to get in there.'

'Even if you *are* American?'

'Yeah. I learned that one the hard way,' Lizzy says dryly. 'I gotta say, it's actually sort of worth the money though – it's super nice. At least five times bigger than this. They have a full restaurant service in there, basically. They bring in these interns from some culinary school in the States.'

'Wow. Fancy.'

'Yeah. Plus they have way more famous people on their events schedule, obviously. And a tonne of places to charge your phone.'

'Celebrities *and* plugs,' Shauna declares. 'That does sound good, to be fair. Ah, but here's the question, though!' Her eyes widen comically as she lifts her index finger. 'Do they have a ceilidh?'

Lizzy just laughs in response, doing her best to ignore the slight queasiness that swirls in her stomach at the reminder. The Scottish Film Board hasn't had a ceilidh either until this year – wouldn't be having one at all had it not been for her cajoling and planning and assuring

Simon that of course a raucous evening of Gaelic folk music and dancing was just what the Cannes Film Festival needed. It would be *great*, she'd said.

And it *will* be great, she tells herself again now. Why would it not be? Even removing from the equation all the elements for which she is personally responsible – which, admittedly, amounts to quite a lot of elements – there is going to be alcohol, and it is going to be on a beach. How badly, really, could that work out?

It occurs to her, though, that she does need to set about finalising the press release fairly swiftly. And she has to update the list of attendees, and she's due to email the venue to arrange a walkthrough, and . . . well. On and on her list goes.

She'd once thought that the whole project, though not remotely in the realm of her actual job description, would be pretty enjoyable. Any time she'd seen an event planner in the movies, it had seemed like the sort of job that could be done in a very breezy and empowering fashion. The reality, alas, has involved a lot more admin and stress than she'd ever bargained for.

She picks a quiet table in the far corner of the terrace, pulling her laptop out of her backpack.

'Alright, you gotta get outta here,' she tells Shauna, 'I have to do some work.'

The younger girl rolls her eyes dramatically. 'Ugh.'

Lizzy plays along. 'I know! I don't know what to tell you, Shauna. It's like people don't even realise I'm trying to have a goddamn vacation here.'

11

Chapter Two

By noon, Simon sticks his head outside. 'Lizzy,' he says discreetly, though there is scarcely anyone around to overhear him, 'do you want to just step inside for a moment? Team meeting.'

Inside the pavilion, much to Lizzy's surprise, everyone is gathered in a sort of huddle – the folks from home plus a bunch of local temps, hired for the duration of the festival to serve coffees out on the deck, and to help with general lifting and laying. Something fizzy that is probably not champagne is being poured into plastic champagne flutes, and Lizzy's co-worker Brendan hands her one.

'Mm, what *is* this?' she asks, after the first sip. 'It's good!'

'Cava and some of that Edinburgh Gin liqueur. Elderflower or something I think?'

'Rhubarb and ginger,' Simon chimes in.

Lizzy takes another sip. The concoction doesn't even taste alcoholic, which is always a dangerous thing.

'So, what's all this in aid of?' she asks. Her boss is a man in his fifties, with a gentle brogue and the neatest, most pristine beard she's ever seen. She likes him well enough – and, more critically, she feels that he likes her – but he is reserved. Fiscally responsible. Not especially known to be the starter of anything approaching a party.

'Well, you know,' Simon shrugs. Something about the way he speaks always makes Lizzy feel that she has to lean in to hear him. 'I just thought, we'll all be pulled in different directions after today; whilst we're all here together, and it's quiet, we may as well start the festival off with a touch of festivity! Plus, you know,' – again, he shrugs, somewhat helplessly – 'we have all this gin.'

'Right,' Lizzy agrees. They really do have a lot of gin, thanks to Edinburgh Gin having come aboard as a sponsor this year. It feels like a major step up from Tunnock's tea cakes and Walker's shortbread, both of which have always been in constant supply in the Scottish Pavilion, and neither of which Lizzy can drum up much enthusiasm for anymore. She very much hopes the gin doesn't go the same way. It is possible, she knows now, to have too much of a good thing.

In the huddle, Simon says a few words, and they all clink glasses before the conversation splinters.

'Are you from Cannes?' Lizzy finds herself asking one of the French temps, for lack of much else to say to him.

Non, he informs her. He has lived in Cannes for three years, but in fact he is from Rouen.

'Ah! *Dans le nord!*' she proclaims, much more jubilantly than the situation probably merits. He, too, looks absolutely delighted.

'*Exactement, ouais. Vous parlez français?*'

'*Juste un petit peu*,' she replies, which is not false modesty. It is, at this point, merely the truth.

'*Mais non, vous parlez super bien!*'

Lizzy just smiles. A lifetime of tourist inundation seems to have left the people of Cannes disproportionately grateful for, and complimentary towards, any linguistic effort whatsoever.

From beside them, Brendan has witnessed the brief exchange, and he reaches out to her forearm. 'That's right!' he marvels. 'I forgot, you actually lived in France for a while didn't you, Lizzy?'

And of course, it's a fine thing to say; a totally normal, nice thing to say. Nonetheless, something tenses ever so slightly inside of her.

'Just for a year, yeah. Or, not even that, I guess. Nine months.'

'Whereabouts, again?'

'Bordeaux,' she says shortly.

'That's right. What took you there?'

What had taken her there, mostly, had been a sudden and overwhelming desire to get as far away as she possibly could from her parents. And, for that matter, from a dentist named Neal. She feels inclined to share none of this.

'I did Erasmus as part of my degree,' she offers instead. 'You know the "study abroad" scheme?'

'Mmm vaguely,' Brendan says, in the tone of voice that Lizzy knows, from experience, means he has very little idea of what she is talking about, but isn't about to admit it

'Anyway,' she shrugs. 'That's where they sent me, so that's where I went.'

'How amazing!' Brendan replies. 'I've always quite fancied Bordeaux myself, what with the wine and everything. Me and Lisa talked about doing a weekend there. Did you love it?'

'It's a beautiful city, yeah,' Lizzy says, trying to meet his enthusiasm with some approximation of it herself. On the inside, though, that little thread of instinctive resistance remains. It just feels like it would be counter-productive, traipsing too far down this particular path – today of all days. When she'd begun her morning with such determination to avoid it. She arranges her face into some expression of sudden alertness, as though she's been reminded of an urgent task to attend to.

'Oh! Hey, I'll be right back, okay?' she says, motioning vaguely with her hand. The difficulty, however, is that even as she begins to back away, there are limited places to actually *go*. Her options are out onto the deck again, or through the curtain divider and into the little reception area. She plumps for the latter, surprised to find a young girl there, sitting at a high-top seat behind the welcome desk. Given the footfall inside the pavilion right now, it very much seems that the post could have survived unattended for a few minutes.

'Hi!' she chirps, with a little wave. 'I'm Lizzy. Everyone's having a drink back there if you want to go say hello? I can hold the fort here.'

The young girl hesitates. 'Are you sure?' she asks, in careful English.

'Totally sure,' Lizzy replies. In fact, this is the best seat in the house so far as she's concerned. She likes to see all the comings and goings.

Hopping up onto the chair that the girl vacates, she slips her jacket off and sets her plastic glass on the desk in front of her. True to form, she notices a big bowl of Walker's shortbread right there, the tartan wrappers practically as familiar to Lizzy as her own face. By now, she's lived in Scotland longer than she ever lived in the States. Yet still, she sounds (mostly) American, and of course she *is* (half) American. She knows that her Americanness likely remains the first thing that many people think about, when they think of her. It's funny to have ended up in this job that is, in a lot of ways, rooted in an identity she cannot fully claim. Undeniably, the thought of being able to say, 'I'm Lizzy, I'm one of the development executives at the Scottish Film Board' without the other person looking confused, or surprised, or otherwise trying to figure her out . . . that does seem like it would be nice. Convenient. She wouldn't mind skipping the zillionth rehearsal of her own biography.

Realistically, though, she knows that obligation would likely exist even separate to her current job. It definitely had predated it. With this thought, as she lifts her glass to drain the last of her drink, her mind drifts once again to Bordeaux. Extremely, *extremely* unsatisfactorily, she can't seem to stop it.

2010, that was the year. Obama was president, and nobody had internet on their phones, and Lizzy was twenty years old.

When she looks back on it now, she's sure that in the first two months of being there, in Bordeaux, some interesting or educational things must have happened to her. She certainly remembers a lot of hard things happening. Just the process of registering the basic fact of her existence

– with the university, and the electricity company, and half a dozen other places – had been an utter hellscape. And that was before taking into account the savage tide of her own fucking *feelings*. In the course of those early weeks, she had definitely cried on multiple forms of public transport.

Largely, though, all of that now feels essentially like preface. Prelude. Prologue. In Lizzy's memory, the whole experience didn't really begin at all until late October.

She remembers exactly where she was, that night – in a tiny apartment that she had never been to before, but that she could soon see was filled with mostly-familiar faces and mostly-familiar Ikea furniture. Caroline had come with her, of course. She and Caroline Gilhooly had barely known one another when they decided to move into their little two-bedroom on Rue Cabirol, but they had been the only students coming to Bordeaux from the University of Edinburgh. It had seemed to make sense. Caroline was from Stirling, and had apparently been Deputy Head Girl in school, a fact from which Lizzy had extrapolated that she had been driven and clever, but that someone else had been just as driven and clever, and perhaps also more well-liked. She had strong thoughts on Africa, having taken an extremely impactful trip there during the previous summer, and strong thoughts on any form of meat entering the apartment.

In truth, Lizzy was already beginning to find it quite a task, co-existing alongside the sheer array of Caroline's strong thoughts on things. But she was doing her best. And, arriving to the party that night, she could remember being grateful for Caroline. Arriving to things was always the time that she was most grateful for Caroline. Just for that ring of the doorbell, those initial two or three minutes, it was nice to have somebody.

What else? Clothes. To this day, Lizzy recalls precisely what she was wearing. A leopard-print dress made of a blousy material – chiffon, maybe, or something chiffon-adjacent. It had puffed sleeves and, in the sale, had cost a grand total of £13.75 the year before. With this, she wore black tights and her trusty black boots, and a hairband with cat ears affixed to it.

The cat ears were critical. They, together with some whiskers drawn hastily on her cheeks with eyeliner pencil, were what made the whole thing a costume.

Chapter Three

The flat was owned – or rather, occupied – by three Irish guys, and in its little kitchenette, Lizzy hunkered down on the tiles, attempting to cram her pack of Desperados into a tiny refrigerator.

'Lizzy, you look so cute! Bonsoir!' came a lilting voice from behind her.

English was the first language for most of the Erasmus cohort, and the second for apparently all the others, such that, right from the outset, everyone spoke English to one another. A sprinkling of semi-ironic *bonjour*s or *merci*s was typically about as Gallic as things got.

Lizzy did sometimes worry about the effect that this would have on her French (which was to say, no effect – or, more to the point, no *improvement*), but mostly, in practical terms, it was a relief. And, in any event, the situation was immutable now. For her to have approached one of the other students *en français* at this stage would have seemed utterly bizarre.

When she turned, Charlotte, from Bristol, was standing there – everyone, now, had acquired a little geo-tag like that after their name. She was dressed as a fairy and holding out a large glass of red wine.

'Stop fighting with those beers and have a glass of wine,' she smiled.

Lizzy hesitated.

'Go on! It's poured now; it'd be rude not to.'

It sort of seemed like it actually *would* be rude not to, and so Lizzy gave up, slamming the fridge door shut – good luck, she thought, to whoever opened it next.

'Thank you,' she said, getting to her feet and accepting the offered glass. 'You guys look so great! How *are* you? How's your week been?'

'Good, yeah. D'you know, Lizzy, it's so weird, I was actually just saying to Emma,' – at this, Charlotte glanced at the redhead next to her – 'I don't think I even know what part of America you're from.'

'Oh. California,' she said, and for good measure, she went ahead and anticipated the next few questions too. 'That's where my mom's from, and then my dad is Scottish, so we moved to Edinburgh when I was fifteen.'

Charlotte's face lit up with enthusiasm. 'Oh, wow! So did you grow up just, like, going to the beach *all* the time?'

Lizzy took a sip of her wine, trying not to wince as it hit the back of her throat. She was not generally a wine drinker, and in the situations where it was unavoidable, her order of preference was very much rosé, then white, *then* red. In other words, so far as she saw it, from least to most . . . wine-like.

'Y'know, not really,' she replied. 'We were more northern California.'

'Ohmygod, wine country, how amazing! Bordeaux must be like home from home!' Emma (also from Bristol) chimed in.

And Emma, while totally wrong on this point, had thus far in Lizzy's estimation shown herself to be basically a nice person, so Lizzy just smiled.

'I guess kinda, yeah,' she replied noncommittally.

What she'd found was that sometimes, at parties – and this was in no way specific to parties in France – the most important thing in a conversation was just to keep it moving. If you had to sacrifice a little accuracy along the way, so be it.

The strictly factual version of this whole California chat had always proved a bit of a disappointment to people, really. The town where Lizzy was born was about as far north as you could get without being in Oregon, and boasted a distinct lack of either vineyards or celebrities. It was known for spectacular redwood forests, some sporadic Victorian architecture and more recently – following the decline of the logging and fishing industries – for the large-scale growth of marijuana. It had actually been a nice place to grow up, but this did not mean it offered any especially great conversational fodder.

Upon her arrival in Scotland at the age of fifteen (*fifteen*; surely the absolute worst possible time to have to move to a new country), Lizzy had been greeted by an initial flurry of excitement from the other girls in her new school. That had faded fast when she'd admitted that the Hollywood sign felt scarcely any more remote upon touchdown in Edinburgh than it had from her particular corner of California.

When the topic came up, she'd always felt slightly self-conscious on a physical level too. Maybe that was ridiculous; she knew it was probably ridiculous, and probably a hangover from the move at the Worst Possible Time. But it was just that Californians generally presented on the world stage in a certain way. That image had been so thoroughly drilled into people's brains; beachy blonde hair, blue eyes, tanned legs and a sparkling smile.

To have been born without any of those things felt, to Lizzy, unfortunate enough in itself. But to have to claim relationship to a place that seemed almost *bound* to bring their absence to other people's attention – that felt just plain unfair.

What God had given Lizzy, instead of anything good, was a decidedly undainty five-foot-seven frame, a nose and chin that competed for prominence, and hipbones that appeared destined always – no matter how much exercise she might do – to be wider than her waist by more than was quite proportional. Also, one crooked canine tooth, on which Lizzy had spent such a portion of her teenage years trying fruitlessly to perform some sort of at-home orthodontics that sometimes, in the evenings, she still found herself unconsciously putting pressure on it with her thumb. She had dark brown hair reaching halfway down her back, and matching dark brown eyes, and had once been declared by her cousins to be 'kinda Portuguese-looking'. Needless to say, these were not her cousins in Scotland, where the subject of Caucasian ethnicity never seemed to come up. By contrast, white Americans were, in Lizzy's experience, pretty interested in discussing the heritage or possible heritage of other white Americans, and her own relatives were no exception. Their assessment of her had seemed like a very specific one, and she'd never been to Portugal, so she had no real sense of its accuracy.

However, when it came to her face and body, she was well aware of the cumulative effect, the basic upshot. There wasn't any way for a girl to get to twenty years old without discovering whether or not she was hot. And Lizzy, very definitely, was not.

*

On the far side of the living room, there were floor-to-ceiling windows that opened out onto a little balcony. Balcony, perhaps, was a generous term – it was largely a decorative feature, too narrow to actually be stepped onto. But, it was providing some much-needed ventilation, and it was big enough to lean out on and smoke, as some people were doing.

There seemed, Lizzy noticed, to be a bit of debate happening in that general direction, and at the centre of it was one of the Irish guys who lived in this apartment. He was someone she'd *been around* before, more so than spoken to. Ciaran, she thought his name was. He was tall and had dark hair that looked like it could do with a trim, and that was more or less all Lizzy knew about him.

His side was towards her, and he was wearing black dress trousers and a jacket. From what she could tell, all the collective focus seemed to be on his shirt. Three or four people gestured at it and talked over each other while he just smiled, shaking his head intermittently.

Lizzy craned her neck to get a better look. In black marker on a plain white t-shirt was scrawled the word 'SORRY'.

'Ah, come on! Sure it's obvious!' he was saying now to much surrounding hilarity and protest.

And in fact, to Lizzy, it *was* obvious. This was for one reason and one reason only: yesterday – much as she presumed Ciaran must also have done – she had googled the phrase 'last-minute Halloween costume ideas'.

'He's a formal apology!' she called over loftily, raising her voice a little to be heard. The huddle turned to look at her.

For two or three seconds, there was silence, then a satisfying, high-spirited hubbub of reaction to her little announcement broke out. She grinned, and Ciaran turned to look at her.

'Bingo,' he called over, with a smile.

She shrugged, not bothering to hide her smugness. Exaggerating it, perhaps, if anything.

'And are you . . . a pirate?' he asked, taking in her appearance. He had a weird accent, she thought.

She rolled her eyes, biting back a smile.

'No.'

'Are you an angel?'

'Obviously yes, but I'm not dressed as one,' she fired back, with the raise of an eyebrow. This was not in a sexy way, because Lizzy would have had no real idea of how to even go about that, and would have been embarrassed to be caught trying. But, she knew for sure that she could pull off wry, and when he laughed spontaneously – genuinely – it felt nice to know that she had hit the mark.

'Are you . . . a cat?' he asked then; evidently, and to his credit, he knew to give up the gag before it got old. Still, something in her couldn't quite let him have it.

'Close,' she said, sympathetically. 'I'm a tiger. But that was definitely close.'

He nodded, taking on the posture of one unquestionably defeated, but gracious in it.

'It's in the cat family,' he agreed readily, with a quick drag from his cigarette.

She couldn't help it then; she burst out laughing, feeling warm and loose and happy. After one glass of red wine, the second and third had gone down pretty easily. He laughed too, and as Lizzy held her glass up to him in salutation, he returned the gesture.

By the time she got back to the little group she'd been in, someone had nabbed her spot on the couch, but she didn't care. Lizzy dragged a folding chair over beside Mia and Hans, German students whom she'd met once at orientation and who – she'd discovered just this evening – were very funny. Also, a couple. Up until now, they'd been sufficiently low-key about their coupledom for Lizzy not to have even been aware of it, which she appreciated. She appreciated, too, that Mia had come to the party dressed as a witch. Not a sexy witch or, indeed, a sexy version of anything else, which was the basic theme around which many of the other girls seemed to have worked. Just a witch, with a fully green face and a drawn-on wart.

'You know, I really like red wine,' Lizzy announced, to nobody in particular. 'In fact, I think that's what I'm going to do this year.'

'What?' Mia asked, over the hum of other conversation.

'Get into red wine. As in like *get into* it. Y'know? Learn about all the different types and stuff. Wouldn't that be a good life skill?'

Hans laughed. 'Definitely. You should go out to the vineyards in Saint-Émilion. They do tours and tastings and things.'

'I *will*, Hans! Thank you! That's *exactly* what I'll do!' she beamed, and then a wonderful idea occurred to her. 'We should *all* go!'

Emma came up then, brandishing her camera. Little pocket-sized ones, often in shiny metallic colours, were as common back then as cell phones and, at least among the girls, were right up there with cell phones in terms of importance. *Phone camera keys wallet lip balm*, that was the recitation on the way out the door.

At Emma's urging, all those in the vicinity bunched together, maybe eight or nine of them in all, and Lizzy felt a rush of affection for these people. Even Caroline.

She hadn't found it easy, so far, being surrounded in this city exclusively by people who didn't really know her. It had been discombobulating and tiring and just plain lonely. Tonight, though, things felt different. The gap between *friendly* and *friends* seemed like it was narrowing a little bit, which was nice. More than that, there was the new sense that maybe the element of the unknown – of *being* unknown – was actually sort of nice too. Liberating, somehow. As though she were suddenly looking in at her life from the outside, and it was 'full of delightful possibilities' like Miss Honey's chocolate box from *Matilda*. She'd watched that movie a lot as a child.

The camera flashed and Lizzy found her mind leaping briefly, as it often did, to what she might be doing in Edinburgh now. For perhaps the first time ever, she concluded that she'd rather be right here, doing this.

Chapter Four

The next morning, Lizzy woke at seven o'clock. Ordinarily, without the prompting of an alarm, she'd happily sleep through 'til noon, but cruelly, when she was hungover – in other words, when she'd most dearly love to just let the hours pass in a state of unconsciousness – she was always awake with the larks.

Her stomach churned and her head throbbed, and as she padded to the tiny kitchen of her apartment on Rue Cabirol, light streamed in through the windows aggressively. It looked like it was going to be a beautiful, sunny Sunday, which she didn't care about whatsoever. Already, the entire day felt like a loss.

She stood at the kitchen counter, letting the water run for a few minutes, before filling a glass and downing it along with two painkillers. After a disappointing rummage around the fridge – although, quite what she was looking for she didn't even know – she managed to unearth some LU biscuits in a cupboard and ate three of them in quick succession, followed by another glass of water.

None of this made her feel any better physically and, in fact, it perhaps even made her feel slightly worse. However, she at least had the small satisfaction of feeling like she'd done the right thing; made some kind of investment in this hideousness dissipating a little faster than it otherwise might have done.

Crawling back into her little twin bed, newly grateful for the near-total darkness that her wooden shutters provided, Lizzy closed her eyes and prayed for sleep.

*

By the time she was able to make it back out of her bedroom, it was after midday and Caroline had disappeared off somewhere – most likely to one of her networking events. When the opportunity had arisen, a few weeks prior, to join Bordeaux Women in Business, Lizzy had known immediately that she'd rather eat her own feet. But Caroline recognised a résumé-builder when she saw one, and she had since begun to proffer satisfied little details of the meet-ups she'd attended, as though Lizzy might be seized with regret over what she too could have had.

In fact, Lizzy was grateful beyond belief for what she now *did* have, which was the apartment to herself on a semi-regular basis.

She stared at herself bleakly in the bathroom mirror, wondering whether she could get away with not washing her hair. Probably, she decided, she could. Quickly, she showered, pulled on some clothes and made her way down to the cobbled street below.

All she really wanted was a family-sized bag of barbecue-flavoured Lays, a bottle of Diet Coke and to wander the aisles vacantly for a while and see what jumped out at her. Not a lot to ask. But it was Sunday, meaning none of these simple pleasures were available. So keen were the French to preserve the sanctity of the thirty-five-hour working week that every super-market in town would be closed. This was how Lizzy came, instead, to be sitting outside Le Café Français – chosen exclusively for its proximity to her apartment – picking at a chicken salad and feeling like death. Red wine, she thought, was obviously just its own thing. Or at least in the quantity that she had drunk it. That was definitely its own thing.

Directly in front of her stood Cathédrale St Andre, spectacular in scale and style, the sandstone of its gothic spires now almost black in parts. Little craft stalls had been set up around its perimeter and Lizzy let her attention drift, watching all the comings and goings – other people really had such wholesome lives – until, suddenly, she found herself jolted back into self-awareness.

Ambling across the square, his arms swinging at his sides, was one of the few people in this city whom she actually knew. Ciaran. Irish, 'formal apology' Ciaran.

Sometimes, it was hard not to feel as if the universe was fucking with you, just a little bit. It wasn't that Lizzy had any problem with seeing him in particular – it was just that she'd pretty much relied on seeing nobody at all today. Inside a matter of seconds, she mentally zipped through the various possibilities. Had he seen her too? Or could she ignore him? If he *had* seen her, would it seem rude if she ignored him? Or was that really his preferred situation? Did—

'Hey!' she heard herself call out then, before her brain could even finish the thought. She barely had to raise her voice – he was no more than six feet away from her.

Ciaran stopped in his tracks, and she could tell by the look of surprise on his face that he hadn't spotted her at all. Wonderful stuff. She'd brought this on herself for nothing.

'I . . . uh, hi,' she added, a little awkwardly. She realised then that she couldn't even have said for sure that this guy knew her name. She felt the urge to introduce herself – or to provide some context for herself at the very least. But that also seemed like it might be weird.

'Hey! How are you?' he replied, all ease, closing the distance between them.

'I'm good, yeah. You?'

'Good! I've definitely felt fresher than I did this morning, like.'

He grinned ruefully, and Lizzy did the same. 'Yeah, me too.'

After that, nothing. Silence that lasted a few crucial seconds longer than it should have. Didn't he know that this was where he should be making to leave? Keeping things breezy? He, after all, was the one who could legitimately claim to have something else to do, some place to go. She was just sitting there; no exit was available to her.

'Uh . . . you wanna sit down?' she found herself asking, gesturing towards the empty seat.

Ciaran did not seem by any means to have been waiting on this invitation, hoping she might issue it. But, when it came, he took it in stride nonetheless, settling himself opposite her.

'Sure,' he said. And then, apropos of nothing, 'I've just been to the cinema.'

'Oh cool, what'd you go see?'

'It was called *The Kids Are Alright*.'

Lizzy hadn't heard of it.

'Cool,' she said, trying to imbue the word with some impression of genuine interest.

'I just really like films,' he added, as if by way of explanation. 'I know that's sort of . . . like, obviously *everybody* likes films. But, yeah. I just sort of see whatever's out, basically.'

'I actually haven't been to the movies since I got here,' she replied.

'Not your thing?'

'No, I mean . . . as much as anybody, I guess.'

'What kinda thing do you like?'

Lizzy just about suppressed the urge to sigh aloud. She hadn't gotten to this stage of her life without realising that when a boy asked your favourite film, there were two acceptable answers, depending on the genre of boy. One was *The Royal Tenenbaums*, and the other was *The Godfather*. She actually liked both, but in her delicate state, she didn't have the energy to be schooled on either of them, and specifically, on the ways in which she had failed to appreciate their full genius.

Instead, she shrugged.

'I like romcoms,' she offered up. This wasn't *un*true, though it did feel, in the circumstances, a little like bait.

Ciaran, however, just nodded readily. 'Yeah. I mean, who doesn't?'

'*You* do?' she asked, slightly incredulously.

He laughed, as though he was surprised by her surprise.

31

'Well, I don't like the shite ones! The way I see it, right, there's a good and a bad version of everything. Are there brilliant movies made about, like, the mafia or the Second World War? Yes, no question. There's also a lot of really terrible ones. I have seven nieces and nephews and—'

'Seven?!' Lizzy couldn't help but interrupt him. 'That seems like a lot.'

'Well, I have five siblings, so.'

'And where are you in the line-up?'

'Second last. I *was* the youngest, for like eight years, and then our Sinead came along.'

Lizzy shook her head. 'Fucking *Sinead.*'

It was the sort of thing she might not have said if she'd thought about it in advance. Other people's sense of humour could be hard to predict. Happily, though, Ciaran didn't miss a beat.

'I know,' he agreed, deadpan. 'Shoulda just quit while they were ahead, like. Anyway, the point is, I do a fair amount of babysitting when I'm home. Which really takes two forms – either (a) I send them out to play, or (b) we watch a bit of CBeebies. Sometimes, like, *quite* a bit. And if you sit and watch kids' TV for three hours, it'll be really obvious, really fast, that some of this stuff is just *better* than the rest of it. So, yeah,' he concluded, 'like I say. Good and a bad version of everything.'

Interesting. Lizzy had never thought about it in exactly that way.

'Okay, so let's talk about your favourite romcom,' she said then, one eyebrow slightly quirked. Somehow, quite unexpectedly, she seemed to have warmed up to this conversation, to the simple fact of Ciaran's company. 'That's what I'm interested in. Let's get back to that.'

He smiled, opening his mouth to respond right as the waitress stepped outside to attend to another customer. He shifted his attention to catch her eye. 'Hang on one sec. Do you want anything?'

It took Lizzy a moment to realise that he meant in the way of food or drink. Despite the fact that she was sitting right there, she was oddly startled that he would even think of her.

'What? Oh! No. Thanks.'

He ordered a café crème, in French, and he had a nice accent. She noticed that. Authentic-sounding but without making a performance of the whole thing.

'Shameful stalling technique there,' she said, once the waitress had gone.

He rolled his eyes. 'Okay, let me think. *When Harry Met Sally*?'

She nodded her approval.

'Pretty much anything with Katharine Hepburn.'

Again, Lizzy nodded. Unquestionably her favourite Hepburn. It wasn't that she *disliked* Audrey as a person. Obviously, she wasn't *against* humanitarianism. But on screen, she'd take gutsy over gamine every day of the week.

'What else? *Notting Hill*? I know these aren't original choices.'

'Hey, classics are classics for a reason, right?' Lizzy replied.

As a matter of fact, she appreciated Ciaran's willingness to bowl right down the middle. A huge number of people, she'd realised, tried to seem offbeat for the sake of it. She herself had made various attempts at quirkiness in adolescence, with this manifesting, by turns, in a variety of different slogan t-shirts, MSN handles and hairstyles, and at one

point, in the purchase of a record player. She hadn't ultimately had the stamina for any of it, and she was starting
to find it tiring in others too. Two years of university had
introduced her to a hell of a lot of people whose prevailing
ethos seemed to be 'I'm not like other people', and sincerity
– being much shorter in supply than irony – had begun to
feel to Lizzy that it must surely be due a comeback.

'You haven't made much of a dent in your salad,'
Ciaran said then, nodding towards it.

Lizzy winced.

'Yeah. I'm a little . . . overhung.'

He laughed. 'That's a more sophisticated version of
being hungover, is it?'

'Exactly,' she said, and gestured towards herself in
what she hoped was an obviously self-deprecating
fashion. She wished, in that moment, that she had washed
her hair. 'I'm a very sophisticated person.'

'That was some singing you were doing last night.'

At this, Lizzy had a sudden recollection of joining one
of Ciaran's roommates – another Irish guy named Liam
– for a raucous, ridiculous, sing-along performance of
'Crazy In Love', in which they both were Beyoncé, but
she alone was Jay-Z. She reached a hand to her face,
shaking her head a little. 'Oh, *God*.'

'I'm serious, you were actually really good! You can
properly sing.'

She had enough of an ego to enjoy hearing that. Still,
though, she sidestepped the compliment.

'Liam's a bad influence,' she said, cautiously trying
another forkful of her lunch. 'Y'know, I've been thinking
maybe this isn't even about the alcohol. Like, maybe I
might have food poisoning or something.'

'Oh right,' Ciaran replied. He said it perfectly benignly, but still, there was something about it. Almost *too* mild an acceptance.

'What? You think I don't?'

He shrugged, some flicker of amusement in his expression. 'I mean, I think if that's what you need to tell yourself in order to get through this hangover, Elizabeth, then you definitely should.'

Huh. So he *did* know her name. Or, kind of. She didn't correct him, just made a snarky face at him, and he smiled widely in response. He had a smile that was very . . . winning. Lizzy had never used that word before in her life, but it was the one that sprang to mind.

His coffee arrived then, with a little speculoos cookie on the side. She appreciated that those tended to be a regular feature in France. Every time she hated this country, it seemed she loved it again within an hour.

'I love how they give you these wee biscuits,' Ciaran said, almost as if to himself, and as he took the first sip of his drink, Lizzy could feel the smile tugging at her own lips.

There was something about his accent. The more he spoke, the more she found her brain instinctively trying to classify it as something more familiar to her – the Scottish she'd spent years surrounded by, or the Oirish-y Irish of Westlife and *Father Ted*. In reality, it was neither, and something about the sound of it kept her on her toes.

'So whereabouts in Ireland are you from, anyway?' she asked.

'Donegal. North. Like as far north as you can get before you hit water, type of thing. While also, confusingly, not being in Northern Ireland.'

'Oh. Yeah. I always thought that was weird,' she

replied. 'Like, when you look at the map, there's just that extra little bit up there that sort of *seems* like it might belong to Northern Ireland, but doesn't.'

He looked . . . well, not exactly surprised. But, by some minuscule shift in his expression, Lizzy could tell that he *was* surprised. Right away, she pounced.

'You didn't think I would know!' she said delightedly. 'You thought I was a dumb American who wouldn't even know geography!'

'Well, geography and history and politics and a load of other shite,' he pointed out, and she tilted her head in acknowledgement. It was possible she wasn't fully abreast of all that.

'I *didn't* think you would know,' he admitted then, with a sheepish smile. 'But not 'cause of the American thing, really. Just 'cause a lot of people don't. Since I moved down to Dublin for university, I've heard some shockers from actual *Irish* people. I was all set to give you my whole spiel. I have it down to like, ninety seconds at this point. The entire history of Anglo-Irish relations and the partition of Ireland.'

'Alright, well obviously you have to give it to me now.'

He just laughed.

'Well?' she said, when nothing followed. 'Go!'

'Seriously?'

'Sure. I got ninety seconds. In fact,' she gestured benevolently, 'let's make it an even hundred.'

And so he told her. And she told him about Edinburgh, and about California too – about her actual real life there, all wide-open spaces and plaid shirts, maybe not so different a childhood from his.

Perhaps it was odd, that they should only have been

covering all this ground now, almost two months after they first entered one another's orbits. But the truth was that up until today – or rather, last night – Ciaran . . . Flynn (she *thought* that was his last name), Ciaran Flynn really had not especially stood out to Lizzy in any way.

In the years to come, to the extent that she talked about him at all, she would repeat that fact, and get some perverse enjoyment from the sheer disbelief on other people's faces.

Chapter Five

At the welcome desk of the Scottish Pavilion, Lizzy's most exciting visitor – in fact, her only visitor – has been Shauna. When she arrives, she dashes straight through to the other side of the curtain partition and then re-emerges, bearing a glass of fizz for herself and another for Lizzy.

'Can't believe I almost missed drinks!' she says. 'Do you want to see my pics?'

Lizzy doesn't know if a human being ever genuinely wants to see the pics – plural – belonging to another. But the delight is radiating off Shauna. And as a matter of principle, Lizzy believes firmly that there is no need to shit on what makes another person happy if you can help it. She accepts the proffered glass and – fuck it – tears open a shortbread to boot. 'Absolutely,' she says, settling in for the ride.

Shauna extends her phone and begins scrolling through the photographs of her morning jaunt, narrating all the while. A dozen blurry shots of the festival's jury members walking into the Palais. Vanessa Paradis having a cigarette.

A bunch of snaps of the different pavilions, and the beach, and the kitschy film cut-outs that you could stick your head through in place of the Joker or Rose DeWitt Bukater. They journey at leisurely pace all the way back to pictures of Shauna's Airbnb – by comparison to which, unbelievably, Lizzy's own rental seems almost spacious – at which point, the other woman clutches at her arm suddenly.

'Oh my God!' she hisses. 'Look who it is!'

Lizzy glances up.

'Don't you think he's such a babe? I was just watching this interview with him last week. Oh my God, he's—' Shauna cuts herself off with a squeak, her eyes wide as saucers, and Lizzy can't discount the possibility that her own might be too.

Because walking past the Scottish Pavilion . . . no, more accurately, walking *up to* the Scottish Pavilion . . . walking *into* the Scottish Pavilion . . . is Ciaran Flynn.

And maybe it's stupid, given that this is a very small town and, of course, she'd known already that he was out there somewhere in it. But actually, Lizzy finds she isn't a whole lot less shocked to see him now than she had been yesterday.

She does, however, find herself a whole lot more irritated. *Is this how it's going to be?* she thinks to herself hotly. She has to just expect him everywhere she fucking goes now? How about being acknowledged in any way, should she expect that? Or does he plan to keep looking right through her?

'Hey,' he says, as he approaches the welcome desk. Shirt sleeves rolled up, sunglasses hooked into the breast pocket, cool as a goddamn cucumber.

Merely in getting her lips to move, Lizzy feels like her brain has to work twice as hard as normal in order to be half as fast.

'Hi,' she manages eventually, and in the endless, agonising seconds that follow, all she can do is blink at him, no more words coming. He blinks right back at her, silence stretching out between them like a desert.

'Uh, hi!' Shauna chirps then, and it forces Lizzy into renewed awareness of her co-worker's presence. She looks over at Shauna briefly, then turns to Ciaran again, pasting a pleasant expression on her face.

'Can we help you with anything?' she asks him, all professionalism now. 'Do you have a meeting? Feel free to just go on back.'

He looks a little confused.

'No, I came to see if I could find *you*,' he says, as though that should be obvious. Lizzy feels a sudden vomity feeling wash over her. It occurs to her that being ignored – while it had enraged her yesterday – might actually have been better than this, the alternative.

'I wanted to just talk to you about—'

'Shauna,' Lizzy interrupts, her head swivelling around once more. 'Would you mind going and, um . . . just checking that we're all set up for the lunchtime panel?'

Shauna looks startled. Her eyes flicker to Ciaran and back to Lizzy, as though she is clocking that something non-standard might be afoot here. She lets it slide, though, and Lizzy is grateful, in this moment, for her own seniority.

'Sure. You mean in terms of the tech, or what?'

'Yes. Exactly, yeah. The tech.'

Admittedly, IT support is not at all Shauna's job, but then, really, her job – at least insofar as it pertains to this free trip to the *Côte d'Azur* – is more or less to do what is asked of her. Without another word, she scurries off.

'Sorry,' Ciaran says, once they are alone, and Lizzy finds she just can't get a handle on him, on his tone or body language. She guesses that should be no surprise. He is, to all intents and purposes, a stranger.

'What are you doing here?' she asks bluntly. 'Like . . . how'd you even know to come here?'

'I looked you up on Cinando.'

Oh. Of course. Cinando was practically designed for missions such as this. The online database listed the name, job title and email address of all the festival's official delegates, and for many people, access to it alone justified the cost of accreditation. It was the way to make sure that everyone knew you were successful enough to be here and, more crucially, the way for you to find out who *else* was here, and how to reach them. That was worth paying for, and handsomely. Not many people were shelling out thousands to see some movies.

It had taken Lizzy a while to grasp that one, actually – that the Cannes Film Festival was not primarily about the watching of films at all; that the films, in fact, were more of a bonus. Like the head massage when you went to have your hair cut; nice if it happened – maybe you even looked forward to it. Maybe you commented on how great it was and how you could just sit there all day. But ultimately, it was not why you made the appointment.

In nearly a decade of coming to Cannes, Lizzy has never seen a single film here.

41

'So you work for the Scottish Film Board?' Ciaran says then, presumably because she hasn't said a thing. 'That's amazing!'

'Thanks,' she replies tightly. And of course, it does strike her that this might be a natural time to congratulate him on, say, his BAFTA. But having spent the past day (or perhaps a *little* longer than that) simmering on a low heat about the man in front of her, she finds she would rather die than do it.

Irritatingly, she can't help but notice that he looks good. As in *good*. He's grown a beard since she saw him last. Not a full one, not the sort of 3D thing that seems to exist separate from a face, but more than a little scruff. And he's filled out somewhat, gotten broader in his arms and shoulders. The difference in him isn't exactly any of that, though. And in fact, in certain regards, he looks exactly the same – his hair is still as thick and unruly as it ever was. It's . . . well, Lizzy doesn't know. Maybe just that in some entirely indefinable and entirely obvious way, Ciaran Flynn is a grown up now.

'Have you had your teeth whitened?' is what she hears herself say to him, her eyes narrowing to a discerning squint.

He laughs, casting a hand across his jaw a little self-consciously. 'Uh, yeah. I didn't think they were *too* Ross Geller, though?'

'They're not. They look good,' she replies, which is true. Her voice still seems to have that dazed quality to it.

'Look, I'm sorry about yesterday,' he says then, and he leans against the desk, the words coming out quickly, as though he just wants to get them said. 'It was just I had this journalist with me. This guy Tristan. He's doing like a "day in the life" sort of thing – except it's turned out to be more like "forty-eight hours in the life" because he's still hanging around today. Anyway, I just didn't want . . .' he trails off with a little shrug. 'Obviously we haven't seen each other in a long time. And . . . we didn't exactly leave things on good terms.'

I'll say, Lizzy thinks grimly. It's possible the thought shows up on her face, because Ciaran shifts awkwardly.

'I just thought if we were going to talk, or . . . whatever, it might better for that not to somehow end up as, like, "colour" for some article, you know?'

He says it like it's some sort of kindness to her, this effort at brand management on his part.

'I was also, to be honest,' he adds, 'just really fucking surprised to see you, Lizzy.'

That part she likes a little better, the frankness of it, and she barks out a quick laugh. She can't help it. She thinks back to that bullish guy from the café yesterday.

'So where does he think you are right now?' she asks. 'The journalist.'

'Oh.' Ciaran looks a little thrown by the question. 'Uh, meditating. Sometimes I actually read these types of articles in the paper myself and I'll tell you what, if other people are bullshitting about their daily routines even half as much as I've been . . .'

It's wry, the way he says it, with the barest hint of a smile and one eyebrow quirked slightly. The whole thing, the force of the familiarity of it, hits Lizzy like a truck.

Being hit by a truck is not, traditionally, known to feel good.

'Look, Ciaran,' she says briskly, and she tries to ignore how strange his name feels on her tongue. 'Whatever. It's fine. You obviously have a lot going on, and actually I do too, so, y'know . . .'

What she feels she says quite clearly in the ellipsis – which is that they should return to their hitherto separate ways and not speak to or of each other ever again – turns out not to be what he hears.

'Well, if you wanted to have a drink, though, or a coffee or something? I'm here for a week.'

Lizzy forces herself to take a breath. She forces herself to contemplate sitting down opposite Ciaran Flynn for a sustained period, talking about Bordeaux, or decidedly *not* talking about it, or . . . she can't think of anything else. What else is there, really, in the Venn diagram of him and her? Yesterday's incident had just added a fresh little top-coat of anger to the stuff that, in truth, has been there for years now, chipped but clinging on. She cannot imagine anything that might be said over the course of a *café crème* that could transform the person in front of her into someone she wants to be friends with. Someone she trusts.

'I guess I . . . I just don't know what the point of that would be,' she says.

Ciaran lets out a short laugh that is all disbelief, no joy. For an endless five seconds, he just looks at her.

'No point, yeah,' he says then, bitterly.

He shakes his head a little, almost as if to himself.

'Jesus, I can't believe I actually felt really bad about yesterday. I have a film at the festival, you know?'

Lizzy does know. She has scrupulously avoided any details of it whatsoever, but she knows. She offers a tiny nod by way of response.

'Yeah. Well, everything is going *insane* with it. Forget about the journalist – when I told my manager I needed an hour to do a personal errand this afternoon, he nearly had a conniption.'

Hark at you, Lizzy thinks. *What it is to be in demand.*

'Seems like I would've been better off not bothering,' Ciaran continues, the muscles in his jaw tensing visibly. He turns to leave, but no sooner is he on his way than he is turning right back around. Like fucking Columbo.

'You know what Lizzy,' he says heatedly, and there is no doubt about it now; he's pissed. 'Back in Bordeaux, that last night? What I did wasn't good. I'd be the first to say it. But you were also, like . . . *not* that great,' he splutters. 'Do you honestly think what you said to me was true?'

Lizzy blinks, finding herself wholly ill-equipped for this turn of events, paralysed by it.

'I'm actually asking you,' he presses, and she watches his Adam's apple bob as he swallows, his voice coming out quietly now. 'I . . . I kind of need to know.'

Lizzy can hardly even process his question. She's aware of feeling warm, and flustered, and she just wants this whole thing to be over.

'I'm not getting into this with you. I'm at *work*,' she says, glancing around pointedly. 'The people back there are my *colleagues*. I'm sure in your world, this whole festival is one big party. Or, I don't know,' she gesticulates expansively, less concerned about making sense at this point than about maintaining some sort of momentum, 'maybe dredging up shitty drama from college is all part of the gig. Maybe that constitutes "research" or something. But I have an actual *job* to do here.'

And, would it have been easier to pull off this particular species of indignance had she not been, in that very moment, wearing a yellow sundress, with a plastic champagne flute in front of her? Might it have been better, for example, if the *actual Mediterranean Sea* were not within fifty feet of her? Yes. Probably it would have been. But, still, Lizzy gives it a damn good try.

It must do the trick, because then he's gone.

Chapter Six

For Ciaran Flynn, there is so much about the film business that still feels very mysterious. By now, though, he's managed at least to grasp one simple fact, which is that the more people show up to a meeting, the worse things generally are.

And in the penthouse suite at the Hotel Carlton, it's standing room only at this point.

His manager is here, of course, and the whole team from the production company, Figment Films. He knows them, all of them having been involved, to some greater or lesser degree, in actually helping him to make *Wish You Were Here*. But equally, lots of people have shown up who, until now, had been a voice on a conference call, if that. Several lawyers, and a tonne of higher-ups from the studio, plus miscellaneous other bodies of unknown origin. They are perched on every available surface, and those Ciaran can see – those whose heads are not blocked by flower arrangements the size of young teenagers – look extremely concerned.

'Okay, guys. I'm just gonna go ahead and ask the question,' says one of the development execs from the studio. Miranda, he thinks. Or Amanda. All the people from the studio are American, and all the people from the production company are English. Ciaran's learned that that's how it works, a lot of the time. The Brits make the thing, the Yanks pay for it. 'Do we need to talk about pulling the film?'

The prospect hovers in the room like an unexploded bomb, and Ciaran feels every single second of the silence that follows. It's remarkable, really, that having Lizzy Munro tell him – more or less – to go fuck himself has not actually turned out to be the low point of his day.

'Pulling the film?' Rupert says, as though he cannot even compute such a prospect. Rupert is the head of Figment Films, and Ciaran has never seen him in any mode other than booming and jovial. His precise contribution to the movie, Ciaran honestly never quite worked out. But he was the guy who needed to approve everything, and he always seemed to be very busy, and he said 'bish bash bosh' a lot.

Maybe-Miranda pauses, as though she is about to deliver a diagnosis of terminal cancer, and it's as hard for her as it is for the patient.

'Yeah,' she says solemnly.

'I'm sorry, I just can't believe I'm hearing this,' Rupert replies. 'Pulling the film from Cannes a matter of days before the premiere? Because some fucking nobody has thrown her toys out the pram? I'm sorry but I can't be the only one who thinks that's fucking madness.'

Miranda-or-Amanda doesn't bat an eyelid. 'I'm just thinking liability-wise,' she says. 'We *cannot* show this film

if we don't have insurance to cover it. That's just . . . I
mean, I don't need to tell you. Obviously the studio is just
not going to do that. Are we going to be able to get insurance if there's a lawsuit before the movie's even come out?'

'I don't think that's a concern. It's just a threatened
lawsuit at this point,' says one of the lawyers.

'And chances are, that's all it'll ever be,' another lawyer
jumps in swiftly. 'This thing goes to court, there's no way
she's getting past the front door.'

Both the lawyers, incidentally, are in jeans. In this
industry, Ciaran has noticed, all the people who routinely
charge, spend or invest the most colossal sums of money
like to wear jeans while they do it.

'I'm just looking at her counsel's letter here,' lawyer
number two continues, swiping at the screen of an iPad.
'Alright here we go. He says: "Having reviewed the trailer
and other promotional material in relation to feature
film *Wish You Were Here*, written and directed by Ciaran
Flynn . . . blah blah blah . . . we note a number of
infringing similarities with our client Penny Ainsley's
screenplay, as forwarded to Figment Films for consideration two years ago."'

The lawyer lifts her eyes from the screen, scanning her
audience. 'And then he mentions a bunch of similarities. I
guess we don't need to go back over the whole list. But
the point is, none of it is actionable whatsoever. It's all just
really broad ideas. There's no copyright in an idea. The
law only protects the specific *expression* of an idea. That's
why we have dozens of TV shows about hospital emergency
departments. Or, I don't know . . . Amish people.'

Everyone nods, which Ciaran takes to be an acknowledgement that there *are* a lot of TV shows about those

things, rather than an indication of any sort of collective understanding of the law.

'Can I just ask,' says some other person, one of the ones whose relationship to this whole situation remains a complete mystery. 'And, no offence Ciaran, obviously. But, this woman Penny – why *didn't* you guys go for her script?'

Rupert shrugs. 'Combination of factors, really. It was under-developed. Just not the right fit for us as a company. And then . . . I don't even know what it would have been, probably six months later, we connected with Ciaran.'

He glances over to Ciaran. 'And you were keen to do something in this area 'cause of your own experience living abroad, weren't you? Where was it you were, again?'

'Bordeaux.'

'That's right, Bordeaux. Anyway. Ciaran had a great track record, really fresh voice . . . all that. And so, y'know, the rest is history; we started developing it with him.' Rupert takes a breath, hitting his stride now. 'I think I can speak for all of us at Figment when I say none of us have even thought about Penny Ainsley for . . . well, years. If ever. When they first said she was talking about legal action, I actually didn't even recognise her name, did I, Jess?'

'You didn't, no,' Jess confirms dutifully. She was among the producers who had been there with Ciaran every single day, doing some actual producing. There is absolutely no one – Ciaran feels confident in saying this – who has put as much time and toil into *Wish You Were Here* as he has. But Jess Turley would be a close second.

There's a slight hush after that. Somebody reaches for a slice of melon on a hitherto untouched fruit platter and, from the huge picture window, Ciaran can see the beach. Other people are, visibly, having a very different sort of day than he is. His childhood home overlooked the sea, and even though the Atlantic's cold, crashing waves were a far cry from the pristine blue sheath of the Med, it still feels unexpectedly comforting somehow, just being near the water. He misses it, in London.

'I think it's clear this whole endeavour is financially motivated,' one of the lawyers says then, to fill the silence. 'Not to mention very deliberately timed. Obviously there's a huge amount of interest in *Wish You Were Here*, especially now that it's screening at the festival. And after Ciaran's last film performed so well, I think it's fair to say that there's a degree of expectation in terms of commercial success. You know what they say,' he adds, with a little smile, 'where there's a hit, there's a writ.'

Ciaran gets the sense that perhaps some part of this assessment is designed to make him feel good, which it doesn't particularly. Nonetheless, he smiles along politely.

'So, in terms of what we're going to do, then,' Jess ventures. 'I really think if we pulled the film now, that would only draw more attention to the whole thing. We'd have to put out a press release announcing the withdrawal, and people would be asking why, and that just all seems like . . . not what we want.'

'I agree,' Rupert says. 'At this point, nobody knows anything. I say we just get through the premiere and bung this woman a few quid before the thing hits general release if we have to – though, I'll be honest with you, it would fucking stick in my craw to do it.'

A young-ish guy from the studio nods. 'I think that's a smart approach. *Yes*, it's frustrating. But keeping this on the downlow is the priority.'

'Oh honey,' comes a drawl from the woman next to him, as though his naivety is almost endearing. 'This is not staying on the downlow. She's gonna tell people. Matter of fact, I thought that's why we were all here. To formulate a strategy for when she tells people.'

Ciaran finds he actually recalls this woman's name, because when she'd introduced herself, she hadn't done it in the same perfunctory, roll-call fashion as everyone else. 'I'm Amy,' she'd said, reaching out to shake his hand, looking right at him. 'Amy Solomon. I handle PR for the studio.' She's maybe fifty-ish, with bouncy, golden-blonde hair, and skin that has seen years of sun.

'Look, you guys say she's basically onto a loser, legally speaking, right?' Amy's continuing now, glancing at the lawyers. 'Alright. Well, whaddya got when you don't have the courts? The *court of public opinion*, that's what. Y'all checked your emails since we've been in here?'

A little flurry of activity follows, a slight sense of release in the room as everyone is given permission to openly look at their phones. The enjoyment, however, is extremely short-lived. Not so much as thirty seconds later, Peter, Ciaran's manager, shakes his head in disbelief, extending his screen out for Ciaran to look at.

'*Variety*,' he says, for everyone else's benefit. 'Looking for a comment from Ciaran and Figment. Piece with Penny's going out tomorrow apparently.'

'Yep, got one too,' Rupert confirms. 'Polly's just forwarded it. *Fuck.*'

'Maybe . . . all publicity is good publicity?' someone suggests feebly.

'Yeah. *No.* This is not good publicity,' Amy Solomon corrects swiftly. To her credit, she does not look at all smug about this turn of events. She looks energised. Purposeful.

'Alright, here's what we're gonna do,' she says. 'Ciaran. You're gonna do some interviews. Friendly outlets, obviously. We can't stop people hearing Penny say she basically came up with this whole project, right? So then they gotta decide – who did? We have to give 'em some reasons to believe it was you. *Authenticity.* That's the word of the day from here on out. Any way *Wish You Were Here* is connected to your life, you talk about. You say you lived in France for a year yourself, right? So that's great. You got a friend or whatever who committed suicide? You've ever even *heard* of someone who committed suicide, and you're gonna talk about it.'

Ciaran opens his mouth to respond, but Amy's not done.

'We're gonna want some corroboration too. We'll brief the actors, of course, but what we really want are some folks who've known you for a while. Friends, family members – "This is the movie he's always talked about making", et cetera. Some tweets, with stories or pictures of you from France, would be good – you can retweet 'em, and then they'll be picked up by all the online outlets. Obviously if we could get somebody to give some quotes for a larger print piece, that'd be the dream. Anybody we could tee up for that?'

'Mmm, I'd kinda rather not drag my family into it, to be honest,' Ciaran says, with a wince. 'The press and . . . y'know, just all of this' – he gestures loosely – 'it's really not their world at all. And, even with friends . . . I sort of have the people I met *through* this business, and the people I knew before it. Not a whole lot of overlap there.'

'What about that girl from yesterday?' someone pipes up then, and Ciaran can't even identify where the voice comes from.

'What?' he asks sharply, eyes darting around.

'The girl that waved at you, when we were in that stupid café. You said you knew *her* from back in the day, didn't you?'

Ciaran's eyes land on the source now. Tristan.

Fucking Tristan from *Life and Style* magazine.

In a 1 to 10 likeability rating, the guy has officially gone into minus numbers now.

It seems like unbelievably bad news that Tristan has somehow managed to end up in this room at all, and right next to Ciaran, Peter looks ready to blow a gasket at the realisation.

The two of them attempt a discreet conversation through gritted teeth, one that amounts to a *what the fuck* (Ciaran) and an *I will handle this* (Peter).

Ciaran can only assume this means that certain threats and inducements will soon be issued on his behalf, in order to somehow extract from Tristan those three little words: off the record. It's not something he even has the capacity to worry about right now, though, because so far as it relates to the rest of the room, he realises he's been silent for a moment too long.

'Uh, yeah. That was Lizzy,' he replies then, careful to keep his voice light and even. 'She's a friend from, uh . . . well. From when I was in Bordeaux, as it happens.'

The attempt to toss it out there casually doesn't work. It doesn't work at all. Ciaran can almost hear the collective intake of breath.

'So, let me get this straight,' Amy says slowly. 'This is a person who actually *lived through this whole time with you*. And now she's *here*? In Cannes?'

'Yeah.'

'Could she talk about, say, how it's obvious – based on stuff she remembers – that the film was inspired by your life during that time?'

'I mean, *loosely* inspired by,' Ciaran corrects, for the record. 'I . . . yeah. I guess she probably could, in theory.'

'Well!' Amy is beaming. 'I don't know if you believe in Jesus, honey, but you'd better be thanking him right about now, just in case. This is fantastic!'

Ciaran is aware, suddenly, of being very warm. And not at all in the nice way he'd anticipated being when he imagined this, his first trip to Cannes. Almost no part of the experience, in fact, has so far turned out to be anything like he thought it would be.

'Amy, I have to just stop you there,' he says hurriedly. 'I don't know what exactly you have in mind, but I can more or less guarantee Lizzy's not going to go for it. We . . . haven't exactly stayed in touch.'

And, as had been made clear to him not two hours previously, that suited Lizzy just fine.

To say that he had been surprised to see her yesterday, at that café, would have been an understatement of staggering proportions. By now, it had been so long that she had begun to seem almost like an illusion to him, one that existed for the time they'd spent together and then dissipated altogether. But, no – there she was. Walking and talking and working in film.

For reasons he's sure anyone would find entirely understandable, the sight of her had brought up a lot of old feelings. The hurt and anxiety and anger had come flooding back at shocking speed.

It was like he'd told her earlier, though. He didn't think he was blameless himself. Not the *most* to blame, if they were going to get into semantics – not the one who started it, really. But not blameless. And thus, no matter how misshapen and sour things had ended up between them, he would have been up for some attempt at forgiving and forgetting. Lizzy, apparently, was very much not.

What was it she'd said to him? *Maybe in your world, dredging up shitty drama from college is all part of the gig?* From this, he'd gathered that she had at least read the blurb of *Wish You Were Here*, and she wasn't exactly going to be first in line to buy a ticket. Absolutely no part of him thinks that she will be willing to assist him with his current predicament, and absolutely no part of him wants to ask her.

'Ciaran,' Amy says then, as though she is dealing with an especially slow child. 'I answer directly to the head of the studio. Jeff has *personally tasked me* with handling this shit show. Believe me when I tell you, we're gonna be at least trying with this girl.'

'Of course!' Rupert chimes in swiftly, back to his usual buoyancy. 'Sounds good to me. Let's reach out, get her on board, bish bash bosh.'

Ciaran looks around helplessly, feeling every single one of the thirty-two eyeballs on him.

It's funny, he thinks, to imagine that – at least if the present situation doesn't leave his film utterly dead in the water – then many of these people will very soon have to walk a red carpet and talk about it to the press. And they'll give him all the credit. They'll pretend he was in charge of every single bit of it.

This is, after all, the central illusion around which the whole movie industry is built. Ciaran had bought into it himself, before he knew better. He never imagined that being a director would involve so much being directed.

Chapter Seven

By day two, things are in full swing, the streets thronging with people. Not far from the International Village, on the sort of generous corner plot that God gave to the French just for establishing bistros, sits Caffé Roma. Beloved for its location and its square footage more so than for the quality of its food or drink, the place is a mecca for delegates during the festival, and Lizzy has spent her day zipping back and forth between it and the Scottish Pavilion. She's run into several old friends, and had seven meetings in total, and, in the midst of it all, found herself commandeered to moderate a panel discussion entitled 'Beyond *Braveheart*: Making the Most of Modern Scotland.'

It's been a good day. Meeting new people is one of those things that everyone says they like, but that Lizzy – at least for the most part – genuinely really does. There's a huge part of her that feels energised and enlivened by being around other people – the same part, probably, that strikes up conversations on planes, or leaps at the chance to sing karaoke, or says *sure, whatever, I can do it!* when a panel moderator fails to show on time.

She's not convinced she can call herself a true extrovert, though, because there also seems to come a point – often, she'd swear she can almost *feel* it descending upon her – when she's just fresh out of attentiveness and enthusiasm and confidence. When she might begin to wonder, for example, if she'd seemed an awkward and unqualified moderator. When solitude, more than company, starts to feel like the thing that's going to fill her up.

By the time she's set to leave the Scottish Pavilion for the day, Lizzy has a window of under an hour before she's due at a restaurant for dinner, and all she wants in that period of time is not to have to smile or talk to anybody.

Everything is busy and buzzy outside, photojournalists with huge hulking cameras on their shoulders already beginning to jockey for position along the red carpet, ahead of the evening's premiere at the Palais des Festivals. Somewhere around sixty films premiere at Cannes over the course of the festival. This can be in a small way – a way that amounts, essentially, to the provision of some rosé outside a screening room – or in a very big way. The big way means the Palais. It means a red carpet so prominent that half the Croisette is closed off for it, and the world's press in attendance, and lots of beautiful people showing up to help promote themselves, a fashion designer and the film, in that order. The stars, of course, emerge god-like from limousines at the last possible minute. However, all the non-famous attendees are required to show up and get their asses in seats a lot earlier, such that by six o'clock, it's not unusual to see the town's pavements crowded with people in tuxes and evening gowns, right alongside those in jeans and sundresses. Lizzy has always loved that mix. She loves the balmy evening heat and the feeling in the air that magical things are happening. Even if they are not necessarily exactly happening to *her*, just the nearness of it is enough.

If she were Ciaran Flynn, though.

If she were Ciaran Flynn, she cannot imagine that a second-hand thrill would be the best offer on the table.

It is, in fact, almost impossible for her to believe that Ciaran Flynn would have nothing better to do right now than hang around outside the International Village and wait for her. And yet, that seems to be exactly what is happening. He is leaning against a wall, his eyes trained in the direction of the security scanner, and as soon as Lizzy clears it, he leaps to attention, making straight for her.

'Look, it's not my dream to be here either, okay?' he says, before she can even get a word in. Maybe her face has already said it all. '*Believe me*. I got the message loud and clear yesterday.'

Lizzy realises that, accidentally, she has frozen on the spot. She catches a hold of herself.

'Okay, so?' she replies, beginning to walk again. He steps into sync with her.

'So, I really *do* need to talk to you,' he says. 'Not about Bordeaux. Or, not exactly. About a different thing.'

Lizzy has no idea what that might be, unless he wants information on the tax incentive to shoot at least sixty per cent of a feature film in Scotland. Which, in theory, she guesses he might. Still, she doesn't slow her pace.

'I just . . . I honestly don't have the time to stop,' she says. 'I'm not being a dick. I have forty-five minutes to get home, get changed and get back out for dinner.'

They're on the Croisette by now and it is swarming with people. Briefly, they are separated by other pedestrians, which Lizzy takes as a prime chance to very firmly set her own course. Ciaran weaves back in her direction, catching up to her.

'Wow,' he says pointedly. 'I mean, are you *kind of* being a dick though?'

That pisses her off.

'I could *start*,' she snaps. Honestly, she is at a loss. How much clearer could she make her feelings? Women, she reminds herself staunchly, are not obligated to give men their time. It therefore follows that *she*, a woman, is not obligated to give this particular man her time. Why he even wants it is a mystery. He'd set fire to what was once good between them – deliberately – and then had managed perfectly well without her company for twelve years.

In the interest of bringing an end to the matter once and for all, she halts briefly in her tracks.

'Look, Ciaran. It's Cannes, okay? It's sunny. You're famous now – kinda.' She wouldn't want to overstate the matter, he isn't exactly George Clooney. 'Just . . . go enjoy that.'

'A chance would be a fucking fine thing, let me tell you,' he replies hotly.

'Excuse me, are you Ciaran Flynn?' some voice pipes up then, as if on cue. Lizzy looks around for the source, spotting a college-aged kid who has approached on Ciaran's right side, all wide eyes and awe.

'No,' Ciaran says bluntly, while at the exact same moment she chirps:

'He is, yeah! He'd love to take a picture!'

And she's petty enough to find it very amusing, the expression on his face as she leaves him there, caught, the force of this stranger's enthusiasm audible all the way until she turns the corner.

Not two minutes later, though, he's calling after her again.

'Lizzy! Wait!'

Much as a part of her might like to just keep on walking even as he calls her name – much as she believes she has the right to, much as that might be kind of badass – she apparently has too much of a good-girl instinct ingrained in her to do it. She finds herself turning around, watches him take a few more strides towards her. When he stops a few feet in front of her on the cobbled pavement, she looks at him – properly – for the first time today. He looks tired, she thinks. For a moment, neither of them says anything. The quiet on the little side street is so noticeable, compared with the hustle and bustle of the Croisette. Then, Ciaran sighs deeply.

'Look, I'm sure by now you've read the *Variety* article.'

She looks at him blankly.

'About the film – *my* film,' he prompts. 'About me.'

And it is on the very tip of Lizzy's tongue, a withering retort to the effect that she doesn't keep up with his press. But somehow, she restrains herself.

'No. I don't know anything about it,' is all she says instead.

'Seriously? That's . . .' he pauses, seems to consider it. 'That's actually kind of amazing, it feels like fucking every man and his dog has read it at this point.'

Huh.

It was true, she really *didn't* keep up with his press, as a general matter. But perhaps she could make an exception, she finds herself thinking, on this one occasion. Perhaps she might make that exception as soon as possible. During the festival, several magazines produced special editions every single day, with people dotted at strategic locations around town to distribute them. Lizzy knows that if she wanted, she could probably get a hold of today's *Variety* within about four hundred metres of where she is standing right this moment.

'Uh, but yeah, so anyway,' Ciaran continues, 'the premiere is next Tuesday night. And basically, today this woman has done a big interview saying that I've plagiarised the film. Like, stolen the whole idea, essentially. From her.'

'Oh,' Lizzy replies, eyes widening a little.

'Yeah.'

Not much more needs to be said. About this, at least, it's not hard to get on the same page. They both know it's bad.

'So, you know the basic gist of the film, yeah?'

Quick as a flash, she's irritated again. It's really quite something, the way that Ciaran appears utterly incapable of believing that her life is not one long process of monitoring his.

Lizzy shakes her head. 'Sorry,' she offers, though even to her own ears, she doesn't sound especially sorry.

'Right,' he replies, seemingly a little thrown. 'Well, it's kind of about . . . I mean, it's set in France. And it's sort

63

of . . . loosely inspired by the year we were there. Or, y'know. Here.'

'What?' Lizzy asks sharply, and just as some internal alarm begins to ring in her brain, an external one begins to ring in her back pocket. She knows, without even looking, that it'll be Oliver on the phone. She'd promised to check in with him right around now. Needless to say, it has not turned out to be good timing. Nonetheless, she smothers the irritation. Sweet Oliver, who has done nothing but make her life better since the day and hour he entered it, doesn't deserve to hear any of that.

'One sec,' she says to Ciaran, before pulling her phone out quickly, pressing it to her ear.

'Hey, bubs,' she says warmly, 'I'm sorry, can I call you in ten? I'm just . . . in the middle of something.'

She lets her gaze drift back over to Ciaran, as though to re-emphasise that she very much wishes this were not the case. On the other end of the line, Oliver launches into a quick burst of chatter, and she can't help but chuckle. 'Hold that thought, okay? I can't *wait* to hear, I'll call you in ten, I promise. Alright. Bye, hon.'

Sliding her phone back into her pocket, she can't help but feel a little exposed by the version of her that Ciaran has very obviously just witnessed. Soft as marshmallow. She gives her head a shake, as though to refocus her brain on the problem at hand.

'Sorry. Uhh . . . so what was that you said? Your movie's "loosely inspired by" the year we were in France? What does that mean?'

'I mean, not that it's directly *about* anything that happened,' Ciaran replies. 'And it's not set in Bordeaux specifically or anything. It's more just loosely inspired by the experience generally, you know?'

Lizzy *doesn't* really know.

'Am I in it?' she asks bluntly. That is her main concern – she might even go so far as to say her only concern. She can feel her heart beating faster in her chest at the very thought.

Ciaran hesitates ever so slightly, which is not comforting. It's possible that the abject horror she feels isn't concealed very well, because a second later, his expression animates too.

'No!' he rushes to add. 'There *is* an American character – but that's it! She's not *you*. I just . . . I don't know, picked some different nationalities and worked from there, basically. I wrote in a German couple too.'

At this, Lizzy feels herself settle a little. That sounds okay. And really, she reasons with herself, what does it matter to her anyway? It isn't like she'll be watching the thing.

'Okay. And so this woman . . .?'

'Penny,' he supplies.

'Her movie is also about being a student in France, is that it?'

'Spain. And it's just a script – it hasn't actually been produced. But apparently, yeah. She's seen our trailer, and read the synopsis, and she has various things she says are similar.'

Lizzy takes that in.

'And you're saying that's just coincidence,' she states, for purposes of clarification.

'I suppose so. I didn't copy her. *That*'s what I'm saying.'

'Alright, well, hey,' she replies, with a shrug. 'Both you guys whored out your year abroad for a movie – fine.

I'd actually be surprised if either of you were the first.'

She tosses it out dryly, without malice and without even thinking about it, and Ciaran laughs aloud. It feels weirdly, unexpectedly good, hearing that sound. The same way it did the first time she ever made him laugh. How does that memory flash into her mind like a lightning bolt? She pushes it away.

'The thing is that the optics are bad, though,' he says. 'That's the phrase that's been used. The optics are bad.'

'Yeah,' she agrees blandly. The whole thing does absolutely strike her as a big problem, even if not, in any clear way, *her* problem. She's conscious of her little slice of time before dinner getting smaller by the minute. 'I guess I don't know what to tell you, Ciaran.'

'Well, what *other* people have told me is I need to do some interviews where I basically explain the genesis of this film and how a lot of it's based on my real experiences. We don't need to denigrate Penny, but we just need to sort of hammer home that this is original to me, you know?'

'Makes sense.'

'Yeah. And – again, this is what I've been told – it would be all the better if there was anything, or anybody, who could, sort of, help back that up.'

She just looks at him, unblinkingly.

'. . . Can you really not see where I'm going with this?' he asks then, a little impatiently. 'There's some stuff in the film that . . . well, that *you* might recognise. Broadly speaking, like. That's what I'm saying.'

Lizzy frowns. 'So you want me to . . . what? Put out a tweet or something? "I knew Ciaran Flynn when he really did live in France", or whatever? I'm not on Twitter.'

He hesitates. 'I think the idea was more like . . . maybe an interview with one of the trades?'

'What?' she asks rhetorically, her brain scrambling to even process such a notion. 'Oh, you gotta be kidding me!'

Despite herself, she lets out a little half-laugh. 'Even wading into this thing from my cell phone would have seemed like a terrible idea, there's no way I'm talking to some magazine! Also,' she adds then, 'just for the record, don't say "the trades" to me, Ciaran. Don't say "the trades" to people in general. It makes you sound like an ass.'

'Okay, you work for a national film board,' he fires back, quick as a flash, his whole face conveying his cynicism. 'You're at a huge international film festival right now. I *know* you've said "the trades" at some point, Lizzy. I know you have.'

Lizzy says nothing. It's . . . definitely a possibility.

For a second, they just look at one another, tension pulsing between them.

'I really have to go,' she says then. 'I'm sorry about your situation – I am. But you're gonna have to find somebody else. I can't help you.'

As if instinctively, Ciaran lunges another few steps forward towards her, before she can leave.

'Look, Lizzy, it wasn't my idea to ask you, okay?' he says, more urgently now. 'I actually thought my days of making myself totally pathetic in front of you were over. But there's a *lot* riding on this film. And the people at the studio . . . for whatever reason, they think it would be good – since by some fucking random twist of fate you happen to be here – if you could maybe just give a couple of quotes.'

It's a surprise to Lizzy to learn that any of those people, whoever they might be, are even aware of her existence. But she misses the chance to express it, because he's not done.

'I know you don't like me,' he continues. 'I get it. To be honest, I *also* generally prefer hanging around with people who don't, like, ignore me or get really arsey with me or make me chase after them in the street. So, y'know. There's that. But if you came to me right now and said, "Here's this thing that's on the verge of ruining my career", and it was in my power to maybe help stop it . . .?'

He lets the prospect linger for a moment, his eyes locked right on hers.

'I swear to God, I would do it,' he says then, his voice some combination of earnestness and defiance that Lizzy can't quite get a handle on. 'We were friends once. I would do it.'

He presses a business card into her hand.

'Just think about it, would you? Please.'

Chapter Eight

The Monday after Halloween, two small things happened in Bordeaux that would come to alter the remainder of Lizzy's life there.

The first was that she received a text from Mia, and when her phone buzzed with the message, Lizzy felt like something inside of her did too. The beginning stages of romance got a lot of air play, but the first gestures of friendship were, in her view, underrated. The *we should do something!* and the exchange of details and the first move that proved it wasn't just bullshit. Some new person – who wasn't trying to get in your pants, who wasn't bound to you by history or family or anything else – wanting to see you. On purpose. Maybe it wasn't quite the fireworks that movies were made of, but there was a certain kind of warm glow that came from that.

No sooner had Lizzy fired off a response to Mia but the second small thing happened.

A friend request on Facebook. From Ciaran Flynn. She was on her laptop anyway when it came through, because looking at the internet was becoming her default activity when she was bored. Right away, she clicked 'accept' and a few seconds later, entirely on the spur of the moment, she found herself clicking on the 'chat' function.

Lizzy Munro
Hey!

Ciaran Flynn
Hey! Sorry, I was Elizabeth-ing you up and down yesterday. Don't know how I managed to re-christen you in my brain 😛

Lizzy Munro
Np! Elizabeth's fine too! Here's a question: wanna come out to St Émilion tomorrow with me and Mia and Hans (don't know if you know them – German)? V. last minute so definitely no pressure! Just if you're around/feel like it!

His response didn't come immediately and what this provided was some time for Lizzy to wonder whether she'd just done a super weird thing. She didn't even really know *why* she'd done it, other than feeling a generalised sense of goodwill following her text exchange with Mia, and Ciaran's direction being the first one in which she'd had an opportunity to spread it.

Was he trying to work out how to gracefully decline right now, though? Worse, did he think she was attempting to initiate some kind of *double date* situation? That prospect, which hadn't initially occurred to her whatsoever, was mortifying.

Then, his name flashed up.

Ciaran Flynn
Yeah, sounds good!

Lizzy felt the slight tension that had built up in her release, like the last bit of air escaping a balloon. Of course he wouldn't overthink it. Ciaran, at least from what she'd observed so far, wasn't burdened by that tendency in the way that she often was. He seemed to be able to take things as they came; he seemed to find things easy – or at least, to be able to resist unnecessarily complicating them for himself.

Lizzy Munro
Awesome – we're thinking the 12.35 train from Gare St-Jean. Obviously feel free to bring whoever!

That last bit was good, she thought. Jaunty. Easy-going. She really could feel that way sometimes, and when she couldn't, she could fake it.

*

When Lizzy looked back on that day in Saint-Émilion years later, she wouldn't be sure if she actually remembered very much about it at all, or if what she remembered were the photographs.

A close-up of the French onion soup she ate in the town square.

Endless shots of every aspect of their tour of a winery: industrial-looking vats, and more picturesque wooden barrels, and on the vines, the occasional wizened grape that had escaped September's harvest.

Hans and Ciaran horsing about in the church cloister, striking a variety of stupid poses in between the arches, Mia doubled up laughing at them.

The sun low in the sky as they all looked out from the bell tower, sandstone buildings and vineyards cast in perfect, peachy light.

Nobody learned anything about wine that they would retain for more than a week, but they all drank a Goldilocks amount of it, and as the four of them headed back toward the train station, past the vineyards in the fading light, the situation was clear: one text and one Facebook friend request later, and they were all friends. Simple as that.

Because tourist season was over, they got the *carré* seats on the return journey to Bordeaux – four in a square, with a little table in the middle that could be folded out. They laid out their baguettes and played Snap with the cards Mia had brought along, and when the conductor arrived to check their tickets, he made some comment that seemed good-natured. Ciaran offered something in response, because he was good at that, Lizzy had noticed – the little conversational asides that she felt she'd never be able to master in French. The notion of 'picking up the language' seemed to be bandied about a lot, in advance of a person moving to a new country – as though such a thing would be effortless, inevitable. Lizzy had not found that to be so.

When she thought about it, most of the new French words that she had learned so far had probably come from Thierry, the five-year-old boy with whom she spent every Wednesday morning. Unfortunately, none of his vocab seemed likely to be of much use to her, since it was hard to imagine a situation in which she'd want to openly insult another person in quite the fashion that Thierry did her. *Tu est chiante!* he would shout, often while hurling – literally hurling – items around his playroom. *Tu est une conasse! C'est moi qui décide!*

He liked that one a lot, actually. He said it over and over, always with gusto. *C'est moi qui décide, c'est moi qui décide!* And the oddest thing was that, in fact, so long as it didn't compromise – at this point, quite *seriously* compromise – his physical safety, Lizzy was entirely happy for Thierry to be the one deciding things. So she wasn't quite sure what his problem was.

The thought jogged her memory, just as Mia was dealing them all in for another round of cards. Tomorrow, it occurred to her, was Wednesday.

'Fuuuuck,' she moaned out loud as the realisation hit, drawing confused glances from the others. 'I have Thierry in the morning.'

'Who's Thierry?' asked Hans.

'This kid I babysit. You know 'cause the French schools aren't in on a Wednesday? And he has a little sister too, Elise. I'm supposed to be teaching them English.'

In truth, after several weeks spent doggedly singing 'Heads, Shoulders, Knees and Toes' and 'Incy Wincy Spider' to these children – or, perhaps more accurately, *at* them – Lizzy had almost totally given up on the idea of teaching them anything whatsoever. Mostly what she now wanted from Wednesday mornings was simply for them to turn, one way or another, into Wednesday afternoons.

'Cute!' Mia cooed.

'*Elise* is cute,' Lizzy clarified. 'All she wants to do is watch *The Princess and the Frog* on a loop. To the point that she didn't even object when I switched her DVD to the English-language version. She's still just psyched every time. So, y'know,' Lizzy shrugged. 'It's possible she's picked up a word or two from that.'

'"Princess" maybe,' Ciaran suggested mildly. 'Or "frog".'

Lizzy smirked a little in amusement. She found herself doing that a lot with him, even when he hadn't said anything all that hilarious. Something about his delivery just appealed to her.

'Exactly, yeah,' she replied. 'Which, let's face it, are both good words to know.'

And he looked back at her, the same amused expression on his face as was probably still on hers.

'So, why do you not want to go?' Hans prompted.

'Oh. 'Cause of Thierry. Thierry is like the devil child. He hates the literal sight of me, and I gotta say, at this point? Not his biggest fan. A couple weeks ago, while I was over there, he actually shat on the floor.'

Hans frowned in confusion. 'What is shat?'

'It's the past tense of shit, Hans,' Mia clarified, as calm as could be. 'Like shitted.'

Lizzy let out a quick snort of laughter.

'Yeah. That. Anyway, he came up to me like "*J'ai fait caca.*" And that wasn't even a phrase I knew in French, but when he said it . . . I understood.'

'Some things transcend language, eh?' Ciaran said.

'Yeah.'

'That's terrible, though!' said Mia. 'Terrible for you, of course, Lizzy. But, for him too. Maybe he has some sort of problem.'

'Oh, no, he didn't have an *accident*. This was like, he popped a squat on the bathroom tiles. On purpose. He was only too *happy* to come tell me about it. Sorry, do you guys know that phrase in English – pop a squat?'

'Some things transcend language,' Mia repeated sagely.

'Anyway, every week is just a total horror show, but I get paid cash so when it's over, I always think "Okay, I'll just do one more and then I'm gonna quit."'

'I don't have class on a Wednesday – I mean, not that I've been attending a lot of classes on any day of the week, but I actually don't *have* any on Wednesdays,' Ciaran said then. 'I can come along if you want the company.'

'What?'

He shrugged. 'Just if you want. Kids like me.'

Lizzy laughed, in such a way as to convey to him his extreme naivety.

'Ciaran,' she said, 'kids like *me*. This is not a regular child.'

'Elizabeth,' he replied, and there was something communicated when he said her name like that; she couldn't put her finger on what it was, but something just between the two of them. 'I'm going to bet you right now that I could – at the very *least* – encourage this wee boy to shit in a toilet.'

Ultimately, that just didn't feel like an offer Lizzy was in any position to turn down.

Chapter Nine

Well.

The devil child, in the end, absolutely *loved* Ciaran Flynn.

That was the truth of the matter. And the most galling part was, Ciaran hadn't even really tried. He hadn't brought candy, or entertainment, or performed anything approaching a skit. Nor, conversely, had he laid down the law and demonstrated a firm hand. All of these were strategies that Lizzy had been busting out on a cyclical basis for the past eight weeks, to varying degrees of failure. She'd gone through every single thing that she imagined her mother might suggest, were she still on regular speaking terms with her mother.

'Wow. This is . . . quite a significant situation,' Ciaran said when he arrived at the house on Cours de l'Argonne, his eyes widening a little as he took in the scene.

Elise, the angel child, was happily watching her Disney DVD. But the living room was in carnage. And out in the little backyard, through the sliding glass doors, Thierry was stalking around, throwing things.

'You think so?' Lizzy asked. She was perversely pleased that the little boy was rising to the occasion and didn't bother trying to hide it. 'Is it not like your *adorable* nieces and nephews in *adorable* rural Ireland?'

'Ah, now. Let's not be churlish about this, Lizzy,' Ciaran replied smoothly, an expression of mock superiority on his face. 'We're both on the same team here, remember?'

Lizzy snorted, and from her spot in the living room, one eye still on Elise, she watched as Ciaran ventured outside.

His presence caught Thierry's attention, and there seemed to be a brief exchange, after which Ciaran hunkered down, lifting a handful of gravel from the landscaped perimeter and dropping it onto the grassy area. Lizzy had to squeeze herself right against the corner of the glass door to even sort of see what he was doing – it looked like he was arranging the stones in some kind of pattern, which Thierry was duly ignoring. His focus remained resolutely on dumping sand from his sandpit onto the grass in a cloud of chaos. Ciaran, for his part, appeared to be ignoring Thierry right back. He simply continued with the task in front of him, whatever that was.

So far, so futile.

Pretty soon, though, the weirdest thing began to happen. Every so often, Thierry began to throw sidelong glances in Ciaran's direction – all of which went unacknowledged. Glances became stares – also unacknowledged. And the next thing Lizzy knew, the two of them were crouched down on the grass together, Ciaran's dark head and Thierry's blond one both bowed in concentration.

They stayed like that for more than an hour.

More than an hour.

Lizzy was dumbfounded.

'What the hell did you say to him?' she hissed, when the two of them came back inside, and the little boy placidly joined his sister in front of a screen.

'I said "*Bonjour, je suis Ciaran.*"'

'That's all?'

'I mean, pretty much.'

She shook her head. 'Unbelievable.'

Mrs Durand, when she returned to reassume responsibility for her children, didn't react with anywhere near the level of unhappiness that Lizzy imagined many mothers might, upon discovering that their female babysitter had shipped in a male companion. She just handed over the money, as usual, and as Lizzy tripped back out onto the street with Ciaran, she felt almost giddy with delight.

'Can we just swing by that bakery on the corner?' she asked. Every week after babysitting, in an aid to the recovery process, she purchased two croissants, which she would take back to Rue Cabirol and slather in butter, savouring every bite. This afternoon, she definitely still wanted the croissants, though it was more a question of greed than of emotional support, which seemed better.

'Sure,' Ciaran replied, and when they went in and placed their orders, he said something to the girl behind the counter that Lizzy didn't quite catch. They shuffled along, hovering at the other side of the cash register, waiting for their coffees.

'How'd you get to be so good at French?' she asked then, curiously.

'God. I've definitely got a ways to go, like. But . . . I dunno.' He shrugged. 'Any amount of good that I am, it's only 'cause I put in a *tonne* of time. Like, really a shit tonne.'

It was a refreshing answer. Lizzy realised in that moment that she'd been conditioned to have compliments either denied and batted away, or chalked up to dumb luck – good genes, natural talent, all that. *I worked really fucking hard at this* was just not a thing a lot of people said.

'Were you top of the class in school, then? Did you get *Paris Match* delivered to your house?' she asked teasingly.

He snickered. 'No. Rented a lot of French films, though. I'm going to go to the cinema this afternoon, actually, if you want to come?'

Lizzy shrugged. She had never seen a movie *en français*, but she had nothing else to do.

'Sure,' she replied.

And that's how it began.

On Wednesdays from then on, Ciaran would come to the Durands' with her in the morning, and she would go to the movies with him in the afternoon. He'd told her before, that day at Le Café Français, that he saw whatever was on, and she quickly learned what that really meant; he saw almost *everything* that was on. Whether it was a documentary or an indie film or a blockbuster, it didn't seem to matter to him. He didn't end up liking all of them, but he was open to liking all of them.

They went to the Utopia Cinema, mostly – a converted church on Place Camille-Jullian that, as it turned out, played lots of English-language films with French subtitles. It had a sweeping ecclesiastical foyer and tiny little screening theatres that had once been convent rooms, and it was amazing how many other people turned out to be going to the movies in the middle of the day. Retirees, largely, and other college-aged students. Lizzy loved seeing the older people especially. A lot of them were so stylish, or so sweet, and some – at least when observed from a distance – were not particularly either, but still they were there. At twenty, Lizzy often already had the sense that she was running out of time, losing ground somehow – that she needed to be doing more, deciding more, enjoying more, before her window of opportunity closed. It was nice to be reminded that the road ahead, hopefully, was a long one; that maybe not every good thing needed to be grabbed at right now or lost forever, as if life were an episode of *Supermarket Sweep*.

The students her own age, meanwhile, were a different kind of enchanting. They wore the sort of big glasses that would become popular in Edinburgh eighteen months later, and after the films finished, the foyer was usually full of them, ordering food and chattering away to one another in French, or sitting outside on the square smoking cigarettes. They seemed *cool* to Lizzy – there truly was no other word for it.

One Wednesday seemed to leap into the next, and just being there, with them and with Ciaran, voices echoing off the walls in that old church or ringing out across the square, crepes and carafes arriving by the trayful . . . it made *her* feel cool, as if she had found herself at the centre of something.

Only one thing about the Utopia turned out to be less

than heavenly, which was that while the foyer had a full bar and bistro – a much more impressive array of food and drink than Lizzy had ever encountered in any movie theatre before – there was no concession stand. This, so far as she was concerned, was an obviously untenable situation.

'It's offensive to me as an American,' she told Ciaran on that very first Wednesday, as they settled into red velvet seats.

He rolled his eyes. 'What about as a Scot?'

'It's offensive to me as a Scot too. You can't have movies without candy. Even very serious, foreign arthouse movies.'

The next week, they saw *Harry Potter and the Deathly Hallows*, which was not serious, foreign *or* arthouse, but nonetheless, Lizzy made sure to come armed with bags of treats from Carrefour City.

And Ciaran, for all his eye-rolling, didn't say no.

Chapter Ten

'It really is quite a significant incentive,' Simon says, ever the numbers guy. He tops up everyone's wine generously. 'Thirty per cent tax relief on all eligible expenditure, with that rising to thirty-five if production happens outside of Edinburgh or Glasgow.'

Around the table at Da Laura, along with Lizzy and Simon, are three powerhouse Canadian producers whose film premiered last night at the Palais, seemingly to great acclaim in the press today.

In, one might say, *the trades.*

'Wow, that's definitely competitive,' one of the producers responds, sounding genuinely enthused. But, it's hard to know, Lizzy thinks. There could be other factors at play here too. Canadian niceness. The universal appeal of a free dinner.

'You know, dollar for dollar you could honestly probably do a little better in, say, Bulgaria or Croatia,' she chimes in, because she's always found the pre-emptive strike, the provision of something fairly close to full disclosure, to work well. 'But then you're gonna be running into other issues in terms of language barrier and facilities and so on. Sometimes it's just not worth it.'

She winces knowingly, as though she herself has been in the trenches of film production in those countries, and has the battle wounds to show for it.

'Oh my gosh, *absolutely*,' the producer agrees, and as she begins a re-telling of some friend's experience on a Hungarian co-pro, Lizzy tries hard to maintain attention. Normally, this is the stuff she likes – the anecdotes, the tales of woe and triumph. Certainly at this preliminary, getting-to-know-you stage, the fewer numbers being tossed around the better, so far as she's concerned.

Tonight, though, she feels drained and distracted, and she knows exactly who to blame for it. She hates how much her fingers itch to grab for her phone and look up that *Variety* article.

On the upside, she can at least do her part of this whole thing pretty well on about sixty per cent power by now. She's had this work meeting countless times already. And that's what it is. If it looks like a dinner party and sounds like a dinner party and smells like a dinner party, but it's happening at the Cannes Film Festival, it's a work meeting.

After nine years in the job, Lizzy knows how to draw out the details she needs, knows how to subtly drop in the information that will sell people on Scotland without them feeling they've been sold anything at all. She has a dozen phrases that almost say themselves by now. Her approach is not exactly aligned with her boss's – she knows that it's probably all a little loosey-goosey for Simon's taste – but it seems to get results. The three biggest film and television projects on Scottish soil inside the past decade were all ones that she brought there.

Truthfully, though, Lizzy's favourite thing about her job is *not* finding a film – one such as these Canadians' next project – that is undoubtedly going to be made *somewhere*, and encouraging it to be made in Scotland. Her favourite thing is to find a film that likely would not be made at all, were it not for the support offered by the Film Board (modest and all as that support generally is). Two years ago, she had plucked a treatment for a short film from the slush pile, helped the filmmakers develop it a little, and then given them ten grand in grant money. The following year, it was nominated for an Oscar for Best Short Film. Rightly or wrongly, she's prouder of that than she is of having enticed any of those big fancy productions to Glasgow and the Highlands.

'The message we're getting from the Scottish government is that they're very much committed to supporting the sector in new ways,' Simon is saying now. She must have missed some connective thread of the conversation, Lizzy realises. But she can catch up fast. 'That's in terms of finances, studio space, crew, everything. We actually have the Scottish Culture Minister in Cannes for our social event this year, which is exciting.'

'Oh, awesome,' says one of the producers.

'We'd love it if you all came along,' Lizzy prompts, 'if you're still around by then. Lots of our heavy hitters in terms of the industry within Scotland and the UK will be there, so it might be a nice opportunity to meet some people. It's going to be a ceilidh.'

'That's, like, square dancing, right?'

There's nothing mocking or mean about the way the producer says it, nothing at all, but still Lizzy feels a faint flutter of embarrassment. It doesn't take much to re-stoke her fear that the whole idea – proposed on a whim around a bleak conference room table back in October – was stupid to begin with.

'Kind of, yeah,' she replies, with a little laugh. 'It's just a fun thing, you know? Screen Ireland do a karaoke party every year, as you probably know, and there's the cabaret event at the American Pavilion – these are kind of staples of the festival by now, and we just wanted to find a way to bring people together ourselves. Like Simon said, we really are in a time of huge growth in terms of the industry in Scotland. So, we figured we could stand to up the ante for our Cannes event; be a little more ambitious than just another drinks reception, you know? The ceilidh itself is just going to be for about an hour,' she adds, by way of reassurance. 'And it's definitely optional. It should be fun, though. Douglas Maclaine is going to call it.'

She sees all three of the producers' eyes light up, in the way that people's eyes do at the mention of a famous person.

'What exactly does that entail, "calling it"?' one of them dares to ask then.

'Oh. Basically just explain the steps, and keep everybody on track as a group. Or, try to at least. It normally ends up in chaos but that's sort of part of the fun.'

'Well, I'm sold,' one of the producers proclaims. 'If you have space on your list, we'd love to come.'

'Absolutely,' Lizzy beams, making a mental note – in among about a dozen other slightly crumpled mental notes – to tell Shauna to add their names to the database.

The database, at this point, is like a child to Lizzy. As precious, and requiring as much maintenance.

'Have you got a busy schedule for the rest of your trip?' Simon enquires of their guests, signifying that they're on the wind-down now; shop talk is over for the evening. 'Or do you think you might get a chance to see anything?'

'You know, that's one of the great parts about having had our movie screen so early on. For the most part, we're kind of done. I mean, we have some meetings and stuff, obviously, but I was just saying to Vicky' – the woman looks towards her colleague – 'that I am *so excited* to maybe actually *see* some films!'

'At a film festival, who'd have thunk!' Simon jokes, and everyone chuckles politely. Or at least, Lizzy chuckles politely. She assumes that's what the others are doing too.

'What have you got lined up?' he enquires.

'Oh my gosh. So tomorrow night we're going to *Onyx* – you know, the new Nicolas Winding Refn film? And then we have Nicole Holofcener's premiere the night after.'

This, Lizzy thinks, is probably her cue. Simon brings her along to these things mostly because her current batting average happens to be good. She knows that. Plus it's important to have a gender balance – Simon whips that one out quite a lot, most commonly when Brendan gets uppity in the office. But Lizzy would wager that there is another, undeclared reason for the regularity of her dinner invitations.

Prior to landing his current gig, Simon had worked for thirty years at Scottish Development International, most recently attempting to entice low carbon energy companies to set up shop somewhere in the country. Before that, it was fintech companies. Before *that*, textiles. Put frankly, Lizzy suspects that – aside from those projects with which the Film Board has been involved during his tenure – Simon Muldoney doesn't actually know shit about films.

'That's amazing! I always love Nicole Holofcener's movies,' she jumps in. '*Enough Said* and *Please Give* and . . . ugh. Just all of them, really.'

'So great, right?' the producer replies emphatically, and as everyone around the table begins to gesture and jabber excitedly, Lizzy can't help but think that this – *this* – is why she still loves filmmakers. Even for all their awfulness and weirdness. Even despite all the emails she's received from them over the years, which have often been genuinely fucking insane in their range, content and sheer volume. There's still a level of enthusiasm, of dynamism, about filmmakers that she just isn't sure exists within many other industries, or at least not in such widespread replication. In among the silliness and stress of these twelve days in Cannes, there are still times when the simple fact of filmmakers congregating, *en masse*, seems to give the whole town as collegial and connected an atmosphere as that square outside the Utopia cinema in Bordeaux.

Just like that, there he is again; Ciaran.

In her brain, Ciaran, Ciaran, Ciaran.

She shoves him out of it. Alarmingly, though, she feels like she might actually be getting worse at that, rather than better.

Even setting her own capabilities aside, it seems he just won't be shoved. Not five minutes later, the conversation is flowing perfectly enjoyably, when one of the producers raises an eyebrow.

'I'll tell you what,' he says, 'speaking of premieres, I had been thinking of seeing if a friend could get us into Ciaran Flynn's new movie on Tuesday? But . . .' he trails off deliberately, clenching his teeth in a fashion that seems to straddle comedy and horror.

'Right?!' one of the other producers says, her eyes widening with the drama. It's a shock to Lizzy to note that there seems, around the table, to be a sense of collective understanding here. Even Simon appears to be up to speed. Maybe Ciaran was right. Maybe his whole situation really *is* the hottest gossip of the day.

She thinks of his face as he left her earlier this evening – the desperation that had seemed to be genuine – and his voice echoes in her brain.

We were friends once. I would do it for you.

She doesn't know whether that's true, or specifically what the 'it' would even entail. So many of the things he'd said had not been entirely clear to her – but she'd been caught on the hop by him, for the third time in as many days; she'd had neither the time nor the inclination to dig down into the detail. What was the thing he'd said, about making himself pathetic? Again? She had no idea what he'd meant by that one. Probably nothing. In films, when people said stuff, it always meant something. In life, a lot of the time, they just said stuff.

'I mean, I guess we don't really know what went down . . .' the producer continues, his tone a lot less impartial than his words.

'Still. Nobody likes a copycat. You gotta figure the woman wouldn't be making these accusations – publicly – and *Variety* wouldn't be printing them, if they didn't hang together. It just kind of leaves a sour taste in the mouth, doesn't it?'

'Honestly, yeah. It does. I guess that's the thing with guys like that who kinda seem to come from nowhere. You just never know. It's a shame though. I really liked his first film.'

'She didn't hold back in the article, did she, eh? Whatever her name was, the other filmmaker,' Simon pipes up, and for Lizzy, that's it.

She absolutely cannot restrain herself any longer.

She's given it a good go, she thinks. But she's only human. She's willing to just go ahead and admit defeat at this point.

She excuses herself from the table swiftly, and in the bathroom cubicle she closes the lid of the toilet, sitting down on top of it. In seconds, she has the *Variety* article pulled up on her phone.

Chapter Eleven

Ciaran Flynn Faces Plagiarism Claims Over Cannes Selection *Wish You Were Here*

EXCLUSIVE: Just days before Ciaran Flynn's hotly-anticipated sophomore film is due to premiere at the Cannes Film Festival, reports of copyright infringement and plagiarism threaten to overshadow its release.

The 32-year-old writer-director has enjoyed a rapid ascent in recent years. His self-produced web series *Not What I Ordered* went viral in 2018, drawing comparisons to Bo Burnham and Phoebe Waller-Bridge, among others. The year 2020 saw the release of his much-lauded feature film debut *Inclement Weather*, and a string of awards followed, including a BAFTA for Breakthrough Talent.

Flynn's latest offering, *Wish You Were Here* is described as 'a coming of age romantic dramedy' produced in association with Figment Pictures, the British super-producers behind such critical darlings as *Dodie* and *Four Lovers*, as well as last year's box office juggernaut *Trifecta*.

Today, *Variety* has exclusively learned that Flynn has been accused of copying substantial aspects of *Wish You Were Here* from British writer Penny Ainsley. Ms Ainsley has instructed legal counsel, alleging infringement of copyright in the feature film script she has been developing since 2019.

Details of Flynn's film, at the time of writing, are scant on the ground. According to a press release, it chronicles the story of 20-year-old Isaac (played by up-and-comer Niall Sullivan). When his younger sister dies by suicide, Isaac leaves his life in rural Ireland to take up his sister's plans instead. Specifically, he journeys to France, moving in with a diverse cast of characters (notably Jools Tanner's Claudia) and becoming caretaker (a so-called 'bro-pair') to a taciturn little boy. Comedy, romance and life lessons ensue – at least, that's what it looks like, based on the trailer.

Ms Ainsley, 37, is an alumnus of the prestigious Sundance Institute Screenwriters' Lab. Her feature script centres on Lola, a young English woman who swaps the confines of her conservative community for an adventure in Spain with a secret boyfriend. However, just a week later, Lola's boyfriend commits suicide, leaving Lola to navigate her grief, and her new life, alone.

Ms Ainsley submitted the script to Figment Films for consideration almost two years ago. She received no follow-up communication from the production company.

'Rejection is part of this business,' she says. 'I'm a big girl, and I've had plenty of practice with that by this stage. So I wasn't necessarily too upset.' However, when details of Flynn's project became public, friends began reaching out to her, struck by the apparent similarity.

Ms Ainsley was too. Flynn, she suggests, has done little more than transform the main character from her script into a man, and send him off to France rather than Spain.

'The core similarity is obvious,' she says. 'We're talking about a fish out of water story – a young student coming to a foreign country and figuring out who they are without any of the things they have always had around to constrain them, or to bolster them. And then there is the broader theme of suicide and how one copes with that particular kind of grief. That's the story I wrote, and it's a story Ciaran Flynn and his producing partners had access to, and I believe that it's the basis for the film they're about to make millions of dollars from.'

Presented with the prospect that such similarities might arise coincidentally, Ms Ainsley is unconvinced.

'It's just a little *too* coincidental, if you ask me. I haven't been allowed to see the whole film yet – my lawyers requested a copy for verification purposes, but were refused. So, who's to say, at this point, where the copying ends? It appears from the trailer that the main character in *Wish You Were Here* becomes romantically involved with someone he meets in Europe, for example. Guess what? Lola does too. And there's even a line in my script where Lola talks about what a mess her life has become, and yet her parents – thinking she's off studying inscriptions in the Alhambra or whatnot – are bragging to all their friends about her. Something very substantially similar to that is featured in the trailer for *Wish You Were Here* – it's just shameless, really.'

According to Ms Ainsley, the alleged theft of her ideas is illustrative of a culture of misogyny that still underpins the film industry. 'Women's labour, creativity and stories are routinely undervalued at best, and stolen at worst,' she says. 'And you can times that by ten for women of colour, or disabled women, or women in the LGBTQIA community. So, this is not new. But at a certain point, we have to stand up against it. Ciaran Flynn is a fully paid-up member of the boys' club, obviously, and I don't doubt he has the ego to genuinely think that it's his right to just pick what he wants – but it isn't. It's illegal, and it's gone on long enough.'

In a statement, lawyers for Ms Ainsley said: 'We have been in communication with the creative team associated with *Wish You Were Here* in regard to numerous clear breaches of copyright law. Should they fail to propose an appropriate arrangement, recognising our client's significant creative contribution to this film, we will not hesitate to seek all available remedies on behalf of our client in court. This matter should be of interest to all who value the arts, and the rights of artists to be fairly compensated for their work and skill.'

Representatives for Figment Pictures and for Flynn did not immediately respond to request for comment.

By the time she reaches the end of the article, Lizzy lets out a heavy exhale she hadn't been aware of holding in. She's clutching her phone in a death grip too, she realises. She feels strangely jittery given this whole situation really has nothing to do with her.

Does it have nothing to do with her?

On the one hand, yes. Of course it has nothing to do with her. She hadn't even been aware of it a few hours ago.

Furthermore, the article, on its face, does sound pretty convincing. Lizzy wouldn't, as a matter of principle, be keen to contribute in any way to what seems to her a relentless, toxic system of women – not just women in film, but women generally – not being believed about the things they say. Nor, of course, is there any love lost between herself and Ciaran. It isn't too big a stretch to imagine a scenario in which he proves to be a huge fucking disappointment.

All of that is on the one hand.

On the other hand, hearing the way everyone at the dinner table had talked about the situation, as though they knew enough to draw conclusions; undeniably that had tugged at some fundamental understanding of fairness inside of Lizzy. And now, reading the article . . . it perhaps *isn't* really true to say that nothing contained within it has anything to do with her. Certainly, she couldn't say that it prompts no recollection or response in her.

She scrolls upwards, reads over certain passages again. There's enough for her to suspect that the similarity between the two projects *might* just be coincidence – Penny could be mistaken about that. Or just plain lying? That's another possibility, Lizzy figures. Her gaze lingers on the photograph of Penny accompanying the article. She's very pretty. The possibility that pops into Lizzy's mind next is . . . well, it's just what pops into her head. She's not proud of it. She curses herself over it. What she knows about this stranger, after all, amounts essentially to the fact that she is a woman who has expressed some criticism of a man. There is no good reason to think that she might be a jilted girlfriend. And in any event, her appearance probably wouldn't especially help confirm or deny such a prospect. A woman did not need to be model-gorgeous in order to find herself at the centre of some romantic drama. The unlearning of shit like that, for Lizzy, never seemed to stop.

Her mind drifts to her dinner companions, and she wonders how long she's been in the bathroom at this point. She probably doesn't have much longer before everyone assumes she has some sort of gastrointestinal issue. That thought horrifies her – it drags her out of rumination and into action. Quickly, she pulls the business card out of her purse. Printed on it, alongside Ciaran's name, is the name and email address of his assistant. In black pen, though, he's scrawled a phone number.

Before she can change her mind, she types it into her phone. He picks up right away.

'It's me,' she says. 'Lizzy.'

'Oh! Hi!'

'Look, Ciaran,' she says then, cutting right to the chase. 'Just give it to me straight. And bear in mind I really, truly don't care one way or another. Did you fuck this woman over? Penny Ainsley?'

'No,' he replies, and though he sounds every bit as clear about that as he had earlier on the street, she wishes she could see his face when he says it – try to weigh him up in the light of all the information she has now.

'Did you fuck her in *any* sense?' she presses pointedly.

'What? No! I don't even know her. Dear Jesus, Lizzy.'

He sounds genuinely insulted. She's touched a sore spot there, it seems. Rich, considering that, at least according to Lizzy's recollection, it's probably not an area whereby Ciaran Flynn has the right to be anywhere close to a high horse. Nonetheless, his vehemence subdues her a little.

'Alright, well . . . good,' she says dumbly.

'Does that mean you . . . might consider . . .?'

She pauses, clicks her tongue against the roof of her mouth.

'Well, I'd need to see the film,' she says, because that much is obvious.

It doesn't seem to be so for Ciaran.

'Oh,' he replies, sounding a little startled, as if, in fact, the thought hadn't even occurred to him.

'If I'm meant to be saying I know for sure this couldn't have come from anywhere but the mind of Ciaran Flynn, I think I kinda need to have seen the thing.'

'Of course,' he scrambles. 'Yeah. Obviously. Sorry. Right. I'll, uh . . . I'll email you. I'll get your address from Cinando.'

'Cool,' she replies, and in her mind, she's already telling herself: this doesn't mean she has to do anything. Not an interview, not a social media post, not any other hare-brained thing cooked up by Ciaran or his minions. She's just going to watch the film. That's all, just watch it. If for no other reason than that the curiosity is absolutely killing her.

Chapter Twelve

The Christmas market in Bordeaux was the stuff of storybooks. In the wide esplanade of Allées de Tourny, dozens of little wooden cabins had arrived, all smelling of cinnamon and dusted with fake snow. Twinkling lights were strung up around the bare branches of the linden trees and a lush fir, decorated with all the trimmings, had been positioned in pride of place at the end of the street. Many of the surrounding buildings were getting into the spirit of things too, their pale, grand façades now floodlit with colour, carols filtering out from mounted speakers. The cumulative effect was the same as it was the world over – for the month of December, the whole city felt shifted on its axis a little, revolving around this new spectacle. Even the bite in the air was somehow made magical by crowds of bobble-hatted heads, by hot chocolates between gloved hands.

When Lizzy showed up, it had just gotten dark outside, and a bunch of people were already there. This was the last hurrah before everyone headed home for the holidays.

Caroline was standing with Emma, and Lizzy waved at the two of them, stopping short of going over for a chat.

Inside the confines of Rue Cabirol, more and more tension was starting to creep in between Lizzy and Caroline. It was unclear to Lizzy why her roommate would especially care that, for example, her university attendance had become somewhat sporadic – lazy days with Mia, Hans and Ciaran often seeming a much more appealing option than schlepping all the way out to campus. But Caroline certainly seemed to care.

'You know, Sylvia said that if we fail things here, it still goes on our transcript,' Caroline had reminded her just a few days prior. Sylvia was their adviser of studies back in Edinburgh.

'Mmm, yeah.'

'So what are you going to do, if you get asked about it in a job interview?'

The implication, which was that she was bound to end up with some fails on her transcript, had not been one Lizzy took offence at whatsoever. She hadn't really registered it, and if she had, she would have agreed the prospect seemed likely. Instead, she'd thought about her roommate's question for a moment.

'. . . If it's going to be a job somewhere in the UK or North America, I guess I'll say, "Those classes were all in French",' she'd replied then, mildly.

But Caroline was not to be deterred.

'What if it's a job in France?'

At the very notion, Lizzy had accidentally laughed out loud.

On Allées de Tourny now, everyone shuffled around in a group for a while, then began splintering off as particular stalls caught people's attention. Lizzy made a beeline for a Nutella crepe. So far as she was concerned, a Christmas market was about two things – atmosphere and food. As for the crafts . . . it would have been a stretch even to have said that she could take or leave them. She could definitely have left them. In fact, she had never really been sure who *was* enticed by, say, a large wooden giraffe, or a dreamcatcher, or a nightlight covered in mosaic tiles.

Soon, it became very clear to her.

Hans Brubacher, that was who.

'*Schnickschnack*!' he said delightedly, his whole face lighting up. 'I don't know how to say that in English.'

'Knick-knacks,' Mia supplied, though the phonetics alone provided a pretty good idea. 'He lives for this stuff.'

And as the two of them trooped off to look at some truly hideous pottery, Lizzy just laughed. Beside her, Ciaran's roommate Liam slung his arm around her shoulders. He was evidently well on his way with the *glühwein* already.

'Well, Lizzy,' he declared grandly.

'Well, Liam.'

'Are you looking forward to Christmas?'

'Yeah,' she said, although she very much was not. 'You?'

'Ah, you know yourself. Be good to get home, like. So, tell me this, and tell me no more. What are your intentions towards our young Mr Flynn there?'

Lizzy followed his gaze up ahead, to where Ciaran was standing at another stall, talking to Matteo and some of the other Spanish students.

'My intentions?'

'The two of you seem to have got very chummy, that's all I'm saying. Cinema dates on a Wednesday now, is it?'

Liam was grinning, and Lizzy felt her stomach churn a little. The time she spent with Ciaran, just him and her, wasn't a secret exactly. But she didn't love the idea that other people knew about it without her having told them. And, apparently, were talking about it. Very little was more sincerely horrifying to Lizzy than the thought of being the subject of gossip.

'Definitely *not* cinema *dates*,' she corrected. 'Is that what . . .? I mean. Where'd you hear that?' Her voice came out sounding . . . not quite normal somehow, but perhaps it was noticeable only to her. Liam was still full of smiles.

'From the man himself!'

Lizzy nearly choked on her crepe. 'What?!'

'Weeelll, he might not have used the word "date",' Liam conceded. 'But there must've been three or four weeks there when I texted him about poker with the lads in the flat, and what was he at? He was at the pictures with you. Or, sitting having dinner and getting pissed after the pictures, I should say. So . . . y'know,' he shrugged extravagantly. 'I surmised. There's a good word, isn't it? Surmised.'

At this, Lizzy couldn't help but smile. The situation felt better now, more containable. 'Yeah,' she said. 'Here's my suggestion to you, though, Liam. *Un*-surmise. We're friends, that's it. If rumours get around, I'm gonna know who to blame.'

'Ah come on now, Lizzy. Sure you would know I'm the very *soul* of discretion. You'll be wanting a mulled wine so?' Liam said expectantly. She looked at him blankly. His Kerry accent was so thick that sometimes it took her a few seconds to catch up.

'Well, *I* do,' he continued. 'C'mon. Lads!' he called out to some of the others, in that way that all the Irish boys did, where people's gender didn't seem to come into it. '*Glühwein!*'

Chapter Thirteen

Several hours later, when Lizzy looked around her living room in Rue Cabirol, she didn't know exactly *how* so many people had gotten there.

Her and Ciaran and Mia and Hans and Caroline and Emma and Charlotte and Matteo and Liam and Andrew. Ten. That felt like a lot in the small space, and typically Lizzy would not have wanted to bring the party home to that extent, firstly because she herself didn't usually want to be responsible for that many people having a good time, but also because of the thought of Caroline's likely disapproval.

When she glanced over, though, her roommate was engaged in conversation with Ciaran, giggling away, and really, Lizzy should have known. When they were around others, Caroline tended to project a much more carefree version of herself. It was a weird one. While a part of Lizzy enjoyed this, the larger part of her was irritated by it. She would watch her roommate laughing loudly, performing friendship – she could sometimes, with boys especially, be downright simpering – and it all just felt a little like hypocrisy to Lizzy. As though Caroline were trying to collect and claim people like certificates, concealing from them her true self. This was, after all, the same girl who tutted when Lizzy arrived home tipsy on Wednesdays. She was not a chilled person. Except, apparently, when she was.

In any event, as Lizzy looked over at Caroline and Ciaran now, it was Ciaran who formed the focus of her attention. She let her gaze linger on him, as though something new might reveal itself to her for the first time.

It didn't.

She cursed Liam for having created this feeling of . . . unsettledness.

The thing was, of course she'd *thought* about it before now – the prospect that Ciaran and she might become more than friends. Although she would have denied it convincingly, the truth was that for at least the past five years, more or less any time Lizzy met someone new and male, the thought had crossed her mind that perhaps this was about to be it; perhaps this was The One. It hadn't ever turned out to be, though, and somehow even the hope had become embarrassing to her. She'd gotten used to thinking of it as a silly thing, a thing to be squashed immediately, a thing that was for other people.

She guessed that must have been what she'd done with Ciaran – to the point that when she squinted over at him in her living room now, she actually did not know whether she was looking at someone she was attracted to, in *that* way, or not. He was just Ciaran.

In any event, it was ultimately all by the by. He had never displayed any interest in her, in *that* way, and she was one hundred per cent sure he had none, and that was just fine. It was the normal course of things. Lizzy did not think she was especially lacking in self-confidence, as an overall matter, but she understood that what it took to be liked and what it took to be desired were not the same. She understood that she had a sincerely terrible nose right there in the middle of her face, and no real bone structure to speak of, and a body that didn't at all belong in the bandage dresses other girls wore. That guys were broadly uninterested in dating her was not a thing she could especially hold against them.

As the night wore on, everyone hit the road one by one, stumbling out of Rue Cabirol with a clatter of farewells and festive wishes. By the time Caroline took herself off to bed, it was just Mia, Hans and Ciaran left.

It had been a fun night but still, Lizzy found she kind of liked it better this way.

'Caroline was in good form tonight,' Ciaran said idly, at some point. Lizzy had no idea what time it was. 3 a.m.?

'She was loving *you* alright.'

'I know, she really was! Oh my God, look,' Ciaran said then.

He and Lizzy were at either ends of one couch and on the other one, Mia was sprawled out. Her feet were in Hans' lap, one of her arms trailing down almost to the floor, her face squashed against the seat cushion in a way that looked neither very comfortable nor very attractive. Hans, meanwhile, was sitting upright, but with his head tilted all the way back and his mouth wide open, snoring.

'Love's young dream, huh? How are they sleeping through this?' Lizzy said, though of course she knew – there was no tiredness that equalled drunkenness in its capacity to knock you out cold. From the crappy speakers of her laptop, 'Snow Is Falling', was playing, tinny but festive, and she tapped the volume down a few notches.

'Any requests?' she asked, glancing over at Ciaran.

'You pick.'

Lizzy thought for a second and then, on a whim, she went for one of her tried and trues, the *Blue* album. In the time she'd been in Bordeaux, she'd found herself listening to a lot of records like that – the ones she grew up on. There was a huge part of her that didn't want to love any of those songs anymore, didn't *want* to keep going toward the comfort of them. But it had turned out to be hard to stop.

'Will we finish this off?' Ciaran asked, holding up the bottle, and she assessed the situation. By then, red wine had become her beverage of choice, and specifically, she'd developed a taste for the cheap stuff. There was about a glass each left, which was a glass both of them would undoubtedly be better off without. The answer was obvious.

'May as well,' she said.

He poured, and she joined in with the music quietly, letting her voice rise and swoop the way it wanted to. Lizzy loved loved loved to sing. And she *could* sing. That was just something she'd always known about herself, in the same matter-of-fact way that she knew she could walk and talk. She hardly realised she had begun to sing right then at all until a minute later, when she caught the way that Ciaran was looking at her. She couldn't describe it. He was smiling faintly, but somehow she knew that he wasn't laughing at her. Still, she suddenly felt a little shy.

'You know, I was almost gonna be named after Joni Mitchell,' she told him then. 'Or Carole, after Carole King. Or Laura, after Laura Nyro.'

'Laura who?'

'Laura *Nyro*.'

'I've never heard of her.'

'Oh my God, so good. She had this record, *More Than a New Discovery*, that I swear my mom played in our kitchen in Ferndale for like a year solid.'

Ciaran smiled. 'So how come you're not Laura, then? Or Carole or Joni?'

'Oh. My dad's mom died, and so I think *my* mom just had to take one for the team,' she said dryly, and even as Ciaran sniggered, she couldn't help but add: 'Not so much her policy anymore.'

He raised his eyebrows, an unspoken question.

'They're getting a divorce,' she heard herself say. She hadn't expected to tell him that. Immediately, she wished she hadn't.

'Oh.' His expression shifted. 'That's . . . shit. I'm sorry.'

She shrugged off the sympathy. 'It's not a big deal.'

At least, that seemed to be the consensus. To think otherwise was childish. And, it was quite clear to Lizzy that in this area of her life – as, apparently, in every other one – she was no longer supposed to be a child.

When the news of her parents' separation had begun to circulate, relatives had said *what a shame*, in much the same manner as they had when her cousin Mark hadn't gotten the grades to do medicine. Even Lizzy's own friends had asked her if she was okay, and the next day, proceeded more or less on the basis that she *was*.

She just couldn't help but find it slightly mind-boggling that had the situation arisen just twelve or eighteen months earlier – back when she was living at home, back when she was still a child – it presumably would have stood a good chance of being recognised by others as the seismic, world-altering nightmare that it was. *How is Lizzy coping?* people might have asked. *How could Robert and Franny do that to poor Lizzy? Maybe Lizzy should see a therapist. Maybe the* whole family *should see a therapist.*

As it was? Not so much.

'Oh. That's . . . I mean . . . wow. Okay then,' she could vaguely remember hearing herself say, right after her parents had first broken the news to her.

'You're probably right,' she'd added, when her mother had suggested that she, busy as she was with undergrad life, would likely not even notice the difference.

What she hadn't done was bawl her fucking brains out, like she had wanted to. She hadn't thrown anything. She hadn't said *I hate this* or *I hate you* or *please, can you not just keep pretending – for me?*

Now, what she had been left with of her family was just her father on the phone, saying 'I know your mum would love to have you stay with her for a bit over Christmas too, eh? Spread yourself around?'

As though an upbeat tone of voice might transform that prospect into something other than an entirely heart-breaking one.

'Is it the sort of situation where it's just better for everybody if they go their separate ways?' Ciaran asked then, gently.

'Well, it's better for them, apparently. I can't say it's really better for me,' Lizzy replied, unable to help the bitterness creeping into her voice, and when Ciaran just nodded in response, she found herself filling the space that he left.

'My mom had an affair,' she said.

Now *that* was something that had attracted other people's attention. So much more interesting than a run-of-the-mill split. It had been unbearable – her father's relatives pressing their hands into Lizzy's, saying *I heard the news*. Gossip, and second glances from old acquaintances on the street, and politeness that had hardly masked the judgement and glee at all.

'With a dentist – *our* dentist, actually,' she continues. 'Name's Neal. How does that even happen, y'know? Who goes in for like, a root canal, and thinks *wow, underneath that surgical mask you must be a real hottie?* Anyway, she's still seeing him. And my dad, apparently, is just, like . . . more or less *cool* with it. So, yeah. They filed the papers just before I came here.'

Lizzy knew that she likely never would have come to Bordeaux at all – never would have been seized with the sudden desire to apply for late entry to the Erasmus scheme – had her parents remained happily married. Or even unhappily married.

'Jesus,' Ciaran said. 'So, is this going to be the first Christmas since it happened?'

'Yep. They each have their own places now, but we're all spending the day together. Not Neal, thank God, but mom and dad and me. One big happy family. And the worst part is . . .' she swallowed, blinking back the tears that – horrifyingly – seemed to have sprung to her eyes.

'I thought that's what we *were*. You know? Like, I just did *not* see this coming.'

'So they weren't fighting and stuff?'

'Nope. I literally never even saw th— I love this song,' she interrupted herself then, as a new track started to play from her laptop. She paused a second, waiting for the words to begin, and then trilled along with them, because she just couldn't help it. That piano, that melody – it just was pure joy, simple as that. With a little smile, she rolled her eyes at herself, at her own indulgence. 'Anyway.'

'You have a *really* great voice,' Ciaran said, and she had a creeping sense of déjà vu, as if perhaps he'd told her that some other time too. She grasped for it in her mind, but couldn't quite remember.

He sipped his wine, and it reminded her to get back to hers as well. She could feel, now that she thought about it, how hours of alcohol had sunk in, had given her that pleasantly heavy feeling in her arms and legs.

'So, sorry, what were you saying?' he prompted then. 'I got distracted. About your mum and dad. Everything seemed fine until it wasn't, basically?'

'Yeah.' He had a way of asking questions that made her want to answer them. What was that? 'I mean, it's not like I spent a whole lot of time just sitting around thinking *wow, I have the perfect family* or anything, you know? But I just . . . thought that they loved me, and they loved each other and . . . I don't know.' She shrugged. That was probably such a juvenile thing to say. 'Some stuff you just think is always going to be true.'

'Were yous all really close, like before all this, then?'

'It was just the three of us so . . . yeah. Especially with my mom. Like to the point where I didn't even go away for college. Or,' she corrected herself immediately, 'university, I mean. I never know what to say.'

He frowned. 'What do you mean?'

'Like . . . let's say with the trash can,' she said, and her voice rose with the change in subject, became a little more spirited. This – the telling stories, making jokes, talking nonsense – was the frequency on which she felt most comfortable. She wasn't sure how they'd veered so far into her personal melodrama. That wasn't fun for anybody.

'Obviously, if I'm in Scotland,' she continued, 'or I'm talking to a Scottish person – or anyone from the UK or Ireland actually – I know that it's the rubbish bin. Right? So, should *I* say rubbish bin? Or, when that comes out of my mouth, in my accent, does that seem, like, pretentious and weird? On the other hand, though, if I just go ahead and say trash can, is that like, oh, here's this American just assuming we'll know all her American terms?'

'Surely people mostly *do* know the term trash can, though.'

'Yeah, but you know what I mean. Does that look like I'm not even *trying* to do as the Romans do, et cetera? And it's pronunciation as well as terminology. Aluminium. Basil. All of that. There's like a zillion of these things every day.'

'Or, probably at least three or four, right?' he offered slyly, and she rolled her eyes.

He opened his mouth, perhaps to provide some further insight, but she wasn't really in the market for it.

'The point is, Ciaran, it's *extremely* difficult to be an American living in Europe. Or a European living in America. Feel sorry for me.'

He grinned. 'I do. I feel very sorry for you. People just have no idea how hard you have it, Elizabeth. And that was *without* your parents losing the absolute run of themselves.'

She laughed, and she meant it, and she didn't know how long they talked after that – about the type of inconsequential stuff that delighted her. But it was long enough for them to finish their wine, and for the album to be almost through.

'I better go,' Ciaran said eventually. He looked over at Mia and Hans, still comatose and contorted.

'What are you going to do about those two?'

She shrugged. 'They're out for the count. They can just sleep it off here, I guess.'

'The pair of them are going to need a chiropractor when they get back to the *Vaterland* by the looks of things.'

She laughed lightly, opening the door for him, and they stood together in front of it.

'Well, have a good Christmas I guess!' she said. 'And happy new year and all that.'

'Yeah, you too,' he said, his eyes softening. 'It might not be as bad as you think.'

She must have made some sort of face, because he switched tacks.

'Even if it *is* as bad as you think, it'll not last forever. At some point, it'll just be over.'

'This is true. Okay.' She opened her arms to him, like an aunt at a wedding. '*On fait la bise!*'

It was just one of those little slogans that all the Erasmus students had come to use with each other, when they were performing the local ritual of air kissing hello and goodbye. In the French way, she and Ciaran kissed each other on the right cheek, then the left, and then, somehow, they were kissing each other's lips.

Lizzy, when she thought about it later, wouldn't have any explanation for that. She'd know for sure that she definitely didn't plan it, but she wouldn't have any idea if, in fact, she started it.

It was quick, just a peck, almost like they had accidentally bumped into one another's mouths. That might have actually been what had happened. They both broke into a short burst of laughter as soon as they pulled away from one another.

But then – this was the weirdest part – they were kissing again. On purpose. It was possible that his hands were on her face, and it was possible her hands reached around his back, and it was possible Ciaran was good at this. Lizzy didn't have time to worry about whether she was, in that particular moment, being good at it.

They parted again, and before he turned to make his way down the stairs, they both laughed again, like kids. That's what they were.

Chapter Fourteen

Any time Ciaran had seen footage of the Cannes Film Festival, it had been of the Palais des Festivals – of actors and directors posing on the famous red steps outside. He'd never thought much about what might be inside that cavernous building, beyond – presumably – somewhere for a lot of people to watch a movie

Sure enough, walking into the Palais for the first time with Peter, his manager points out the general direction of the Louis Lumière auditorium – the two-thousand-seat theatre where, completely terrifyingly and completely thrillingly, *Wish You Were Here* would be showing in just a few short days.

Principally, though, this place is a convention centre. Ciaran's not sure how he hadn't quite grasped that information before today. It's thirty thousand square meters, divided up into endless little booths, each rented for the duration of the festival by production, distribution or other film-related companies. Entities, Peter says, that are too low on the pecking order to have a suite at a hotel. Ciaran can't argue with that. But surely, he thinks, it speaks to a certain degree of success – or at the least, to a certain degree of ambition – just being here in Cannes at all. Weaving through hundreds of interior booths that get not so much as a glimmer of natural daylight, the image that pops into his mind is of an ocean liner's steerage compartments. The hard days and hope that coexist right alongside the majesty.

The place is swarming with people, and it's incredibly hard to believe it's a Saturday – weekends, Ciaran is learning, are of no consequence during the festival. Tucked away on the third floor, a little removed from the main action, is a twelve-seat screening room that he knows for sure he'd never have located by himself. Nonetheless, he shoos Peter away just as fast as he politely can. After that, ten minutes pass, and there is no sign of Lizzy.

If there were enough space for it, Ciaran would absolutely be pacing. As it is, he drums his fingers on his thigh, feeling jittery. It's always like this. He'd rather show something he's made to one thousand strangers than to one person he knows. He *thinks* Lizzy still qualifies as that, in some sense at least. And so far as he recalls, she'd never been shy about expressing her thoughts, unfiltered, in the aftermath of a film. Somehow, he doubts that's changed much. What if she hates it?

By way of distraction, he picks up his phone. The compass and the bird call to him, there's no denying it. Ciaran doesn't believe there's a person in the world whose life has somehow led to the point of being discussed on the internet, and who has not ever looked themselves up on the internet. He sure had. But it hadn't taken him too long to realise that even setting aside all the bad stuff people said, the good stuff, too, was like a diet of pizza and candy floss: probably not very good for him in the end. These days, he relies on Peter to tell him anything he might need to know. Today, he's been informed already that the *Variety* article has been spliced up and shared via 'a few other outlets' and that there has been 'a little bit of noise about it' online. Though it takes some effort, he manages to hold off on the four taps it would probably take to ascertain the extent to which Peter has downplayed the situation. Even so, that restraint only goes so far. A certain amount of reaction takes a more direct route to him. On WhatsApp, he has forty-three unread messages, ranging from capital-letters-outraged on his behalf, to emoji-led concern and sympathy, to wholly unconcealed nosiness. It's from one of these correspondents that he manages to glean that #CopycatCiaran is trending. He can feel the humiliation burning through him at the mere thought of it. Aside from this whole debacle with Penny Ainsley being cruelly timed and potentially extremely bad for business, it's also just plain old embarrassing, the knowledge that many people now think of him – and may always think of him – as a liar and a cheat.

He has just about convinced himself that any damage limitation efforts are futile, and that Lizzy has evidently bailed, when she walks through the door.

'Hi,' she says, and there's some part of him that still doesn't seem to be used to the sight of her. She looks . . . great, basically. There isn't really much more to say about it than that. There never has been.

'Sorry I'm late, this place is such a rabbit warren,' she says, sounding a little frazzled. She gathers her hair up in a fist, shaking it a few times, as if to create some air on the back of her neck. 'I swear to God, if we added it up over the years, I bet I've lost hours of my life in here at this point.'

Over the years? She's obviously an old hand at this whole Cannes business, Ciaran thinks. She could probably teach him a thing or two.

'Y'know, when I said I wanted to see the film, I was kind of thinking more that you'd send me a link,' she adds.

'I just thought, y'know . . .'

He trails off with a shrug. Truth be told, he doesn't exactly know what he'd been thinking. Maybe that the chances of anyone enjoying any film were upped by viewing it on a screen larger than a slab of butter. Maybe that it would be helpful if he were there with Lizzy, to explain or deny. Whatever it was, in this present moment, he wishes he *had* just sent her a link.

In any event, she doesn't seem to be waiting around for his explanation. She slithers into one of the seats in the back row.

'Alright, will we get the show on the road? I have to get to a meeting at Caffé Roma by 3.45, so I'm a little under the gun.'

Ciaran takes the seat beside her – they're big and bulky enough that he's still a good distance away from her. It doesn't feel like he's encroaching on her space. Back in Bordeaux, at the Utopia, they'd always been squished together like sardines, knees knocking, elbows brushing on the armrests. But, things were different then.

He looks down at a console that apparently is going to control both the lights in the screening room and

116

also the film itself. 'Okay, let me just . . . I've had a very extensive lesson from my manager on all these buttons.'

He's pretty sure he knows what to do, but still, he hesitates, glancing over at her.

'Do you want me to give you like a summary first, or do you have any questions, or . . .?'

'I think let's just watch it,' Lizzy replies, and the fact that she seems so breezy, so business-like, somehow makes him feel even more antsy.

'Okay,' he says, turning back to the device. Again, something stops him just as he's about to press the button.

'I feel kinda weird about you watching it,' he admits, the words out of his mouth before he has the chance to stop them.

He doesn't look for her response. Instead, reflexively, his face contorts – he sticks his tongue out and shakes his head a bit, as though to clear away the clutter, make more room for logic in his own mind.

'Okay whatever,' he says then, almost as if to himself. 'I suppose you would have seen it eventually anyway, right?'

She cocks an eyebrow the tiniest bit. 'Missed the first one,' she mumbles.

And, of course, this is not a fact that Lizzy necessarily needed to point out to him. Arguably, it is a bit rude that she chose to. But it seems to have just spilled out of her mouth, as though she too were speaking more to herself than anyone else. And honestly, what Ciaran mostly feels is an urge to laugh. The past few years have been a whirlwind of people being very nice to him. A crazy amount of people have taken it upon themselves to fawn over his work, only to later reveal, in some inadvertent fashion, that they had not, in fact, seen any of it. Ciaran didn't mind at all that they hadn't. But the hypocrisy – the totally voluntary and unnecessary hypocrisy – could be a bit of a sickener. It's strangely refreshing, to have someone just give it to him straight.

'Well it was very well received,' he offers slyly.

She looks at him, deadpan.

'So I hear,' she replies, and somehow he knows – he *knows* – that she's a little amused too. It's just such a precise feeling, the one where they each are finding the same unspoken thing enjoyable at the same time. He doesn't know how that's lasted all this time.

He clicks off the lights in the room, and with another click, that distinctive trumpet fanfare announces the beginning of the film. This is it. Ciaran ignores the butterflies in his stomach, because that's really the only thing to do with them, and after a few minutes, they've subsided considerably. This is his film, he remembers. He's proud of it. That's been sort of hard to hold on to over the past few days.

Still, though, as the first scene fades into the second, he becomes aware of a vague, niggling sensation. Some not-quite-right-ness about this, some part of his usual cinema experience that's missing. Then, it comes to him. In the darkness, he reaches down, pulling a few packets of Maltesers from his bag. Silently, he offers one to Lizzy.

For a moment, she just looks at him, the big screen casting her face in half-light, and he wonders whether maybe she's about to refuse.

She doesn't, though.

'Thanks,' she whispers, reaching out to take them from him.

You couldn't have movies without candy.

Chapter Fifteen

They're about forty minutes into the film when it hits him.

And in the midst of the tidal wave of horror and disbelief, what Ciaran knows for sure – the only thing he knows – is that he'll never be able to explain this to anyone.

After all, by now, he's seen *Wish You Were Here* more times than he can even count. Maybe twenty-five times.

How, in the re-telling, could he ever possibly make sense of the fact that on this, his maybe-twenty-sixth viewing, something brand new about it occurs to him for the very first time.

He seems – he fucking really seems – to have made a film about the woman sitting next to him.

Seriously.

Not her as she is now, of course. But her as she'd been years ago, back when they first met, back when she'd been Claudia's age.

Ciaran could die right here in his seat, and consider it a mercy. His mind reels as he tries to find some thread of plausible deniability he can pull at. It's true that the film is not *all* about Claudia. Isaac, the male lead, does have some other shit to deal with – job problems, flatmate problems, *my sister killed herself* problems. And, there definitely are some details about Claudia that Ciaran doesn't especially remember being true of Lizzy.

And yet.

If Isaac is the film's engine, Claudia is its beating heart. Suddenly, it is so *so* clear to Ciaran that she is sarcastic, in exactly the way that Lizzy had always been; sparkly, in exactly the way that Lizzy had always been. He even – Christ almighty – has Claudia *singing* at one point. The actress had done a great job with that, actually. She'd given just the kind of performance he'd hoped to draw out from her – no timidity but no ego either. Just naturalness. Joy.

All the way along in making *Wish You Were Here*, it had been a tricky thing, trying to square his own deep-seated aversion to schmaltz with the desire to acknowledge that sometimes, life *could* be magical. Sometimes, a human being *did* briefly get to feel young and free and in love, all at once. Ciaran thinks that scene with Claudia in the karaoke bar, in particular, does a pretty good job of getting the balance right. But, as it plays in front of Lizzy Munro in high definition, it is also, staggeringly and undeniably, the low point of his own myopia.

As the minutes tick by, he sits there frozen, trying to unpick how on earth this could have happened.

A film was just such an unwieldy, amorphous thing. A thousand decisions and almost as many decision-makers sought, painstakingly, to mould it into some sort of shape, but still, it spilled out into cracks, it gathered in places you didn't exactly put it. It did what it wanted a little bit.

Had he thought of Lizzy, way back at the very beginning, when he was mapping out a story set in France, when he was attempting to put the bare bones of some characters on the page? Of course he had.

Had he thought of her *throughout* the process, though? Even with the benefit of hindsight, Ciaran doesn't think so. Not consciously at least; not consistently. Maybe here and there. Here and there, he'd thought about all sorts of people he'd known throughout his life, all kinds of situations he'd been in or had so much as heard of. The characters in the film – he'd imagined, all the way up until today – were probably some composite of all of that. When he had told Lizzy yesterday that nationality was the crux of the similarity with Claudia, he'd meant it. He'd sincerely thought that was true. Now, it seems like an unbelievably transparent cover.

Because the very worst bit is this: Claudia – in the end – *picks* Isaac. She does not, for example, string him along and then scream like a banshee at him, and then have the nerve to act like the injured party. She does not abandon him and cut him off forever. No. None of that. She loves him and she finds him and she tells him. In other words, there is, Ciaran can see now, a lens through which the whole project comes off as some sort of mortifying fan-worship of the woman who is presently sitting beside him, just about tolerating the situation into which he's dragged her.

As the ninety minutes wear on, he chances some sidelong glances at Lizzy, trying to gauge her reaction. She gives nothing away, though. Her eyes don't move from the screen.

Finally, as the credits start to roll, she clears her throat a little. 'Wow,' she mumbles, almost inaudibly. 'Okay.'

Ciaran swallows. She's not looking at him, and he cannot read her whatsoever.

The good news, he thinks – getting back to the *original* problem here – is that if Lizzy isn't in too much of a hurry to file a restraining order, she will surely have no difficulty in attesting to the fact that this movie is based on something real. That it is not, in fact, a rip-off of someone else's story. That much should be all too obvious to her.

'Um, can we switch the lights back on?' she asks, turning to him.

'Yeah, of course,' he says, and he fumbles for the console, pausing the film while he's at it.

A second later, they each blink in the brightness. It seems very silent, the song that had been accompanying the credits suddenly halted mid-chorus.

Lizzy opens her mouth to speak when, on the arm of her chair, her phone jolts to life. Ciaran sees the screen light up. Oliver, it says, with a heart next to it. The same guy who'd called her yesterday, no doubt. The one she hadn't even been able to fob off without sounding slightly besotted.

He watches as she glances down now, hesitating for a second before hitting the red 'decline' button. Somewhere in Scotland, Ciaran thinks, there's a man who should never, ever see *Wish You Were Here*.

Or, maybe he should. Maybe he'd get a kick out of it. *My girlfriend's in that*, he might tell people, as a bus passes with the poster on it. *Or, kind of. It's the cringiest story you've ever heard in your life.*

Again, Lizzy clears her throat.

'Alright, so,' she begins, 'obviously there's a tonne of stuff in there that—'

'Knock knock!' comes a sing-songy voice, interrupting them. Ciaran hardly knows whether to be relieved or frustrated as Amy Solomon strides through the door. Big hair, sunglasses, wrap dress – this, Ciaran is learning, seems to be her standard look.

'I've been waiting outside for like twenty minutes for it to end! Hi, you must be Lizzy,' she says warmly, extending a handshake.

'That's me. It's nice to meet you.'

The moment Amy hears Lizzy's reply – or, much more likely, the accent in which it is delivered – she is so plainly thrilled that it's all Ciaran can do not to physically squirm. He rushes to avert his eyes when she beams over at him, and his mind clouds a little bit as the two women get acquainted. By the time he snaps back to attention, he seems to have missed a whole section of conversation.

'I guess you know all about that,' Amy's saying, with a chuckle. 'Being a fellow Cali girl and all.'

'I mean, not LA though. I grew up way north,' Lizzy clarifies, in that same vaguely apologetic way that, Ciaran remembers suddenly, she always used to. 'And then we left when I was fifteen. I try to get back most years, to visit family and stuff. But I've actually never even been to LA.'

Amy apparently is gobsmacked by this information, and spends a little time demonstrating it before getting down to business.

'So. Lizzy,' she says then. 'You've seen the movie now. And I think Ciaran's explained our predicament, right? It's non-optimal, obviously.'

'Non-optimal. I like that. That's a really good way of not saying "shitty",' Lizzy replies, and Ciaran can't help but snigger.

Amy raises an eyebrow. 'I'm a publicist, honey. I have a thousand ways to not say "shitty". So. Can you help us out? We'd sure appreciate it.'

'I guess I'm still not exactly sure what you want? Ciaran mentioned something about giving some quotes for the press, or . . .?'

'Right. Here's what I'm thinking. I have a dozen inter-views lined up for Ciaran tomorrow but the biggest piece is going to be in the *Hollywood Reporter* – Alexandra Goldman's doing it. Very sympathetic. She's scheduled for an hour sit-down with Ciaran, and – if you say yes – I can have her primed and ready for the fact that he has lunch right after with an old friend that he just can't miss. An old friend who, actually, he knows from when he himself lived in France. Who'll probably stop by the suite to pick him up. Who might even be able to provide some useful background for the article. You see what I'm saying?'

Lizzy hesitates. 'Well, I was just telling Ciaran before you arrived – there's plenty in the movie that, y'know, is news to me, and so I figure is just from his imagination. Or,' – she turns to Ciaran – 'you copied from this girl Penny, I guess I don't know!'

That this would be Lizzy's first comment on what she's just seen is frankly stunning to Ciaran. He's *stunned*.

But, she's looking at him like she's expecting a certain

reaction, like she might find some fun in actually provoking a certain reaction, and so he makes a stupid face at her. She makes one right back at him, as though they are both children on a playground, before turning back to Amy.

'Um, but yeah,' she continues, her tone softening a touch. 'There's . . . I mean, obviously there's stuff in there that I recognise. For sure.'

It feels deliberate, the way her gaze is fixed steadfastly on Amy when she says that, and Ciaran just cannot believe the kindness she's extending to him in this moment. The embarrassment she's trying to spare him. He feels his cheeks flush with heat.

'Wh—'

'Oh my God!' Lizzy cuts into whatever Amy had been about to say and she turns her head to look at him again, aghast this time. 'Your little sister, she didn't . . .'

It takes Ciaran a second to catch her meaning.

'Oh! No,' he assures her. 'She's fine. That bit's completely imagined.'

'Okay. Good,' Lizzy says, with a little exhale, and for a second, the two of them just look at each other, neither seeming sure what to say.

Amy breaks the silence. 'Alright!' she says briskly, and Ciaran watches her eyes narrow, flitting between him and Lizzy like she's sizing them up. For a moment, she says nothing. Then, she lands on Lizzy.

'Here's my question for you, girl,' she says. 'Do you believe that Ciaran wrote this film?'

Lizzy's glance flickers towards him briefly before she gives Amy the tiniest of nods.

'Yes.'

Amy's smile is somehow gentle and triumphant at once. 'Then that's all I need to know. Will you speak to Alexandra tomorrow? The parts you can't corroborate, just don't talk about.'

Lizzy puts her hand on her neck and stretches a little, with a wince. As though she's considering it.

'I wouldn't want my picture in there,' she warns. 'Or my last name.'

'Done.'

Lizzy gives another little nod. 'Okay then, yeah,' she agrees quietly. 'Done.'

After that, Amy wastes no time in getting on the phone, right then and there, talking at about a million miles a minute. It's an immediate reminder to Ciaran of how many people are invested in this thing, and the stress that has become a constant over the past few days re-roots itself in him just like that. To be totally truthful, he's still not sold on the idea that Lizzy's input is necessarily going to make a meaningful difference to the situation (much less is he clear on the specifics of what exactly she plans to say). But, somehow or other, she seems to have become a box that the studio wanted ticked. On that level alone, her cooperation is a huge relief.

With Amy chattering away beside them, he and Lizzy look at one another awkwardly.

'Thanks. I'm, uh . . . I'm definitely going to owe you one,' he says, and he wonders if this, right now, is where she confronts him about the reality of what she's just seen. He can hardly bear it, but he can't see any way around it.

The confrontation doesn't come, though.

'Sure,' she chirps, all crispness, in such a way as to

convey to him that, yes, she is doing this, but it doesn't make them friends. And that's when Ciaran realises. She hadn't been sparing his dignity before – or, not entirely. She doesn't actually want to talk about it either, the most obvious truth of the film. At least, not a moment before she has to.

That probably should be no great surprise, he thinks then. If there was one thing Lizzy Munro had always been good at, it was wilfully ignoring the blindingly fucking obvious.

*

By comparison to the dark cavern of the Palais, everything outside appears as if in technicolour, the afternoon sun hitting Lizzy as she dodges across the road. The producer she's meeting has likely beaten her to Caffé Roma, and she mentally tries to recall something of his filmography. It's a little difficult, though, to put the film she's just seen out of her head. Watching that had been . . . something.

It had been more or less as Ciaran had told her – the city was not Bordeaux, the characters were not the real people they'd known there. But still, Lizzy had somehow been able to see flashes of Bordeaux – of the sorts of shitty apartments and pretty squares in which she'd spent most of her time. Still, she had been able to see seeds of people she remembers.

Had some part – some unappealing, ungenerous part – of her been hoping *not* to like the whole thing? Hoping to be able to discount Ciaran Flynn, the wunderkind, once and for all?

Maybe.

But the truth is that she *had* liked it, and she thinks other people probably will too. It's about romance and youth and siblinghood and healing, and the ways in which France and a five-year-old can hand you your ass daily. It's also a tight ninety minutes in length, which so far as Lizzy is concerned, is as long as any film needs to be. She wouldn't say it's the most radical, most experimental thing she's ever seen in her life. But that's not – at least in her assessment – what it's trying to be. *Wish You Were Here* is smart and hopeful and genuinely, actually, funny. It's cleverly cast, it's beautifully shot . . . it does what it sets out to do well. *Good and a bad version of everything.* Lizzy's remembered that one.

Selfishly, of course, her main concern at the outset had been The American. Claudia. That the role had been quickly revealed to be rather a bigger one than she'd anticipated definitely hadn't helped matters there. However, as it turned out, her worry had faded fast. Nothing much of her own weirdness and neuroses had made it into the character – if anyone, Isaac, the male lead, got a bigger dollop of the sort of confusion and self-doubt and loss she remembers feeling on a regular basis at the age of twenty. And of course, this was to say nothing of the obvious fact that so far as romance was concerned, Claudia's French sojourn had a very different ending – and for that matter, beginning and middle – than Lizzy's own.

Of the people who knew her back then – that is, the only people who'd even be aware of the brief intersection of her life with Ciaran Flynn's – Lizzy is entirely content that not one of them would see any substantial link between her and Claudia. Even if, purely by virtue of nationality, they sought to try and make one. . . well. The character is confident and carefree, and played by a pretty, young actress. Honestly, Lizzy can think of worse things.

By the time the credits had rolled on *Wish You Were Here*, her major takeaway had been that Ciaran, in sketching out some semblance of his life in France for the world to see, had an opportunity to majorly fuck her over. Frankly, she wouldn't have been altogether surprised if he had taken it.

But he hadn't. And maybe one good turn deserved another.

That's why she's agreed to do this interview thing, mostly.

Plus, if she's being really honest, she'd found herself a little verklempt, when the lights came up in the theatre back there. She was not made of stone, after all. It had been hard, in the circumstances, *not* to remember the person she knew, or thought she knew, all those years ago. It had been hard to see his name on the credits and stop herself from thinking *wow, you really did it*. Maybe some pathetic and sentimental part of her is going along with all of this for that boy, too.

Chapter Sixteen

January in Bordeaux was not good. It was, in other words, *bad*.

When Lizzy put her key in the lock and stepped inside Rue Cabirol on the twelfth, the place felt cold and dingy and un-lived-in. Things she had stopped seeing before the Christmas break – the stains on the shower tray, the flaking paint on the window shutters – became *all* she saw, and even the primary appeal of the place, which was its location, no longer felt quite so appealing. Cathédrale St Andre, when she looked at it now, seemed ominous and austere, the seats outside all the surrounding cafés, lonely and bleak.

The weather was much as it had been before Christmas, but with all the trappings of the holiday season now disappeared, the city felt decidedly less magical. A mild winter, Lizzy learned, was still winter. Exams she didn't much care about were still exams that had to be endured. Caroline stalked around the apartment, reciting facts in French like some sort of Gallic lunatic, and it was, overall, the Januariest January that Lizzy had ever experienced.

Of course, not every bit of the dread and apathy and glumness inside of her could be put down to new-year blues. Some of it was the memory of, the lingering hangover from, December.

Fairly quickly upon her touchdown in Edinburgh, Lizzy had received the best news she'd had in a long time, perhaps in her entire life, which was that her mother had broken up with Neal the dentist.

Her father had been the one to tell her this, and Lizzy had tried to react only with mild, grown-up interest; as though she didn't especially mind one way or another, as though the only thing that mattered was that her mom – that both her parents, really – were now living whatever lives felt most authentic to them, and all the other evolved stuff she was supposed to have bought into (and in fact, *did* buy into, when it came to other people's families).

Secretly, though, Lizzy had been relieved beyond words, and when her mother arrived on Christmas day and swept her up into a fierce hug, Lizzy had let her do it.

The whole holiday season that followed – her mom stopping by her dad's flat most days, the pair of them getting on as well as they ever had – had been like waking slowly from a bad dream. Lizzy had just about floated on air all the way through until the new year, and by early January, it had come to feel normal to go into town for lunch with her mom, to talk and laugh like they used to.

'I'm thinking about maybe doing a master's degree,' her mom had said, spreading butter onto a scone. Lizzy's face brightened in support of the idea.

'I'd need to wait until after the divorce is finalised, obviously. Until all the dust has settled in terms of finances and things.'

And just like that, something inside of Lizzy had crumbled.

'So that's . . . you're still doing that?' she'd asked, her voice coming out stilted even as she strove for casualness.

'Oh, sweetie,' her mom had said softly, reaching out for her hand across the table. 'Yeah. We are. You know we are.'

The look on her face was unbearably sympathetic; it was a look that had made Lizzy suddenly feel almost violent. She had snatched her hand away.

'But I thought you broke up with . . . that guy.' As a matter of principle, she disliked saying Neal's name aloud.

'I did, yeah.'

'So . . . what?' Lizzy had asked searchingly, and then the dread came fast. 'Tell me there isn't somebody else already.'

'Lizzy! No, of course not!'

'Of course not!' Lizzy had repeated, with a mirthless sort of laugh. 'I don't think you get to say "Of course not" anymore, Mom, like that would just be out of the question. How the hell do I know what you're gonna do?'

Her mother hadn't been able to keep the surprise, the slight affront, off her face. Nonetheless, she'd swallowed it, said nothing about it.

'Your dad and I separating . . . it wasn't about Neal,' she'd replied instead. 'I know that's hard for you to believe, but it wasn't. Not really.'

'Well then what was it about, Mom?! Seriously.'

This question was the crux of what had plagued Lizzy

for months, and that it should be erupting like a zit, oozing out unattractively, here, in the Costa Coffee on Princes Street, was not something she had anticipated. But neither did it feel like something she could stop.

'You guys are the same now as you ever were. I don't know why you wouldn't want to be married anymore unless one or both of you wanted to *fuck* somebody else. And, so far as I can see, that doesn't seem to have been on *Dad's* radar.'

At this, her mother had looked downright shell-shocked. That wasn't the way they spoke to one another. It just wasn't. In the five seconds of awful silence that followed, there was probably an opportunity to roll things back, make things better, but Lizzy didn't take it.

'What?' she'd said instead, insolently. 'We're both adults now, right?'

Her mom shook her head a little. 'I guess we are,' she'd said, sounding sort of dazed. 'How'd that happen, huh?'

She had breathed out a sigh, and for a second, she'd just looked across the table. Lizzy could feel the heat burning in her cheeks.

'I'll tell you what, though,' her mother had continued then, 'no matter how grown up you get, me and you and your dad will always be a family. And as long as you guys are in Edinburgh, that's where I'm going to stay, okay? You don't have to worry about that. Going back to the States is not on my radar. And I'm definitely not looking to date anybody right now. At some point in the future . . .? I guess, who knows. I might meet somebody, and I might be attracted to them, and they might be attracted to me. That's just a part of life, right?'

That her forty-five-year-old mother, now down one husband and one boyfriend inside the space of a year, could say this with such apparent ease had been absolutely staggering to Lizzy. When she – who was young, and single and *supposed* to be out there sowing wild oats or whatever – could hardly imagine having the confidence to utter it herself; could hardly imagine feeling that things, in that particular sphere of her life, would likely just fall inevitably, reciprocally, into place. And somehow, that had enraged her.

She had not even been able to summon the words to respond.

*

Preoccupied as she had been, in Edinburgh, by other problems, the thought of what had happened with Ciaran before the break had been a niggle – *there*, no doubt, but fairly easily tucked away in some private corner of her brain.

Back in Bordeaux, though, it was harder to avoid thinking about. He hadn't been in touch – not a text, not a Facebook tag, nothing – and Lizzy was mortified. Her memory of that last night felt . . . unreliable. But it was clear that she had embarrassed herself, and probably also embarrassed him, and the whole thing was just *awful*.

By the twenty-third of January, her final exam came around at last. All of the others had been oral and had consisted, in the end, of a few rudimentary questions about the topic at hand, followed by a swift pivot to the more general matter of how she was enjoying France.

The last one, however, was written – a three-hour monstrosity that she walked out of after only ninety minutes, because she simply could not think of one more word to write down. Lizzy was certain she had failed and was on an almost-empty tram back home when her phone buzzed. Ciaran. In her already-fragile state, she could hardly bear to look at the text.

Are you finished with exams? he'd written.

Literally just done, she typed back.

Maybe this is weird, but would you want to go to Paris? came the next message.

What?

Of all the things that Lizzy might have anticipated from him, this would not have even made the top ten. Paris? She had been to Paris only once, when she was nine, which meant she almost felt like she hadn't been at all. She'd like to see it again, and it was just a four-hour train ride from Bordeaux. Maybe that would be something to look forward to – a spring trip.

When? she wrote, and his response came quickly.

Whenever really. This afternoon?

Lizzy laughed out loud on the tram, drawing glances from the few other passengers. Could she do that? she wondered. Did she even want to do that?

There certainly was nothing practical standing in her way. Thanks to her Wednesdays with the Durands, she had the money, assuming they wouldn't be booking dinner at the Ritz. And her schedule was wide open.

Of course, it was still true that she and Ciaran hadn't spoken for over a month. The fact that he'd made this suggestion, though, seemed to indicate that he was prepared to overlook her momentary idiocy. That he thought their friendship was salvageable from the wake of it. Undoubtedly, they'd have to push through a certain initial barrier of weirdness, but if he was willing to do that, Lizzy reasoned, then perhaps they may as well do it in Paris.

Why the hell not?

*

He was already on the train by the time she arrived – indeed, it seemed like more or less everyone intending to travel on the 13.57 TVG to Paris was already on it by the time Lizzy boarded, at 13.56. The packing process had been a bit of a scramble and it was possible that she didn't have any complete outfit with her other than the one she was wearing. She pulled her little wheelie suitcase through four, seven, ten carriages until she found him, installed by the window in a *carré* with his feet up, illegally, on the seat opposite him.

It was, in some instinctive way, good to see his face.

'Hi,' she said, settling herself at a diagonal to him.

'Hi,' he replied.

Each of them grinned, a little awkwardly, and even though Lizzy had spent the last thirty minutes planning her opening gambit, he beat her to it.

'Look, I'm really sorry about before Christmas,' he said, and even as she started to shake her head, he ploughed on. 'I don't know what . . . obviously we both had had a bit to drink, and I just—'

'No, oh my God, *I'm* sorry,' she interrupted him.

He seemed to barely hear her. 'I wanted to text you, and then I just didn't know if you were pissed off, and I didn't hear from you and—'

'No, I just felt so stupid—'

'I suppose I just—'

Their words kept overlapping, bumping up against each other, such that Lizzy couldn't grasp the specifics of what Ciaran was telling her. She thought she got the general gist, though, which was firstly that he wished they hadn't ever kissed in the doorway of Rue Cabirol, and secondly that he seemed to feel responsible for the fact that they had. Needless to say, the first part was not a surprise to her. The second part . . . well, that was much less expected, and certainly at odds with the narrative she'd spun in her own mind over the past five weeks. But then, by now, she'd thought about those – what? maybe ninety seconds? – so much that she had little concrete sense of what was real and what was not.

In any event, it was a spectacular thing to discover that – at least from what she could glean in the midst of her own frenetic babbling – he did not now appear to think of her as a girl with a crush. Desperate. Pathetic.

Both of them, at around the same time, seemed to run out of steam – or, more accurately, breath. They looked at each other silently.

'You wanna just . . . never speak of this ever again?' she suggested then.

He exhaled a little laugh through his nose. 'Absolutely.'

*

When they arrived at Gare du Nord, it was raining, and it proceeded to rain almost constantly for the next four days. They had the best time.

They checked into a youth hostel in Montmartre,

chosen because it was the first one they came upon, and because it was twenty-eight euro a night. Ciaran was in a four-bed male dormitory and she in a four-bed female one. Because it was low season, though, she turned out to have the room to herself.

In the mornings, they ate as much from the breakfast buffet as they could manage, and tried to convey to the few other guests in the kitchen that they were friendly people, but not there to make friends. Then, they walked all over the city. Under the wide awnings of bistros and greengrocers and souvenir shops, they waited out the worst of the downpours, and when the rain dwindled to a drizzle, they got on with the business of taking all the photographs that other people took. The Sacre-Coeur and the Eiffel Tower and the Eiffel Tower at night; him with the Eiffel Tower, her with the Eiffel Tower. They weren't a single bit artsier than any of the students who'd ever come before or would come after them, and it didn't occur to them even to try to be.

'It's actually pretty shite, isn't it?' Ciaran said, as they stood in front of the Moulin Rouge.

'Yeah.'

'I think we have to give a lot of credit to Baz Luhrmann for making this seem legitimately like a place where something romantic and exciting might happen to you.'

'Before you died of consumption,' Lizzy added.

Ciaran looked around the street, which was grey and wet and populated by bleak-looking strip clubs and sex shops. 'Yeah. Although, I mean, Jesus. You might be begging for the consumption to take you, mightn't you?' he said, which maybe wasn't even all that funny. But, with damp hair and aching feet, Lizzy laughed her head off.

Inside of ten years, the city's red-light district would be re-branded, first into South Pigalle and then into SoPi. Boutique hotels and American-style coffee shops would spring up, and an influx of new cocktail bars would begin to slowly convert a city of wine-lovers. The seedy would start to look a little kitschier, and what grit and grime remained of the place would serve mostly to make twenty-somethings feel edgy even as they lodged their parents' rent cheques.

On the bus on her way to work in Edinburgh, Lizzy would read an article one morning on the *New York Times*' website entitled 'SoPi: How Hipsters Ruined Paris' and would be catapulted back to that moment on the street with Ciaran with such force that her entire day would be thrown a little out of balance.

It didn't seem special at the time – it certainly wasn't glamorous – but it was joyful and it was real, and no part of it was made to last.

*

By the time they decided to go home – which was what Bordeaux felt like in comparison to the unfamiliar Parisian streets – it was primarily because of Thierry and Elise. Wednesday was coming around fast.

On their last evening, they went to Studio 28, a narrow little cinema near their hostel, famous for having itself featured in the movie *Amélie*. The film they saw – selected on the basis of being the only one showing – was a thriller.

'Not great,' Lizzy proclaimed, when the lights went up, the credits still rolling on screen. It had been nice to be sitting down, and nice to be dry, but these things of themselves didn't quite make for a five-star review. Or even a three-star review.

'Really not great,' Ciaran agreed, as people around them began to stand up and gather their things. And there was a pause before he added:

'Still. It'd be class to do that though, wouldn't it? Make a film.'

Tugging her big coat out from under her seat, Lizzy made a non-committal sort of sound in response. It wasn't something she'd ever thought about.

'I'd kinda like to make a film,' he said, after another moment, and something about the way he threw it out there – lightly, but carefully somehow, like he was testing the waters – made her feel intuitively that he was actually telling her something here.

She set her coat aside for now, and looked him in the eye. He really did have nice eyes. Sea blue, she thought she'd say, if she had to describe them. Maybe that was stupid.

'You could,' she replied simply.

Because Lizzy knew what it was to want something that seemed silly. She wanted, sometimes, to be famous; she wanted, almost always, to be beautiful. She wanted her parents to get back together. She wanted someone wonderful to fall in love with her and occasionally post cheesy things on the internet for the people she went to school with to see. She knew what it took – or, no, she could well *imagine* what it might take – to say out loud the silly thing that you wanted and didn't have, and probably would never have.

Ciaran looked unconvinced. 'Where I'm from . . . it's

not exactly the sort of place where you can just say you want to make a movie,' he said, getting to his feet and reaching for his rucksack.

Lizzy had seen pictures – he'd brought them up on Google Images to show her once. Donegal had vast beaches and cliffs and unspoiled countryside; pretty little white stone cottages that had probably been in families for generations, and pubs that looked like they would actively encourage communal singing. From this combination of the internet and her imagination, the place certainly seemed very cinematic to her. But, of course, that was not the same as having anything to do with the cinema industry. So she took his point.

Still, though. As she stood up beside him, she frowned. 'Is anywhere that kinda place really?'

Apart from maybe LA – it probably *was* perfectly normal, there, to just up and declare an intention to make it in Hollywood – she couldn't think of anywhere else.

'I dunno,' Ciaran said. 'But some places are especially not. And the arse end of Donegal would be one of them.'

He pushed the door out into the lobby, holding it for her.

'Yeah. I see what you're saying,' she replied. 'But . . . I don't know. I still think that's a cop-out. You live in Dublin now. They're bound to make tonnes of movies in Dublin. Or, some, at least.'

'Mmm. Maybe.'

'So, why'd you pick business studies? If you actually want to do something creative like that?'

'Just . . . y'know. Good, solid degree. I think my dad was hoping I'd maybe go ahead and just start helping *run* the business, to be totally honest.' Ciaran's father,

Lizzy knew by now, ran a kitchen-fitting company. It sounded like a fairly substantial enterprise.

'None of the rest of them have taken any interest and it's only our Sinead after me, so it's a bit of a tricky one. Sort of like I'm essentially the last hope, or something. Anyway. The point is, if I hadn't even wanted to go to university at all, there would have been no pressure, like.'

'And how 'bout if you said "I want to study film" or something like that?'

Ciaran winced. 'I sort of brought it up over Christmas, actually. The idea of transferring, I mean. I dunno. You know how sometimes your parents are all like "it's your decision" but somehow it's very obvious what decision they're telling you to make?'

Lizzy nodded. She knew exactly.

'Well, yeah. *That*. I think if I switched now . . . I mean, it would probably be grand. I don't think it would be like "never darken the door of this house again" or anything. But my parents – my dad especially – would just think it was totally insane. He'd probably be right.'

By then, they could see the front entrance of the theatre. It was, unsurprisingly, raining on the street outside.

'Will we just go to whatever it was called, Caratello's?' Ciaran asked.

'Perfect, yeah.' They'd been there last night, it had been nice, and it was close.

Hoods went up.

'I think filmmaking is probably the sort of thing you don't even really need to have a degree in anyway,' she told him confidently, as they tramped through puddles on cobbled streets. 'You could probably just learn on the job and work your way up.'

And truthfully, Lizzy had absolutely no idea of what was involved in making a film. She had no idea if Ciaran would be any good at it, no idea how much money you could expect to make or how much money you'd need to start with. But none of this mattered. They were not yet at an age where practicalities had to come into the discussion of anything so nebulous as one's future career.

Chapter Seventeen

'You are back!' the maître-d' at Ristorante al Caratello said, as soon as they arrived.

The restaurant was warm and unpretentious, with terracotta walls and bold artwork that was not attractive in itself, but that seemed to work in the context. There were dark wooden tables and squat wooden chairs, and – perhaps as a reward for their loyalty – Lizzy and Ciaran were seated in a prime spot overlooking the street. The windows had fogged up, but still, they could make out the blurred comings and goings. It was sort of delightful, the sense of all the life that was out there, and that burst through the door occasionally, blasting them – less delightfully – with cold air. Over pizzas and red wine in little round goblets, they had a long discussion about what, from a scientific perspective, caused windows to fog. Neither of them exactly knew, but they were both willing bullshitters and Lizzy had the feeling of content-ment that came with knowing they'd arrived where they were going to stay for the night; they could settle in and get tipsy, and have only a quick walk home ahead of them.

'So about your movie,' she began, once desserts had arrived. 'What would you make it about?'

'Oh.' He got that same bashful look on his face as he'd had when they talked about it earlier. 'I don't know.'

'Well, think!'

He shrugged. 'Could make it about this, I suppose. Not this, like, specifically having dinner in this restaurant—'

'Might not have much of a dramatic "arc",' she interjected, a teasing lilt in the final word so that she couldn't be accused of grandiosity.

'I mean, not *yet*, Elizabeth,' he fired back. Was there something slightly flirtatious about the way he said that? About the raise of his eyebrow, the sound of her full name coming out of his mouth? Or was she going insane?

'But, no,' he continued, before she could think too much more about it. 'I mean "this" as in France. Erasmus.'

Lizzy cocked her head to the side. She tried to imagine what that would look like – which events in their lives could be spun into some kind of significance, who among their friends might make leading men or leading ladies.

'Mmm, I don't know,' she said. 'I think maybe this is the sort of experience that feels really, like . . . interesting and weird and transformative for us right now, because it's happening to us. But other people might be kinda like "I don't know if we need to see a bunch of middle-class white kids swanning around Europe and finding themselves", you know?'

She paused, reaching for another sip of her wine, letting

it tickle the inside of her nose and slide warmly down her throat.

'I mean, maybe that wasn't exactly the angle you were thinking of taking,' she offered then. It took about three seconds for the both of them to come apart with laughter.

'Oh, no!' he corrected, deadpan. 'It completely was – you're spot on there, Lizzy. I thought people would love that! Had the tagline and everything. "Erasmus: it's just like being on the dole, but your parents are still proud of you."'

Lizzy laughed so much she almost spat out her wine.

*

On the street outside, Ciaran planted his hands on her shoulders and turned her around, like they were children playing a game of blind man's bluff.

It was half past eleven, on a Tuesday in January, but still there were people on the streets of Montmartre – not masses, just enough to hit the sweet spot between crowded and creepy. It was also, miraculously, not raining. They'd been able to sit outside, in a little heated patio area, for an espresso and a cigarette before home time. Lizzy had never bought a pack of cigarettes in her life, and nor would she dream of doing so, but she wasn't averse to bumming one here and there. She was, in fact, getting less and less averse to it. The government and, more notably, her parents had gone to great pains throughout her adolescence to convey to her that smoking wasn't sexy, wasn't sophisticated. Unfortunately, in the right circumstances, it actually could be both those things and she was beginning to suspect that everyone, if they were being really honest with themselves, knew it.

'You have to close your eyes!' Ciaran instructed her now, standing on a cobbled street. His voice was just a tad bit louder than normal, and she could tell the alcohol had hit him in the weird way that it always seemed to when combined with the cold air. It had hit her too.

'They *are* closed! Also, I don't know why I need to be spun around for this.'

A beat.

'Actually yeah, I don't either,' he said then, and he halted both of their movements, his two hands still planted on her shoulders as he stood behind her, a head and shoulders above her.

'Keep your eyes closed,' he warned. 'Okay. So remember: it's how many if you turned three hundred and sixty degrees. Not just how many in your direct eyeline.'

'I know.'

'Well, guess then!'

'I don't know. Nine!'

'Well *obviously* it's not going to be *nine*, Lizzy,' he said, sounding utterly disdainful.

'That's my guess,' she repeated obstinately, and as she opened her eyes, he rotated them both in a slow, jerky circle. They took in the street they were on, and the two others that they could see halfway down, counting the fluorescent green crosses.

'Four,' he concluded. 'I think that's a lot.'

'It *is* a lot,' she agreed, feeling charitable.

'I'm telling you,' he said staunchly. 'They fucking *love* a pharmacy in this town, Lizzy. It's beyond belief.'

Laughing, she turned around to face him. She hadn't really noticed the weight and the warmth of his hands on her shoulders when they were there, but she found that she did notice the absence of them.

She noticed the four or five inches he had over her too – that was another thing that had come to her attention during this trip. Lizzy herself had always been tall. It had been apparent fairly early on in her life that she wasn't ever going to be the girl on top of a cheerleader pyramid (or, really *anywhere* in such a pyramid). She wasn't going to be hoisted onto someone's shoulders at a music festival. But she *did* have to look up at Ciaran, when they were standing like this, in a way she wasn't often conscious of doing. There was something nice about it.

'This has been a good trip,' she said, and it was true. The anxiety of Christmas at home and exams in Bordeaux now seemed like another lifetime. 'You're very fun.' She grinned at him as she said it, leaning right into the corny. Sometimes, earnestness just felt safer that way, with a some silliness mixed in.

'You're very fun too,' he replied, and then he paused, his expression suspended somehow, like something was on the tip of his tongue.

She was about to ask him what was up – that was on the tip of *her* tongue – but then he dipped his head a little, moved in closer towards her. She could hardly even process his face at that proximity to hers, couldn't quite seem to grasp what was about to happen, not even as he hesitated for a last second, searching her expression for . . . well. Who knew what he was searching for, and who knew what he found, but then he was kissing her.

And she was letting him do it.

Her arms were rising of their own accord – floating helplessly in mid-air for a moment before locking around his back – and then her lips were parting against his, and she remembered this exact feeling, suddenly, from that night before Christmas break.

Of course, the whole thing was very unwise. They weren't drunk, exactly, but they definitely weren't sober either. Not only was Lizzy certain that Ciaran would regret this in the cold light of day, the odds were good that she probably would herself. She didn't want to be the sort of girl who made herself weak for a boy. Someone who'd get buzzed on wine and make out with him at random on the street, just because he started it. Who could – with one loose word from him tomorrow – start to be talked about. Who could develop a reputation. Who could be hurt and made foolish.

The very thought of any of those things filled Lizzy with panic and shame.

The problem was that it was just difficult to think of them, with his mouth on hers. Ciaran edged backwards on the kerb, until he was against a building's stone façade, and she went with him easily. He slid both hands under her coat and up over her ribcage, his lips moving to trail along her jawline. Instinctively, Lizzy tilted her head a little, and as he hit one particular spot just below her earlobe, she let out a soft moan from the back of her throat.

Suddenly, with that sound, the reality of the situation slithered in between them. She became newly aware of the sensation of his hands on her, spread across almost her entire torso, and the thought occurred to her that with her big sweater, she probably felt bulky and lumpy to him.

'This is crazy,' she murmured.

He just smiled in response, and when she looked in his eyes, they were hazy somehow, his pupils dilated. Jesus. Maybe he was drunker than she realised. Or they both were. Did he have more of the wine than her? She couldn't remember.

He went back to kissing her, his mouth moving steady and unhurried, and it was too much.

She stepped back from him a little and closed her eyes briefly, trying to get herself together. She tried to rid herself of the phantom sensation that he was somehow still just *everywhere*, all over her body; tried to ignore the deliciousness of it.

Her gaze flickered past him, then, to the neon sign of their hostel. It was only about ten paces away, give or take.

'We really should probably . . . go to bed,' she said then, and she watched as, almost imperceptibly, his eyes widened.

'As in, like, to sleep!' she spluttered, tripping over her own tongue in her haste. 'Just, y'know. Early train in the morning. And I think we *might* be hungover,' she joked. Truthfully, Lizzy felt suddenly stone-cold sober.

'Oh,' Ciaran said, sounding taken aback. For a moment, he just looked at her searchingly. How had she never noticed the blueness of his eyes before this trip? It was as though she was seeing him for the first time. A cliché, but the truth.

And then – exactly as she had known would inevitably happen sooner or later – she watched the moment his rational brain switched on.

'Okay. Yeah,' he replied, and she'd never heard his

voice sound quite like that before – so low and scratchy. 'You're right. You're definitely right. God, of course you are.'

See? she thought to herself.

And as they walked the few steps to their hostel's front door, Lizzy wondered how they were possibly going to negotiate all this in the morning. Maybe the clock could be wound back from one . . . incident, but two? Already, she was dreading that conversation.

As things turned out, she needn't have worried.

At half past eight the next morning, Ciaran bounded down to breakfast just like normal. He was in his jeans and hoody, as usual, and as Lizzy watched him pour himself a bowl of cornflakes, somehow he didn't even *look* like the person from last night. When he opened his mouth to speak, his voice sounded nothing like that one she remembered, either.

'D'you sleep okay?' he asked idly. 'I had my Moroccan friend snoring like a foghorn, as per.'

And that was that. They never talked about the previous night ever again.

Chapter Eighteen

The day of the interview with the *Hollywood Reporter*, Lizzy has an appointment down at Plage Raphael in the morning, to go over plans for the ceilidh. It's a private stretch of the beach owned by a hotel, on which there is ordinarily a restaurant. Next Monday evening, though, the restaurant will be closed, all its patio furniture moved down onto the sand in order to make space for the ceilidh on the wooden decking.

Taking in the surroundings, Lizzy sighs with satisfaction. It's exactly how it looked in the photographs. Granted, she has never planned a wedding, but nor does she think she is likely to, hence she can scarcely imagine ever being more invested in any event than she has been in this one over the past six months. It has been torturous, and she is absolutely never doing it again, practically every week having presented some unexpected new predicament to be resolved. It *is* sort of rewarding, though, to see everything begin to come together at last.

She's feeling so enthused that she decides to

commence her communication with the hotel manager with a little bit of French. Monsieur Henri takes this treat and runs with it to a degree that she probably wouldn't, frankly, have chosen – but, she gets the gist. Mostly, from her end, it involves smiling and saying *d'accord* as they walk around the perimeter of the space together and he points things out. This, he says, is where the projector will be set up; that is where the bar will be stationed.

All is going swimmingly until towards the end of the tour, when Monsieur Henri gets a slightly pained expression on his face, and leans in towards her conspiratorially. The hotel has been approached by a jeweller, is what Lizzy can gather. A very *significant* jeweller, that wants to rent Plage Raphael for the same night as the ceilidh. Might it be possible that the Scottish Film Board could make do with less – maybe forgo just the little area on the other side of the bar, just the little strip of beach in front of it? The hotel *would* so hate to let down *any* of its valued patrons.

Lizzy's first instinct is to assume that she's misunderstood this somehow, but the longer the manager goes on, the more furrowed his brow becomes, the more it seems like she has not. Mercifully, she still remembers the French knack of conveying, in a mere two words, that a situation is unacceptable.

C'est impossible.

People used to say that to her all the time back in Bordeaux, and for a long while, she'd laboured under the misapprehension that the phrase translated as 'it's impossible.' In fact, what she had learned – eventually – was that it was a lot closer to 'I don't want to do that.'

Sharing Plage Raphael with some jewellery company – no matter how significant – is very much not something Lizzy wants to do, and so she deploys the phrase liberally, with accompanying hand gestures. From the resigned sort of expression that comes to settle on Monsieur Henri's face, she can only assume it's worked. The whole thing does take a while, though. It pushes her visit into just slightly more time than she'd allocated, which is her own mistake. A rookie one, at that. She should know by now that a fairly chunky margin for strife and absurdity needs to be built into any schedule of events that is ultimately going to play out in this country.

By the time she gets away, it's almost 12.45, and Lizzy sets a swift pace up the Croisette towards the Carlton, not only because she is, generally speaking, a person who doesn't know how to walk any other way than fast, but also because she is now, specifically speaking, cutting it fine. En route, she types a hurried, one-handed email to Monsieur Henri, making her thoughts on the jeweller situation entirely clear. In other words, she emails him in English.

It really is such a unique stress, she thinks to herself idly, once she's done – the stress of trying to communicate in a foreign language. Any time she has to do anything in French that goes beyond ordering in a restaurant, the sensation of grasping for words that are hovering just out of reach comes flooding back to her. The frustration, the powerlessness of it. She remembers it, too, every time she encounters a non-native English speaker, as happens fairly frequently in Edinburgh. All these years after the one she spent living abroad, if Lizzy had to pinpoint the primary benefit of the whole thing, she'd wager that this sense of compassion might be it. Not knowledge of another language, or understanding of a different culture, not experiences of meeting new people or trying new things. All good stuff. But, compassion. That's the main thing, she thinks – maybe the *only* thing that might actually be helpful to the world and not just to you. Some degree of empathy for what it is like to be foreign, and overwhelmed, and trying and failing.

As she swoops around a journalist talking energetically to a camera, the Carlton comes into view, and it occurs to Lizzy that she has probably never spent so much time thinking about Bordeaux as she has in the past few days. Perhaps it's not a bad headspace to be in right now, though, given what she's about to do.

Walking into the hotel, its opulent entryway a hive of activity, a sudden jolt of nerves hits her. This whole plan came together so quickly – has been so jumbled in her mind with all the other things she has to get done – that she hasn't really had the chance to be anxious up until now. She reminds herself: this is good karma. And it's not going to take that much time out of her day. She can take a quick trip up the high road on this one.

Though she's short on time, she makes a pitstop at the restroom off the lobby to freshen up. It's probably more psychological, more ritualistic, than anything, because there is a limited amount to be done. Her hips aren't getting any narrower, her smile isn't getting any straighter, her profile isn't getting any more elegant. Nonetheless, she puts on a fresh coat of lipstick. She blots away the sheen from her forehead with a square of toilet paper and tries to zhuzh up her hair a little, and when she looks in at her reflection, she thinks there's a small, but satisfactory, improvement.

Once upon a time, Lizzy's relationship to mirrors had had two speeds – excessive consultation or steadfast avoidance. Looking back, she can see that she probably fluctuated somewhat unhealthily between the two all the way from early adolescence into her early twenties. It had been Oliver, in a way, who'd helped put a stop to that – helped her see that prettiness, or lack thereof, was really such a silly thing to let herself be consumed by. She looks more or less okay most of the time, she thinks now. She isn't hideous or freakish, the way her brain used to tell her – and likely still would tell her, if she let it. Instead, she tries to remind herself repeatedly of the factual reality: no, she is not beautiful, and nor does she have much interest in any of the mental gymnastics that might allow her to pretend to herself that she somehow is. She isn't. That's just a fact. But she probably is at least ordinary. On a day like today, when she's put in some effort, she can look nice, in an overall sort of way.

It's enough.

Or at least, she knows that it should be. And most of the time it is.

Chapter Nineteen

Knocking on the door of the Carlton's penthouse, Lizzy can hear a gentle hum of activity from inside. It occurs to her that plenty of people might find even this portion of proceedings – standing outside a hotel suite in Cannes by herself – to be vaguely questionable. For a while there, back when all the sexual abuse stories first came to light, going to a hotel suite by yourself had become the new walking home alone in a short skirt. Outside of the industry, Lizzy had heard people – including a lot of women – ask, 'Why would you go to someone's hotel room? How could you not know that was a come-on?' She'd always felt something had been a little lost in translation there. What people didn't understand was that in Cannes, all the major players rented suites. And, they really weren't bedrooms at all – the bedroom furniture, in fact, was typically removed altogether to make way for conference room tables and meeting nooks and promotional roller banners. Hotel suites were, for all intents and purposes, offices. Nice ones, with views of the Med.

After what seems like an age, a woman in a lanyard comes to the door and takes Lizzy's details. Standing at the little makeshift reception desk, Lizzy scans the surroundings. Everything looks appropriately professional – no one seems likely to materialise in a bathrobe any time soon. She can see fresh flowers everywhere, and at least half a dozen bodies in different rooms off the central foyer. In one of the doorways, Amy Solomon appears. She makes no move to approach, but gives a double thumbs-up from a distance, like an eager pageant mom. Lizzy smiles in response, as gamely as she can manage, when, quite without warning, Ciaran himself comes striding out of another of the rooms. Hair washed, eyes bright, shirt pressed and rolled up casually to the elbows. He looks like a man who smells good.

'Lizzy!' he says warmly, a little more loudly than seems to be necessary. 'Right on time. You ready for lunch?'

'What?' she frowns in confusion. 'Oh! Right, yeah, lunch. Can't wait. Are you, uh, done with your interview?'

That seems – once she catches up – like the sort of thing she should be saying. Maybe? It's immediately clear to her that she's probably going to be less good at this than he is.

'Almost,' he replies, all ease, as he leads her into a sitting room. 'Come and meet Alexandra, she's from the *Hollywood Reporter*. Alexandra – Lizzy.'

From a plush cream sofa, Alexandra rises to meet her. She's wearing a beautiful kaftan and has big brown eyes, and she seems, Lizzy thinks, incredibly *young*. Could she be one of those girls who skipped college to focus on her blog, and was now having the last laugh? She makes a mental note to google that later. Probably, if she were any sort of competent adult, she would have googled it *before*.

'Hi!' Alexandra says brightly. 'Sorry to encroach on your lunch date.'

'Oh, no,' Lizzy replies, shaking the reporter's hand. 'Not at all.'

'I hear you guys go way back, huh? You know each other from when Ciaran lived in Bordeaux? Or, when you both lived in Bordeaux, I guess I should say.'

'Right,' Lizzy says. Seems like this girl really *has* been well primed by Amy, or Ciaran, or some combination of the two.

Ciaran nods towards the empty armchair. 'Sit down,' he urges. 'We have a few minutes before we have to go, don't we?'

Lizzy attempts a benign smile, sinking down onto the chair and feeling as though she is about to be interrogated for some sort of low-level crime.

'So that must have been such an incredible experience,' Alexandra says. 'A year in Bordeaux. A lot of living your best life in the vineyards, I'm imagining. Or is that a cliché?'

Ciaran looks over in Lizzy's direction, as though ready to defer to her, but something about her must tell him she could use the help.

'We did do a few wine tours, yeah,' he replies smoothly, and she doesn't have time to think about whether it's ultimately good or bad that he still has some ability to read her like that. 'I don't think we were above a cliché in any way whatsoever. Not quite reading Camus in our polo-necks and berets or anything, but, yeah. There was a fair bit of drinking cheap red wine and smoking Gitanes and all that stuff.'

He leans in, as though to talk directly to the digital recorder that has pride of place on the coffee table. 'Obviously I've seen the error of my ways there and am now a non-smoker. Smoking is bad, kids.'

Alexandra giggles. 'The folly of youth, right?'

What can this girl be, Lizzy finds herself wondering again – twenty-two? Twenty-four at most? How on earth has she landed this gig? More power to her, however she's managed it, but what's the backstory there? Equally intriguing is the thought that maybe she is here in Cannes, reporting for one of the largest publications in the industry, because she is in fact a very normal thirty to forty-five years old. In which case, how is *that* possible? She doesn't look at all like she's seen a surgeon's scalpel. Could it just be a drinking-a-lot-of-water situation?

Lizzy would much prefer to be the one getting to ask the questions.

Alas, that's not how this works.

'So, have you guys just always stayed in touch?' Alexandra prods, and she's looking directly at Lizzy now, clearly on the hunt for something – anything – that can be quoted. In that effort, she likely thinks that she's tossed out the softest of softball questions. Lizzy, however, finds herself already a little thrown. She'd said she'd do this, but she doesn't plan to lie in the process.

'Um. Not *as such*,' she replies. 'Just . . . life, you know? We've seen each other quite a bit here in Cannes, though, so lots of fun opportunities to, uh . . . catch up,' she says, unable to resist a sly glance in Ciaran's direction.

His eyes meet hers, and the quick little flash of amusement, or recognition, or *something* that passes between them whooshes right by Alexandra.

'Of course! Actually, it's kind of cool that you're here,' the reporter says, getting down to business. 'Ciaran and I have just been talking about *Wish You Were Here*, and this whole *unfortunate* situation with the copyright claim. What's your take on that? Like, as a friend?'

Once again, the phrasing isn't ideal. Lizzy wouldn't say she's necessarily qualified to be offering any thoughts *as a friend*. However, the heart of the question is not unexpected and she's given it – the one basic thing she knew she'd be asked – some forethought. She's prepared something of a script for this.

'Well, my take is that if he copied from somebody, then I think he should . . . I don't know. Whatever happens to people who do that,' she says candidly. 'The film gets pulled from the festival, he has to pay damages, whatever. But I saw the film yesterday. And I just . . . don't think he copied.'

'Got it. And is that because you recognise a lot of it? Ciaran and I were just talking about how so much of the story really is directly inspired by his own experiences of living in France as a young man.'

Huh. Lizzy's ears prick up at the terminology. 'Directly inspired by' is not quite 'loosely inspired by'. But, whatever. She guesses that at this point, Ciaran's job is not to undersell the situation – if anything, it's the opposite. Hers too, probably.

'Yeah,' she says. 'So, I mean, I guess the first thing is that I remember – even all the way back then, when we were living in France – him telling me that he would be interested in making a film about the experience.'

Alexandra's eyes light up. 'You do?'

'Yeah. I mean, it was all kind of pie in the sky at that

time, you know? Like, we were students. But I do remember him telling me he wanted to do it. We were in Paris. I remember him joking he had the tagline and everything, and it was going to be something like "Erasmus: it's just like being unemployed, but your parents are still proud of you." Which we thought was very funny, 'cause it was kind of true.'

She can hardly help but sneak another look over at Ciaran, and she's not sure who starts it, but a tiny smile seems to rise to both their lips. It's just a nice memory, there are no two ways about that. Lizzy clears her throat a little bit, focussing her attention back on the reporter.

'And now . . .'

'Right!' Alexandra jumps in. 'Isaac actually says that to Claudia in the film! I saw the "Press and Industry" screening this morning,' she adds, by way of explanation. 'That was such a great line!'

'Didn't quite make the posters in the end,' Ciaran jokes politely, and Lizzy smiles along, equally politely. It's a reminder of the artificiality of the situation; of the fact that they are not here for a catch-up. They are here to perform for the benefit of this stranger.

'And, I don't know, there's just a lot of little things,' she continues, to that end. 'Like, I had a babysitting job, taking care of this little boy, Thierry. And Ciaran used to come and help me out with him.'

Alexandra makes an interested sort of face, scribbling something in her notepad. Honestly, Lizzy judges the notepad a bit. It just seems like a very unnecessary prop, given that this whole thing is being recorded anyway.

'Can you believe Thierry would be *seventeen* now?' Ciaran interjects.

And in fact, Lizzy cannot believe that. Her eyes widen. 'Oh my *God*. That's just insane. Well,' she cocks an eyebrow. 'I'm sure he still misses one of us a lot.'

'Agreed, it was obvious he secretly loved you,' Ciaran replies, quick as a flash, and Lizzy snickers. For real this time. It's a tonic – it just makes her feel a little looser somehow, a little more like herself.

'That's a lie,' she tells Alexandra dryly. 'You definitely won't want to print that. Anyway. In the movie, obviously, Isaac ends up taking his sister's *au pair* job. And, it's hard to explain exactly, but I can just see a lot of the relationship Ciaran had with Thierry in the one Isaac has with the kid.'

'So, you've got the receipts, so to speak?'

'Yeah, I guess so. You could put it like that. The point is just that I find it impossible to believe that Ciaran didn't come up with that stuff himself. He would have had no need to steal from anybody else.'

'Great. Anything else especially stand out for you? In terms of the film?'

Lizzy thinks. The biggest, most powerful thing that Ciaran has gotten right, in her opinion, is the atmosphere. When she looks back at the year that she spent – that *they* spent – in France, a lot of details have disappeared by now. There are particular events and trips that she barely remembers happening at all. And of those she *does* remember, in many ways they too seem to have melded together in a sort of video montage in her memory. Ciaran had obviously seen it long before she could – how well the whole experience would lend itself to cinema. Lizzy likes a novel as much as the next person, but she doesn't think there is any novel that can convey, in quite the way that a film can, the infectiousness of a bunch of friends laughing hysterically. Or, the gorgeousness of golden evening light. All the swallows and glances between human beings that are loneliness and lust and anxiety and awe. Visuals, at their best, just seem to carry so lightly what words can sometimes hardly grasp.

Nonetheless, what Lizzy needs in this precise moment are words.

'I think a lot of it just feels very authentic to the experience we had,' she offers. 'Starting with, even, just things that *sound* like Ciaran to me. From what I remember, at least. Like, when stuff took forever or was really bureaucratic – which was, like, *often* – he would say it was a "whole arsing-about session". I noticed that one made it into the film, for Isaac.'

Beside her, Ciaran chuckles.

'And what else was in there?' she wonders aloud, feeling herself getting into the swing of this a little now. 'Oh! "Jesus wept!" That was a Ciaran thing, too. "Jesus *wept*." Like when something was just ridiculous – which, again . . .'

'Was common,' Ciaran supplies, and when she turns to look at him, somehow they're both grinning.

'It's funny,' he says, with a shake of his head, 'I wouldn't even think of those as things I particularly say?'

Lizzy just shrugs a little in response.

'I guess we don't always see ourselves, right?' Alexandra chimes in – again, she's scrawling something in her notebook. 'This is great. You're every journalist's favourite person, Lizzy – somebody with a memory for details!'

'I don't know about that,' she replies. It occurs to her that what she does not want is for Ciaran to think that she has spent the past twelve years fondly, pathetically replaying every utterance from his lips. 'It's weird. Some stuff you don't even know you remember until it's . . . y'know. Right there in front of you on a forty-foot screen.'

'That's . . . yeah,' Ciaran says, sounding almost rueful. 'Ain't that the truth.'

Lizzy's not sure what to make of that, exactly. She searches his face, but she can't find it, the thing she feels like she's missing. Added to that, she's aware of Alexandra watching the both of them like a hawk. The best thing, maybe, is to move swiftly along.

'So, yeah,' she continues. 'I guess there are lots of little things like that. Not necessarily exact plot points or specific sections of script or anything, but little flashes here and there that seem like Ciaran to me, or like other people we knew back then.'

'Right,' Alexandra nods. 'On that note, I *gotta* ask: how 'bout you? Am I looking at the real-life Claudia right here?'

'Oh, no!' Lizzy replies swiftly. She'd been half expecting this question too. 'I get why you would ask that, because of the American thing and whatever but . . . no. I mean, man. I *wish* when I was twenty I'd had my shit together as much as Claudia does. I was just a big ball of neuroses.'

She looks over at Ciaran, expecting hearty agreement and getting . . . well, she doesn't know *what* she's getting, from the expression on his face. She ploughs on.

'Plus, you know, with Claudia and Isaac, obviously that's, like, a love story. Ciaran and I were never a couple.'

Again, she looks over at him, waiting for him to

jump in. For about four seconds, the room feels very silent.

'I can vouch for that. Not a couple,' he pipes up then, at fucking last. Wasn't she supposed to be here as backup for *him*, not the other way around? For him to at least give the conversation his full attention did not, in Lizzy's opinion, seem too much to ask.

'Got it,' Alexandra says. 'No busting out the high notes at karaoke for you then, huh, Lizzy?'

She tosses this out like it's nothing, as though she's barely even expecting a response beyond perhaps a chuckle of agreement. Why Lizzy cannot simply provide that, she doesn't know. It must be the desire to keep things buoyant, or plain stupidity, or both.

'Oh no, that's definitely possible, I can be a total ham that way,' she quips instead, and as soon as the words are out of her mouth, she wishes she could snatch them back. Alexandra's head cocks to one side, her pen poised.

'Are you a singer?'

Lizzy can see the wheels turning in the reporter's mind. Truthfully, things in her own mind are starting to feel a tiny bit fudgy, in a way she immediately decides to ignore.

'Oh, not like Claudia is,' she says, trying to get ahead of the situation. 'I mean, Claudia's *a singer*. I'm just a person who likes to sing.'

At this, Ciaran makes a strange, choked sort of sound that Lizzy can't identify; half protest, half guffaw. Both she and Alexandra turn to look at him.

'Sorry,' he says, like the interruption wasn't deliberate at all. 'It's just . . .'

Lizzy can see him hesitate and then she can see him decide: fuck it.

'For the record, she's an incredible singer,' he tells Alexandra. 'You can go ahead and quote me on that.'

Alexandra doesn't write anything down, though. She just smiles.

Chapter Twenty

When they're done, Ciaran walks her back downstairs, even though she assures him there's no need. The hotel is full of people in festival lanyards, and he attracts more than a few glances from them. It must be such a strange thing, Lizzy thinks – being known by people whom you don't know at all. She wonders if it has stopped being strange for Ciaran. If he notices the special attention he generates, he doesn't show it.

Once they reach the lobby, he slows his pace, and she matches him, until they come to a hover near the concierge. There is nowhere left to go but through the revolving doors and back out into the street,

'Thanks for doing that,' he says. 'I know it was a bit . . .'

'It was fine,' she assures him, on autopilot. In truth, though, she does feel slightly unsettled. It doesn't seem like she's going to be able to move on with the rest of her day in quite the seamless fashion she'd anticipated.

'Maybe a *little* stressful,' she admits, and he nods.

'I probably wouldn't say no to a cigarette right now if you had one, let's put it that way.'

Slowly, she arches an eyebrow. 'What kind of a non-smoker does that make you, huh?'

He looks right back at her, undaunted, a smile pulling at his lips. 'I average about six a year these days, I'd say. Doesn't count if they're other people's cigarettes, everybody knows that.'

Lizzy bites back a smile herself. 'Everybody *does* know that,' she agrees, as seriously as she can manage. It's the most bizarre thing. Having spent the past four days and twelve years very much not wanting to speak to Ciaran Flynn, standing opposite him now, she feels like, oddly, she sort of *does* want to speak to him. She'd once read that forcing yourself to laugh out loud – even when it was fake, even when you felt miserable – could successfully brighten your mood for real. That was science. To do with the release of endorphins, or something. Could it be, she wonders, that some similar chemical reaction has occurred here? That the performance of connection with Ciaran has made her maybe, possibly, feel some?

'Would you want . . . I mean. We could *actually* get lunch,' she suggests disjointedly.

'Eh.' His expression freezes. 'I can't. There's like ten people waiting on me up there,' he says, with a nod toward the elevator. 'I have more interviews, and then I have the photocall with the cast later on, and then this party, and it's just a whole thing.'

'Oh!' She's embarrassed to have asked. 'Of course, yeah. That's fine.'

Silence. Neither of them seems to know quite how to extract themselves from the conversation.

'Fucking *insane*,' he says then, conspiratorially, shaking his head a little bit. 'That the film got into Cannes.'

And in this moment, he looks so boyish – so very much like the twenty-year-old that Lizzy remembers – that a giggle escapes her lips.

'*Insane*,' she agrees. 'How'd you learn how to make a film, anyhow?'

Simplistic as the question sounds, it's something she's been wondering. Twelve years ago, she'd been aware of the desire in him, the enthusiasm. But, as is now made clear to her on a pretty regular basis in the context of her job, having those things is definitely not the same as having any actual know-how.

'I don't know, I'm kind of just winging it,' he says. 'It turns out that's what most people are doing?'

He scrunches his face up, as if he's genuinely perplexed by the realisation, and it makes her laugh. She suspects that might be the whole point.

'I was a production assistant for a few years after uni,' he adds then. 'So, I wasn't really doing anything that could be called filmmaking, obviously – I was more just a general dogsbody. But it was good, even just seeing how other people did it, up close. And then I took a couple of courses at the London Film School – made some pretty terrible short films that basically nobody ever saw, or probably ever should see.'

'I think that's true of a lot of directors,' Lizzy replies. It's been the thing that has comforted her, in fact, on the few occasions on which she's granted funding to someone who has proceeded to totally shit the bed. A disappointing film, she's always tried to remind herself, could perhaps at least be a bridge to somewhere.

171

'Yeah, that's what they tell you – "This is all part of the process" and whatever. Which is fine, and true, but it's still just a slightly mortifying thing, isn't it? Getting caught trying. Like, when you're very obviously doing the absolute best you can at something and the result is still . . . not that great. Sometimes now, if you can believe it, people actually ask *me* about filmmaking and I always say that it's amazing what you can get, like, reasonably good at if you can just stand being bad at it for a while first.'

Lizzy takes that in. She had once quit a six-week aerial yoga class after two weeks. She has always had a fairly binary view of the things she was and was not good at. Music, yes. Sports, no. Making people laugh, yes. Driving, no.

Ciaran was different. She remembers that about him now. He had never seemed to subscribe to the view that talents were handed out by God or the universe, and you took what you got, like a child in the school dinner line. In his opinion, the want-to could create the how-to.

And it seemed that he might have been right about that. Even if his route here had not always been clear to him – even if he had once thought that his chances of being able to *get* a job in this industry, as distinct from being able to actually do such a job, seemed a very far off prospect.

'Your dad came around to the whole thing, then, huh?' she finds herself asking. 'Having a filmmaker in the family instead of a kitchen fitter?'

'Well, it was touch and go there for a few years,' he replies, and she can tell by the look on his face that he's not entirely kidding. 'That's for sure. It's not fun to be twenty-seven and telling your parents you can't afford a flight home. My dad was finally selling the business at that point, and I wasn't really getting anywhere fast in London, and . . . I dunno . . .' He trails off, with a slightly uncomfortable little shrug. 'We weren't, like, *estranged* or anything. But . . . we also probably weren't a million miles from it to be totally honest. Now, though, yeah.' His eyes brighten. 'There's actually this local paper at home – the *Donegal News* – and I swear to God, sometimes Da phones them up himself. Like, there's just no way they're contacting him about every random thing to do with me.'

'I don't know,' she counters. '"Local boy bound for Cannes" – I think that's pretty newsworthy.'

'Oh! No! That *would* be fine. But that's not the level we're talking. I mean, like "Local boy enters post-production on web series." "Local boy thinking of buying a holiday home in Ballyliffin." Could be anything, and there's the quote from Paddy Flynn. Sometimes!' he continues laughingly, 'He's in there talking about *other people's films*. "Father of local filmmaker" or whatever. As if he's just a general cultural commentator now!'

Lizzy chuckles, but even as she does, Ciaran's smile is fading.

'. . . That's actually kind of the shit part about this whole situation with Penny Ainsley, to be honest,' he says. 'Or, y'know. One of the many shit parts. People keep telling me about the twenty-four-hour news cycle, but back home, I don't know. Stuff like this doesn't really *cycle out* of the news. People'll be chatting shite about this for years.'

Lizzy just nods in sympathy. Then, in her hand, her

173

cell phone buzzes. It's Oliver, and she smiles a little automatically, just at the sight of his name.

'Sorry, I kinda gotta take this,' she says, raising her phone in Ciaran's direction. His eyes flicker to the screen, and immediately, he seems to retreat, his spine straightening slightly.

'Absolutely, yeah,' he agrees hurriedly. 'I should, uh, probably get back up there anyway.'

'Alright, well.' She shrugs. 'Good luck with the premiere tomorrow. Hope the article does . . . whatever it's supposed to do.'

'Thanks. And thanks again for doing this, seriously. I really appreciate it.'

He looks so sincere. It's convincing. But, when Lizzy thinks back, it remains all too easy to recall the snarling spite of that last night in Bordeaux.

At this point, she really does not know if Ciaran Flynn is a good person who sometimes has the capacity to be awful, or an awful person who sometimes has the capacity to be good. It probably doesn't matter anymore. As Lizzy walks out into the sunshine, bringing her cell phone up to her ear, she thinks: *Well. That's that.*

Chapter Twenty-One

Shortly after they returned from Paris, Ciaran got a job bussing tables at Le Café Français. He never seemed to be scheduled for a Wednesday, though. He still showed up at the Durands' every week to help kill the time on her shift playing Lego with Thierry, or doing something else with the little boy that involved a lot of construction and not much conversation. And later on, he and Lizzy still went to the Utopia together, taking turns to pick the movie each week, sitting outside on the square afterwards until day smudged into night.

The weeks started to gallop in, and the weather improved, and Lizzy had plenty of time to enjoy it now that the thought of attending class never so much as entered her mind.

The days turned out to be very easy to fill. Sometimes, she had a practical task of some sort to attend to – laundry to wash at the *laverie* on Rue du Loup, or a document to print at the internet café, or some debacle to attempt to resolve in relation, for example, to her bank account, the apartment's various utilities, or the rent rebate with which the French government was supposed to provide her each month. Those days felt veritably *jam-packed*.

Even without any particular errand, though, Lizzy found that she could still occupy herself pretty well with what amounted, essentially, to the classic combination of sleeping late and then bumming around. People who felt this would not be a satisfying way of life, she realised, simply hadn't given themselves enough time to bed into it. Those early days in Bordeaux, when she'd felt the empty hours stretch out dauntingly before her – when she'd almost longed to get back on the monotonous upward climb that had been the past fifteen years of full-time education, just to feel normal . . . they were but a dim and distant memory now. She had a new normal.

She walked the streets to suss out new coffee shops, and she lay in the *jardin public* with her iPod, and at some point, on some unremarkable day, she spent almost a full hour plucking her eyebrows to an extent that she would eventually come to regret bitterly. It also seemed an ideal time to start reading *Le Monde* – every French teacher she'd ever encountered had been almost fanatical about its critical importance when it came to the mastery of the French language, and now that Lizzy saw the newspaper stacked outside the *épicerie* on a daily basis, she started to give a lot of regular consideration to the prospect of, at some point, buying it.

One other thing that she sometimes did, during this period, was make out with Ciaran.

Only sometimes. Only when he started it. And he only ever started it when they could sneak away from other people, when their senses were blurred a little or a lot by red wine. It was the Paris scenario, repeated. They never discussed it.

Lizzy thought about it, though. It became, over time, kind of the *main thing* she thought about.

More or less everything about the experience was a new one for her.

When she was twelve years old, she had never kissed a boy, nor remotely wanted to. A girl in her class named Kate Conway had called her 'frigid' in front of everybody, and Lizzy hadn't even known for sure what that meant, but she knew that people sniggered or looked sympathetically at her, and she knew that her entire body felt hot and tight with embarrassment. She knew the term was related, somehow, to her having never kissed a boy. She knew it meant that she was defective in this regard.

The way to resolve the issue was obvious. Per the orchestration of various classmates, she'd kissed Billy Emhoff outside the cafeteria at lunch the following week. It wasn't nice, but that wasn't the memorable thing about it. The memorable thing about it was that afterwards, Kate Conway had mocked her, and Billy's friends had mocked her, and even Billy himself had mocked her. It went on for weeks. It was just a new, even more acute, kind of embarrassment.

Lizzy certainly was not the first girl to have the sense of being damned if she did and damned if she didn't. But, she was twelve, which meant she *felt* like the first, and the only.

Then came her teenage years, and a growing awareness of the ways in which she was odd-looking, ugly-looking. On the rare occasions that boys had paid

177

her any attention whatsoever, a weird phenomenon had developed. Very quickly, Lizzy had found herself repulsed by said boys. Not disinterested, not apathetic, not unsure. Repulsed. It wasn't that they themselves were repulsive. One or two of them, she'd actually liked for a while, before they demonstrated any reciprocal interest in her. It seemed to be the interest in her that was, of itself, the problem. She just couldn't shake the feeling that there was something inherently suspicious – somewhat difficult to respect – about that. Indicative, she felt, of a pretty low bar. Unless entirely desperate, how could anyone claim attraction to what seemed to her, any time she looked in a mirror, so objectively unattractive?

With Ciaran, though, things were different.

For whatever reason, she hadn't ended up repulsed by him. The opposite thing, in fact, had happened. She had come to wait for, hope for, those moments when the air around them would change, when they would find themselves in some darkened corner and decide to be different people for a while. It began to occur to Lizzy that she might even have an opportunity to rid herself of the virginity issue sometime soon, if she so chose.

Thus far in life, she had not been waiting – as in, Waiting. It was just that the chasm of difference she had once imagined would surely exist between high school guys and college guys had turned out to barely leave room for daylight. She had simply never encountered anyone with whom she even slightly wanted to have sex. By consequence, that members of her preferred gender had typically shown little or no interest in having sex with *her* was really not the sadness it might otherwise have been. Nonetheless, at the grand old age of twenty, Lizzy was ashamed of her virginity.

When she looked back in years to come, she wouldn't be sure of exactly why that was. The proliferation of adult actors confidently simulating sex on teen dramas perhaps didn't help matters. And the drinking game *Never Have I Ever* – within which her peers regularly offered up their apparently endless array of sexual adventure for communal entertainment – certainly had a lot to answer for. This was the era of Kim's sex tape, of girls on the dance floor of every club mouthing along to misogyny, of the deification of Carrie, Samantha and co. One way or another, Lizzy's comparative lack of experience had come to feel, impliedly, like an extremely weird thing, a thing she should probably do her best to conceal.

For her to have felt this way at any age, really, but especially at such a very young one, would eventually strike Lizzy as every bit as insane and enraging as the notion of a twelve-year-old child being designated frigid had already begun to seem. But, she wasn't there yet. She was where she was.

As that spring in Bordeaux wore on, punctuated every few weeks or so by these addictive, inexplicable encounters with Ciaran, Lizzy began to think of sex as a feature, or possible feature, of her own life for the very first time. Undoubtedly, there was an appeal to the thought of just letting one thing lead to another – encouraging it, even. This was, first off, an inherent sort of appeal that was actually quite shocking, Lizzy having begun to think herself likely incapable of ever experiencing it. Secondarily, there also was the practical interest in simply not being a virgin any longer – ridding herself of the burden of that particular label.

But then, Lizzy had learned early on in life that shame didn't always dissolve the way you thought it would – it sometimes was merely exchanged, for a different variety. Potentially a worse one. And, according to any sensible analysis, that did seem likely to be where this thing with Ciaran was headed. Because *of course* the circumstances were not ideal. *Of course* Lizzy knew that while Ciaran thought she was funny and smart and interesting in the coffee-drinking hours, she could not possibly be his top pick, really, for a particular set of end-of-the-night activities. What it came down to, for him, was just that wine had happened, and it was fun in the moment, and they were semi in the habit now.

Lizzy knew all of that.

She knew it.

And still she didn't stop.

'This is a bad idea,' she murmured against his lips, one night at the end of April. Down in the entryway of his apartment building, beside people's bicycles and post-boxes, they were both a little buzzed. The usual. Not sloppy but not sober. ''Cause of . . . well. We don't need to rehash the reasons.'

'Right enough, yeah, the reasons,' Ciaran agreed breathlessly, and Lizzy wondered, then, if she'd ever, exactly, *had* that discussion with him – or just in her own head a zillion times. Either way, he evidently understood the situation every bit as well as she did. They were sailing so close to the wind every time they did this, putting their perfectly good friendship on the line.

'The thing is, though,' he continued, with the smile that had come to make her bones melt, 'if this is a mistake . . . then, we've already made quite a few mistakes really, haven't we? We could just . . . make another one?'

And she giggled, pulling his face back down to her, kissing him hungrily. She couldn't help it. Her tongue flicked playfully against his in the way that felt almost second nature now, and her arms looped around his neck, and quite how the next thing happened was unclear. Some way or other, though, his hand ended up between her legs. The newness made her freeze, pull away from his lips for a second. Through the flimsy cotton of her sundress, she knew he must be able to feel heat, throbbing. That's what she could feel, at least. It made her nervous, embarrassed, until she looked in his eyes, and then somehow she wasn't either of those things. Or rather, she was other things *more*. Ciaran moved his hand, experimentally, and when she gasped, he exhaled, leaning in ever closer to her. His other hand cupped her jaw as he repeated the movement, over and over, and she found his thumb, biting down on it.

Thirty seconds later, she was coming. And going.

When she fled, flushed, from the apartment building, it was because she felt excited and confused and alive and afraid. That made no sense, she knew, and the good news – if a person wanted to look at it that way – was that there was absolutely zero prospect Ciaran would want to discuss any of it with her the next time she saw him.

Chapter Twenty-Two

Things were probably always going to go to shit, and in the end, when that happened, it happened fast.

'So, what exactly is the situation with you and Ciaran?' Caroline asked, completely out of the blue one morning at the very beginning of May. It was rare, these days, that their paths crossed in the flat at all. Lizzy tended to make it her business to be elsewhere.

On three occasions throughout the spring, lightbulbs had fused in Rue Cabirol, and on all three occasions, Lizzy had taken responsibility for replacing them. Last week, when the one in the bathroom had gone, she had decided to just wait. And see. It was more about the principle of the thing than the money (although, incidentally, it had been a trip, these past few months, finding out that so many of the functional items that had seemed to exist on a rolling basis in her parents' home – Sellotape, spare batteries, cold and flu capsules – were actually disgustingly expensive). The result of all the waiting and seeing was that it had been five days of peeing in the dark, and Lizzy was feeling generally somewhat sour on Caroline.

'What do you mean, "what's the situation?"' she replied.

'You know. Are you two . . . *dating* or whatever? I suppose that would be the American way to put it.'

Lizzy probably would have had more appreciation for her roommate's effort to bridge the cultural divide if, in so doing, she'd also managed to take the vaguely appalled look off her face.

'What?' Lizzy arranged her own features into shock at the mere idea. 'No! Oh my gosh. Definitely not. Just friends.'

She could do this easily by now, because by now, tonnes of people had broached the subject with her. Liam, back at Christmas time, had turned out to be the first of many. Mia, in particular, had become pretty persistent of late, and increasingly Lizzy was desperate to just tell her friend everything that had happened – to pull it apart with her and try to make sense of it. But the greater part of her felt like she wouldn't even know what to say. The last time she'd seen Ciaran had been almost a week prior, when she'd fled from the foyer of his apartment building. How would she find the words to describe that?

'Is he, uh, seeing *anybody*, then, do you know?' Caroline enquired, all would-be casually, the faintest tell-tale bloom rising to the apples of her cheeks.

Lizzy just about choked on her breakfast cereal. 'Um, no,' she replied, striving for something like nonchalance herself. 'Not that I know of, no.'

Needless to say, the whole interaction was extremely unwelcome, and unsettling, and the best thing would likely have been to just put it to the back of her mind. That was not what she did.

*

The next day, Lizzy and Ciaran sat at the Durands' kitchen table, watching through the glass doors as Thierry and Elise played together outside. Wednesday mornings were, by this stage, almost entirely drama-free, the days of stomping and screeching long gone. The kids had even managed to learn a little *anglais* along the way. Both were able – and, more to the point, in Thierry's case, *willing* – to greet their mother, upon her return, with a 'Good afternoon, Mom, how are you?' Mrs Durand, having now shelled out over a thousand euro for what amounted to this one English sentence and some alone time every single week, seemed to think she'd gotten an absolute bargain.

From the garden, there came a child's yelp and Lizzy craned her neck to check whether it was of the happy variety. Once satisfied that it was, she turned back to her coffee and to Ciaran.

'So Caroline mentioned you yesterday,' she started then, as casually as she could muster.

'Oh right?' Ciaran replied.

'Seems to be quite a fan.'

He looked unperturbed. 'She comes into Café Français a fair bit,' he said, which was not something Lizzy had known, and not something she found she much liked the idea of. How long had that been going on, she wondered. Weeks? Months? What did the two of them talk about? 'Maybe I've dazzled her with my drink-serving capabilities.'

'I think she likes you. As in, *likes* you.'

Ciaran snorted. 'Does she bollocks!'

Immediately, Lizzy could sense the tension in her – more than she'd even realised she'd been holding – start to drain away. So that was how they were going to treat this. Like a joke. She was down for that.

'Seriously!' she protested, with a little laugh.

He paused, cocking an eyebrow.

'And would that be a problem for you?'

Suddenly it didn't feel so funny. She felt heat rising in her. 'I mean, *no*, I just . . .'

''Cause if it was . . .' he offered, teasingly, but this wasn't a subject she wanted to be teased about. How could he tease her about it? It felt . . . below the belt. So to speak. It felt mean.

'It wouldn't be!' she snapped. 'Why would it be?'

Ciaran just shrugged, saying nothing, leaving it all on her to back them out of this cul-de-sac he'd led them into.

'Obviously that's just . . . whatever,' she said, doing her very best to get to breezy. 'Messing around. You haven't, um . . . told anybody about that, have you?'

Ciaran set his coffee cup down, so abruptly that it made a little clatter on the table, some of the liquid sloshing out. She looked down at it, and then squinted back up at him. There was a hard expression on his face, one she'd never seen there before.

'No, Lizzy,' he spat, tightly, and she'd never heard him sound like that either. 'I fucking haven't.'

She didn't know what to say, and the time he gave her to come up with something wasn't enough. She could feel his eyes on her, staring at her, and no words were coming. The next thing she knew, Ciaran was pushing his chair back from the table. With some further reproach she couldn't quite make out, he was getting up, striding out of the kitchen – striding, in fact, right out of the Durands' house, with not a word, not a glance backwards.

He *stormed off*. In real life. Just left her sitting there, alone and reeling at the kitchen table, with two small children effectively holding her hostage.

What the hell was that about?

Lizzy had no idea, and she was no closer to working it out by the time said small children traipsed back inside, rosy-cheeked and asking for brioche. Almost immediately, Lizzy could see Thierry's eyes darting around, searching for his friend.

'Ciaran's gone,' Lizzy told him bluntly. 'Not here. *Gone.*'

And maybe this kid's English was better than she gave him credit for, because right away he scowled in response. He stamped his foot, and all the assurances from Lizzy that followed – all the various baked goods she thrust at him – made no difference at all. Eventually, just like old times, he began – unintelligibly and with all the power of his five-year-old lungs – to yell.

Lizzy didn't blame him one bit. It *was* confusing. The rug *had* been pulled from under him. She felt, honestly, a little like joining him.

Chapter Twenty-Three

Even for the brief period in which Lizzy pretends she might not read the *Hollywood Reporter* piece, she knows that's all she's doing: pretending. Then, it's just a question of getting a spare moment alone.

After a long lunch with Simon and another bunch of producers, she makes a dash for it, and she's scurrying past the harbour when she sees Ciaran's face – dozens of his faces, actually, being handed out one after another on glossy magazines.

The teenager distributing them thrusts a copy right at Lizzy, and it stops her in her tracks. She'd planned to just pull the thing up on her phone – a hard copy seems so much more real somehow. And, the *cover*. She hadn't seen that coming. It's a close-up shot, Ciaran's eyes so blue that she'd think they'd been enhanced if she didn't know better. She accepts the proffered magazine and takes it to the nearest bench. Before her is a picture-perfect marina – clear water with multi-million-dollar yachts on one side and dinky little sailboats on the other, and Lizzy notices not one bit of it. Her heart is beating fast as she flips to the article.

It's not laid out in a question-and-answer format. Rather, it is more like what she guesses would be termed a 'profile' – a pages-long rumination and analysis, photographs scattered throughout, quotes integrated elegantly into the piece itself. Lizzy scans for her own name. When at last she sees it, she reads through the paragraphs quickly, grasping for the gist.

And . . . it's *fine*.

She lets out an exhale.

It really is fine.

First of all, they haven't put in her last name, like Amy promised they wouldn't. And it's a pretty accurate summary of the conversation as she remembers it, at least in terms of words said. On a closer re-reading, Lizzy does notice some pretty florid prose from Alexandra thrown into the mix too.

> The pair have the innate ease with one another that only comes from a deep knowing, from years of shared history; with Lizzy in the room, I feel I'm getting a look at the real Ciaran, the one his friends and family describe as remarkably unaffected by his swift rise to fame.

What else?

> 'We always got a lot of mileage out of the words we pronounced differently,' remembers the California-born Lizzy fondly. 'Though that might have been a mark of how little we had to do more than anything else.' Her favourite thing about Ciaran, she says, was that, 'He always made

me laugh a lot. While also understanding I was the funny one, obviously.' One can't help but suspect there might be something of Lizzy's dry wit in the movie's resident American girl, Claudia, though of course the suggestion is coyly rebuffed by both Ciaran and Lizzy herself.

Lizzy stumbles for a second over that part, there's no denying it. Could that be true? Would she want it to be true? The whole thing makes her feel weird to think about, and she doesn't know whether that's fear of egotism or just plain fear. *Whatever*, she decides then. It's probably a reporter's prerogative to editorialise a little.

Incidentally, she had only provided that particular comment because Alexandra – in those last ten minutes before she'd left the suite – had directly asked her *what's your favourite thing about Ciaran?* What a question to ask. It is little wonder, Lizzy thinks now, that people find certain celebrities likeable. Little wonder that those around celebrities could appear fawning and sycophantic. When there were journalists out there, apparently, with pens poised, saying *tell me something super adorable about that guy.*

Or the reverse, presumably.

The main thing – at least, she imagines, so far as Ciaran and his people will be concerned – is that Alexandra has come to the desired conclusion, loud and clear:

Wish You Were Here is a departure from Ciaran's freshman offering, of that there is no doubt. But, unmistakably, it is no less the product of his innermost self, no less inspired by his authentic truth. When I say goodbye after an hour in the Irishman's easy company, I ask him: what does he think people will make of the movie? 'I guess they'll like it or they won't,' he tells me, with a weary smile, and I suspect that for Ciaran, the chaotic events of recent days have perhaps been clarifying. Certain facts have been reduced to their simplest form. People will like his film, or they will not, but either way, it is his.

Lizzy takes a second, letting the words sink in and then – she may as well go all the way down the rabbit hole – she picks up her phone and types Ciaran's name into Google. As she does so, she tosses a quick glance over her shoulder, as if some part of her expects the man himself might pop up and catch her red-handed.

A bunch of articles appear. Some are new interviews with Ciaran, ranging from a head-on confrontation of the issue ('Ciaran Flynn Hits Back At Copycat Claims') to a more softly-softly approach ('Award-Winning Director Says Latest Offering Is His Most Personal Yet'). A lot of the things Lizzy clicks on, though, seem to simply repackage quotes from the *Hollywood Reporter* piece. She guesses maybe that's why it's important to set the desired tone with a big outlet like that. And, Alexandra herself appears to have quite a following, with bylines in *Vogue* and *The Atlantic* and any number of other publications. Described over and over as a 'writer and cultural critic', she seems to be a name people know, a voice they trust.

If none of this is accidental – if it has all been carefully and deliberately calibrated, and at speed, by Amy Solomon – then Lizzy would have to say it's pretty impressive. It does strike her, though, that there might still be one corner of the internet in which the inmates are running the asylum.

On Twitter, the top result when she searches Ciaran's name is a post from Emma Lewis. It takes a second for Lizzy to realise that she knows this person at all – that's how long it has been since she's seen, heard from, or thought about Emma Lewis. But, when she clicks on the profile, she can see that, yes, it's the same redheaded girl who'd been on exchange in Bordeaux along with her and Ciaran. Her bio reads 'Mummy to @ChesterTheDog. Feminist. Empath. Tea-drinker.' She has 542 followers. She has retweeted some article about Ciaran and created a whole thread in response to it:

> Love this piece! I spent a year with #CiaranFlynn in Bordeaux, back in our university days, and you guys, I have THOUGHTS [1/8]

> As any of you who follow me will know, I am all about lifting up women's voices – but as an old friend of Ciaran's, I can't say it wasn't painful to see #PennyAinsley publicly smear him earlier this week. [2/8]

> The Ciaran I know is honest, kind, original – a true artist and creator in every way. We all could see it back in Bordeaux, and we can see it now. [3/8]

> Ciaran doesn't need to steal other people's ideas! He's a BAFTA winner for God's sake! Lol. And as soon as I saw the trailer for #WishYouWereHere, I knew I was in for a treat, something that only his unique vision could create. [4/8]

In this article, and others that have come out today, Ciaran has said that the film is based STRONGLY on his own experiences living in Bordeaux. I can tell! I was there! [5/8]

There is so much REAL stuff that I remember and relate to even just from seeing the trailer. I think I might have even spotted myself in there lol! #RedheadsUnite #gingersrock #redhairdontcare Can't wait to watch the full film when it comes out in cinemas. [6/8]

I truly can't imagine how hard it must be to pour your heart and soul into something and have it trampled all over. But those of us who know the truth are here to support you all the way, Ciaran! Our #Erasmus community will be bonded for life [7/8]

and #WishYouWereHere is honestly such a beautiful way to honour that. We love you #CiaranFlynn <3 <3 #IStandWithCiaran [8/8]

Huh. Emma had barely known Ciaran, so far as Lizzy recalls. But, no matter. The thread has 15.7k 'likes'. Lizzy wouldn't claim to be an expert on Twitter, but that seems to her a shockingly large amount. Below it, she can see that when she scrolls down a little further, there's another tweet from Emma:

Wow this blew up! See, there is SO much love for you out there #CiaranFlynn! For those asking, you can follow me on Insta @Emmstagram – sending love and light! Xxx

192

And another:

Just for fun! #Throwback #Erasmus #WishYouWereHere #IStandWithCiaran

To this last one, she's attached a photograph. It's of a group of about seven or eight of them, that night they all went to the Christmas market. Lizzy hasn't ever seen it before. Everyone is looking at the camera, except for her and Ciaran. They're looking at each other. Their cheeks are noticeably chubbier than they are now, and ruddy from the cold, and even though she tries so hard to be less self-critical these days, Lizzy can't stop herself from noting that the way her head is angled is far from the most flattering angle for her chin. Or for her crooked tooth. They both look incredibly *happy*, though. That's the other thing she just can't help but notice. The happiness jumps off the screen of her phone, grabs at her guts. Lizzy stares at the picture – at their two faces, frozen mid-laugh – for longer than she probably should. Maybe if they hadn't ended that night making out in a dimly lit hallway, then things would have been fine. All that mess could have been avoided, and she wouldn't be stuck, now, wondering what was real.

Or, is that what she's wrestling with?

Maybe not.

Because she's starting to suspect that perhaps *all of it* was real. The good and the bad. It's just a question of what matters more, now. How should she remember Ciaran Flynn? Him at his best, or him at his worst? She's put so much time into the latter that a change of strategy at this stage doesn't exactly seem smart. And yet, every time that she's seen him here in Cannes, it has felt like she's lost a little more ground. There still seems to be something – some fundamental thing about him – that she just . . . likes. In the simplest, purest sense of that term.

Anyway. With a quick glance at her watch – she has another meeting in thirty minutes – she scrolls past the photograph, clicking onto the 'IStandWithCiaran' hashtag. There are hundreds of comments, maybe thousands; it makes Lizzy's eyes hurt trying to scan them all. It's crazy to see how many people have chosen to weigh in on a situation about which they know essentially nothing. But then, she guesses, that's the internet. Most of the comments are generic, and sweet. Some . . . less so.

Fuck – and I cannot emphasise this enough – you @PennyAinsley. The words bandwagon and jumping spring to mind. #IStandWithCiaran

This bitch Penny seems like a jealous cunt, amiright? #IStandWithCiaran

Wah wah wah! Too bad @PennyAinsley, nobody cares. #IStandWithCiaran

I guess you really can't buy class @PennyAinsley, I hope you die in a fire lmfao #IStandWithCiaran

@PennyAinsley you literally are such an ugly attention seeking whore, it's pathetic

On and on it goes, and Lizzy clicks on Penny's account. It has been deactivated. She tries to reason away the unease she feels, seeing that. Maybe the account was deleted a long time ago. Maybe Penny's one of these new, cool people who is definitively Offline. Maybe she *hasn't* decided to flee the internet because of relentless harassment from Ciaran's groupies.

In her hand, Lizzy's cell phone starts to ring. Unknown number.

Shit! she thinks. Did she have a meeting she'd forgotten about? Could some new disaster have arisen in relation to the ceilidh? She calculates how long it would take her to get down to Plage Raphael from here if she had to.

'Lizzy!' comes a warm, honeyed voice on the other end of the line. 'It's Amy Solomon. From the studio!'

'Of course,' Lizzy replies, trying to conceal her surprise. 'Amy! Hi.'

She wonders how Amy got her number – wonders why asking that question would, somehow, seem ruder than the fact the other woman had clearly done some snooping around.

'I just wanted to give you a quick call, thank you again so much for swinging by the interview the other day. We all super appreciate your input. Have you seen the piece?'

'Yeah, I actually just read it.'

'It was great, right? I think having you there was really that extra little bit of legitimacy that we needed. Just helped tilt the whole landscape of the coverage in the right direction, y'know? Alexandra is . . . let's say *well-disposed* to the studio, but she's not a dummy. You can't pick a dummy for these things or there's no point.

Anyhow, I was just talking to Ciaran, and it would be wonderful if you might be free to come along to the premiere tomorrow night.'

'What? Oh, no, that's okay,' Lizzy protests automatically.

But Amy protests harder. 'No, really! You'd be our special guest. Please come. The limos are leaving from the Carlton at 7 p.m.'

'Limos?' Lizzy says blankly.

'I know, right? So crazy to hire them to drive, like, a hundred meters or whatever it is. But I guess that's just the way things are done.'

Lizzy feels very much like she's missed something along the way here. 'Hang on a second. Is *Wish You Were Here* premiering at the Palais?'

She asks this as though she is enquiring whether the film is premiering on Mars, and when Amy responds, in the affirmative, she does so like it's the most normal thing in the world. Practically mundane.

Lizzy would like to think she's not a total idiot. She'd known all along that it was a studio movie – American money, and plenty of it, she'd guess. She knows that Ciaran is somewhat of a 'name' at this point, and that the two stars are as well. She knows the producers have form. So, it isn't as though she expected this film to premiere in a room of a hundred people. But there is quite a jump between that and the most high-profile venue in town, and all the hoopla that comes with it.

'Wow. That's a big deal.'

'So you'll come? You really should, Lizzy. It'd be great for the Scottish Film Board too.'

Lizzy cracks a smile. This woman is never not selling.

There's something likeable about her though. Maybe it is just that Lizzy enjoys a straight shooter.

'In what way – *whatsoever* – will the Scottish Film Board even come up?' she asks laughingly.

'Well, you'll *bring* it up, obviously. You never know who you might get chit-chatting with at the after-party. It's on the *Serenity*.'

Lizzy guesses that's a yacht. She's never been on any of the yachts in Cannes and she lets her gaze drift out towards the ones that are in front of her right this very moment. Amy probably makes a valid point about the networking potential. Even setting that aside, there's an appeal, just for sheer nosiness' sake. When would she get an opportunity like this again, to walk the red carpet in Cannes, explore the inside of one of those fancy yachts? Maybe never.

'Would I be coming just to come, or to, like . . . do anything?' she asks uncertainly.

'What do you mean?'

'Like . . . what I did with the *Hollywood Reporter*, that type of thing.'

'Oh! No, nothing like that,' Amy replies. 'You'll just walk up the carpet, no stops. In terms of inside the Palais, or at the after-party, there'll be photogs and TV folks around, obviously. But it'll be fluff stuff. You can talk to 'em or not talk to 'em. Of course if you *wanted* to say something . . . y'know, *helpful*, that sure would be . . .'

'Helpful?' Lizzy fills in.

'Right. But you don't have to say anything at all if you don't want to.'

That sounds good to Lizzy. As for the Ciaran of it all . . . who knows. Presumably he'll be pretty busy; maybe she'll barely see him. And to the extent she does . . . crazy as she would have found the prospect a few short days ago, maybe that'd be okay. Maybe a part of her actually wouldn't mind seeing him, wouldn't mind one last chance to try and figure him out.

'And Ciaran knows you're inviting me? Definitely?'

'Honey! Of course! He would have called you himself, but he's in the press junket all day today, poor thing. So I said I'd just give you a call. I'll tell him you'll be there, then, will I?'

Lizzy clicks her tongue against her teeth. 'Uh, yeah. Why not? Yes,' she repeats, with a little more vim. 'I'll be there.'

Chapter Twenty-Four

The first priority, of course, is what to wear. Not in order to make a splash or to make heads turn – Lizzy's goals are much more modest. Blend in, look appropriate. That's it.

Every year, she brings one sort-of-fancy dress to Cannes, just in case. It's midnight blue, falling to just above her ankles in swishy narrow pleats. Gold beading and sequins are dotted delicately from waist to throat, then encrusted, in more dramatic fashion, across the shoulders and down to elbow-length sleeves. Lizzy brings it because she always feels good in it, and because it doesn't really wrinkle. She's never ended up wearing it at any of the festivals past, though. By now, the thing has become more like a talisman in her suitcase than anything else. The prospect of actually needing it had seemed so remote this year that she hadn't even thought so far as accessories. Though a little scuffed, she figures her flat gold pumps should probably do. That just leaves a purse. And a bra – the back of the dress dips low, requiring some kind of strapless feat of engineering that she can only hope will be available at short notice in such a tiny town. Then, she gets a hold of herself. Surely if any tiny town is going to anticipate an underwear emergency, then Cannes – at least for twelve days in May – is the one.

By four o'clock the following afternoon, with the hours falling away before she's due to show up at the Carlton, Lizzy dashes out of the Scottish Pavilion, a woman on a mission. Her entire working day, in truth, has felt like a mere formality – something to be endured and now, finally, escaped.

'I gotta go, I'll talk to you later!' she calls out as she passes Shauna at the front desk.

'Cool. Oh, hey!' the other woman's voice rises, and Lizzy stops in her tracks. 'Some guy was just here looking for you, but you were in the middle of your meeting. From the . . . rifle place or whatever?'

'The what?'

Lizzy stands aside, lets Shauna meet and greet a bunch of people traipsing in for the last panel event of the day.

'The place where we're having the ceilidh,' Shauna clarifies, once they're alone again.

'Oh! Plage Raphael. Monsieur Henri. What did he want?'

'He just wanted to talk to you – he was quite hard to understand to be honest. I said you'd email him.'

'Okay,' Lizzy replies, and she must look a little worried because suddenly the younger girl does too.

'Is that alright? Should I have got Simon?'

'No! No. That's fine, I'll deal with it. Thanks!'

She's practically out the door when Shauna calls out

to her once again. 'Are you coming to that Raindance reception tonight by any chance? I thought it might be a good way to meet new filmmakers. They won't have any money, yet, obviously, but still. Good to know who's on the up, and develop relationships and all that.'

Lizzy smiles. She has high hopes for this girl, she realises. How has it happened, without her even really noticing, that she's no longer the protégée – that she maybe, sort of, *has* a protégée?

'I can't,' she says. 'I have a different thing. You *absolutely* should go, though. I'll be sure to tell Simon you're flying the Scottish flag. He'll be thrilled.'

*

On Rue d'Antibes, Lizzy zooms around a few stores, both her tasks successfully accomplished in little more than an hour. Urgency, as it turns out, focuses the mind. She returns to the Airbnb thoroughly impressed by her own efficiency, and with plenty of time for a leisurely dinner. Whatever food might be presented to her in the course of the evening seems extremely likely to be thimble-sized, such that she's put in place a contingency plan. She polishes off a large baguette, a macaron and an apple, all the while typing a lengthy email to Simon. Asking her boss to do something does feel a little contrary to the natural order of things. But at the same time, he has done almost nothing at all in relation to the ceilidh thus far, beyond sign the contracts – one follow-up phone call to Monsieur Henri does not seem a huge demand. In fact, if it's a money issue, then all the better that Simon be the one to handle it directly.

She relays everything she can think might even possibly

be of relevance – the wet weather back-up options that had been forwarded to her just last week, all at eye-watering prices; the minor decking crisis that had been averted the week prior to last; that whole weird interlude about the jewellers from the other day. Then, with a decisive snap, she closes her laptop. For one night only, she's got other matters to attend to.

Clicking on some Carole King, she hums along as she begins doing her makeup. She takes her time with it, applying a little more foundation than normal, being a little more careful with her eyeliner pen. Next, it's on to hair. For lack of the skills to do much else, she adds some waves with the curling wand and leaves it loose around her shoulders. All the while, her playlist darts from Carole to Lizzo to Dolly to Brandi, and her voice gets louder and louder alongside them, until she's way past the volume that, out of consideration for her neighbours, she typically allows herself in Edinburgh. Of course, there are neighbours here too, but she cares about them a lot less. She just . . . can't resist.

What it comes down to is that, in life, there are a lot of things that Lizzy thinks are pretty special. Twinkling lights in the darkness, receiving a card in the mail, the feeling of going to bed in a different country than the one you woke up in. Red wine with food, certain bookshops – all good stuff.

But then there are other things. Newborn babies. That moment in a cinema or theatre when the lights go down, when the collective hush descends. And, singing at the top of her voice.

Those things, to Lizzy, are better than good. To her, they are kind of magical. Holy.

She lets her voice rise freely alongside the music that is filtering out from her phone, and it is exactly what she needs right now. It makes the whole thing – a process that, centred as it is on the basic fact of how she'll end up looking in the mirror, could so easily be anxiety-ridden – actually feel fun.

Even better, she manages to hang on to that feeling the whole way to the Carlton. It's less than a kilometre away, but she has to go the long way round because the middle section of the Croisette is already closed off for the premiere. As she makes her way along the back streets, she can sense people giving her a second glance – the way she gives other people a second glance, when she sees them all dressed up – and a fizz of excitement zips through her. It's been a long time since she's gotten to do anything in this town that she hasn't already done a dozen times before.

She'd received an email from one of Amy Solomon's assistants with a schedule, literally down to the minute, of the evening's proceedings and by the time Lizzy gets to the Carlton, she heads straight for the studio's suite, as instructed. She doesn't know what she had been expecting, exactly, but the volume of people who are up there comes as a bit of a surprise. She checks in with a stern-looking woman guarding the door and swiftly finds herself amidst a swarm of strangers. All of a sudden she feels very spare. Why on earth, she wonders, is she in this room? She has, after all, had nothing whatsoever to do with the making of this film. A ticket to the premiere, maybe that would have been one thing. But to be here, in the suite? To be, pretty soon, bundling into a limousine with all these people on the way to the red carpet? How could she not have realised that in those contexts, she would feel – would, factually, *be* – an utter interloper?

She's on the verge of turning on her heel to leave when she's accosted by Amy, finding herself enveloped in a hug.

'You look just fabulous!' Amy says, which may or may not be true. Compared to some of the women now in her direct eye-line, Lizzy suspects she probably looks like she's at a backyard barbecue. But, that's okay. She seems to have landed somewhere in the right range. And between underdressed or overdressed, she'd go for the former every time.

'Thanks! So do you,' she smiles.

'Let's do some quick introductions, 'kay?' We only have fifteen minutes before we all gotta be downstairs.'

A whirlwind of names and faces follow, and it's some comfort to Lizzy to note that in among this group are quite a lot of people who she imagines had little, if anything, to do with *Wish You Were Here*. At least six people are just the spouse of a studio executive.

Weirdly, some of them – not the spouses, but others – seem to know her. Or rather, know *of* her. 'Oh! Lizzy!' they say, eyes brightening in recognition when they hear her name. 'Of course.' It's all very odd. She pretends it isn't, because sometimes, that's the only thing to do.

Eventually, at a far corner of the suite, Amy taps a tux on the shoulder. 'No introductions needed here, I guess,' she says jovially, and when the tux turns around, Ciaran Flynn is the one inside it.

'The man of the hour. I'll let you two chat, I gotta run to the restroom before we leave,' Amy says, and as she disappears, Ciaran smiles – almost a little shyly, if such a thing could be possible.

'Hi,' he says. 'Thanks for coming. It's . . . nice to see you.'

'Thanks for inviting me. It's nice to see you too,' she says, and as soon as she hears the words out loud, she realises that they seem to be true. Entirely out of the blue, Lizzy is reminded of a long-forgotten moment, in her mom's flat in Edinburgh. She'd been back from Bordeaux for maybe a couple of months at the time, and her dad had come over for dinner. Around the table, things had been feeling nice – cosy and normal and easy – until she'd said something snide. She doesn't even remember what it was, but she remembers the way her mom had tried to make light of it, before excusing herself to go to the bathroom. Lizzy had sat there with her dad, and suddenly everything felt very silent. Awful.

The problem was that her mother's betrayal – not so much the affair itself, or even the fact of her parents getting separate flats, but the deliberate *betrayal* at the heart of it all – remained one of the most shocking, most painful things Lizzy had ever experienced. She actually felt some sense of loyalty to the shock, to the pain – even if, in truth, they had begun to ease a little. Every so often, she still felt almost compelled to make the point: *I haven't forgotten.* The idea that her family, collectively, might slide into some new narrative – one where she'd been dramatic about the whole thing to begin with but had soon come around – was like a screwdriver in the stomach. She'd wanted, at the least, for her mother to stay sorry; that didn't seem unreasonable to her.

205

All the same, sitting in the kitchen that night, it hadn't been hard to see that *she* was the one who had just taken the joy out of things. She'd suddenly realised how exhausting it was – this constant oscillation, the reaching out slowly and then retreating fast. She'd done it just now, she'd done it at Christmastime – she'd been doing it over and over, in explosive and in more internal ways, ever since her parents' separation.

'You *can* just forgive her, you know,' her dad had offered, in his usual quiet way. 'If you want to. It's okay to just let yourself love her again.'

And of course, this thing with Ciaran is very different. Lizzy doesn't know that she needs to forgive him. She certainly doesn't need to love him. But, liking him – in the platonic sense of the term? Honestly, she realises, as she looks at him now, it *would* be a relief to give in to that. At least for the duration of this one evening, she might prefer to be happy than right. Maybe he had been a bad almost-sort-of-something-like-boyfriend to her, twelve years ago. In fact, she'd go so far as to say he definitely was. Maybe he would have been a bad actual-boyfriend to her. Maybe, to this very day, he's a bad boyfriend in general.

But, the fact of the matter is, he's not her boyfriend, and he's not going to be. He's the one familiar face in this room – aside from Amy – and Lizzy wants to be able to let herself just enjoy the experience of being here. If a little compartmentalising is what's required, she finds herself willing to do it.

It strikes her, looking at Ciaran standing there by himself, that if other people have managed to wangle a plus one to this thing, he shouldn't have had any problem.

'Did you not bring your family or . . . anybody?' she asks.

He shakes his head. 'I think I just wanted to get the lay of the land with everything, you know? Which probably was a good call, given the way things have worked out. To be trying to wrangle the Flynns *en masse* in the middle of it all might just have been . . .'

'Yeah,' she nods, not needing the adjective.

'I literally haven't had a minute,' Ciaran says, his voice lowering. 'Like, high-class problem and everything but, dear Jesus. I'm sick of the sound of my own voice.'

'Any more contact from Penny?' Lizzy asks. Strangely, this seems to be the topic that comes most naturally with him now. It feels safe, somehow. Their common project.

'Nope. The craic is she hasn't even *seen* the actual film. So, the lawyers say we probably won't hear anything else from her until it goes into cinemas, at which point, who knows. She'll probably come up with a dozen more things I apparently nicked off her.'

'And what do we think is the motive here?' Lizzy asks. That's always been a little unclear to her. 'She just wants a payday, basically?'

'Most likely. I mean all she can foreseeably get out of this is money, so it's hard to know how it could be anything else. Gets her name out there too, I guess. Gets people talking about her.'

Lizzy nods. *Not always for the better*, she can't help but think grimly, her mind flashing back to some of those tweets yesterday. Ciaran, however, doesn't appear to be thinking along remotely similar lines. His whole expression is one of unrestrained aggravation.

'For the first while I was just, like, slightly shell-shocked by everything,' he continues. 'I couldn't even be that angry, you know? But the more I think about it, the more I can't get over the *nerve* of ju—'

'Guys!' comes a nasally, American accent then, rising high above the collective conversation. (*Is that what I sound like?* Lizzy wonders, every single time she comes across such an accent. She fears that, at best, she might sound more like it than unlike it).

'Guys!' The woman is wearing a headset, like Britney Spears circa 2001. She hadn't been included in Lizzy's whistle-stop introductory tour. 'I'mna need you all to head to the elevators, the cars are here. Ready when you are! But, like, now.'

Lizzy looks at Ciaran.

He looks at her.

All around them, people start to move, chatter ramping up in volume.

He raises both his eyebrows, some curious hybrid of trepidation and calm amidst everyone else's straightforward, high octane excitement. 'Show time, I guess.'

Chapter Twenty-Five

Lizzy finds herself sandwiched in the back of a limousine with Ciaran, Amy and three others. They travel at a snail's pace along the Croisette – it really would be quicker to walk – until they reach a bottleneck at the end of the red carpet. She can hear the cacophony of fans, can start to see the hordes of press photographers, TV cameras and lights. Their driver rolls down his window and speaks to a security guard before pulling over to the side.

'We have to wait,' he explains, craning his neck to look round at them. 'Three cars ahead of us on the schedule. So, they arrive, the people get out, they walk up the carpet, and then it's you.'

It is as though the limousines are aeroplanes coming in to land. The whole process is like a military operation, guys in *Men in Black*-style suits, dark glasses and head-sets swarming the area, bringing order to what seems, from the outside, like a fairly close cousin of chaos.

Lizzy cranes her neck to take in the whole scene. A further four limousines are waiting behind them.

'That's the actors,' Ciaran says. 'And their people. They weren't in the Carlton, they've been staying down in Cap d'Antibes.'

Lizzy nods. It's the only thing he's said to her for the entire journey, because Amy Solomon and some other guy – Ciaran's manager, Lizzy can't remember his name – have been talking at him in an almost unrelenting stream. He's due to stop and speak to this outlet and that one and the other one, they're telling him now; it should take no more than ten minutes, tops. Then he'll take some 'singles', by which point the actors will be coming up behind him and they'll do group shots. They can all go over to sign some autographs for fans but not for longer than five minutes. ('No signing blank pages,' the manager dude says. 'And no blue ink if you can help it.' Lizzy doesn't understand that one, but she can tell it's not the time to ask.) Then everyone needs to make their way up the steps, apparently, for the final group shot at the top of said steps, before their asses are due on seats in the theatre at eight o'clock sharp.

It's a lot to take in, and Lizzy isn't even the one who *has* to take it in. Ciaran is quiet, nodding seriously through the litany of instructions. He's tapping his heel the tiniest bit, she notices, his leg twitching with it repetitively. Anxiously, maybe. She has the strangest urge to reach out and still his knee with her hand. Of course, she knows better than to do it.

Eventually, he repeats back all the information he's been given, like a schoolboy saying a poem by heart. Amy clutches a hand to her chest, making as though to dab a tear from her eye. 'My work here is done. You're gonna kill it out there, hon.'

And then, in what seems like a snap of her fingers, that's where they are.

Out there.

As soon as they exit the car, people are yelling Ciaran's name, urging him to look this way and that, pointing their cameras in his direction, holding posters and Sharpies aloft.

'Good luck,' Lizzy murmurs instinctively, as she shimmies past him, and it's a surprise that he can even make her out, amidst all the noise.

'Thanks,' he replies, holding her gaze for a second, looking a little dumbstruck.

He snaps out of it fast, though, striding over to one of the television reporters just like he's been told. Amy and the manager linger a few feet behind him, at a diagonal so they're out of the shot, and Lizzy makes her way up the carpet along with the others from the car. None of their little group is famous, but still a few people holler at them, urging them to stop for pictures. Perhaps, as a red carpet photographer, it's just smart to cover your bases.

By the time they reach the top end of the carpet, a huddle of other people are already there – faces Lizzy recognises from back at the hotel. They're lingering and chatting at the side of the iconic red staircase leading into the Palais, as though it's any other cocktail mixer, as though they are not in the midst of this giant, near-deafening spectacle.

'So, what's the idea,' she asks one of the producers, whom she remembers as being friendly. 'We just hang out here?'

'Yep,' the producer says. Jess is her name, Lizzy thinks. 'Ciaran and the cast will come up, do the photo at the top of the steps. Then they go inside, and we all follow them.'

Lizzy nods, looking around her, taking it all in. She remembers, as a very small child – probably no more than four or five – desperately wanting to go to the car wash. She was a bit afraid of it, but that was the same part of her that was drawn to it. When her parents finally agreed to pay a company to do what the rain more or less did for free, she'd found the whole experience . . . interesting. Not as exciting as she thought it would be, and not as dramatic and scary either. It was mostly just a lot of not knowing exactly what was coming next – more water? Suds? Those big brushes? Some other thing she hadn't even considered? Just five solid minutes of uncertainty and, by consequence, curiosity.

Lizzy hasn't thought about that in at least twenty years. But for whatever reason, it is what springs to mind as she stands on the red carpet in Cannes, engulfed by sound and flashes of light.

The hysteria reaches fever pitch once the actors arrive and she looks over at Ciaran, flanked by them, smiling proudly for photographs. She watches him sign autographs and contort himself into shapes to take selfies, and he's good at all this, she thinks. Lizzy would never have described him as a wildly extroverted person – a person who loved the limelight, demanded attention. But he'd always had a certain ability to roll with the punches that seems like it would probably come in handy here. He looks like he belongs. Her living room in Rue Cabirol, his Converse trainers on the coffee table, feels like another lifetime.

*

The theatre is enormous, split into three levels, and as they walk into it, the whole audience stands and claps respectfully in greeting. It's nice, but a little weird. Several rows in the dress circle have been reserved for the film-making team and their guests, and as Lizzy sinks down into her seat, as the lights dim and the film begins, there's the sense of an exhale. After the frenzy of the carpet, the prospect of ninety minutes in darkness sounds pretty good to her right about now, no matter that it involves watching a film she's already seen just a few days ago.

Lizzy is, as a general matter, a re-watcher of films she likes. Her very *favourite* kinds of movies are the ones where there is stuff to find, the second and third and tenth time around. New jokes and details and layers to appreciate even once the suspense is gone.

In the case of *Wish You Were Here*, it's a huge relief, actually, to have the suspense gone. Without it, she can tell – even within the first few minutes – that she's able to see the thing more clearly. Little touches, ones she hadn't had the mental space to enjoy before, present themselves to her, delightfully.

Then, entirely unbidden, that woman's phrase from the *Hollywood Reporter* piece pogo-sticks back into her brain.

One can't help but suspect there might be something of Lizzy in the movie's resident American girl, Claudia.

Could that have been right? Could she have missed something there, on the first viewing?

Lizzy really doesn't think so.

No.

Nationality, she reminds herself, does not a blueprint make.

There *was* that whole thing about the singing, though, that Ciaran had mentioned in the interview. Had he just been paying her a compliment there, separate altogether from the film? Or, something else?

Nationality and one common interest, of course, do not a blueprint make either.

But still, Lizzy can't seem to stop herself from considering it, for the first time. The possibility. And all of a sudden, two things are true. One: she is desperate for Claudia to show up on screen in about ten minutes' time. Two: she can hardly bear the thought of it.

In front of her, a bit of a kerfuffle catches her attention. Various people, Ciaran included, seem to be leaving – crouched down, they're creeping out of the theatre. She tries to minimise the inconvenience of her own body as a few people in her row start to move too, squeezing out over the top of her.

'Are you coming?' Jess whispers, on her way past.

Lizzy hesitates.

'Obviously you can stay if you want!'

One way or another, it's a decision that has to be made fast.

Lizzy doesn't know where she'd even be going to, or for what purpose. No matter the details, it seems a pretty certain bet that she'd be giving up any semblance of restorative anti-socialising.

That quote from the magazine repeats like a chant inside of her, though. And she knows an escape when she sees one.

Chapter Twenty-Six

'Half those people from the studio probably haven't even seen the film before now,' Jess says, as they make their way down a corridor with a bunch of others. 'And then even with the creatives, some people like to watch it with an audience. Usually I'd stay myself. But this week . . .' She shakes her head, looking suddenly exhausted behind her sparkly eyeshadow. 'I kind of just need *one* day where I don't see *Wish You Were Here*, y'know?'

They arrive into what Lizzy guesses would be termed a 'green room' even though it's not green. There are drinks and snacks laid out, and big leather couches that people are already beginning to sink into. Ciaran is nowhere to be seen. Maybe, subconsciously, she's looking around for him, because Jess supplies:

'Ciaran's been whisked off to do some press with the actors. Should only take about forty-five minutes or so, though, and then they'll be in.'

'Wow. It never ends, does it?'

'It's pretty full-on,' Jess agrees. 'We've been lucky with

215

this one, though. The cast are brilliant. They've played such a blinder this past few days, what with . . . everything. And Ciaran too. He just makes it so easy. Directors can be . . . well, I suppose I don't need to tell you. I'm sure in your job you know all about it.'

'I really do,' Lizzy replies. Whether it's imploring directors to do something, or trying to call a halt to them doing something, she's had to become master of the compliment sandwich: the thing she wants to say shoved between *we are so thrilled to have you in Scotland* and *this is obviously such a special film.*

She finds herself a spot on one of the couches, glass of whisky in hand, and the time passes quickly. She's still not one hundred per cent sure of everyone's names, but it's a smallish group – only about ten of them in all – and with high heels kicked off and top buttons undone, everybody starts to seem a bit more human.

Her attention is drawn to the door when Ciaran and the four actors eventually troop back in, and a few minutes later, Ciaran drifts over towards her.

'You all done?' she asks.

'Yep,' he nods. There are no seats left, so he perches himself on the arm of an adjacent chair and she twists herself around a little on the couch to face him. 'Once was enough for you, then?'

It takes her a second to work out what he's talking about. The film.

'Oh. Y'know. Just wanted to hang out with the cool kids.'

He smiles. 'You on the whisky too?' he asks, glancing towards her glass, and Lizzy notices he's nursing one just the same.

'Yep.' There had been a time, maybe around age twenty-nine or thirty, when she'd thought of drinking whisky as somewhat of a power move. It often seemed to be a conversation starter with men and, embarrassingly, she had kind of enjoyed that for a while. It hadn't taken long, though, to realise that the initial hit of attention – the slightly patronising tenor of it, the narrow range of response it seemed to allow for in her – was really not worth it. She had, she suspected, maybe gotten a peek into the lifelong cross borne by female football fans.

These days, whether it's a Laphroaig or the pinkest, slushiest of strawberry daiquiris, Lizzy mostly just wants to drink her fucking drink in peace. Happily, that seems to be precisely what Ciaran intends to let her do.

'Cheers to that,' is all he says, tilting his glass to clink it against hers. At this close range, he looks like himself again – the image of him, out there on the red carpet, is the thing that seems like the figment now.

'Cheers. Hey, I meant to ask you, did you see that Twitter thread Emma Lewis wrote the other day?' she asks. She likes a little gossip as much as anybody.

'Saw that, yeah,' he replies dryly. 'I'm not actually on Twitter, but my manager showed it to me.'

'Did he set that up? Or did Amy, or somebody?'

'Nope. Amy *was* on at me to get some friends and family to post on social media, but I kept fobbing her off. That whole thing from Emma was . . . organic, as they say. Or as far as I know, anyway.'

'Are you still friends with her?'

Ciaran shakes his head. 'Haven't heard from her since the day and hour we left Bordeaux. Matter of fact I feel like I barely heard from her when we were *in* Bordeaux.

Unless I'm just totally blanking stuff out, which is possible.'

'She sure seems to remember you fondly,' Lizzy teases.

He snorts. 'Doesn't she? She laid it on a bit thick. "Even here at this Christmas market, we could tell he was a visionary", and all that craic.'

Lizzy laughs. 'A lot of people "liked" it, though,' she adds then. 'I actually didn't know . . . I mean, I had no idea of the *scale* of interest in, um . . . you.'

She only realises when she gets to the end of her sentence that it could seem like a jibe. Ciaran doesn't look at all insulted, though. The truth, Lizzy has to admit, is that she seems to have been way off-base during those first few days of the festival. Ciaran Flynn might not be a perfect person, but he really doesn't seem to be up his own ass, in the way she'd initially decided he was. Something tells her she wouldn't have to compliment-sandwich him.

'No I know,' he says readily, 'it's insane. I mean, that's just people on the internet, though. Mostly in day-to-day life, nobody gives a fuck about me.'

'They did out there,' she counters, with a tilt of her head in what she imagines to be the direction of the red carpet outside.

'That's not real life either though, is it? That's theatre.'

Lizzy doesn't disagree.

'Must be pretty weird.'

Ciaran exhales lightly, as though he doesn't quite have the words. 'Unbelievable. I don't think I would have expected, as a director or a writer, to really be that visible, you know? But, I don't know. People just started to ask to interview me, and do stories on me, and I started getting invited to events and . . . there you go.'

'Do you like it? Being recognised and stuff?'

For a second, he pauses. 'Nobody's ever asked me that,' he says. 'Isn't that weird? Um . . . mostly, yeah. I don't know if it's cool to admit that or not, but yeah. I mostly do. The fact that I've gotten to make some stuff, and people have seen it, and they like it, and they like me? That's pretty great, let's not lie.'

'I think it's a different ball game for actors, though,' he continues. 'Or, pop stars or whatever. As I say, for me, any attention's largely just at, like, press events or premieres. Even to the extent I've had people come up to me randomly on the street or whatever in Cannes, it's a very specific set of people who are here, you know? This is not a regular population. Once you get to the stage of, like, mass recognition . . . I'd say that could be pretty tough.'

'I guess if you're an actor or a pop star, mass recognition is kind of the goal,' Lizzy says.

Ciaran cocks his head. 'Mmm. But then, maybe by the time a person has enough information to make a proper decision about whether they want that kind of attention, it's actually too late. Like, by definition, you can't know if you're going to enjoy being really super famous – never mind be any good at it – until you've experienced being really super famous. At which point the toothpaste's kind of out of the tube.'

'I guess I buy that. Yeah. I've never really thought about it that way,' she replies. 'I don't know, though,' she adds, a second later. Maybe she *doesn't* fully buy it. 'You're saying that right now, things are at a certain level for you, and you feel like it's enough, right? You can *imagine* what more would be like, based on what you already have, and you know you don't want it.'

'. . . True. Suppose not everybody has the imagination I have, is the thing,' he says, and even as Lizzy rolls her eyes, she can't hold back a smile.

'Nah,' he continues, more seriously. 'I dunno. I think maybe it's just . . . incremental. Creeps up on you. Like you're at a certain point and you think "this is good" – or it's *fine,* at least. And then it gets a little bit more, and that's still good and fine, and a little bit more, and a little bit more . . . until eventually, at some point, that extra little bit becomes the bit that's too much.'

'Maybe,' she agrees, feeling satisfied that they've just about sufficiently analysed this subject now. 'Interesting, anyway.'

'Yeah. I have to say, turns out I've kinda missed hearing your thoughts on stuff, Elizabeth.'

And, it's not like it means anything, really. It's not like it was deliberate, it's not even as though he is the only person to have ever called her that – her full name. But there is some strange shift in the atmosphere as soon as the word is out of his mouth, and Ciaran seems to realise it too. His cheeks maybe flush a little. Or that could be her imagination.

'I'll tell you what the *weirdest* thing is, though,' he says then, his voice rising, and just like that, she can tell that they're back in cocktail party mode. 'About being somebody that people know even a wee bit.'

'What?' she asks indulgently. If he is inclined to move swiftly on, she's certainly inclined to let him.

'The *fan art.* I've been sent a *number* of hand-drawn sketches of myself at this point. And I just – honestly, with the best will in the world – don't even know what to do with them. Like, it feels wrong to just throw them out, but I also really, really don't want them in my house.'

He trails off, looking utterly helpless, and Lizzy guffaws. She can't help but think that it might be a little dangerous, how good it feels to laugh with him again.

*

Half an hour later, shoes have been put back on, ties and bow-ties straightened, and they all wait outside the theatre, ready for their re-entry once the credits start to roll. Ciaran and the actors are going to do a short Q&A on stage, apparently, and then it's off to the after-party.

'Do you think they've enjoyed it?' someone asks, in hushed tones.

'I friggin' hope so. I don't know why we spent three nights freezing our asses off in that pond if not for other people's validation,' cracks one of the actors – Jools, the one who played Claudia.

Lizzy snickers. She likes this girl, she's decided. In the (admittedly very limited) time they've spent together, she seems to be a lot more amusing than the beautiful typically need to bother becoming.

'They're hardly likely to egg us if they don't, I suppose.'

'We'll know at the party, though,' Ciaran says, and he looks a little antsy, Lizzy thinks. 'If people start giving us really obscure compliments on, like, the sound design or something.'

'Not that sound design isn't terribly important,' Jess chimes in.

'Terribly important,' Ciaran agrees, though it sounds more wry in his Irish accent than in Jess' cut-glass English

221

one. 'But it might not be the first thing that springs to mind, if you've just been swept away by the magic of cinema, is all I'm saying.'

'Oh, I've got a good one for that, actually,' Lizzy pipes up, and it's a little startling, once the words are out of her mouth, to find everyone's eyes suddenly on her. 'For when I haven't liked a film. I mean, obviously one option is just not to comment, which is great if you can get away with it. But if I'm in a situation where I *have* to say something, I look at the person, and I say . . .' She pauses, letting a little anticipation swell. '"*Wow*. What an achievement."'

It always goes down well, and this time is no exception. Around her, everyone laughs, satisfyingly.

'That's genius!'

'Yeah, I'll be stealing that one!'

'It's great because, like, everybody's got an *idea*, right?' Lizzy continues. 'But, having the follow-through to actually make something? I *do* think that's an achievement at some level, almost no matter how it turns out. So, it's just the perfect line. I don't even have to feel like a bitch when I say it.'

The doors are opened, then, and on the way into the theatre, Jools tucks her arm through Lizzy's.

'I gotta say, would've been nice of Ciaran to introduce us *before* we filmed the movie, huh? Would have saved me a whole lot of trouble, that's for sure.'

She grins, tossing it out like it's nothing. Like it might have some result *other than* turning Lizzy's mind into instant oatmeal. She's slightly stupefied, scrambling to make sure she's correctly understood the implication, and the effort to find an appropriate facial expression – much less a verbal response – takes a good five seconds too long. By the time she manages it, Jools very definitely has other priorities. Because inside the auditorium, the entire audience is on their feet, applauding. And not in the polite way they did at the beginning. They're applauding wildly.

Chapter Twenty-Seven

On the gangplank of the *Serenity*, Lizzy finds herself just staring up at the yacht for a moment, like a tourist in New York City. Set over four levels, it's a beast – glossy and gaudy and glorious. Once she steps aboard, waiters circulate with endless trays of Veuve Clicquot, and on the ground floor, a DJ that other people seem to have heard of is playing, creating a reverberation through the whole boat. The place is packed. Lizzy does a circuit and takes it all in, wondering how many others were, mere hours previously, sitting in tiny rented rooms, shoving convenience food into their mouths. Or studying themselves in the mirror, fixating on a strand of hair, smoothing their palms over curves as if to somehow shrink them a little. She would wager not very many. In ordinary circumstances, she might well reach the opposite conclusion these days, having come to believe that although they hid it well, other people – other women – tended to be more like her than not. But this is a very particular crowd.

An incredible number of those among it, as well as

being rich and beautiful, are also famous. Lizzy has been around some celebrities before – primarily Scottish ones – such that she knows the rules. She knows not to stare, not to ask for photos. She can keep her shit together. This is really a different league, though. More famous people, at a closer range, than she has ever seen in one place. And a pretty random mix, at that. Bradley Cooper, but also Donatella Versace. Marion Cotillard, but also Dua Lipa. This is the Cannes Film Festival as Lizzy's never quite seen it before.

And yet, as she takes in her new surroundings, there's a certain amount of fundamental familiarity about the situation too. It's finger food and free drinks, and the knowledge that this thing is only going to be as enjoyable as she makes it.

By now, the days of having a Caroline Gilhooly – or someone like her – there to lean on as she arrives to parties are long gone. Lizzy knows what it's like to walk into a room and know nobody, or next to nobody – to be obliged to be the starter of conversations with strangers. It's a dynamic that she's gotten more comfortable with over time, by virtue of practice and necessity. Is that always the same as it being easy? No, in fact, it is not. However, what she's learned is that if you're willing to do it at all, others assume you find it an absolute cakewalk. She has lost count of the times that co-workers have foisted networking events or presentations upon her, claiming their own shyness or awkwardness – as though these were immutable characteristics. As though Lizzy herself was not shy at times, as though she didn't have the capacity to feel like the most awkward person alive.

Of course, she knows there are those who would describe her – and, not always inaccurately – as *sassy*. A spitfire. A *real live wire*. And failing all of that – failing any ability to be interesting – she can usually at least be interested. The actual chat therefore does not tend to be the problem – Lizzy would acknowledge that she does appear to be naturally pretty good at that.

The *initiation* of the chat, on the other hand – that can still be agony. Thankfully, at this point, she has at least picked up a few tricks along the way, cultivated some kind of party-craft. The bar, the buffet, maybe the women's bathroom – those are the best places to strike up a conversation, she's discovered; places where there are things to comment on, places where people linger. She's often wished she were still even a casual smoker, purely for the lingering potential.

If absolutely necessary, Lizzy has also developed what she thinks of as the nuclear option, which is simply to pretend she already knows the person she wants to meet. She'll walk right up to them with a smile and a *great to see you!* and when – inevitably – the object of her attention looks thoroughly confused, she'll paste a similar expression on her own face. 'Didn't we meet at Berlin?' she'll ask. Or, 'Weren't you at the Producers' Network thing the other night?' And no, of course, they *didn't* meet at the Berlin Film Festival, they *hadn't* spoken at some other party. But that doesn't matter. They'll unravel the mix-up, laugh about it together. It's an in.

The point is that if she has to, Lizzy can make it happen for herself. Nonetheless, over the years, she has often thought how wonderful – how easy – it would be if *she* were the one that others spotted across the room;

the one *they* made a beeline for, opening line locked and loaded. If she were the sought instead of the seeker.

Aboard the *Serenity*, Ciaran is the sought – or one of them, at least. And Lizzy can't help but think that, in reality, it looks like its own sort of stress. Of course, Ciaran is on cloud nine – how could he be anywhere else, after the reception the film just received? He catches her eye a few times over the course of the night, though, as she flits around different parts of the yacht, and every time, she has the sense that he is perhaps trying to get to her, and can't. Any attempt to move so much as three feet seems to result in some sort of accost.

By 1 a.m., standing on the top deck of the boat and sipping champagne, Lizzy wonders if maybe she's got the better end of the deal after all. Zero pressure. Just a very nice, very high-profile New York director named Zak, and a starry night sky, and not a whole lot to complain about.

'And, I mean, how *crazy* that you guys just ran into each other!' Zak says delightedly, once she's relayed the basic facts of her acquaintance, and reunion, with Ciaran. 'You really hadn't seen each other in – what, ten, fifteen years?'

'About that, yeah. You know how it is. Our lives just kind of went in different directions.'

'I mean, not that different, right? You're both at the Cannes Film Festival!'

Lizzy's initial response is to protest; to point out that there is a world of difference in the capacity in which she is attending this festival and the capacity in which Ciaran is. But she lets her grip loosen on that instinct, just for a second. Maybe it *is* a pretty wild thing, that they have both ended up in this industry; have both ended up successful in it. Not just him. Her too, in her own way. She'd done enough to get here, at least.

'Is that kind of what brought the two of you together, then?' Zak continues. 'You guys were both movie buffs?'

Again, Lizzy hesitates. Is it odd, that she's never thought about that? She's trying to work out the answer when Zak's attention shifts, a smile spreading across his face.

'Speak of the devil!' he proclaims, extending his hand. 'Congratulations, man. What a great night. Friggin' *loved* the movie.'

Lizzy turns to find Ciaran approaching on her left, reaching out to meet Zak's handshake.

'Thanks so much. That's such a huge compliment coming from you. It's all been a bit more dramatic than I'd like it to have been in the past few days, but . . .'

He trails off knowingly, and if he feels the need to do that every time now – to demonstrate a certain degree of self-deprecation, to couch things in some good-natured chagrin – then Lizzy can see immediately how tiring that must be.

Zak, at least, blows right past it. 'Hey. Always somethin', right?'

'So I'm learning,' Ciaran replies, and then he turns to look at her.

'Hi,' he says quietly, with a little smile. There's some inexplicable sliver of intimacy to it.

She clears her throat. 'Uh, hi.'

'I hear you guys go way back, huh?' Zak says jovially.

'Suppose we do, yeah.'

'Very cool.'

'Zak was just asking me if we, like, bonded or whatever 'cause we both were into films,' Lizzy adds.

Ciaran just tilts his head upwards a little, in acknowledgement.

'What do *you* think?' she prompts, because she finds
she's actually interested in his take.

He considers it for a moment. 'I don't think so,' he
says then. 'Not really. I mean, I suppose we *were* both
into films. But I think we would've found some stuff to
talk about without them.'

He's smiling again in that slightly secretive sort of way,
and Lizzy suspects the same expression might be on her
own face.

It's definitely not hard to remember sitting together in
Place Camille-Jullian, tossing back and forth the merits
and demerits of *The Princess Bride* or *Garden State* or
Psycho. But she can remember telling him about her
parents' divorce, too. She can remember him talking,
here and there, about his father – the man who loved
him and was not like him. She can remember *how many
pharmacies do you think are on this street?* And *imagine
the excitement, when humans first discovered all the stuff
you can do with an egg.* What an enormous amount of
time they'd passed together, talking. Movies weren't even
the half of it.

'Y'know, it's funny, before that year, I don't think I
even would've thought I *was* into films,' she finds herself
saying, and she looks at Zak as she does. That just feels
easier somehow. 'Or, at least, not especially. Not more
than other people. But then, after university – college,'
she corrects herself, adjusting for her audience. Out of
the corner of her eye she could swear she sees the glint

of a smile on Ciaran's face. 'I was just kind of flailing around, y'know; didn't know what to do with myself, hadn't applied for any jobs. And somebody – my mom, actually – said I should think about the things that made me happiest and go toward those.' Lizzy rolls her eyes. 'Like it's just that easy, right? She was doing a *tonne* of yoga at the time. Anyway. Weirdly, the thing that popped into my head was this little cinema we used to go to in Bordeaux.'

At this, she can't help but chance a quick glance over at Ciaran. He's looking at her intently.

'The Utopia,' he supplies then, for the benefit of their companion.

'Right,' Lizzy says, turning back to Zak. 'So, we would go there every week – it was a little arthouse place, not like a multiplex. They'd show all different kinds of movies, and do events sometimes – talks and stuff like that. And there was just such a great mix of people, y'know? We would hang out after, and everyone would be talking about the films and . . .' she shrugs, takes a breath. 'I don't know. It was just a nice vibe. It felt so . . . safe, but also so alive, at the same time. Does that make sense?'

'Oh my gosh, absolutely,' Zak says.

'Yeah, well. I wanted to try and . . . somehow go toward that feeling, I guess.'

'That's amazing! I love that!' Zak replies, but Lizzy hardly hears him. She is, at this point, unavoidably conscious of Ciaran – of his physical closeness, of his eyes still resolutely fixed on her.

When she turns to look at him, his gaze shifts away quickly, as though caught, and Lizzy looks away too. For his part, Zak glances between the pair of them, a quizzical expression on his face. Seconds tick by. It all feels the very opposite of slick, the opposite of the sort of breezy, boozy networking that this yacht was made for.

'Umm, y'know what, I'mna just . . . freshen this up,' Zak declares then, with a vague flourish of his glass, his voice rising in a sing-song lilt. 'Yeah. That's what I . . . think I probably need to be doing right now.'

Whether consciously or not, he's already backing away, and Lizzy would swear there's the beginnings of an impish smile on his lips.

'Great to see you, Ciaran, congrats again!' he tosses out, and then he's gone, retreating into the mass of other bodies. Without him, even as the party continues all around, things suddenly seem very quiet.

Lizzy and Ciaran turn to face one another at last.

'I didn't know that, about the Utopia,' Ciaran offers then. 'I mean, I suppose how *would* I have known it, but . . . that's really cool.'

She just shrugs, feeling more than slightly awkward. She has never liked the idea that, were it not for meeting Ciaran Flynn, she might be on an entirely different career path right now. That she might, in other words, have something to thank him for. She's rejected the notion, pushed it away even in her own mind. But it's true. Of course it's true. And for some reason, she's just admitted it to him. She casts her eyes around the vicinity, hunting for a new subject.

'This is a very fancy party,' she notes.

'Agreed,' he says. 'I kinda thought we might actually be setting sail somewhere, though. I've never been on a yacht before.'

231

She's surprised by that. 'Me neither.'

And, weirdly, Ciaran looks surprised himself. 'Really? Would've thought this would be old hat, you being the seasoned festival-goer and all.'

'Yeah, my parties aren't usually attended by Ted Sarandos,' she says, with a laugh. 'Or,' – again, she lets her eyes dart around, seeing who they land on, 'Christian Bale!'

Ciaran follows her gaze, and he lets out an incredulous sort of laugh too. It seems he finds this whole situation not much less bizarre than she does herself.

'Anyway. It's getting late,' she adds, glancing down at her watch. 'I should probably hit the road.'

'Can't hack it anymore, Elizabeth?'

She smirks. 'I guess not. I gotta be up in the morning. If I'm not there to spread the good news about Scotland . . .'

'All hell breaks loose?'

'Not really, people can just look it up on the internet,' she says, and he sniggers.

'I'm sure it's all in the way you tell it.' He tilts his head toward the dock. 'C'mon. I'll walk you.'

'Oh,' she replies, with a toss of her head. 'You don't have to do that. This is your party.'

'So I can leave if I want to, right?' he says. 'Also, this is *so* not my party. This is the *studio's* party. Let's go.'

Chapter Twenty-Eight

In Bordeaux, a little more than forty-eight hours had passed since Ciaran had walked out of the Durands' house, and Lizzy had turned their conversation – if it could be termed a conversation – around in her brain a dozen times. She'd looked at it from all angles. And still she didn't think she'd quite gotten the measure of it. Already, she was beginning to doubt the accuracy of her own memory, which didn't help. One way or another, though, it was pretty clear that she had angered Ciaran. Or hurt him, even.

From what she could recall, the tipping point seemed to have been the suggestion that she did not want other people to know about the way their nights sometimes ended. This was absolutely true. She *didn't* want people to know about that. He didn't want them to either.

Or, *did* he? Maybe she didn't know what the fuck he wanted. The more she thought about it, the more that seemed to Lizzy like the most accurate summary of the situation. Maybe he wanted her to tell people. Maybe

233

he wanted her to, like . . . be his girlfriend? Everything about Lizzy's experience, with Ciaran specifically and with boys in general and with herself, suggested that this was so extremely improbable. But the thought did cross her mind, in the midst of plenty of other thoughts crossing it too.

It was now Friday night, and Liam Cooney's twenty-first birthday party had been on the books for weeks. Facebook invitations had been issued, a hungover brunch pre-emptively talked of for the following afternoon. Everyone would be there.

In the end, though, Lizzy found she just couldn't face it. The thought of seeing Ciaran made her feel itchy inside.

'Y'know, I think I'm gonna skip it,' she told Caroline, a half hour before they were due to leave. 'You go ahead. Tell Liam happy birthday from me, okay?'

A couple more days to let the dust settle would be no bad thing, she figured. In the meantime, she could just chill at home this evening, lean into the luxury of a little alone time.

Alas, as she heard the front door slam behind Caroline, it dawned upon her that she had no bathtub in this apartment. No candles, no face mask, no television. In other words, many of the key elements of a cosy night in were unavailable to her. She did, at least, have music, and she put on *The Civil Wars*, letting herself sing along. The melodies were rich and gothic and soothing, but still, they didn't help to settle her. As time went on – as eight o'clock became nine o'clock, as nine o'clock became almost ten o'clock and there was nothing whatsoever left in her bedroom to organise – Lizzy felt, if anything, *less* settled.

She was stepping out of her jeans, reaching for pyjama bottoms, when she reached for a dress instead.

*

Liam himself answered the door, once she got over there.

'You made it!'

'Of course, it's your birthday! Happy birthday!' Lizzy said, raising her voice a little to be heard over the din of music and people.

He offered her a quick, one-armed hug, ushering her inside. 'Thanks! I can legally drink in America now!'

'Just three short years after you could've gotten blown up in Iraq, right?' Lizzy replied, deadpan.

'See, that's why we need you, Lizzy. Not one of these selfish bastards in here has even *mentioned* the Iraq War tonight,' Liam said, and she snorted out a laugh. She really, actually, loved Liam.

'Drink?' he asked then. 'What'll you have?'

Suddenly, Lizzy realised, with some embarrassment, that she'd shown up empty-handed. Liam didn't seem in the least inclined to call attention to it, though.

'Oh, anything, thanks,' she replied gratefully. 'I'll go on a booze run in a little bit.'

Following him into the kitchen, she stood in the door frame, taking in the scene. Costumes aside, it was broadly the same setup as the Halloween party she'd been to in this very apartment all those months back. But it was different, too. She felt like she belonged here now.

In the corner of the living room, Mia was standing with Charlotte and Emma, and they waved when they spotted her, all smiles. It was warming, that sense of being wanted, and she responded in kind. Still, though, her eyes darted about the small space. They weren't really who she was looking for.

'Hey Liam, is Ciaran here?' she asked. It seemed incredibly weird for him not to be. Unless he was deliberately avoiding her.

Liam handed her a glass of wine, and she mouthed a thanks.

'Yeah, he's about somewhere. Maybe he's beat you to it on the drinks run? Or, try his room there.'

With a gesture to the girls that she'd be back in a minute, Lizzy walked down the little corridor that led to Ciaran's bedroom. The unease she'd been feeling for the past two days kicked up a gear, made her chest tighten as she knocked on his bedroom door. It was a cursory sort of knock, though, likely drowned out in any event by the noise of the party. She waited only seconds before pushing the door open, peeking her head inside.

The main light was on, and there he was, on his bed. She'd found him. Right away, every bit of Lizzy's trepidation about seeing him dissipated altogether.

Not in the way she might have hoped for, though – it didn't give way to relief or familiarity or any other nice thing, as it had done on so many other occasions this past semester. This time, it transformed in a flash into something hard and cold, settling like an icicle under her ribcage.

Because Ciaran wasn't alone.

A girl was in there with him, and Lizzy knew that girl immediately. It was Caroline.

The two of them were kissing, like mating animals, both naked from the waist up. His jeans were undone, and her hand was inside them.

236

Lizzy stood in the doorway, frozen in place, and the next parts she watched as if in slow motion: Caroline shrieking, Ciaran leaping up, all the clichés of being caught in a compromising position.

Lizzy let out a sound that she didn't recognise, a mangled squall, an exhale expelled like vomit. The thing was, she'd known this feeling before in her life – the feeling of being completely and utterly blindsided. The feeling that right here, in front of her very eyes, were the ways of the world, and she had just been too stupid, too much of a child, to see them until now. What was wrong with her, that she couldn't ever seem to keep up?

Caroline was casting around – looking for her bra, presumably – and it occurred to Lizzy that her roommate was pretty. She hadn't ever especially noticed that before, but now she did. Caroline wasn't beautiful, but she was the ordinary amount of pretty that Lizzy would have happily settled for. And Lizzy had seen before that for all the many respects in which Caroline might have been kindly described as highly-strung, she still was willing to go with the flow when it suited her.

Was that the explanation for this turn of events? Just one thing leading happily to another? Or was it ambition, redirected slightly? Lizzy didn't know or care. One way or another, somehow even Caroline Gilhooly evidently knew how to do *this* – how to go into someone's bedroom during a party and take her clothes off and be normal.

It felt like an age that Lizzy stood there, but of course it probably wasn't. At some point, she became aware of Ciaran, coming closer and closer into her line of vision, his face contorted, his hand reaching out as if to land on her upper arm.

237

The prospect was intolerable, and it jolted her into action. She turned, and she fled.

Seconds later, she could hear him bounding through the apartment, coming after her.

'Lizzy, stop!' he called, creating – it sounded like – a little bit of commotion in the process, others becoming alive to the first whiff of a drama unfolding.

She ran down the stone staircase, taking them two at a time, and out the main door.

'Lizzy!'

She was on the street by then, and still he was behind her, gaining on her now.

'Stop!' he cried again, grabbing her shoulder.

She spun around. 'Do *not* touch me!'

Ciaran and Liam's place was at the top end of Rue St Catherine, the less-nice end, near kebab shops and a McDonald's and stores that, in the daytime, had carousels of cheap, clingy clothing positioned outside them. Anyone who said that the French didn't binge drink, that they restricted themselves, as a matter of culture and policy, to a few civilised *verres*, hadn't been to the top end of Rue St Catherine after midnight, that's what Lizzy always thought.

Around them now, it was noisy – little clusters of people in high spirits, and somewhere in the distance, a busker was singing 'Losing My Religion'. Between her and Ciaran, though, there was dead silence.

They looked at each other.

'Fuck you,' she said quietly, deliberately. She'd never said that to somebody out loud and meant it.

Ciaran, for a moment, seemed stunned. Lizzy could see in his eyes that she'd hurt him, and she felt a jagged twist of satisfaction inside her. That was what she'd wanted. Some sense of her own power reclaimed, yes. But, also, in plainer terms, just to try and hurt him back at least a little.

It must have been *only* a little, because it didn't take him too long to recover.

'Oh, so you give a shit now, do you Lizzy?' he said then, the sound of his voice letting her know he'd been drinking. 'You didn't yesterday. You didn't the last three and a half fucking months! I swear to God, I've never met more of a . . . of a *prick tease* in my life than you!'

A punch clumsily thrown was still a punch. Turned out, it could still nearly knock you off your feet. Lizzy physically recoiled, feeling her breath hitch in her chest. So, *that*, she thought, was what it all came down to. Such a fool she'd been, to imagine anything else.

'Well, I'm sorry,' she managed, her voice wobbling with rage, among other things, 'that you didn't *quite* get what you wanted from me. But, hey,' she glanced back up towards his apartment, people leaning out the window smoking, faint strains of music filtering down. 'You should get back up there. Caroline might still have her tits out. Maybe she won't mind your MO. You only make a move when you're half wasted, right? The girls too? Maybe that's how you like 'em, Ciaran – not in their fucking *right minds*.'

She paused, trying to swallow the feeling of her heart-beat in her throat.

'You *knew* ho . . .' She felt her voice break, unable to finish the end of that sentence. She tried a new one, with new vigour. 'And you took advantage of me!'

His eyes narrowed, and she didn't understand what

that was about – maybe confusion, or anger, or, worst of all, some kind of sympathy for her. She found she didn't have the energy, anymore, to try and work him out. There seemed to be very little point. Not when the sight of him, half naked with Caroline Gilhooly, couldn't ever be unseen.

As his lips parted to speak, she shook her head to herself, breathing out a sour little laugh. Pointedly, she looked down at his belt, left unbuckled in his haste, then back up to his eyes.

'I think we're done here.'

And as she turned to go, this time he didn't follow.

'Yeah,' he shouted after her, just before she turned the corner. 'I think we really are, Lizzy! Fuck *you*!'

*

She made it all the way until she was back inside her own apartment before she crumpled, her chest heaving, tears rolling down her cheeks.

Somehow, she was twelve and twenty at once, the words resounding in her ears.

Frigid.

Prick tease.

Frigid.

Prick tease.

She didn't know what to do with any of it, didn't know what to do with herself. Did she want to sleep, or break something, or go outside and run as fast as she could, or down an entire bottle of wine? In the end, she stuck with the crying. She lay on her little twin bed and cried and cried, until, at some point, the phone call seemed to make itself. Months of resentment turned out to be no match for muscle memory, for the hardwiring of biology.

An explanation of the situation tumbled out, watery and uneven, and then came her mother's voice on the other end of the line.

'Oh, *sweetie*,' she murmured, as soothing in that moment as any lullaby. 'I'm so sorry. I hate hearing you upset like this. Why don't you just come on home?'

Such a prospect had not even entered Lizzy's mind as a possibility.

'But . . . the semester's not done,' she blubbered. 'And we have exams, and everybody would know I left, and . . .'

She trailed off, unable, really, to think of any more reasons.

'Well, whatever you want to do. You don't have to decide anything right now. Just take a few days, huh? Think it over, see how you feel.'

Burrowing down into her bed a little more, Lizzy tried to picture the next few months of her life, tried to find something decipherable there. It had all blurred into a drab sort of watercolour. What she could imagine, on the one hand, was having to see Ciaran, or having to avoid him. Living in this apartment with Caroline, and fielding other people's questions, and the performance she'd have to put on in order to deflect their concern, silence their gossip.

On the other hand, was the sudden possibility of just . . . not doing any of that.

It struck her as such a blessed relief that in the end, there wasn't much thinking the situation over, no seeing how things went whatsoever.

Lizzy packed up all her belongings into two suitcases

and the very next day, with barely more than a sentence to Caroline, she walked out of Rue Cabirol and onto a plane.

She didn't sit any of her summer exams, thereby failing every single one of them.

No one, in a job interview, ever asked her about it.

Chapter Twenty-Nine

They walk along the beach, past the Cinéma de la plage. It consists of a big screen, set up for the duration of the festival on a plinth in the shallowest part of the sea. In front of it are a few hundred deck chairs, and every night, there are free public screenings. Not of festival films – of something from the archives, something campy and crowd-pleasing. *James Bond*, *The Goonies*, things like that. The deckchairs are all empty now, the evening's event having long since ended, but the circular lights that surround the screen are still on. Lizzy has no idea how the whole thing works, in terms of the proximity between water and electricity. But, it's Cannes. Unseen people make all kinds of magic happen here.

'What was on tonight?' Ciaran asks idly. He's pulled his bow-tie off now, his white shirt open at the collar.

'*Grease*, I think.'

'Classic choice. You wanna sit for a minute?'

She's a little caught off-guard by the suggestion. 'Uh, sure,' she agrees.

They each settle into a deckchair, and Lizzy thinks how nice it is, that they're available like this. It reminds her of the green seats dotted liberally around all the parks in Paris. She's sure that this country has its problems – ones she's never had to get bogged down in during her time as an exchange student or a tourist, and that she had never even gotten around to reading about in *Le Monde*. But, so far as she's concerned, there is something delightful about the fact that so many public spaces in France seem to consist of items that are not nailed down. It speaks, in her opinion, to a certain sense of community spirit; to a population that could be relied upon not to ruin its own fun – not to throw stuff in the water, or graffiti it, or steal it, or otherwise be dicks about the situation.

She kicks off her shoes, and wiggles her toes in the sand, mostly just for the novelty value. She's never been on a beach in an evening dress before.

When she looks over at Ciaran, there's a weird expression on his face.

'Lizzy,' he says, something pent-up about his voice, like he's been waiting to get this out. 'I know you don't want to talk about Bordeaux and everything that happened. But I . . . I'm sort of conscious that we might not ever see each other again after tonight. And so I just . . . I just have to ask you. The thing you said, about me taking advantage of you. Did you really mean that?'

Lizzy feels somewhat blindsided by the question. She doesn't want to ruin what has been an undeniably great night. Nor, in truth, is she all that keen to invite her vulnerable, messy, twenty-year-old self to the party. But, he's asked her a direct question. There seems no option but to give a direct answer.

'Well . . . I mean. Yeah.'

Ciaran blanches. 'Right. Okay.'

There's a beat of silence, nothing between them but the gentle lapping of the water as it shifts and sways.

'Fuck,' Ciaran hisses then, almost as if to himself. He brings his fingers up to his temples. 'I just don't know how I could have missed . . .'

His voice peters out, and he shakes his head a little before dropping his hands, looking over at her.

'I thought about that a lot – obviously – after you said it, and I couldn't think . . . even to this day, when I look back at any time we . . . y'know, kissed or whatever . . . I swear to God, in my memory, it just . . . always seemed like you were into it.'

Ciaran looks at her with wide, helpless eyes, and Lizzy frowns.

'Well, *yeah*,' she says. 'That's what I'm telling you.'

'What?' He also, now, looks thoroughly confused. 'What do you mean?'

'Ciaran!' she says, exhaling his name on a half-laugh. 'Come on. I was, fucking . . . *pathetically* into it!' There seems little to do, at this point, but call a spade a spade. 'I was more or less waiting around for any time you might be drunk or bored enough to look in my direction. Which you knew. And you just . . . passed the time with me, for *months*, until you got a better offer, basically.'

He opens his mouth, but he can't seem to get the words out. His expression freezes in an almost comical fashion, as though he's a cartoon that's been paused.

'I mean, look,' she adds pragmatically. 'It was a long time ago now, and we were both young and . . . I guess these things happen. But that *is* what happened. There's no point in pretending it isn't.'

It is, after all, just the two of them here now. No journalists, no colleagues, no celebrities.

Ciaran, however, does not seem to especially appreciate her magnanimity.

'Um, it's so *not* what happened!' he replies hotly, his face springing back into animation, and Lizzy is so utterly shocked that she finds herself mimicking him, like a toddler.

'It so *is*!'

They look at one other, wordlessly, tension suddenly pulsing like a heartbeat between them. And when everything had been going so well. When it had proven so easy, this evening, to slide back into just, sort of . . . being on the same team.

Too easy, perhaps.

And after all, the agreement Lizzy had made with herself back at the hotel suite, to put the past in the past . . . that had technically been a one-night-only deal. It's well after midnight at this point. Some pumpkins are probably past due for arrival.

Ciaran's expression contorts as he looks skyward, a mixture of anger and disbelief and the powerlessness one feels when dealing with a crazy person. Her being the crazy person. In response, she feels her own temper slide into second or third gear.

'I'm just . . . sorry,' he says, shaking his head. 'I'm just trying to work out how you *possibly* could say that I was . . . whatever you said. Just killing time with you.'

Lizzy cocks an eyebrow. 'Well, when you fucked my roommate, I guess that was a pretty good indication.'

'Okay, first of all,' he says tightly, 'I *didn't* fuck your roommate, an—'

'Close enough,' she interjects. 'I'm sure you guys sealed the deal once I got out of town.'

'Believe me when I tell you, we very much didn't. And *also*, second of all, that only happened at all because—'

'I wasn't putting out?' she cracks. 'Yeah. I got that part.'

Ciaran's eyes flash with irritation. 'No,' he replies. 'Because, as I remember it, you had had an absolute freak attack at the thought of anyone we knew finding out about us. Or no, hang on, sorry; there *was* no us. Wasn't that your whole thing?'

She doesn't answer. The conversation feels like it is spiralling very definitely out of her control now, becoming less and less like a situation in which her role will mainly be to accept his apology. She feels almost dizzy with it.

'It was like you were ashamed of me, or something,' he adds, much more quietly. 'And obviously you were about a billion miles out of my league, but that's still a shitty way to make somebody feel, Lizzy. What I did with Caroline was shitty too, but it was only because I was so fucking *heartbroken*.' He pauses for breath. 'Maybe that's dramatic. It probably is, we were twenty. But that's how I felt.'

Lizzy says nothing. The contortions required to wrap her brain around this information just don't seem to be compatible with forming sentences at the same time.

'. . . What?' she manages eventually, brow furrowed. 'You thought I was . . . out of your league?'

'Lizzy, I thought you were . . . well, I mean, you *saw* what I thought, I suppose,' he says frankly – verging on

247

brusquely, even, and then he rolls his eyes a little. 'In fucking 4K HD and Dolby surround sound.'

Lizzy feels her stomach clench like a fist. She takes a breath, takes the plunge, because she can't avoid it anymore, the thing that has been itching at her all night. Maybe longer.

'You mean in the film? With . . . with Claudia?'

He nods.

'But . . .what about "loosely inspired"?' she asks dumbly.

'Yeah, "loosely inspired" was more or less bullshit,' he replies. 'At least when it came to you.'

Wow.

There is really no misunderstanding that one. Lizzy certainly hadn't perceived Claudia to be a perfect character, and in fact, at points of the story, she was plain stupid. But she was spirited and talented and . . . lovable. She was the girl the boy wanted.

Lizzy has no clue what to do with this information. She feels utterly dazed, and maybe she looks it too, because Ciaran cocks his head sceptically.

'Oh, come on,' he says. 'You knew that.'

'Um . . . nope. Not really.'

'Seriously?'

'Seriously.'

He takes that in for a moment. 'I suppose I don't have much room to talk,' he says then. 'I swear to God, I didn't even realise myself until we watched it in the Palais and you were right there beside me, and . . . anyway, I know the whole thing is weird and probably borderline creepy. I know you have a b. . .' he falters a little. 'Well, obviously in the meantime you've moved on with your life, is what I mean to say. You didn't ask to get dragged into any of this. But, yeah. For the record, if you thought, back then, that I was anything other than crazy about you . . .' He shifts in his seat self-consciously. 'That would be . . . incorrect.'

Lizzy feels her heart thunder furiously in her chest.

'Ditto,' she replies then, quietly, and immediately she can see her own confusion, her own surprise, reflected on Ciaran's face.

It's very difficult to know where to go after that, conversationally. A huge part of Lizzy is still struggling to compute – to really, fully accept as true – all the things he's said to her in the last sixty seconds. Maybe he feels likewise. The two of them just sit there for a moment, barely able even to look at one another. Out in the distance, there are still some boats, their lights twinkling against the night sky. Feeling antsy, Lizzy cranes her neck, looking back at the Croisette. It's quiet, all the bistros and stores closed by now, of course. But, in hotel suites and hidden pockets on back streets, drinks will be being served until sunrise.

'You wanna . . . keep walking?' she suggests. What she needs right now, she thinks, is to be in motion. 'Let's walk!'

'Sure,' he agrees, and as they rise, she scoops her pumps up from the sand, hooking her middle and index fingers into them. For a few paces, she and Ciaran walk together quietly, and she feels not one bit better than when they'd been sitting down.

'So, just so that we're a hundred per cent clear,' he starts, after another couple of paces, 'at no point did you actually think of me as some sort of sex pest? Like, I didn't ever . . . do anything you were uncomfortable with?'

'No,' she replies. That one's an easy answer.

Ciaran breathes a literal sigh of relief.

'Okay good. Thank Jesus.'

'When I said that . . . the "taking advantage" thing. I don't know, I guess it just came out. But if I implied that you were, like, *harassing* me or anything, I never, ever should've done that.'

'It was so long ago. Maybe I picked you up the wrong way. But, there's always just been a bit of . . . *what if*, you know? You start to wonder if you're remembering stuff right. And the truth is,' – his eyes shift a little uncomfortably – '. . . we *had* had a drink, a lot of the time. Or, all the time. Up until that point in my life, I don't actually think I'd ever gotten off with *anyone* stone-cold sober. Which is . . . obviously not great. With you and me, I thought that was just 'cause that's when I felt bravest, you know? But then as the years went on and I looked back, I'd wonder: was it also 'cause that's when I felt like you'd be most likely to go for it? Maybe it *was*, even subconsciously. And so, what did *that* mean?'

He looks at her searchingly, and Lizzy thinks about it for a minute. There is probably an interesting discussion to be had here about the intersection between the age-old notion of Dutch courage, and the relatively newfangled one of informed consent. About the things alcohol gets the blame and the credit for. It's not one she feels especially fit for at 2 a.m., though. She sighs heavily.

'I don't know. But if that was bad, I'm *as* bad. I used to feel like the end of the night was the only time you . . . wanted me. Like that was the explanation for it, you know? And I didn't put the brakes on, either. I wasn't thinking *oh, Ciaran doesn't know what he's doing, I should really protect him from himself.*'

'I don't think I was ever that drunk, to be honest.'

'I don't think I was either,' she replies, and she realises then that somewhere along the way, they seem to have stopped walking. They are just standing there, on the beach, looking at each other. She makes to start moving again, and he falls into step with her.

'I suppose the thing is, we were probably all at least tipsy for a good seventy per cent of that entire year,' she adds loftily. 'So in fairness, it would probably have been hard for us to catch one another *totally* sober.'

It's a vast exaggeration, of course, but he goes with it.

'This is true. Plus the good news is, the whole thing has made me, like, borderline obsessive about consent. Women have to ask me about seven times before I'll even hold their hand these days.'

Lizzy snorts. They're veering left, now, away from the sea and up towards the Croisette. She realises, with a slight sense of panic, that they're running out of time. Anything she wants to say on this subject, she needs to say now or forever hold her peace.

'What you said about me being ashamed of you . . . that was never it. I hate that you thought that,' she says quietly.

'What was it, then?'

She sighs. 'I don't know. I think I was probably ashamed of *myself*, a little bit? I know that probably sounds ridiculous. But you have to understand, I just felt like *why am I making myself so stupid for this guy?* You know? When he doesn't even . . . Anyway. Whatever.

Plus my mom was, like, the fucking talk of the town in Edinburgh at the time because of her affair – or at least in my mind she was – so I had all these hang-ups about gossip and probably about relationships in general. I might have also had some sort of mild, like, body dysmorphia thing going on, but we can just skate on past that,' she says, her voice speeding up, her face contorting a little goofily. The instinct to grab for humour when she's stumbling is as alive and well in her as it has ever been. 'I don't know. You caught me at a kinda screwed up time, basically.'

'Maybe if I had been a bit less of an uncommunicative Irishman, eh?' he jokes, but she's unconvinced.

'Maybe. I don't know.' The idea that somebody she liked and was attracted to would have liked and been attracted to her . . . the idea that it wouldn't have been merely out of desperation or confusion . . . the idea that they could have just started dating and maybe started sleeping together and it would have had at least a shot at working out. . .

Perhaps that was all true. But even if Ciaran had told her a dozen times, Lizzy isn't sure she would have believed him back then. It's not necessarily the easiest thing in the world for her to believe, even now.

'I never should have said you were . . . you know. A tease,' Ciaran mumbles, as though he can hardly bear to utter the word. 'That was bad. I was just angry and hurt and drunk – that night, I really *was* drunk, I can tell you that for nothing. I'm so, so sorry.'

And, the thing is, it's really not like Lizzy has thought about it every day for the past twelve years. She hasn't been crying herself to sleep over it at night. But she hasn't ever lost the ability to conjure, with perfect clarity, the look on his face, the tone of his voice, when he said that to her. *Prick tease.* Any nice memory of Ciaran has somehow short-circuited right to that one, to the white-hot burn of embarrassment and fury and hurt.

Now, though, it's the weirdest thing.

When she thinks about it, puts herself back on Rue St Catherine with him that awful night, she finds she doesn't feel . . . anything much.

Or, no, that's not true. What she feels, for both herself and for him, is the aching hybrid of frustration and compassion that she imagines a parent might extend to a child. All the other stuff, though – the pain she's kept right where she could reach it for years – seems to have melted away.

'The whole Caroline situation was really, *really* not my finest hour either,' Ciaran continues. 'You don't have to believe me, but what you saw honestly was the extent of what happened. And there was absolutely no part of it that was actually about her.'

Lizzy takes that in, gives the tiniest of nods.

'I believe you,' she replies quietly, though such a thing would have seemed impossible not twenty minutes prior.

'I'll have to apologise to her too, if I ever see her again. Who knows. At this rate maybe she'll show up at Sundance.'

Lizzy laughs, a little absently. How could it be, that twenty minutes had – and maybe always would have – untangled this knot?

They reach the little ramp that leads up from the beach, and as her feet hit concrete, Lizzy lifts one foot then the other to put her shoes back on. Instinctively, she reaches out to Ciaran for balance and when she straightens, she looks at her own hand, clutched around his upper arm, as though it belongs to someone else. *His* hand, she realises then, has made its way to the base of her back, just resting there lightly to help steady her. She'd swear she can feel it in every cell of her body.

She swallows thickly and for a moment, she thinks he's about to kiss her, whether for old times' sake or for some other reason. As it turns out, though, her ability to predict him – at least in this particular domain – is no better than it ever was. With a start, Ciaran drops his arm like he's been burned, giving his head a quick little shake. Lizzy takes her hand back too, and she grasps for some words – any words – to put in the space between them. Whatever it was that darted into his brain just now, she'll probably never know.

'That's, uh, actually me right up there,' she says, gesturing towards the other side of the street.

'I'll walk you up,' he offers.

'Oh, no, it's fine. I can literally see the apartment,' she protests. Not quite true, but almost. Literally in the modern sense.

'Are you sure?'

She nods.

'Alright, well.' He shrugs, as though he isn't sure what to say, given everything else that's been said. 'It's been . . . *enlightening*,' he says, with a bit of a laugh.

'It has,' she agrees, a smile rising and fading fast. 'I'm sorry about . . . everything.' The truest thing she can think.

Ciaran just holds out his hand to her. 'Call it even?'

Her fingers close gently around his. 'Deal.'

Chapter Thirty

When Ciaran wakes the next morning, the previous night feels a little like it might have been one long fever dream. There's his tux on a heap on the floor, though, the proof that it had all really happened. He thinks of walking up onto the stage after the screening, that huge audience on its feet and applauding – among it, people he's watched and admired since childhood. Among it, Lizzy Munro, her eyes and her smile and her dress all sparkling.

It's been an incredibly stressful week – preceded, in fact, by a fairly stressful year – but in a flash, that moment had made every single bit of it feel worthwhile. It might have been the very best moment of Ciaran's life.

The reviews, he knows, will be online by now, and as he reaches for his laptop, it's with a sense of nervous-excitement rather than nervous-terror. He is buoyed not only by last night's reception but also – while it might seem cocky to admit aloud – by his track record in this regard. The truth is that up until now, his career has been characterised by good reviews. On some occasions, really quite staggeringly, unexpectedly good reviews. Reviews that seemed to imbue his work – sometimes even him personally – with a level of significance in the world that he was not sure was actually real, but that was nonetheless quite nice to read about.

What he gets, this time around, is . . . not that.

Ciaran scans the headlines that pop up from a quick web search, his stomach dropping sharply.

Three stars.

Charming but insubstantial.

Two stars.

Little more than a romcom at heart.

On and on it goes, as he clicks through various links. There are some positive comments in the mix too, but none that resound anywhere near as loudly as the negative ones.

Cloying and predictable.

Sadly lacking in the gravitas of Flynn's freshman feature.

Disappointing.

Lightweight.

Each one is like a dagger to the heart. The good news, Ciaran guesses, is that most of the reviews make either no mention at all, or very cursory mention, of Penny Ainsley. He seems to be getting full credit for writing and directing this apparently largely disliked film.

Is that good news? He's not entirely sure.

As he reads and re-reads the pieces, turning their most choice phrases over in his mind, it's almost impossible to stop the defensiveness rising up in him, to restrain himself from mentally arguing back. He can't help but

notice that *Wish You Were Here* is often compared –
unfavourably – to *Inclement Weather*.

His first film had been a different beast altogether.
Based partially on his own family, it had been about
three generations of men and their relationship with
Gaelic football and each other. It'd had a more muted
colour palette, a blacker sense of humour, a slightly more
melancholy ending. *Wish You Were Here*, by contrast,
was something entirely distinct in scope and tone.
Visually, it was lighter, softer – more feminine, in a way.
And thematically, too, it was lighter – a little more
playful, more hopeful. Could all of that, Ciaran wonders
now, have anything to do with the critical reception?
Are people somehow conditioned to see more depth in
darkness?

That doesn't seem right to him. At the most basic level,
to the extent that any film – any pretend, made-up thing
– has value at all, he can't accept that a sad one inherently has more than a happy one.

Who knows, though, he thinks then; maybe he's read
too much into it. Maybe *Inclement Weather* was simply
a better piece of work. Either way, he suspects he could
be well on his way to being Irish again in the British
press. They'd begun to claim him as their own at the
very first hint of success and he has no doubt they'll
disown him just as quickly.

He shuts his laptop and pushes it away, swallowing
thickly. He doesn't know how long he has been sitting
there, staring at the screen, but he realises now that he
has begun to feel almost physically sick – not just with
disappointment but with utter, paralysing fear.

By this point in his career, he understands that a film

studio measures success by two things only: prestige and profits.

In the case of *Wish You Were Here*, Ciaran thinks it's fair to say that whatever slim hope of prestige that might have remained after Penny-gate is now well and truly circling the drain. The recollection of a meeting he'd attended a few months back, on the topic of 'strategies for awards season', now seems laughably presumptuous.

Onwards, then, towards profits.

This film has got to make money, or he'll never be allowed to make another one. That's the bottom line.

Of course, in recent months, Ciaran has begun to secretly suspect that he might never make another film again *anyway*. But not being allowed to make one – being edged out of the industry he'd had to work so hard to elbow his way into, being thought of as a flash in the pan who just couldn't be trusted with the big bucks – that turns out to be a different prospect altogether.

As he jumps in the shower, readies himself for the day, the specific figure that rings in his ears – louder and louder, like the incantation of a curse – is a cool sixty million dollars. That had been the budget for *Wish You Were Here* – a massive jump from that of his first film, and a huge vote of confidence on the studio's part, but still some distance away from the cost of most Major Motion Pictures. Throughout an eighteen-month period from pre- to post-production, it had – incredibly – actually felt like *not quite enough* money to accomplish the job at hand.

Now, all Ciaran can think is that if the film makes a cent less than sixty million dollars, he can kiss goodbye to that kind of investment ever again. More established writers or directors – ones who were comfortably in the black, who had already made many millions of dollars more for corporations than they would ever cost – they were allowed a stinker every now and then. But that wasn't Ciaran's position. There was no cushion, no reserve of goodwill waiting on him. If this one failed, he would just be very, very much in the red.

*

By noon, he's been summoned upstairs to the studio's suite, and once there, it doesn't take long to establish that an already pretty bad situation (non-optimal, he corrects himself grimly) has gotten worse. Even less optimal.

A lengthy think-piece has appeared on *Vulture* entitled 'The Dumbing Down of Cannes,' within which 'Ciaran Flynn's latest offering' is cited as the prime example of that apparent dumbing down. Director Luis Romero Sanz is quoted:

'This is what happens when you programme film festivals for popularity. You end up with silly films. Romantic comedies are fine, but they are not cinema. They are not art. *Inclement Weather* [Flynn's first feature], yes, it showed promise. But a director who makes one good film and a . . . web series. That is not a director who should be in Cannes, and it is high time someone said so out loud. We are not trying merely to cater to the masses here. As custodians of this festival, and of the unique medium of film, we must ask ourselves, where does this end? Will we be showing TikToks in the Théâtre Claude Debussy next?'

Dotted around the suite, people are reading the article – all two thousand words of it – in tandem, to much outrage and eye-rolling. And if it were someone else's film, Ciaran would likely be able to summon plenty of outrage too. His own eyes would hardly be able to roll far back enough in his head. As things are, though, it's hard to feel like his current mess of feelings would be especially welcome inside this room. They'd seem far too much like neediness, like weakness.

He mostly listens for the hour that follows, and when his phone rings, he steps out to the suite's foyer, grateful for the escape. He looks at the name on the caller ID, more than a little surprised to see it.

'Hi,' he says.

'Hi,' comes Lizzy's voice in return. Somehow, in that interaction, in the beat of silence that follows, everything is communicated. They've both seen the reviews, and they each know that the other has.

'How're things?' she asks then.

'Eh,' he replies, more of a sound than a word.

'Is everybody freaking out?'

Ciaran's gaze drifts back to the other room.

'I mean, not necessarily *totally* freaking out,' he says, which is true.

Mixed reviews (that's what everyone has started to call them: 'mixed') weren't *helpful* to the financial success of a film, of course, but neither – apparently – were they necessarily fatal. There were other factors. How attractive was the cast? How famous? How much money had been spent on marketing, and in what specific ways? What else happened to be out at the cinema that weekend? All – Ciaran has been assured – is not yet lost.

A conference call has been planned for next week, once everyone has returned to their respective cities and the dust has settled. There has been talk of regrouping and circling back and following up on the reimagined game-plan going forward. Other people appear by now to have collectively committed to a taut, thin veneer of optimism that Ciaran is doing his best to get comfortable underneath.

Still, he casts a hand over his face wearily. 'It's obviously pretty . . . gutting, though. Yeah.'

'Of course,' Lizzy murmurs, and something about the tone of her voice makes him feel that – for just one minute – he can allow himself to treat the morning's events not as a business problem. Or at least, not *only* a business problem. Because, while he understands that hurt feelings and embarrassment are very far from the main issues here, the truth is that Ciaran's feelings *are* hurt. The truth is that he is *achingly* embarrassed. He thinks about last night's applause – wonders whether it was faked, whether everyone in that auditorium had banded together in what they all knew was mere politeness and pity.

'Did *you* like it?' he asks then. 'The film. I don't think I ever actually asked you that.'

'Yeah. I really did.'

'Like "such an achievement"?'

'Like "such an achievement" *and* I really liked it,' she says, with a smile he can hear. He chuckles in response, but his heart isn't exactly in it.

'Cool. I'm glad. Anyway, we've all just been chatting here, and I think we're going to go ahead and fly back to London tonight.'

'Oh?'

261

'Yeah. I think everybody just wants to . . . get the fuck out of Cannes, basically.'

Lizzy pauses.

'I get that,' she says then. 'Try not to beat yourself up about the reviews, though, huh? It's only, like, a handful of outlets – there'll be a tonne more to come when the film goes on general release.'

'Mmm.' He's not convinced. 'Did you see the *Vulture* piece?'

'Yeah. I mean, that's not *even* a review. That's just mean-spirited, pseudo-intellectual bullshit. First of all, that guy they quoted hasn't made a film in, like, nine years, so I don't know what he has to do with this whole discussion in the first place. And what was the argument? A lot of people might see and enjoy this movie? Jesus. Alert the gatekeepers!'

Again, Ciaran offers up a half-laugh. 'You're probably right,' he says, and there's another moment of quiet between them before he begins again.

'I'm happy we got to talk last night anyway. Probably shouldn't have taken us over a decade to do it, like, but . . .'

'Better late than never, yeah.'

'Thanks again for everything,' he says. 'I hope it hasn't caused any problems for you, with work or with . . .'

He trails off, assuming Lizzy can fill in the blank on that one. It seems, however, that she cannot.

'With what?' she asks.

Suddenly, Ciaran feels approximately fourteen years old. 'Uh, with your boyfriend,' he mumbles.

'. . . I don't have a boyfriend,' Lizzy replies, the confusion evident in her voice.

'Oh,' he says, abruptly.

'Yeah.'

It takes him just a little too long to catch up to the surprise. Before he can speak again, she beats him to it.

'Um, so anyway,' she continues, her intonation rising. 'It's all good. I guess I'll look you up if I'm ever in London, huh?'

'Yeah, do,' he replies. 'Definitely do. Any time.'

Ciaran can't help but feel, though, as if something has punctured, disappeared sooner than he could grasp it. It's extremely unsettling.

'Cool,' Lizzy says, and could it be that the brightness in her voice perhaps sounds a little thin now too? 'Well, safe flight back, I guess.'

'Thanks,' he says. 'You too . . . or, not you too. Well, you too eventually I mean, but . . .' he huffs out a laugh, at himself, and it makes her laugh too. 'Sorry,' he adds. 'Okay. Bye.'

*

When everyone disperses at last from the suite, Ciaran walks back down to his own hotel room and outside of it, his manager hovers, like a priest at a wake.

'I'm fine!' Ciaran says. 'Honestly! I'm fine. Car's coming at six for the airport, yeah? I'll give you a knock on my way down to the lobby.'

He all but shuts the door in Peter's face, and as soon as he is alone again, he reaches once more for his laptop. Just to check.

There are no new reviews, though, and in their absence, he opts to re-read the ones he's seen already.

Undoubtedly, this is a terrible idea in general, not to mention a waste of his last few hours in Cannes. But, whatever. He has long since let go of the idea that he'd be swimming in the Med at any point during this trip. As he stares at the now-familiar text, his eyes blur a little, his mind drifting.

What it drifts to is absolutely no less masochistic.

What it drifts to is Lizzy. And, specifically, to how incredibly good she'd looked in that silvery dress last night. So at ease, somehow. She'd made all the women who'd been hoisted into corsets and contoured to bejesus look faintly ridiculous. From across the room – or rather, the deck – he'd watched her chatting enthusiastically to the head of a US cable network, quite clearly charming the pants off him; later, he'd spotted her smiling a little awkwardly as a photographer urged her into a posed photograph with someone else. She wasn't too-cool-for-school, the person who walked around drinking martinis, all sallow, ironic detachment. Neither was she outrageous – the one who waltzed onto a yacht and made it their mission to take everyone on it by storm.

What was she, then? Ciaran didn't know how to explain it, other than to say that Lizzy Munro seemed to have a way of just . . . staying herself. She was the friendly, sane, interested, interesting, attractive person you hoped you met at a cocktail party, and yet so rarely did.

As for everything she had said afterwards, on the beach . . . well. What a mindfuck *that* had been. When he'd gotten back to the hotel last night, Ciaran had tried to rewind, to work out where exactly their miscommunication began in Bordeaux, what was the point at which he could have been a little clearer, a little braver, maybe set them on a different path. It was hard to remember, though, after all this time. And, really, he wasn't so sure that there had been any such moment at all.

Lizzy, almost as soon as he met her, had been any number of new and wonderful things. And she was American to boot, which was to say she was – at least in his mind back then – inherently glamorous. He was a boy from a tiny village in Donegal, gently mocked by his siblings for his two left feet on the football pitch, for all the random interests he sometimes couldn't hide. Then he was a boy at university in Dublin, gently mocked by classmates for his northern accent, for all the things he didn't know about city life. He hadn't much minded any of that. He could take a slagging and he could give it back just as well. But still. He had always felt that he was a person who lingered a little left of the bullseye. There had been a baseline assumption on his part that someone like Lizzy could not have been interested, in any real way, in someone like him.

Apparently she could have been, though. Apparently she *had* been.

Lying in bed last night, Ciaran hadn't been able to work out whether it was better to know or not to have known that information. It probably didn't much matter in the end, he'd told himself. Things that never happened were much easier to romanticise than those that did. And in any event, it was water under the bridge. Lizzy had moved on since then. Standing with her on the Croisette, it had taken a lot to remind himself that she had a boyfriend now.

Except that, on the phone earlier this afternoon, it turned out that she . . . *didn't* have a boyfriend? How he had gotten the wrong end of that particular stick, Ciaran has no idea. Who else would Oliver with the heart be, the one who kept calling her? He knows Lizzy doesn't have any brothers. A best friend maybe?

Whatever the explanation, Lizzy, it seems, is currently single.

And of course, she could well and truly have gotten over a years-old crush without this having manifested in the form of a present-day boyfriend. Ciaran is aware of that.

But nonetheless, as he sits in his hotel room, staring vacantly at words he's ceased to truly be reading, reality presents itself to him as clearly as if it were written right there on *Deadline.com*.

The thing that has been gnawing inside of him all day, making him feel restless and dissatisfied, is perhaps not about *Wish You Were Here* at all – or at least, not entirely. It's Lizzy. The thought of her then, and the thought of her now, and the sneaking suspicion that, just maybe, the two of them had buried something that wasn't dead.

Before he can talk himself out of it, he finds himself reaching for his phone, his mind whirring.

'I was thinking,' he begins, as soon as his manager picks up, 'I might actually stay on here for a few days after all. Take some meetings.'

That was the sort of vague thing you probably couldn't get away with in other industries, but that nobody even remotely questioned in this one.

Chapter Thirty-One

'I'm thinking of Rachel Weisz for the lead role,' says a young producer, sitting across from Lizzy on the Scottish Pavilion's back deck.

There was a time in the not-so-distant past when Lizzy would have been swept along with that, been thoroughly impressed and convinced by it. As it is, she has come to understand that very many producers are out there – walking around all over the place, in fact – thinking constantly of actors who are not even slightly thinking of them back. Nonetheless, as this particular producer launches into an impassioned monologue on the ways in which Scotland might make a credible dupe for the Yorkshire moors, Lizzy does her best to look attentive, tries to give him a fair shot. What she knows by now about finding a diamond in the rough is that it requires digging through an awful lot of stuff that seems extremely unlikely to be diamond.

Her heart just isn't in it today, though – not the way it usually is.

She's had three espressos but still she feels . . . flat, somehow. Every thirty minutes for the past two and a half hours, a new person has come to sit opposite her, and she has asked the same questions and made the same jokes, and her voice – along with the rest of her – is just tired. Discreetly, she presses her fingers into the hinge of her jaw, massaging a little. This, she thinks, is why most people only stay in Cannes for three or four days. Being here for the entire duration of the festival . . . Lizzy knows it's not like being up a chimney, or down a mine, but it can be hard to be *on* for that long. Fatigue starts to set in.

Truthfully, though, that's maybe not all that's wrong with her today.

It was sort of ironic, really. She'd hated the thought of sharing this town with Ciaran Flynn, and now she finds she doesn't like the thought of him leaving it any better. He'd sounded so downhearted on the phone. And what was all that weirdness, about some phantom boyfriend? There had seemed little point in discussing it, him having already one foot out of town. Nonetheless, it had been odd.

When Ciaran had first turned back up in her life, she had certainly wished – in a way that was instinctive and perhaps made her a bad feminist – that she could claim to be part of a pair.

She's not, though.

She has, in fact, been single for large swathes of the past twelve years. And she can honestly say that – at least for the most part – the thing she dislikes about it is not the actually being single, in the present tense. It is more the thought that she might at some point grow to dislike it, when it's too late, when whatever limited currency she has in the dating game has slipped away altogether. The thought that loneliness and regret might lie just up ahead is terrifying.

Of course, there are flashes of those things, even now – moments of feeling melancholy and unchosen and as though she is falling behind in conspicuous ways that everyone has to pretend not to see. But, they tend to be brief. And there are other moments too – the pleasure in being able to decide, without consultation, to just have beans on toast for dinner. Watching a friend's husband tell a story in the pub and the deep, abiding knowledge that there is no way in hell she would want to be going home with that guy. Things mostly even out, Lizzy thinks.

Her meeting wraps up – thankfully the last on her list for the day – and as she stands to shake the producer's hand, send him on his way, her gaze drifts to the far side of the deck. There, clacking away on a laptop, sits Amy Solomon.

'Amy! Hi!' Lizzy calls out automatically, feeling the panic rising inside her as she squeezes past half a dozen other tables to close the distance between them. 'Is everything okay?'

She can't help it that the sight of this woman screams 'crisis' to her. Amy waves away her concern, though, her blow-dry bouncing jauntily.

'Oh, yeah. Bummer about the reviews today, huh?'

'Yeah,' Lizzy replies, feeling a lot more genuinely bummed out, when she's reminded of them, than the other woman sounds.

'It'll do well at the box office. That's what counts.'

Lizzy definitely doesn't think that critical response to a film is the be-all and end-all. But, nor does she necessarily think that box office receipts are either. So, she just shrugs. 'I guess. So, um, nothing's up?'

Amy shakes her head, all ease. 'I just thought I'd swing by.' With a smile, she brandishes a Tunnock's teacake, presumably procured from the front desk on the way in. 'Heard the snacks were good here! You wanna sit?'

Lizzy does. 'Did you talk to Ciaran today?' she asks.

'Yeah, he's doing okay,' the older woman replies, and she tilts her head to the side in an inquisitive, appraising sort of way. It makes Lizzy wonder if she has something in her teeth.

'You know what he coulda made after *Inclement Weather*?' Amy asks then, and the question seems to be rhetorical. 'Anything. Like literally pretty much whatever he wanted. His agent told me he got offered a comic book movie.'

'A comic book movie?!' Lizzy exclaims. That seems like a stretch.

'Yeah. I'm telling you. That's what it is to be a thirty-something white guy who's the dish of the day. I mean, don't get me wrong – do I think he's talented? Actually yeah. I really do. But I'm just saying how it is. You know that.' Amy pauses, polishing off the last bite of her teacake. 'Anyway, the point is, he had a lot of options. And he chose to make something that was sweet and sincere and friggin' *all about* you, girl. You've figured that one out by now, right?'

'Uh,' Lizzy clears her throat, feeling suddenly self-conscious. 'Yeah. I mean . . . that's what I hear, yeah.'

How completely unbelievable it still seems. To the point that she, maybe, *doesn't* altogether believe it? Or, she does and she doesn't. She knows that's what Ciaran told her, and it's not that she suspects insincerity on his part – it's not that at all. It's just . . . well, it's hard to explain. Suffice to say Lizzy is pretty keen to get another gander at *Wish You Were Here* as soon as humanly possible. Somehow, she thinks that might be what it takes – seeing being notoriously integral to believing. Or, in this case, seeing *again*.

'So, what's the deal?' Amy prods. 'Tell me you're not just gonna do *nothing* with this information . . .?'

Lizzy shifts uncomfortably. Even this morning, when she'd lain in bed turning everything over in her mind – when she'd played and replayed that moment just before she and Ciaran had parted ways last night – she hadn't known the right answer to that question, or the true one. Now it seems like a moot point.

'I don't know,' she mumbles. 'He's gone back to London now anyway. Or, he's on his way back.'

Amy just looks at her.

'Alright, well, hey,' she shrugs, after a moment. 'If you're not interested, you're not interested. That's a hundred per cent your call. The guy could make ten movies about you and you still wouldn't owe him a cup of coffee. So, then, what about you? What's next?'

'What do you mean?'

Amy scans the Scottish Pavilion, gesturing vaguely. 'From what I hear, you're pretty much running this show, girl. You got this big party coming up, right?'

On that note, it occurs to Lizzy that she really needs to catch up with Simon about said party – find out whatever was the latest from Monsieur Henri yesterday. That she has not had a barrage of angry phone calls from either party seems like a good sign, but she'd like to stay in the loop. Alas, within squinting distance, Simon seems to be gathering his things now, making as though to leave. Meanwhile, Amy hardly pauses for breath.

'And you were the one who handled *Lightning Bugs*, I hear?' she continues. 'And *The Baker Boy*. You sourced those projects, developed 'em?'

Lizzy nods. She has no idea how Amy would know any of this information, but somehow, it's wholly unsurprising that she's made it her business to find out.

'Pretty impressive.'

'Oh, that's the best part, though,' Lizzy replies, gliding over the compliment. 'It's hard to *find* good stuff. Especially at the level of budget we can offer – you pretty much are talking about first-time or early-career film-makers. But once you do? Yeah. I love working on the script and figuring out the logistics and just . . . helping make the thing into what it's supposed to be.'

Amy smiles warmly. 'That's really great. So, whose job do you want around here, huh?' She nods towards the inside of the Pavilion, towards Simon's retreating back.

'That guy's? So, what? You gotta just wait for him to retire? That's how it works on this side of the pond, right?'

Lizzy laughs out loud. She can't even count how many questions that is, and in terms of response, wholesale agreement seems to be the only option. As it happens, Amy actually *is* correct on more or less all fronts. Not quite all.

'That's Simon, he's our chief exec. I don't think I *would* want that job, though, to be honest,' she says, lowering her voice.

'No?'

Lizzy shakes her head. 'It's a lot about raising finances and accounting for finances and . . .' she trails off with a wince. 'I'm not really a numbers girl. In an ideal world, I'd just want the money to be there, y'know? I don't especially want to be the one getting it there, or taking care of it once it is.'

'Well, you know where you gotta get your ass, then, right?'

Lizzy says nothing.

'Hollywood, baby,' Amy replies with a smirk, and Lizzy smiles along.

'I'm serious,' the other woman continues. 'You should be doing development at a network or a studio. I got a contact over at William Morris. You come out to LA and take some meetings and I'm telling you, she could have you fielding five offers within two weeks.'

Again, Lizzy just smiles. 'I don't know about that,' she says, and it's not false modesty. Not even a little bit.

'Are you kidding me, girl? You have all this experience – all these *connections* – in the European market. Plus, you studied, where? Same place as Wills and Kate, right? And then the south of France? People would eat that shit up in LA. It's all the benefits of hiring some dude from London but they don't even have to fuck around getting you a visa.'

Lizzy doesn't bother pointing out the factual inaccuracies. Amy, she knows by now, is not the sort of person to let the precise reality get too much in the way of an appealing narrative. Plus, she guesses the gist is true. It's hard to believe that after all these years of low-level angst about her half-and-half-ness, her never-quite-whole-ness, that very thing could somehow become an advantage. It's a nice thought. And yet:

'I just don't think I'm an LA person,' she says simply. She can't imagine she'd fit all that naturally into a short-shorts, green-juice world. Upon learning of her Californian roots, people, on various occasions throughout the years, have informed Lizzy that she has 'more of an east coast vibe', and she has taken it as a compliment every time.

'You don't like the beach?' Amy replies sceptically. 'The mountains? Literally the best Korean barbecue on God's earth?'

'Would that include Korea?'

'Yes!' Amy says, with not one jot of uncertainty, and Lizzy would bet anything that Amy Solomon has never set foot in Korea. She sort of admires it, that kind of baseless but absolute conviction. She wouldn't mind feeling a little bit of that herself. About anything.

'Let's say you come out for a year,' Amy continues. 'You hate it. What's the worst that could happen? That guy Simon would have you back in a second. Hell, a year's worth of Hollywood connections? He'd have you back with a raise.'

Lizzy frowns dubiously. But, she can't lie. Some tiny part of her brain is enjoying the fantasy, some synapse is fired up in a way it hasn't been in a long while.

'Look, I'mna guess you've spent a whole lotta time over this past couple days thinking about when you were twenty. All the stuff you did and didn't do back then, or whatever. True?'

'True,' Lizzy admits quietly, feeling suddenly exposed. It's always strange, when somebody sees more than you thought you'd showed them.

'Okay. And you're, what, fifteen years down the track at this point?'

A slightly excessive estimate, but Lizzy does not correct her.

'Take it from someone who's got another fifteen years on you,' Amy continues, and Lizzy thinks that has surely *got* to be a conservative estimate. 'The time is now. Sometimes, you just gotta suck it and see, hon.'

Lizzy barely restrains a snigger. If that's an expression, it's not one she's ever heard before, nor a philosophy she's ever really subscribed to. Then, right that second, as though the universe itself is obliged to do Amy Solomon's bidding, her cell phone buzzes in her lap.

And on the screen, it's Ciaran's name.

She almost does a double take at the sight of it. In her mind, at this point, he is somewhere over the English Channel. She picks up, and once they've exchanged greetings, he gets to the point quickly.

'So, turns out the studio want me to stay a bit longer,' he says. 'I don't know, press the flesh in the interests of my shitty film or whatever.'

Lizzy looks over at Amy curiously, as if for some confirmation. An admission, maybe, of wheels she'd personally set in motion. Nothing is forthcoming, though. The other woman just sits there, looking at her, like butter wouldn't melt.

'Anyway. I was just thinking," Ciaran continues, on the other end of the line. 'Would you be interested, at all, in drinking copious amounts of alcohol with me? Maybe tonight?'

She chuckles lightly. 'For old times' sake, huh?'

'For old times' sake, but also . . . y'know. Just 'cause.'

It's probably mortifying, the little flicker of excitement that rises inside Lizzy, and she finds herself very aware of Amy's company. The pavilion may be too noisy for her to hear Ciaran's end of the conversation, but by her wide grin, it looks as though she is getting the gist alright. Into her phone, Lizzy attempts to keep her voice low and her smile small, as though those things might create some measure of privacy.

'Um . . . yeah. I could do that,' she replies. As soon as the words are out, though, she can hear how they seem to fall short of what she actually means. She tries again, cards on the table this time. 'I'd like that.'

Chapter Thirty-Two

In principle, Lizzy would not be in favour of someone, for instance, having their manager call a restaurant in Cannes and do whatever needs to be done in order to free up a table for eight o'clock that very evening.

In practice, the foie gras pâté at Relais des Semailles is unbelievably delicious. Who is she to question the precise details of how she came to be the one eating it?

The doors of the tiny restaurant have been thrown open to let some air in, and tucked away in a corner table, Lizzy can just about make out the windy, uneven streets of the Old Town, people meandering with bare arms and legs even as daylight fades. A few tables over, she can see Jessica Chastain, looking fabulous in a jump-suit and tucking into a steak. Or else Bryce Dallas Howard. Or, she guesses, potentially neither of them.

Whoever it is, Lizzy notices now, is wearing bulky trainers with her jumpsuit, in the way that beautiful people can pull off. Lizzy finds this somewhat comforting, having wondered, upon arrival, if she herself was perhaps too underdressed, in her bottle-green floral shirt, tied in a knot above the waistband of her jeans.

But, no, she'd decided; the shirt was silky and evening-ish, and together with the swipe of burgundy across her lips, she thought she got away with it. And, more to the point, she's comfy. There isn't any way to really feel good without feeling comfy, that's something she's figured out by now.

Over appetisers, she and Ciaran have had a forty-minute debrief on the response to *Wish You Were Here*, and on the response to the response among the folks at Figment Films and at the studio. Lizzy's happy to see that Ciaran himself does not seem as cut up about the whole thing as she'd feared he might be. Anxious, yes. Disappointed, of course. He was only human. However, it had been obvious right away that he wasn't falling apart, wasn't on a mission to get completely wasted tonight, no matter what he might have said on the phone earlier.

'I mean, don't get me wrong,' he says, and it seems like his final word on the matter. 'This morning it was definitely a bit like: "Kill me now," y'know? "Just fucking go ahead and shank me in an alley."'

She laughs out loud at that, and she takes it as a very good sign that Ciaran himself does too.

'But I got a few hours' sleep this afternoon and I'm feeling . . . well, I wouldn't say a *lot* more chilled, but *slightly* more chilled now, at least about the money side of things. It's just out of my control, isn't it?'

'Yeah. And you know, the other thing I think that's always good to remember,' she offers chirpily, 'is that really, the vast majority of people out there don't care about your film.'

Ciaran takes a moment, as if to absorb this. His eyes narrow to a squint, his mouth twitching in amusement.

'Right, yeah. So, advocating for movies and TV shows . . . would that be, like, a *big* part of your job, Lizzy?'

She lets out a burst of laughter. 'I'm actually trying to be helpful to you here. Like, seriously. I get that this matters to you. And it *should*. But I'm just saying. For almost everybody else, this is, like, a blip on their radar. If even that. We spend so much time worrying what other people are thinking about us, and the truth is? Mostly? They're just not thinking about us at all.' She takes a sip from her wine, raising an eyebrow slyly. 'Even you, Mr BAFTA Rising Star.'

He smiles back at her, and he looks so good in his silver-grey shirt, and she thinks they might be on a date. It just seems like that's what this is. In practice, if not specifically in name. She doesn't have the required time to properly contemplate that – to list the factors supporting and countering the theory, to weigh up the ramifications, both positive and negative, should the theory prove correct. She just has to get on with living it.

Living it, actually, is sort of great.

'How'd you manage to get so wise, eh?' he asks.

'It all just came in a package on my thirtieth birthday. Did you not get that?'

'No. Was it from Amazon?'

A smile pulls at her lips. 'Yeah.'

He tilts his head, as though comprehension is dawning. 'Ah see, that's why. I don't do Amazon because of, like, my principles and everything,' he says and they both snigger.

'Seriously,' he prods then. 'How'd you get to be all zen?'

She pauses.

'You want my actual answer?'

'I do,' he replies assuredly.

'Uh . . . well. This is kind of a cheesy story. But, I have a little brother now. He's ten.'

Ciaran's eyes widen. 'No way!'

'Yeah. Dad got a young wife. Not, like, horrifyingly young. She was thirty-eight when they met. She's actually very nice, and it's cool, and . . . whatever. It was kind of rough for me, when Elaine got pregnant, though. I didn't say anything but . . . you can imagine. Like, if it had been up to me, did I *want* them to have a kid? Not really, no. Cut to, the baby's born, and he's almost three months early.'

'That's . . . a lot, isn't it?'

'That's a lot,' she confirms. 'I felt so guilty, like somehow maybe subconsciously I made this happen or – I know, ridiculous,' she adds, seeing the look on Ciaran's face. 'But I'm just telling you how I felt. Anyway, the day he finally came home from hospital was maybe the happiest day of my life, no joke. I remember looking at him – he was still this tiny, perfect, little thing – and just thinking "wow, I've spent a lot of time thinking about my own bullshit problems." Y'know? When I basically had everything a person could want. Any day you're not at a hospital is a pretty good day, that's what I learned in the four months Oliver was in there. I think maybe I got a tiny dose of the kind of perspective that new parents get – without actually having to give birth,' she says, with a smile.

Ciaran smiles too. 'So, I take it your brother's all good now?'

'Yep. He's perfect. Once he got home, he just went from strength to strength.'

'What's his name?'

'Oliver.'

Ciaran's expression shifts. 'Oh,' he says, sounding strangely startled by this information.

'What?'

He brushes it off. 'Uh, nothing. Nothing.'

The waiter comes to clear away their appetisers, and there is that odd, deferential suspension of conversation. Lizzy doesn't remember, from her own waitressing days, whether she liked it better when people clammed up during this part, or just kept on talking. Most probably she had disliked both, which was to say, she hadn't really cared either way.

'So, the whole thing with your mum and dad, and the divorce and everything . . .' Ciaran continues, once it's just the two of them again.

'Oh, yeah. You know, with that, it's a boring story,' she replies. 'I just kind of . . . got over it. There was no big event or anything. Just, time passed, and it got less painful. Turns out sometimes that really does happen.'

He tops up both of their glasses, and she murmurs a thank you.

'I guess I got older too, you know?' she continues. 'Realised that sometimes stuff is just complicated. I think with the affair and everything, my mom just needed some way to end it – the marriage, I mean. They didn't hate each other, so they both needed a reason.'

'It's pretty crazy when you find out your parents are actually just people, isn't it?'

'Totally. I mean, don't get me wrong. I still think the whole thing could've been handled better. No question. But, my mom and dad were *forty-five* when they separated.

Which obviously – now – seems super young to me. At the time, though, I honestly was a little like "Jesus, you've come this far, why can't you just live out your twilight years in peace?"'

Ciaran laughs, as Lizzy takes a sip of her wine.

'And you're still liking Edinburgh?' he enquires.

She thinks about that. At a certain point, you've lived somewhere for so long that nobody ever asks you whether you like it anymore. She's stopped asking herself.

'Y'know, it's a great city. And it's home at this point. Would I still be there if it weren't for my family . . . I don't know.'

'Yeah?'

She shrugs. 'It's small, you know? So there's limited work in terms of the kind of thing I do, or might want to do.' And then, she doesn't know why she tells him this, but she rolls her eyes when she does. 'Amy Solomon thinks I should go to LA. See if anybody wants to hire me out there. Of course she claims they'd be lining up.'

'Oh wow! Amazing! Are you going to do it?' he asks.

'I don't know. LA,' she says dubiously.

'What about it?'

'I just don't know if I'd like it.'

Ciaran nods, as though that's a perfectly valid point.

'I like it,' he offers then. 'I've only ever been out for a couple of weeks at a time – during which, I have to say, I did get asked about my star sign a *lot*. But, overall, I liked it way better than I thought I would.'

She smiles, but still, she's unconvinced.

'I think maybe I'm just not quite hip enough for LA,' she replies, putting on self-deprecation to mask the self-doubt. 'Don't quite have the face for it, you know?'

Ciaran leans back a little in his chair. 'Okay,' he says. 'That's the biggest load of balls I've ever heard in my life, Lizzy. And as you know, I work in the *film business* now.'

She laughs out loud at that, which makes him laugh too, and that's how the waiter finds them, when he returns to deliver their dinner.

She'd ordered lamb, after much deliberation, and it smells divine. There is nothing, she thinks, like the satisfaction of having chosen well.

'Would you not ever want to do music?' Ciaran asks curiously, cutting into his beef bourguignon. 'You're so good. Seriously you are.'

'Oh my God, you haven't heard me sing in twelve years! I think there's a possibility you might have *slightly* overestimated my talents.'

Or *significantly*, she thinks.

He shakes his head, undeterred. 'I remember.'

And something about the way he says it, something about the steadiness of his gaze, makes her believe him.

Feeling warmth spread inside her like liquid, Lizzy considers it for a moment. Truthfully, it's not the first time the suggestion has been put to her, and she finds it flattering every time. She understands that's how people most earnestly compliment any sort of creative talent – by suggesting you could make money at it. Nonetheless, she shakes her head.

'Nah. I think sometimes it's okay for something to be a hobby, you know? Sometimes it's better that way.'

Ciaran nods, a little raise of his eyebrow telling her that the past twelve hours have perhaps taught him just how true that is.

'How about you, anyway?' she asks, changing the subject. She feels like they've been talking about her for a long time. 'Do you like London?'

'I do,' he nods. 'It's been good to me, so I can't complain.'

He says it, though, like someone who knows he *shouldn't* complain, rather than in the manner of one with no complaints.

'Oh, go for it!' she urges, waving a forkful of her dinner wildly. 'Complain! I don't mind.'

He chuckles. 'No, I think it's just that thing of, like . . . to get something, you have to give something away. Don't you? Every single time. And it's fine if the thing you're giving away, you don't even like that much. You know? You've outgrown it, or it's about to break down anyway, or . . . I dunno, whatever; you think it's pretty small in comparison to what you're getting. But sometimes that's not how it is. Sometimes, you have to give up something that you actually fucking *love*. Something that's good, but just different. And that's what it was like, leaving Ireland.'

Lizzy just nods in response. She likes hearing him talk. That feels like a big thing to like about somebody.

'So, what I mean to say, basically,' he adds then, 'is can we go to Ma Nolan's Irish bar after this?'

Lizzy snickers into her dinner. He's grinning too.

*

They linger over coffees and desserts, the sky outside darkening now to petrol blue, waiters circulating with little tealights for the tables.

'So you said you weren't seeing anybody at the minute,'

Ciaran says, apropos of absolutely nothing. The swirling anticipation in Lizzy's stomach kicks up a notch, becomes harder to ignore.

'No. You?' she asks in return, and it feels mostly like a formality. There's no ring – she'd clocked that one earlier in their reacquaintance than she'd care to admit – and nothing about him, in the time she's spent around him in Cannes, has seemed like someone who has a girlfriend. Though of course, she'd acknowledge that did not always mean a man didn't have a girlfriend.

'Nope. Has there been anybody . . . y'know. Significant?'

'There was Steven, I guess. We dated for . . . two years, ish?'

'That's a while.'

'Eh,' Lizzy replies. She's not so sure that's always true.

For the first six months, after all, you are maybe only 'seeing each other', and for the last six, you're on the wind-down. So, that really only leaves a year. A year of living-apart togetherness can go by fast when you are also dealing with a full-time job and a full-time family; when you are rushing to spin class after work, and batch cooking chilli, and seemingly constantly hunting out old photographs at the demand of some chief bridesmaid in a group chat. What you remember can boil down to a handful of good boxsets and weddings, a long weekend in Reykjavík, and – in the end – a clean kill.

'Just wasn't right, you know?' she adds, because she feels like Ciaran wants more from her on the subject. 'Fizzled out, I guess. How about you? You on your second ex-wife at this point?'

'Still on great terms with them both,' he jokes. 'Nah. There hasn't been anything serious. Since things took off a bit more in terms of the films and whatever, that's made relationships sort of . . . complicated.'

'Mmm.'

'Some people are really into the "filmmaker" thing,' he explains. 'But, like, *too* much, you know?'

'So, wait,' Lizzy says, frowning in mock confusion. 'The women who make you fan art . . . are you saying you *don't* consider them girlfriend material? Seems like you're missing a trick there, my friend.'

He laughs, and it's so satisfying to her every time, amusing him.

'Not so much. And then the people who are more chilled about the job tend to be people I've met through work, but there are issues there too.'

Lizzy scrapes the last of her crème brûlée from the edges of its ramekin. 'Like what?'

'Just, you know . . .' he makes an uncomfortable sort of face, as though he isn't quite sure how to explain it. 'Like . . . okay,' he continues, with a little more purpose. 'Here's an example. I had this junior producer, right. Junior's a relative term here, by the way, as in "junior doctor". Anyway, you know, we sort of stayed in touch after the film wrapped. She seemed like maybe she was into me, and she was nice, and pretty and whatever. But, at the end of the day, like, effectively I'd been her boss.'

'Yeah,' Lizzy says. 'So, what happened in the end?' she prods.

'Oh. Nothing. She basically just started to slightly annoy the fuck out of me, so the issue sort of resolved itself that way.'

'Maybe you started to annoy the fuck out of her too,' Lizzy suggests slyly.

Ciaran doesn't miss a beat. 'Absolutely, yeah,' he replies, deadpan. 'I've no doubt I did.'

He picks up his coffee cup, draining the last of it and setting it back down with a sigh. 'Anyway,' he continues then, suddenly sounding a little despondent, 'all of this will probably not be a problem for too much longer. I'll probably never make another film in my life.'

Lizzy rolls her eyes, but in kindness. 'Ciaran. Honestly. You gotta try and just *not think about* those stupid reviewers.'

He shakes his head. 'Nah, I don't mean 'cause of those. Or, I mean, maybe *also* 'cause of those but . . . d'you want to know a secret?'

'Always,' she replies, leaning deliberately into the drama.

'I don't have any more ideas. As in, like . . . none.'

Lizzy's face contorts into an *eek*. 'Wow,' she says. 'Shit.'

'Yeah,' he agrees emphatically, and for a second or two, neither of them says anything.

'D'you know,' Ciaran adds then, 'I've actually confessed this to a few people, and you're the only one who hasn't told me I'll "think of something".'

'Well, maybe you *will* think of something.'

'Maybe I won't.'

'These are the options,' she agrees plainly. 'I'll tell you what though, Ciaran. If I were a betting woman?' Her voice softens as she regards him for a moment. '. . . I wouldn't bet against you.'

Chapter Thirty-Three

They don't, in the end, go to the Irish bar after dinner. Instead, they end up in Le Petit Majestic, a hole-in-the-wall place tucked behind the Croisette. There is nothing particularly charming about it, but it stays open later than anywhere else in town, and has earned a sort of reputation based on its very shittiness. Inside, there are a few Formica tables and chairs, but outside is really where the action is. As late night creeps into early morning, dozens – sometimes hundreds – of people gather outside Le Petit Majestic, drinking three-euro beers and hoping to find themselves in conversation with a beautiful, or useful, or at least entertaining stranger. Even those at the very top of the totem pole have been known to swing by when the premieres and parties are over – the equivalent, maybe, of a McDonald's after the Oscars – and more than few blockbusters have reportedly begun life right here, in a back street in Cannes. Lizzy does not know how true that is. Specifics seem to be thin on the ground. But everyone has bought into the myth, and she sort of has too.

She stands against the exterior wall, taking in the activity around her, and eventually Ciaran re-appears, with two Kronenbourg 1664s.

'Sorry,' he says, passing one over to her. 'Got a bit waylaid.'

'One of your many fans?' she asks teasingly.

He says nothing – which tells her she's got it in one – and lifts his drink to his mouth. Something about the sight of it – about his lips and the condensation on the bottle and his Adam's apple as he tilts his head back a little – is just incredibly, incredibly hot. That's when Lizzy knows for sure that she's gone. There just isn't any denying it anymore. She's a girl with a crush.

And the thing is that she knows, in a way she hasn't ever known before in her life, including with Ciaran, the first time round – including with Ciaran as recently as last night – that he wants her back. It remains pretty hard, intellectually, to believe that. This town is a veritable zoo of beautiful women, after all, and he could likely have his pick. But she feels it in her blood and bones. At least for right now, she knows that it's true.

Over the next hour, probably half a dozen people approach for a chat – a couple due to random proximity, most of them specifically in order to meet Ciaran. Ordinarily, that would be fine by Lizzy. She typically enjoys a free-wheeling, low-stakes conversation with a stranger, especially when she's buzzed. It is, in fact, one of her favourite parts of being in Cannes. But, what little alcohol she's had feels like it's hardly touched her tonight, and she finds she's really not so interested in other people's company.

'I have a vision for, sort of, this very dark, dramatic cello score but I just cannot find anybody,' says a very nice Swedish stranger. Ciaran has asked her about her film because that, Lizzy's noticed, is what he does. He makes it about the other person. Whether that's a mark of his sincere interest in their projects, or a symptom of how deeply bored to death he is of talking about his own, is unclear. Either way, she finds it sweet.

'It's so hard, with composers, to explain exactly what you want,' the Swedish woman continues.

'Yeah,' Ciaran replies. 'I actually know this brilliant cellist I could put you in touch with if you want. I mean, obviously no pressure to go with him, but he's great.'

'That would be amazing! Thank you!'

'Cool, well sure I have your card,' Ciaran says, gesturing towards his pocket. 'I'll do an email intro. His name's Seamus Farr – really young guy, like twenty-five, so he's just getting started. But, honestly, amazing.'

'Oh!' Lizzy pipes up. 'He did the score for *Inclement Weather*, right? That was gorgeous.'

As if in slow motion, Ciaran turns to her.

'Oh, you watched it, did you?' he asks loftily.

She frowns in confusion, until she gets his drift. That day in the Palais. Could that really only have been four days ago? Why had she felt the need to mention to him that she hadn't seen his first film? She'd probably said all kinds of stupid things.

'The other night,' she admits, and he looks so thoroughly delighted with himself that she rolls her eyes, flashing him her middle finger even as a smile tugs at her lips.

He holds his hands up, as though in defeat. 'Hey, you held out for like, two and a half years,' he replies. 'That's pretty good going. Would've been nice, obviously, if you'd seen it in the cinema. Box office figures and all that. But whatever.'

'I heard you did alright,' she replies breezily.

With a barely suppressed grin, Ciaran turns to their new acquaintance.

'We have a very unusual friendship,' he tells her seriously, as if it's a real explanation, as if this too is not all for Lizzy's amusement. 'Elizabeth here is just not that supportive.'

'Oh, I think I've been pretty supportive,' she counters, and she watches as the recollection of the past week's events dawns upon him.

'Mmm. Yeah. Fair, I suppose.'

And all of a sudden, Lizzy just can't wait any longer. She feels like she is about to vibrate out of her own skin.

'Hey Agnes, would you excuse us for just one second?' she says, and as the other woman nods, she grabs Ciaran by the hand, leading him all the way around the corner and away from the crowd.

The two of them land, laughing, against the wall of Le Petit Majestic. They're angled towards each other, their shoulders pressed against the stone façade.

'What are we doing?' he asks, even though it's obvious by now. Everything about this whole situation, she realises, has been obvious all night, if not longer than that. It's been a matter of when and how.

He looks at her, all attention, and she exhales a little.

'Tell me if this is weird, okay?' she says, and then her hands are reaching for his face, and she's kissing him.

Ciaran sucks a breath in through his nose, playing catch-up for a second or two. After that, though, he's right there with her. She can tell. Both of his arms wrap around her, pulling her as close as he can, and it's the sort of kiss Lizzy hasn't had in a long time. Giddy and frenzied, powered by adrenalin. The sort of kiss that feels exciting, that seems to promise everything. When eventually they pull apart, they both are buzzing and breathless with it.

'Not weird,' he confirms, tilting his head back a bit to look at her. 'Or, maybe a wee bit weird. But in a good way, I mean,' he adds quickly. 'I'm *very* happy you did that.'

She smiles, feeling like her heart is about to beat out of her chest. 'Why didn't you do it?'

'I was, like, respecting your autonomy as a woman and everything.'

'Ohhh,' she says, 'waiting for the green light, huh?'

'Exactly.'

'Man,' she mutters, shaking her head. 'You accuse somebody of being a sex pest *one time* . . .'

'Fuck off,' he says affectionately.

'Ciaran, I'm gonna give you a tip, okay?' she says, her voice dipping a little lower, her arms curling a little tighter around his neck. 'You can go ahead and consider me a walking green light at this point.'

'Okay me too,' he agrees readily, and as he grins at her, she grins right back, letting the new reality settle around them for a moment.

'I like the beard,' she finds herself murmuring then, trailing her fingertips along it lightly. 'Have I told you that? I think the beard's a really good choice.'

Ciaran makes no reply, he just urges her back in towards him again. And this time around, when their lips meet, it's different. A little bit less frantic, a little bit more languid. They let themselves sink into the kiss, tasting one another again, and it's probably crazy to imagine that along with the newness, there's some familiarity too, some hint of the long-forgotten. But that's what it feels like to Lizzy. His tongue traces along her bottom lip, and she lets her lips part wider, one hand making its way into his hair. Movement for movement, breath for breath, they match each other, and it is as though there could be no better, more obvious thing for them to be doing right now than this. Every second they've spent doing anything else suddenly seems like such a colossal waste of time.

Soon – she has truly no idea how long it might have been – Lizzy begins to be vaguely aware of her whole body warming, as though it's radiating heat. And when Ciaran dips his head to kiss along her jaw, moving slow and open-mouthed down her neck, she feels it in her stomach and in the arches of her feet and everywhere else besides.

'Jesus,' she hisses unconsciously, at the end of a long, slow exhale.

'D'you want to go . . . somewhere that doesn't have all these people?' he murmurs, his breath tickling her skin.

All these people?

Lizzy feels almost light-headed. She had, in fact, somewhat forgotten about the existence of *any* other people. They'd become one mass of ambient noise. But then, the truth is that for this entire evening, more or less everything besides Ciaran has been background. Just scenery and supporting characters. As her eyes dart about, though, she notes that, yes, even here, away from the main throng, there are a shit tonne of other people. And when she looks back at Ciaran, she notices his flushed cheeks and dark eyes, and she wants them all to herself.

'Yeah,' she replies, her voice coming out little more than a whisper.

'Where are you staying again?'

'Just off Rue d'Antibes,' she says. It isn't far away. Nowhere, in Cannes, is really very far away from anywhere else.

'D'you want to go there? Or, I'm just in the Carlton?'

Lizzy takes his hand. 'Let's go.'

Chapter Thirty-Four

You don't have to do anything you don't want to do,
Lizzy had been told, over and over in her formative years,
by her mom and her health class teacher and celebrities
trying to be good role models. *You deserve to be
respected. You teach people how to treat you. Don't let
yourself be taken advantage of. You can always say no.*

That message had sunk in, deep. And it had been a
good thing, in certain ways. She was not someone who'd
ever had any problem telling some handsy guy on a
dance floor to fuck off. She had understood very clearly
what doing that said about her: that she was not stupid,
not to be messed with, not about to do anything she'd
regret. Not easy.

But, what happened when she *didn't* want to say no?
She'd had a whole lot less instruction there. What did
that mean about her? She'd had to try and work that
one out for herself throughout her twenties.

There certainly was a long period of her life in which
Lizzy would have thought that coming back to a man's

hotel room on the spur of the moment like this was not what a good girl did. And – much more to the point, so far as she was concerned – was not what a genuinely empowered woman did, either. She would have thought it an act of self-sabotage, bound to make for a mediocre night, at best, followed by a terrible next morning, at minimum.

She's listened to some very instructive podcasts in recent years, and she doesn't believe that to be the case anymore. Or at least, not necessarily. But, it's still not something *she's* ever done, or wanted to do. She still doesn't find much to relate to within the main source of her information about other people's sex lives – namely, confessional essays, published online by women whose debut novels are apparently forthcoming.

In the backseat of the taxi, he fingered me and I hated it and hated myself, but also I loved it.

At the Xerox machine, I ran into Brody. He was skinny and intellectual, just like me, and sometimes, on our lunch break, we fucked, passionately yet passively, in the toilet cubicle on the fourth floor.

That's the type of thing Lizzy seems to read a lot of – and, it's all fine. No judgement. It's just that it does not tally whatsoever with what sounds like fun to her personally, no more than an article extolling the virtues of the Christian side hug might.

Bursting through the door to Ciaran's hotel suite, though, his hands on her hips . . . that feels like a lot of fun.

The place is huge, and smells like a spa, and that's all she has a chance to absorb about it because very swiftly, she finds herself pressed against a wall. Then they're kissing, kissing, kissing again, deep and delicious, like they might never stop. His tongue swirls across the pulse point on her neck – he'd known *exactly* what he was doing earlier, kissing her there – and when she moans aloud, Ciaran bucks against her at the sound.

'Fuck,' he hisses out. 'Sorry. I didn't mean to . . . we can slow this down, if you want.'

Lizzy stares up at him, and again she's struck by how dishevelled he looks, how his breathing is a little laboured. *She* did that. It's a thrill to realise it.

She kisses him sweetly, tugging his shirt out of his jeans, and sliding her hands up his back. He feels warm and solid and safe, and the nearness of him, the way he is looking at her, makes something inside of her ache.

'I don't want to slow down,' she murmurs. 'Do you?'

He shakes his head, leaning down to kiss her again – gently at first, and then with all he's got. His hands are suddenly everywhere, and she wants them everywhere, and as he thrusts against her again, she gasps, arching into him in return.

Somehow, in a few clumsy steps, they make it from the little sitting room into the bedroom, and she gets to work on his shirt. As quickly as she can, she undoes the buttons until they're all opened, and he flings the thing off. He has the sort of body she'd imagined, that first day he came to talk to her at the Scottish Pavilion – maybe now she can admit she might have imagined it. Broad shoulders and strong arms and a flat stomach. Fit, but not intimidatingly so.

Lizzy kisses across his clavicle, down his shoulder a little bit. She doesn't have to stretch, hardly has to bend at all – she is the perfect height for this task and it's probably not a skill she can ever put on a résumé but right now, it feels like the most glorious revelation. She lets her tongue dip out experimentally along the way.

'Jesus fucking Christ,' Ciaran says, his voice coming out strained, and when he clutches at a handful of her hair, tugging the smallest bit, something inside of Lizzy tightens. She likes that, she realises. She hadn't known before.

He works his hand under her silky blouse and up her back, as if he's seeking some new terrain of his own to explore and suddenly, that's all Lizzy wants – her bare skin on his. What might that feel like? She guides his hand to her waist, gathering some of the material up, with his fingers under hers.

He pulls away a little, to look at her.

'Can I?' he murmurs, and she barely lets him get the words out.

'Yes,' she says immediately, and then he's fumbling with the buttons, all fingers and thumbs, working down them slowly, each one revealing a bit more.

For the first time, Lizzy becomes aware that she is not only the observer here – she's the observed, too. The realisation makes her heart pound all the faster. Maybe for something to do as much as anything else, she reaches for Ciaran's belt buckle. He's straining against the material of his jeans and she swallows, beginning to feel ever so slightly overwhelmed. Not because anything bad is happening, just because a *lot* is happening. Her own hands become a little uncoordinated.

'Hey, Lizzy?' Ciaran says then, somewhat breathlessly. Her hands still, and his do too. She looks up at him.

'Are you freaking out? Like, a tiny bit?' he asks.

And for some weird reason, she's okay with admitting it. 'Yeah,' she replies, her voice barely more than a whisper.

Ciaran smiles, exhaling a little in what seems like it might be relief. 'Okay, me too.'

Absolutely no part of her expects this response.

'Why?' she asks incredulously. The very notion is bizarre to her. Not only because Ciaran is gorgeous but also because he is a man. The first thing most boys absorbed about sex was that it would be so much fun, and the first thing most girls absorbed was that it would hurt. That, at least in Lizzy's experience, very much laid the groundwork in terms of the distribution of anxiety going forward.

'I dunno, it's just . . . new isn't it?' He shrugs a little shyly. 'I want to be . . . what you want.'

It's surprising, and sweet – so often, he seems to be both of those things - and as Lizzy looks up at Ciaran's face, her response comes effortlessly.

'You're already what I want,' she breathes out.

After that, they have no more need for words.

Chapter Thirty-Five

Ciaran hasn't been woken by anything but an alarm clock in a very long time, such that he can hardly believe the luxury of it as he opens his eyes slowly the next morning, sunlight filtering in through the curtains. And that's not even the best part. It takes a second for everything that has happened to re-root itself in his brain, but when it does, a thrill pulses through him, moments from last night coming back to him like snippets of film. He has always been able to see things that way, in his mind's eye.

It all seems almost too good to be true, and looking over to his left now, some part of him half expects to find an empty space beside him.

But, no. There she is. Propped up a little against the pillows, Lizzy's put on one of the waffle dressing gowns he'd spotted on the back of the bathroom door. He doesn't know what that means, or if it means anything at all.

'Mornin',' he says, his voice coming out husky.

'Morning,' Lizzy replies. It seems like maybe she's been awake for a while.

'What time is it?' he asks.

'Like, 8.45.'

Ciaran can't read her with any certainty, but it does seem that if she wanted to leave, she might have done it already. Just the fact of her still being here feels like a pretty good sign. He tugs himself upwards a little so they're on the same level, and entirely without his say-so, a smile creeps onto his lips.

'Last night was . . .'

He shakes his head, unable to find the words, and Lizzy doesn't do much better.

'. . . Yeah,' she manages, on an exhale.

He nudges his shoulder against hers, and she giggles. It erupts like giddy relief, making her nose crinkle, and it sounds exactly like he feels.

'I've never done that before,' she admits. 'Ever.'

Maybe he looks surprised, because she rushes to clarify.

'Oh! No, I don't mean . . . I *have* done *that*. I mean sex on the first date, one-night stand, that whole deal.'

Ciaran nods in understanding.

'Is that what this is?' he asks then, because he just can't help it. 'A one-night stand?'

Her cheeks pinken the slightest bit. 'I don't know.'

'I don't know either.'

Lizzy slides down in bed, burrowing under the blankets until just her face is visible. Ciaran does the same, and they stare at one another.

'Do we have to have a really serious discussion about this now?' she asks, scrunching up her face, as if in trepidation. Ciaran knows she'd likely reject the adjective

301

as applied to her, but he thinks she looks completely adorable right now. There's just no other word for it.

He cracks a smile. 'Probably, yeah,' he replies. '*Or* – I know this might be crazy talk but bear with me – we could just . . . enjoy it for a minute, maybe?'

She smiles back at him.

'I could do that,' she says, a little shyly, and he lets himself shift closer to her, running his foot up her calf. Her skin is warm and soft, and suddenly his mouth goes a little dry. Suffice to say that over the past few days, it has not been difficult to recollect, with painful clarity, the way he always used to feel around Lizzy Munro. When he had ached to just be near her. That he would at last get to see her like this, touch her like this, feels like a little bit of a miracle.

'How long are you staying in Cannes 'til?' she asks.

'How long are *you* here?'

''Til Tuesday. We have the ceilidh on Monday night and then I fly out the next morning.'

'I could stay 'til then,' he offers, and Lizzy nods.

'Okay. Cool,' she says, in that same bashful sort of way.

He grins. Suddenly, five full days and nights seem to stretch out gloriously ahead. 'Shall we order some breakfast?'

'Sounds good. I'm gonna jump in the shower really fast, okay?'

'Yep, cool.'

And as Ciaran watches her, padding into the bathroom in her thin white robe, he still feels somewhat like she might be a fantasy, a take he's watching from behind the monitor on a film set. He gets up himself, then, pulling on his boxers and walking over to open the curtains. The sun streams in fully, bathing the whole room in bright light. He gazes out at the sea, and that familiar sensation washes over him like a wave. It's the sense of freedom, of calm, of joy, of his own smallness, his own connectedness – all the things, in short, that other people feel when they look out at that expanse of blue. Ciaran doesn't think it makes him anything extraordinary. He had just forgotten it, in the hustle and bustle of film shoots and edit suites and Tube lines. He has a good life in London, he reminds himself staunchly. The city gave him everything he has. But undeniably, there is something about getting out of it that makes him feel like maybe he might have Stockholm Syndrome.

From the bathroom, he can hear the water turn on, and then something else.

Lizzy is singing.

Her voice rises and trills and Ciaran doesn't have a clue what the song is, but suddenly it's his favourite.

*

They have breakfast not quite in bed, but *on* the bed, at least, pastries and fruit spread out across the duvet as the two of them sit on top of it cross-legged. Lizzy bites into the last of her croissant, scooping up errant bits of flaky pastry from the duvet, and Ciaran glances at the clock on the nightstand.

'Do you have to do work stuff this morning or anything?' he asks.

'I had three meetings but I, uh, emailed and rescheduled them,' she replies.

He smiles. So she'd wanted, maybe, to spend the time here. With him.

'Cool,' is all he says.

'I mean, I should probably be taking the opportunity to clear the backlog in my inbox, but . . .'

Ciaran shakes his head, as though the very notion is insane. 'I think with emails, if you can't answer within twenty-four hours, the thing to do is leave it like a week and a half.'

'Oh really?'

'Absolutely,' he says, all confidence. 'You want to let that danger zone pass where you just look sloppy – I'm talking, like, the three-, four-day point. That's not good. Hang on a bit longer and pretty soon you're into the territory of, like, "Wow, this person is just so busy and in-demand, I should be grateful they've gotten back to me at all."'

Lizzy laughs. ''Kay. I'll buy it. I probably do need to show my face at the Pavilion at some point today, though. I just want to check in, make sure my boss hasn't ended up in some major showdown with this guy from the ceilidh venue. I think at this point we've probably had all the hiccups we're going to have, but still. How 'bout you, anything on your agenda?'

'Nope. Nothing major,' he says. Nothing at all, more like. He reaches over to the cafetière and divides the dregs into their two cups. 'I *have* sort of been thinking though. About this whole Penny Ainsley thing.'

She frowns. 'What about it?'

'I don't know. You just go over everything in your head, you know? Those few days before the premiere were so insane. It was like I could focus on whatever was the one thing immediately in front of me and that was it. And honestly I was pissed off, that somebody could come along and just screw everything up. Now that the dust has settled a bit, though. . .'

He pauses, with a bit of a shrug, a bit of a wince.

'I definitely never read her script. I'd never even heard of her until her complaint. But some people at Figment had. I'm not sure who. She sent a pitch – or a script, or *something* – in to them. Cut to, then, however long later and I'm developing *Wish You Were Here* at Figment, right? And I do remember at some point, there was a discussion about how we needed Isaac to have more of, like, an emotional journey. Something a bit more weighty, you know?'

'Right,' Lizzy nods, and Ciaran gulps down a lukewarm sip of coffee, setting the cup aside. This is where it gets murky.

'So we talked about various possible problems to give him. Does he have some kind of childhood trauma, or does he start drinking too much, or . . . whatever. I don't know how we came up with the sister's suicide. I don't know if I said that first, or if it was somebody at Figment. I really don't.'

Lizzy clicks her tongue against her teeth. 'So what are you thinking?'

'I don't know,' he says, with a sigh. 'I just think . . . like, obviously the producers were massively involved in the film. They helped shape the thing all the way along – maybe they *did* mould it into something that was a bit like Penny's project. Best of both worlds type of thing. And maybe not even deliberately, you know? Maybe just subconsciously.'

'Or consciously.'

Ciaran nods glumly. 'Yeah. Who knows. If her script *was* similar, though – if it maybe had some good ideas and some stuff that needed work, the same as mine did . . . I dunno.' He casts his mind back to the reviews, to the phrases that still echo in his brain at extremely regular intervals. 'Maybe she would have actually done a *better* job, in the end.'

Lizzy says nothing, just reaches out a hand, scratching her fingertips against his knee. Ciaran sighs again.

'*Or*,' he continues, 'she really is just a money-grabbing madwoman, who can't get a gig and is raging about it. Either way, it's a shitty situation, isn't it?'

At this, Lizzy lets out a little sigh herself. There's no getting away from that one.

'It is. I'm sorry.'

A half-smile rises to his lips. 'Why're *you* sorry?'

'I'm just sorry you have to deal with all this,' she says, and it's such a simple thing, but as she leans forward to drop a kiss on his lips, Ciaran can hardly believe how nice it is to hear. That's another thing he realises, all of a sudden, about his life in London. He has work-friends there, and friends-friends there, but maybe – in a certain way that had somehow totally escaped his attention – he has also been really, really lonely.

He puts his hand over Lizzy's, working his fingers through hers.

'Well, we'll see. Festival's not over yet. Maybe I can figure out a way to unravel this whole Penny thing somehow. Anyway. Here's a question for you, Elizabeth,' he says then, his tone brightening. He hadn't meant to talk so much, to get so serious. 'Would you by any chance want to go . . . swim in the sea?'

Chapter Thirty-Six

Lizzy hasn't brought a swimsuit, so she dashes into H&M and picks one off the rail, which – mercifully – fits when she wriggles into it down on the beach. It turns out to be a good strategy, actually – skipping out on the photographing herself in the mirror, the turning this way and that to assess it from all angles. She's left feeling nothing much about this swimsuit other than that it's navy with white polka dots, and it's the thing that's enabling her to get in the sea.

The water's cold, the way it always is at first, but Ciaran hardly seems to feel it. She's not even up to her thighs when he ducks all the way down, emerging with soaked hair, smiling. He looks like some kind of cologne commercial. Except for the smile, she thinks then. He could maybe do with working on a more sultry expression.

'This is all I've wanted to do since I got here,' he says breathlessly.

'Yeah?' she replies, and once she takes the plunge, she finds him swimming up behind her.

'Well, maybe not *all* I've wanted to do,' he adds, his arm sliding across her middle.

Lizzy giggles, letting herself lean back against him. He feels totally solid and slightly unreal at once. She isn't sure how long they spend in the water after that, bobbing along weightlessly, tasting the salt on one another's lips, messing around like gleeful children. She only knows that it feels like a flash and the part of the day that follows – the part without him – seems to inch along at an agonising pace.

By the time she gets to the Scottish Pavilion, having made a pitstop at her Airbnb along the way for clean clothes, the place is bustling with festival delegates. Alas, though, no Simon. Is it her imagination, or does he, this festival, seem to have been failing somewhat at the 'being available' portion of things?

'Has he said anything about Plage Raphael?' Lizzy asks Shauna. '"The wheels have totally fallen off the bus?" "Where the fuck is Lizzy Munro?" Anything like that?'

'Nah, he seems happy enough,' Shauna replies. 'He was actually chatting away this morning about how things have gone way more smoothly with the ceilidh than he thought they would.'

Internally, Lizzy breathes a little sigh of relief. Maybe she is a control freak, but it has been niggling at her, the not knowing exactly what was happening.

'Wonderful!' she beams, feeling as though she is glowing from the inside out. The whole world, today, seems to be made of wonderful things.

*

By half past seven, she has at last made it back to Ciaran's suite at the Carlton. In the little sitting room, they're settled on the sofa, a feast spread on the coffee table in front of them. Wine and lots of bread, plus a variety of things to be put on bread. Cheeses and parma ham; tapenade and pâté and sun-blushed tomatoes.

They'd flicked on a French television show for a while, to see how much they could understand, but the results were too depressing, so they've switched; some true-crime thing is on in the background now, Ciaran chiming in with choice commentary at regular intervals. ('That's his first mistake, there, isn't it? Maybe don't put the axe on your credit card, mate. Wee pair of gloves would be no harm either. Christ almighty! He hasn't even turned off his phone, Lizzy! The cell towers'll be pinging all over the place now – we've all listened to *Serial*.')

For her part, Lizzy can well imagine that this – cable TV and dinner from a supermarket – would not be everyone's number one way to spend an evening on the Côte d'Azur, but she is happy as a clam. She already knows that the party they'd vaguely talked about going to – the extremely exclusive Warner Brothers one that Ciaran could get them on the list for – is not one they're actually going to be attending.

As she unfurls her legs from underneath her, he grasps her feet, pulling them into his lap. The gesture makes her feel weird in a good way. So much about this whole thing with him seems to make her feel weird in a good way. He runs his hands up and down her shin absently, and she wonders does it feel a tiny bit stubbly, on the way up. Or, no. That's not it. It's that she knows it *must*. And it's hard, trying to hold on to what she believes in principle – which is that hair grows from women's legs as naturally as it does from men's and should be as unremarkable – when it feels so instinctual, the wish that she were offering him Barbie-smooth skin right now. Is that just what she wants, and it's okay to want it? Or is it what she's been conditioned to want, and she should fight against it? The whole thing is exhausting to think about.

Under her hip, her phone is digging into her, and she reaches to dislodge it.

'I'm pretty surprised Oliver hasn't called tonight already,' she says idly. 'He just got a phone, for emergencies, like two weeks ago. So, there've been a *lot* of emergencies since then.'

Ciaran smiles. 'Here's a fun fact about Oliver,' he tosses back. He doesn't seem to have any thoughts on her legs, other than maybe that – for whatever reason – he wants to keep touching them. 'I actually thought that he was your boyfriend for a period of time.'

Lizzy doesn't even slightly follow. 'What?!'

'I saw his name come up on your phone a few times, and I just . . . I don't know. Put two and two together and came up with your kid brother was your boyfriend.'

She snorts, shoving his thigh with her foot. 'You're an idiot.'

'Then you said on the phone that you were single – 'member the morning after the premiere? And I thought . . .' he shrugs. 'Maybe a few more days in the south of France'd be okay.'

'Hang on. So, the studio didn't make you stay?' she asks. She's been wondering about that, actually. It hadn't seemed like he'd had any work stuff to deal with today, but she hadn't wanted to bring it up, in case the whole thing was a sore subject.

'Nope,' he says, a sheepish sort of look on his face. He stayed for her. He doesn't say it, but Lizzy's not deaf. She hears it.

They smile bashfully at one another – they smile like fools, probably – until Ciaran turns back towards the television, unmuting it.

'Right, what have we missed here? This fella's probably googled "How to fit your wife in a freezer."'

Lizzy sniggers, and before she sets her phone aside, she takes a brief glance at her email inbox. There are, of course, more bolded black headings than she can count.

It's like this every year – by a certain point of the festival, it becomes a losing battle, a question of accepting the backlog – and all the more so for Lizzy this year because of the ceilidh. Almost constantly, there are begging messages arriving from strangers seeking invites, or from existing invitees seeking plus ones. Even as she looks at her screen now, a new email whooshes to the top of the list in real time, about as welcome as a fresh turd. This one, though, stands out from the rest. It reads: **Douglas Maclaine – URGENT.**

Chapter Thirty-Seven

'What's up?' Ciaran asks, and it's then that Lizzy realises she's letting out a low, long groan, like roadkill in its final moments. She looks up from her phone.

'Douglas Maclaine, you know he was supposed to be calling the ceilidh?'

'Yeah . . .'

'Yeah. Well. Apparently, he's checked into rehab as of two hours ago,' she says. Saying it out loud makes it horribly real.

'Jesus. Drugs or booze?'

'*Exhaustion*, officially. But, booze. Manager says he's been a functioning alcoholic for the last eighteen months. I mean . . . fucking *fuck*,' she says, pressing her fingers into her temple. 'Could he not have just hung on? Functioned a couple more days? What's a little extra liver damage at this stage of the game, really? I'm sure The Priory would've taken him in a week's time.'

Ciaran snorts. 'So, what, you need to line up a replacement now?'

'Yeah, pretty much. I mean, I guess so,' she says, feeling utterly helpless.

'Ah well. I'm sure you'll get somebody.'

He says this so assuredly that Lizzy actually has to take a second to process it. She'd been fully expecting that he'd be right alongside her in the journey toward spiralling out entirely – on some level, she'd maybe even been looking forward to the company. She lets herself exhale heavily.

'. . . You really think so?'

'Yeah. Fuck, worst comes to worst, *I* could give it a go.'

Of all the things she might have expected, this was not it.

'*You* know how to call a ceilidh?'

'I mean, I've *been* to a fair few ceilidhs,' he says, which is not something she'd known about him.

'You have?'

She probably shouldn't be so surprised. The tradition, after all, has its roots in Scotland and Ireland alike.

'Oh yeah. Strip the Willow, Gay Gordons, I know all about it,' he says, tossing the names of the dances out with a little swagger that she knows is to try and amuse her. Against the odds, it does sort of work.

'People would be big fans of a ceilidh in Donegal,' he continues. 'Fun for all the parish et cetera. Have I ever actually *called* a ceilidh? Technically, no, but how hard can it be? It's mostly just counting people in and that, isn't it? I could look it up on YouTube.'

It's not lost on Lizzy that this is probably precisely the attitude that led Ciaran to a BAFTA at scarcely more than thirty years old. Nonetheless:

'You're sweet,' she says. 'But I'm sure I can find someone who . . .'

'Knows the fuck what they're doing?' he supplies.

She laughs. 'And is available with, like, *no* notice, yeah.'

A Scot here for the festival, perhaps – someone with a secret talent and a benevolent frame of mind. Or, there must be Irish or Scottish community groups in Nice that could help. She'll get Shauna on the case.

Despite the situation being really no better than it was just a few minutes prior, Lizzy finds she *does* seem to feel a little more relaxed about it. If Ciaran did that, she has absolutely no idea how.

'Thank you, though,' she adds, leaning forward to brush her lips against his. She'd intended for the kiss to be brief, but when she pulls away, he urges her back in toward him, making it last. Just like that, all thoughts of Douglas Maclaine, or anything else for that matter, are banished from Lizzy's mind. She shifts so that her thighs are either side of Ciaran's, and as his hands make their way up her back, his mouth dipping down into the v of her dress, it's the same as it was last night, the same as it has been any time he's touched her since. That sensation of being drunk on him. He's just so good at this, Lizzy thinks – if, in fact, that's true of anyone on a standalone basis. She's beginning to think maybe it's not. That maybe, instead, there are *combinations* of people who are good at it.

Across the past twelve years, she's counted herself incredibly lucky that none of the sexual experiences she's accrued have been traumatic. Some of them she would definitely describe as positive. Nonetheless, there has always been a certain awareness, on her part, of bases being reached and rounded. There has always been a degree of effort involved in sidestepping what she didn't want and maybe – *maybe* – trying to engineer what she did.

With Ciaran, it's so different as to be like an entirely new experience. It's instinctive and intoxicating and as she arches into him now, she somehow doesn't have to waste a single second wondering whether she seems too much, or not enough, like a pornstar. It turns out that all the time she's spent over the years – whether she was having sex or not having it – feeling as though she might be slightly freakish and abnormal in this domain . . . all that time, the only thing she needed was to be driven mad with desire. That really seems to take care of so many other issues.

They manoeuvre themselves on the couch so that she's lying underneath him, and it's such a completely joyful surprise, Lizzy thinks, to find that this can all be *easy*. Maybe not always – if the last ten seconds are anything to go by – graceful, but easy.

In some distant part of her brain, it occurs to her that perhaps the ceilidh, too, could be that way if she let it. That maybe the option right in front of her is as good as any she might torture herself trying to find. Or, in fact, better. After all, part of Douglas's appeal had been his name – his fame. Some random festival delegate or ex-pat wasn't going to tick that box. But Ciaran could.

He's tugged down her dress now, and he's doing something spectacular with his tongue. It clouds her mind and makes her stomach somersault, want blurring into need.

'Actually Ciaran,' she finds herself saying hazily, right as she's inching her fingers just below the back of his jeans, '*would* you call the ceilidh?'

There's a second's pause before he bursts out laughing, loud and unrestrained, his upper body collapsing on top of her. Lizzy's eyelids, half hooded in lust, blink all the way open. She laughs then too, as though she's heard the question right along with him.

'Sorry! I guess I could have picked some other time to ask you that, huh? I don't know why I . . .' she shrugs, another giggle escaping her. 'It just floated into my head.'

'You know I *offered*, right?' Ciaran says, lifting himself up a bit so as not to crush her. 'You don't have to seduce me for my . . .' – he searches for the terminology, looking thoroughly amused – 'folk . . . dance . . . organisational skills.'

Lizzy rolls her eyes. 'I don't even know if you *have* any skills.'

'No, no no,' he tosses back. 'Not what I'm hearing whatsoever, Elizabeth. You want me.'

There's a glint in his eye as he says it, and she sneaks under his t-shirt to scratch her fingernails across his skin, holding his gaze all the while.

'I'm desperate,' she murmurs, because two can play at this game. She watches him swallow, watches his expression seem to glaze over a little.

He kisses her then, like he means it, easing her legs apart so that he's nestled flush against her. When he presses into her just right, Lizzy can't help the sharp intake of breath that follows, and he grins. That's how it goes. They each get their little victories.

'I'll give it a shot if you want me to,' he says. 'Will we discuss it later?'

And as it happens, that suits Lizzy just fine.

Chapter Thirty-Eight

The following day starts off every bit as well as its predecessor, with warm arms around her in bed, and twenty minutes luxuriating in a shower so large that Lizzy possibly could have done a cartwheel in it, were she capable of doing a cartwheel as a general matter.

But maybe it's true that nothing gold can stay. She's only been gone from the hotel suite fifteen minutes, the damp ends of her hair still drying in the sunshine, when her phone rings. She smiles when she sees the name on the display.

'Missing me already?'

On the other end of the line, Ciaran laughs, a little uneasily. 'Uh, yeah. But also,' – he pauses for no more than three seconds, plenty of time for fear to clutch at Lizzy's chest – 'Peter's just phoned me. There's an article on the *Daily Mail* website. "Article" would probably be putting it generously, really. It's mostly just pictures. Of you and me.'

'What?'

'Yeah.'

Lizzy realises that she seems to have stopped right in the middle of the pavement, and she shuffles to the side, out of other people's way.

'Details, Ciaran. What pictures?'

'Pictures of us at the beach yesterday. Some fucker obviously spotted us, and saw pound signs.' His voice is tight with irritation.

'What, like paparazzi?' Lizzy can't believe she's saying this – can't believe such a notion is being raised in her real life. And yet, when she hears her own voice out loud, it seems to sound relatively normal, even as panic rolls over her in hot, pulsing waves.

'Doesn't look like it. They'd be better pictures. This just looks like somebody with an iPhone.'

'Okay. Um . . . okay.'

'I'm so sorry, Lizzy.'

'It's not your fault,' she replies, as if on autopilot. And of course that's true. But honestly, in this moment? It does sort of *feel* like his fault. She's very glad to be getting this news over the phone. If they were in the same room together she suspects she wouldn't be able to stop her feelings showing up on her face. She might be mean. She might shrug his hand off her shoulder in a way he didn't deserve.

'No, I know, but . . .' He lets out a sound that's somewhere between a groan and a growl. 'Who even gives a shit about some director going for a swim with his . . . with a woman? Nobody, that's who. Nobody actually *wants* this. But they'll still click on it if it's put right in front of them,' he says bitterly.

'Yeah.'

318

She agrees with him, fully. She just doesn't have it in her to get too worked up about the principle of the matter right now, when all her brainpower is taken up by its practical impact on her personally – and, specifically, ascertaining the extent of that. She needs to see this article.

Ciaran sighs deeply. 'I suppose it's like you said the other night,' he says glumly. 'Other people basically don't care. They look at it for thirty seconds while they're having their breakfast in the office, and then it's gone. It's fucking annoying, but nobody's in a hospital bed, here, right?'

That's when Lizzy realises what's happened. Inadvertently – she would never have done it on purpose – she's sold herself to him as some species of Cool Girl.

And the truth is, it's not a total fraud. A lot of the time, she really *does* have a pretty good capacity to see the bigger picture he's painting – the exact one she'd painted for him. She can laugh and say *fuck it* and decide not to care. It's clear to her that this is the part of herself she needs to drag out into the light now. The analytical-self-critical-maybe-also-hypocritical part, while equally real, must be squelched.

'Exactly,' she replies, all pragmatism. 'Whatever. It just . . . is what it is.'

'People are dicks,' he says emphatically.

'They really are.'

He chuckles lightly, sounding a little bit cheered. 'I'm so sorry, though. Seriously. This is shitty.'

'It's not your fault, Ciaran' she repeats, and she finds she can mean it a bit more this time. 'It really isn't. You don't have to beat yourself up over it. It's *fine*. Like you said – it's shitty, but it's fine.'

319

She gets him off the phone, and in seconds, her thumbs are working overtime across the screen. How, she wonders, has this actually become sort of familiar to her? Looking up articles in which she has some sort of personal stake. She's not especially built for this particular brand of suspense, that much she's learned.

Ciaran Flynn Packs in the PDA in Cannes Beach Romp

It's been a rollercoaster week for director *du jour* Ciaran Flynn in Cannes, and yesterday, he took some time away from the spotlight to relax with his latest love. Sources say the mystery brunette is thirty-two-year-old American industry-insider Lizzy Munro.

The pair frolicked playfully in the sand, body-confident Lizzy boldly showing off her ample curves for all to see as Ciaran looked on adoringly. Later, they took to the Mediterranean, getting wet and wild. The steamy display culminated in a sexy clinch in the ocean, the twosome clearly smitten. 'They were all over each other,' reported one onlooker. 'Definitely looked very loved up. Lizzy's not shy, that's for sure.'

The movie executive opted for a flattering vintage-inspired polka-dot one piece during yesterday's romantic beach outing. As she flaunted her bikini body in the crystal blue waters, Ciaran cheekily let his hands wander to her voluptuous posterior. And although the Irishman is usually more at home behind the camera, he looked every bit the hunky leading man.

Sources say the couple began dating casually some time ago, but things are now heating up. 'They tried to keep it private, but Ciaran really likes her, and he doesn't care who knows it. He's been telling friends she's "the one". Lizzy feels the same way. She's dated around a lot in her twenties, but she knows she's in her thirties now. She's absolutely ready to get serious and obviously wants to lock Ciaran down sooner rather than later. They're adorable together.'

. . . there's more, after that. Basic info about Ciaran, about *Wish You Were Here* and – yes – about his recent brush with scandal. But, Lizzy suspects that in the midst of it all could be 'Filmmaker Ciaran murdered his whole family before taking to the red carpet in Cannes on Tuesday night', and nobody would even notice. They are just words. It's quite remarkable how many of them the writer of this thing has managed to string together in order to meet the simple goal of filling some space around the photographs.

Because, really, it's all about the photographs. Ciaran had been right about that. Lizzy feels the breath sucked out of her, when she sees them.

There are seven altogether. Three of them are okay-ish. But that doesn't matter. Her response to photographs of herself is hardwired at this point. When she sees one that isn't terrible, she knows that it is a lie, and when she sees one that *is* terrible, she knows that it's the truth.

She scrolls up and down over them again and again, zeroing in on every detail – the plumpness of her thighs, the nothingness of her hair, the *her nose*-ness of her nose. She hadn't been remotely aware of these photographs being shot, which of itself is unnerving. And now here they are, offered up for the judgement of everyone who knows her and plenty of people who don't. All too swiftly, Lizzy is reacquainted with the understanding of her appearance as a thing that has always taken some making up for.

She thinks back to the way she'd been glad of Ciaran's celebrity last night, when she'd enlisted him for the ceilidh. She thinks of being in Monoprix with him before that – he'd met her when she was done at the Scottish Pavilion and they'd walked there to pick up their picnic dinner. In the supermarket, a few people had approached, wanting to chat or take a picture, and honestly, there had been a level on which Lizzy had done more than tolerate it. There was just something about being the one who already had what others so clearly wanted. Specifically, Ciaran Flynn. His time, his interest, his touch.

Now, looking at these pictures, some illogical part of Lizzy's brain computes them as payback for that . . . whatever it was. Self-satisfaction. She feels furious and violated and embarrassed, and she wonders why she's not crying. She *wishes* she could cry, if that would mean some sense of purge. No tears come, though. So, instead, she just slips her phone back in her pocket, and walks the remaining distance to the Scottish Pavilion.

What else is there to do, really? She has nowhere outside of herself to put all the feelings. She just has to make room for them, take them with her.

*

If there is an upside – which she'd be inclined to think there really isn't at all, but if there *is* – then maybe it's how easy the whole debacle makes it for Lizzy to work out which of her colleagues secretly read the *Daily Mail*. That seems to be most of them. At her table out on the deck, Lizzy barely manages to get her laptop out of her backpack before Brendan is over to her like a shot.

'Hi Lizzy,' he says, casual as anything.

She puts a benign, pleasant sort of expression on her face. 'Hey Brendan,' she replies. She catches the eye of one of the temps who's passing by. 'Christophe, would you grab me an espresso when you have a sec? A double?'

'Tired?' Brendan asks meaningfully.

'Eh, y'know.' She opens her laptop. 'We can't complain, can we? How's everything going with you, anyway?'

'Oh, fine, yeah. And you? Anything . . . *exciting*?'

She smiles, gesturing out toward the water. 'Always exciting to be in Cannes, right? That view definitely beats my usual.'

In the circumstances, Lizzy does feel like she could probably have pulled off an icy *can I help you with something?* Equally, though, she finds she's somewhat enjoying this approach, in a perverse sort of way. If Brendan wants to know anything personal about her life, she's going to make him work for it. *I'm a nosy fucker who reads gossip websites every single day of my life*, that's what she'd like him to admit, and not a thing less.

He stands before her, mouth agape, looking altogether dissatisfied.

'Absolutely,' he says. 'Well, I'll . . . I'll leave you to it then, shall I?'

He doesn't seem at all keen to leave her to anything, though. What does he think she might offer up in this moment, Lizzy wonders? *Actually Brendan, I know we've never spoken about anything more personal than what we've brought for lunch. I know I wouldn't trust you with so much as a house plant, but might you like to hear some more details of my recently-reported 'tabloid exploits'?*

Not likely.

'Cool!' she chirps, not wasting a second before she lets her gaze shift decisively to her laptop screen. A woman can be 'frolicking' on the beach one moment, and doing something extremely important on a computer the next; that, she feels, is the clear message.

As soon as Brendan shuffles off, she allows herself a momentary eye-roll, even if only for her own satisfaction, before glancing down at her phone. Texts have started to trickle in, including one from her mom:

Hi my busy Lizzy – imagine my surprise to find five people have sent me links to PAPARAZZI pictures of my one and only child today! What in the world is happening?!! Are you okay? I'm teaching all morning but I'll call you at lunch. Love you – Mom.

Lizzy tugs at the inside of her lip as she reads it. The thought that her parents have been confronted with this whole thing hits like a fresh wallop, even though she wouldn't say that either of them are particularly shock-able – least of all her mother. Between her students at Edinburgh Napier, and her friends from the refugee centre and her classmates in that sushi-making course, Franny

Munro, PhD, probably has the most varied social circle of anyone Lizzy knows, and the most *live and let live* attitude to boot. So, it's not that Lizzy fears judgement. In fact, she can already hear her mother saying *you have absolutely nothing to be ashamed of. If you're happy that's all I need to know.*

For some reason, it's this that makes the tears spring to Lizzy's eyes. Here, at her place of work, where she can't even enjoy them. She *had* been incredibly happy yesterday, on the beach. But, somehow, she finds she can't quite taste that happiness anymore. A delicious thing has curdled.

She blinks back the tears furiously, raising her hand to her temple to shield her face a little, and as she does, she becomes vaguely aware of a presence beside her. Hovering. She glances up to find Shauna standing there, looking a little more timid than usual.

'What's up?' Lizzy asks impatiently. She very much doesn't have time for another co-worker on a fishing expedition right now, not even one whom she generally likes a lot better than Brendan.

'Uh, sorry, it's just that guy is here again,' Shauna begins. 'The one from the ceilidh venue. Mr Henry?'

'Oh! Sorry, Shauna, I was just a little distracted. I'll come talk to him,' she says, and her brain switches gears instantly as she rises, smoothing her hand over her face. It had been on her list today to give Plage Raphael a call, run through some finer details. That Monsieur Henri has once again taken it upon himself to come to her does, however, seem like a bit of a red flag. In the course of the quick walk to reception, she cycles through various difficulties that might foreseeably have now arisen down at the venue, and she glances around for Simon. He is nowhere to be seen, which is unfortunate, not only because he'd handled the last round of dispute, but also because she wouldn't mind some backup if there's a brand new one to come. Historically, she has proven more than fit to manage things without him, but she's just feeling a little fragile right now.

Perhaps, she thinks, the projector screen that she had been assured would be available would, in fact, not be. Perhaps the band was to be forbidden from playing beyond a certain volume, or past a certain hour of the evening. Perhaps the Film Board might somehow be forced to cede a bit of space to that jewellery company, after all.

This list, admittedly, is non-exhaustive. But nowhere in the recesses of Lizzy's mind does she even contemplate the thing that Monsieur Henri tells her.

What he tells her – standing there casually at the Scottish Pavilion's reception desk – is that the ceilidh cannot be held at Plage Raphael.

Cannot be held there *at all*.

There has, he explains, been a misunderstanding. A very regrettable, unfortunate and unprecedented misunderstanding. It was not the case, as he had previously thought – and, indeed, had conveyed to Lizzy – that Cartier had been calling to enquire about the prospect of booking Plage Raphael on Monday. Rather, Cartier had been calling to discuss the arrangement it had already made. Somehow – by some flawed sequence of events that the hotel couldn't quite pinpoint, but was looking into and taking very seriously – two contracts had ended up being signed in respect of the same space, on the same night.

Alas, someone therefore needed to be cut loose. And it wasn't the billion-dollar company.

Monsieur Henri explains all of this – a situation that could essentially be summarised in the words 'double booked' – in an agonisingly protracted fashion, and for her part, Lizzy is certain that any preconceptions the manager may be harbouring about loud and inarticulate Americans, she well and truly validates. Some of the delegates schlepping into the Pavilion in the midst of it all actually look quite alarmed.

'Miss Munro. I offer you my sincerest apologies,' Monsieur Henri says eventually, in what she can sense he may feel is a conclusion to the matter. 'This is very embarrassing for us. It is not normal. What can I say? Of course, anything that we can do to assist in your alternative arrangements, we will be glad to do.'

Alternative arrangements? Lizzy takes a long, deep breath in and out.

'Monsieur Henri,' she says, her voice tight and quiet with fury and despair. 'It's *Friday*. My event is happening on *Monday*.'

If there is a way to more clearly convey the gravity, the hopelessness, of the situation, she cannot think of it.

Monsieur Henri just nods sadly.

'Yes. I have been trying to make touch with you, but . . .'

He trails off, as though, really, this whole predicament is a question of her ineptitude. Lizzy almost gasps with outrage.

327

'Well, you didn't try very hard! And didn't my boss call you, like, the day before yesterday? Simon Muldoney? Why didn't you just tell him all this?'

Monsieur Henri shrugs. 'Simon? I have no call from Simon . . .'

'Simon *Muldoney*,' Lizzy repeats, although of course it's no use. With instant, heart-sinking clarity, she can see what has happened here – or rather, not happened. For everyone's sake, she thinks, it is perhaps better that Simon isn't around right now. She doesn't think she'd do a very good job of concealing her feelings. Again, she forces herself to breathe, slowly and tremulously.

'I come to the pavilion, Miss Munro,' Monsieur Henri continues, still in that same doleful tone of voice. 'I email you three times . . .'

Lizzy's jaw tenses. She hadn't noticed any emails from him, but neither could she say for sure that there had been none. That reality – serving, as it does, to slightly loosen her grip on righteousness – somehow only adds to her anger.

'So, what? When I didn't get back to you right that second, you thought you'd just see how things went? What were you going to do, wait for us all to turn up on Monday? That's ridiculous!'

Whatever the man's response to that, she barely hears it, because she is so furious. And not just with him. Not just with Simon. With herself too. It would be fair to say that the last few days have been among her least responsive ever on the work front. She hadn't even felt too badly about that. She'd told herself that it was fine; that after nearly a decade of extremely responsive days (and, for that matter, nights) she could grant herself a little of the sort of slack other people took as though it was owed to them. But where has it left her – all that time thinking about premieres and yachts and the feeling of Ciaran Flynn's tongue on her ribcage?

Pictured on the internet in her underwear, essentially, and now caught with her pants down here too.

Chapter Thirty-Nine

Lizzy needs to get out of the pavilion – she just feels as though she can't breathe in there – and she walks through the town aimlessly, weaving her way through crowds of people, grateful for the quiet as she gets further and further away from the main drag. In front of one especially picturesque façade, she passes an influencer having her photograph taken. The young girl looks, by any standards, absolutely ridiculous as she pouts and poses in the middle of the street, two men with lighting equipment surrounding her. She's also making life very inconvenient for all other pedestrians. But no doubt, Lizzy thinks bitterly, the pictures will come out great.

She isn't sure how long she's been walking when Ciaran calls her. Enough time for her to have eaten a humongous ice cream cone and to have come up with absolutely no ideas as to how to resolve this latest mess with the ceilidh. Douglas Maclaine's trip to rehab, by comparison, seems like barely a wrinkle. No doubt he is off in some rural idyll by this point, reciting the Serenity Prayer, *and more power to him,* Lizzy thinks. Right about now, that sounds pretty damn good to her.

'How can they be allowed to just ditch you?' Ciaran asks, once she's explained the situation. He sounds the kind of incredulous and incensed that she's largely moved past by now. In terms of the stages of grief, she's done denial, anger and bargaining, and is now hovering somewhere around depression and/or acceptance.

'I guess they more or less *had* to ditch one of us,' she says. 'They're reimbursing what we paid, obviously. And . . . I don't know. We could potentially try and sue for breach of contract – I'd have to get Simon to actually *look* at the contract again – but I think they probably just know that realistically we aren't going to go to the expense of doing that. Plus, aside from anything else, presumably we'd have to do it here, in France. In French.'

'Absolute shower of *shites*,' Ciaran says emphatically, and that's another one of his favoured phrases, one she'd forgotten about. She laughs, but there's not a lot of energy to it. She's not, truth be told, really in the mood for conversation.

'And here I was worried you'd be all annoyed about that fucking thing in the *Daily Mail*,' he adds.

'Oh, man,' she replies, putting a little theatricality into her voice. 'Yeah. How my ass looks in a swimsuit is so far off my radar at this point.'

A white lie. But, undoubtedly it is the thing that *should* be true. And perhaps if she says it out loud, it will become so.

'Your ass looks great in a swimsuit,' he returns, his tone lowering roguishly. Lizzy can almost *see* the sweet and dirty expression on his face when he says it. But even as she gives a little laugh for his benefit, something hisses at her. *That's not true . . . you don't need to tell me things that aren't true.*

'What's your boss said anyway?' Ciaran continues, oblivious.

'I haven't told him yet. I mean, he's my boss, it's not like I can go off on him because he didn't do me a favour.'

'Well, no, but I mean surely he has to . . .'

She shakes her head, though she knows Ciaran can't see it. 'This was my responsibility,' she insists. The cold, hard truth of the matter. 'I just would like to have some sort of alternative to present to him, by the time I tell him.'

'What are you thinking?'

'Dunno. Every hotel, boat and private beach in town will be booked,' she says flatly. 'Maybe fucking twice.'

'Have you rung round already?'

'No, but they will be.'

There's a second's pause, during which Lizzy can tell he thinks she should make some calls, just in case.

'Well, look, I'm sure we can find *somewhere*,' he says instead, valiantly. 'Maybe not any of the usual places but there's bound to be somewhere.'

'I guess.'

'There'll definitely be somewhere,' he repeats easily. His confidence doesn't soothe her, though, in the way that it had last night when the news had come about Douglas. It actually kind of irritates her.

'I mean, I've never been in this exact situation, but I *do* know what it's like to have a location fall out at the last minute,' he continues. 'And the worst thing you can do is try and find something that's basically the same as what you had. 'Cause nothing will ever measure up, will it? But sometimes, something totally different works out great.'

'Yeah,' she says shortly. 'Maybe you're right. I actually can't really talk right now, though, I have to go . . . deal with this, somehow.'

'Okay, well I can—'

'I'm not asking you to fix this, Ciaran,' she cannot seem to stop herself from interrupting. 'Seriously. It's fine.'

'Oh,' he sounds a little taken aback. 'Okay.'

She feels her cheeks flush in contrition. But, still, there's a large part of her that just wants to be off the phone. 'I'll call you later, alright?' she says, a little more softly.

'Yep,' he says, his tone matching hers. 'Cool. Bye.'

And Lizzy hangs up with an exhale, feeling like an ungrateful, ungraceful failure of a person. A very sweaty one. Only now does she realise that she's been walking uphill for some time. Her hair is sticking to the back of her neck in the heat, and she's not entirely sure where she is. There isn't another soul around. Just up ahead, though, is a little streetside bistro, with a few plastic tables and chairs outside. Striding over towards it, she picks a spot in the shade, and eases into one of the seats. It'll likely be fifteen minutes, she knows, before any employee even considers paying her some attention, but on this occasion she doesn't mind at all. It's nice just to be sitting.

Special offer, reads the menu in front of her, *Aperol Spritz €12.* This does not strike Lizzy as much of a bargain, but nonetheless, there's an appeal. If she applied herself, she could probably be hammered within an hour.

However, what she knows by now about alcohol is that it is a mood-enhancer. That is to say, it enhances the mood you're already in. *More* of the mood she's already in seems like it would be a horrendous idea.

She fans herself with the menu, and lets her gaze pan the surroundings idly. Further up the incline, she can see parts of a castle peeking out over the trees. Or, a fort, maybe. She's not sure what the correct terminology would be.

Last year, it had been described to her as a castle, by a very charming guy she'd met at a party down at Long Beach. A bunch of people were heading up there, he'd said, to have a nightcap and see the view. Did she want to come?

Even at the time, Lizzy had been alive to the potential for a great story there – meeting a film composer in Cannes, and going where the night took her, and ending up at a castle to watch the sunrise. That sounded like the beginning of a romance film. The trouble was that it had also sounded, potentially, like the beginning of a horror film. She hadn't really known the composer, much less his friends. She'd passed.

Anyway.

Lizzy is going to go with the term 'castle' to describe this structure in the distance. She stares up at it now – the parts of it she can see. It's an austere, angular-looking thing, not a whole lot of ornamentation or romance about it.

But, it has a good view. She's heard that much, at least.

And all of a sudden, she finds herself pretty keen to check it out.

*

An hour later, give or take, Lizzy's sitting on the low stone wall that surrounds the castle, eating a tuna baguette that she'd picked up at the bistro. It turns out to have slices of boiled egg in it, which is unexpected but also not. Among the many facts she's learned about the French over the years is that they love adding a little surprise egg to things. She's wolfing down the last bite when Shauna approaches over the brow of the hill, Ciaran right behind her.

'Hey!' Shauna calls breathlessly, her face looking a little . . . dewier than usual.

'Hey,' Lizzy replies, jumping down from her spot. 'You guys met already, great!'

'Ah sure,' Ciaran says easily. 'We're old friends from that day I came to the Pavilion.'

Beside him, Shauna looks over at Lizzy, her whole face an expression of unabashed incredulity and glee. She can't quite restrain a little half-choked exclamation, and Lizzy's eyes slide over to meet Ciaran's, a quiet acknowledgement passing between the two of them – he's here, because she'd asked him to come, but this is not the time for them to talk.

Meanwhile, Shauna clears her throat, putting on her grown-up face. 'Um, so what are we doing here?' she asks. She looks the stone tower up and down, takes in the modest courtyard surrounding it. 'It's no Edinburgh Castle, is it?'

'No. Although I've never actually been into Edinburgh Castle.'

'Oh God, no, me neither,' Shauna says, as though the notion would never even occur to her. 'It's like twenty quid or something ridiculous now I think.'

'Yeah, well. What'd you notice when you walked up here?'

Shauna looks at her blankly. 'Apart from it being a bastard of an uphill climb?'

Lizzy snickers. 'No entrance fee,' she prompts. 'No barrier. And not a lot of people around, huh? Probably 'cause, yeah, like you said, it's kind of a hike to get here, when all the action is down there.' She looks out in the distance, the Palais and the marina and the Croisette visible below them, the Mediterranean sparkling all the way to the horizon. The view, undeniably, *is* pretty great.

'S'pose so, yeah,' Shauna says, seemingly for lack of anything else to add. Lizzy decides to get to the point.

'Tomorrow night, we're gonna have the ceilidh here,' she says, her heart beating slightly faster at the idea made real. Again, she looks over toward Ciaran. She can't tell, from his face, what he's thinking.

Beside them, Shauna just about explodes. 'What?!' she exclaims. 'What are you talking about?'

'We can't have it at Plage Raphael. It's a long story,' Lizzy replies, though what it is, really, is a short story that she doesn't especially want to re-tell.

'Fuck,' Shauna says quietly.

'Yeah.'

'So you thought . . . here?'

'There isn't anywhere else. Or no place I can come up with, at least. It's here or nowhere, I think.'

The other woman squints, surveys the place for a minute. 'I suppose it could work,' she says then. 'But, Lizzy, you're sure we don't need . . . I dunno. Some type of licence or permit or something?'

On the contrary, Lizzy thinks it's quite likely that they *do* need a licence or permit. Or, at the very least, an unspecified *something*. She also has zero faith in that being provided within the course of the next forty-eight hours. Such a prospect would seem fairly unlikely in most countries, and doubly so in this one, where it had once, after all, taken five weeks, a translated copy of her birth certificate, and ten minutes of open weeping at an administrator's desk in order to procure a replacement for her misplaced student card.

Given the day she's had, she's absolutely sure she would be capable of producing some tears in the *mairie*'s office, if she thought they alone would do the trick. But, she knows better. There would be money involved. Documentation. Processing time. Things, in short, that she does not have.

As she takes in the uneven surface of the ground, the stonemasonry that's got to be a good eight-hundred years old, there's certainly a part of Lizzy that can see a health and safety calamity waiting to happen. But then, if this place has lasted centuries, she has to figure it'll likely last another couple of days. Needs must. Had she come up here last year, with that composer and his friends, the chances are that she would simply have had a great, good or underwhelming time. She would probably have lived to tell the tale.

And probably, on Monday night, everyone else will too.

*

They walk the perimeter to survey the space, and once Shauna turns the corner, Lizzy and Ciaran hang back, their pace slowing. She looks over at him, with a chagrined half-smile.

'Sometimes you gotta think outside the box, right?'

He looks around him. 'This is . . . definitely that, yeah,' he agrees, but the chuckle that follows seems perfunctory somehow.

'I'm sorry about earlier,' she ventures. 'I was just . . . I don't know. I was stressed out.'

He nods, a little stiffly. 'Sorry if I was kinda . . . steam-roller-y.'

That's exactly what she'd felt he was, but she knows his intentions were good.

'No, you weren't,' she finds herself replying. Perhaps, though, she is not quite at her most convincing either, because even with apologies duly exchanged, awkward-ness seems to linger slightly between them.

'I've had quite a dramatic day myself,' he says then, and it feels like an offering of sorts – like he's ready to turn the page. Be back to how they were this morning in his big bed. That feels like a long time ago now.

'Oh yeah?' Lizzy replies, injecting some brightness into her own voice.

'Yeah. Maybe this is a really stupid idea, but I asked . . .' He hesitates, trailing off. 'Actually, you know what? We can talk about that later.'

She looks up at him curiously. 'You sure?'

'Completely. Let's talk about, I don't know, how fucking *awesome* this ceilidh is going to be,' he continues, a grin spreading across his face.

She laughs along, and yet even as he lifts his arm up and around her shoulders, starts chatting away easily, Lizzy can sense in herself a remaining reserve – a certain distance – that hadn't been there before. Is it that she's newly aware – all too aware – that she can't afford the type of distraction he presents?

Or is it that the humiliation of seeing those pictures on the internet – of reading herself characterised as some impossible amalgam of 'slutty and shameless' and 'fat and brave' – somehow keeps catapulting back into her brain?

Either way, she feels off for the whole remainder of the day.

And then in bed that night, Ciaran sleeping soundly beside her, Lizzy does a stupid, stupid thing. She reaches for her phone on her nightstand, and she looks at Twitter.

Chapter Forty

The next day, she does it again. This time, at a little bakery, while Ciaran's paying their bill after breakfast.

What she'd learned last night, scrolling in the darkness, was that people on the internet had identified her, in that photo Emma Lewis posted – the one from the Christmas market in Bordeaux. By morning, the latest development is that someone has now made a collage comprising of it, one of the better shots from the beach, and another photograph that Lizzy hadn't even been aware existed – one captured, apparently, in the brief seconds after she and Ciaran exited the limo at the premiere. The cumulative effect, Lizzy has to admit, is pretty sweet. The collage has been captioned:

Find someone who looks at you like this girl looks at Ciaran Flynn.

12.2k likes. Below the post, the top reply is:

Um, find someone who looks at you like Ciaran Flynn looks at this girl.

17.9k likes. The numbers go up even in the time that Lizzy stares at the screen. It's slightly hypnotising, watching them. People have said all sorts of other nice things and every comment is a fresh hit of dopamine. She can actually sense in herself the pull to reply to some of them – to fire off some word of thanks or self-deprecation.

Of course, she knows better than to do so. Even feeding the beast that doesn't seem so beastly is probably a terrible idea. And it's sure not all memes and validation and female solidarity out there.

It very much is not.

Some comments are positive on their face, but laced with an unnerving proprietary undertone – a false familiarity patched together out of whatever information is publicly known or decipherable about Ciaran, and by extension, about her.

Then there are the downright horrible comments. It had seemed, last night, as though she must surely have exhausted those, but no – a new day brings a brand-new set. This, apparently, is a renewable resource.

Sorry but I could fully build a house on that arse.

All y'all hating on Ciaran Flynn's new gf need to relax, he will clearly be done with this chick in a month tops.

Sigh some girls literally will do anything for attention, it's kind of pathetic. She's literally just hanging off him everywhere he goes at this point.

Average. Could be a 7 out of 10 IF she dropped a few pounds. Not the standard I look for in a female.

Ciaran Flynn can slide into my DMs any time, I guarantee this bitch won't do for him what I would lol, she looks like she has such a stick up her butt.

What is on her face though 'cause I'm 75% certain it isn't a nose.

I guess you have to respect it when a guy who definitely could be dating an actress or a supermodel, um . . . definitely isn't.

There's the vague urge to respond to some of those too – to clap back via numerous four-letter words and a degree of sass that Lizzy knows she could pull off, but doesn't really feel. Mostly what those comments – and the dozens of others like them – make her feel is just plain small. Ugly.

Ciaran returns, and she drops her phone, puts a smile on her face. The last thing she wants is to discuss any of this with him, to have to admit that she's hurt by it. The last thing she wants is for him to read those tweets. Because of course he'd see the meanness in them right away – the jealousy and the cruelty. But Lizzy knows that he might see something else too, just as she does herself. He might see the truth in them.

*

It distracts her all morning, though. She finds herself horribly conscious of her own flesh and bones in a way she hasn't been for years, the criticisms that used to play on a pretty frequent loop in her ears beginning to buzz again. Up at the castle, even as she is meant to be directing operations, she's on edge, a sense of dread working its way into the pit of her stomach and staying there. She's tired – four hours of sleep, she's convinced, might be worse than no sleep at all – and overwhelmed, and the constant sense of herself as an object for dissection does not help matters one bit.

By the afternoon, Ciaran is finishing up something of a dry run at the far end of the courtyard, attempting to verbally guide six of the temps from the Pavilion through the process of a simple ceilidh dance. It is, from what Lizzy can see, maybe not a *roaring* success, everyone involved totally unglued with laughter.

'Lizzy, don't look at this!' Ciaran shouts when he spots her, hardly able to even get the words out. 'It'll be better than this, I swear! Go away!'

She smiles in response, but she just can't seem to completely feel it. She hates that.

Backing away until she's around the corner, on the other side of the castle, she takes the opportunity to pull out her phone – at least the sixth time she's done so today. She squints at the screen in the sunlight, refreshing the search, and instantly, any remaining joy is utterly sucked out of her.

Another article online. New pictures, new comments.

Lizzy scans everything fast, like she is ten years old again, presented with a dinner that she doesn't like and keeps being given and must simply try to get down quickly.

The remarks on her appearance sting the most, of

course. But, even setting those aside, it's just the photographs themselves – the fact of them having been taken in the first place, the all too candid nature of them. Having to look at her body like this – reflected back to her the way that others see it – feels like a very hard thing. As though it is a quiet attack she needs to quietly withstand. She leans back against the castle wall, grateful for the support behind her, forcing herself to take some deep breaths.

Lizzy is completely sure that nobody will ever ask her what she learned from this trip to Cannes, but if they did, she knows what her answer would be. What she's learned is that so many of the stories she has told herself have not been quite true. About Ciaran, yes, but also about herself, about her own life as it was and as it is. This whole thing with the way she looks is a prime example. A fortnight ago, she would have been confident that she'd more or less put all that toxic, pointless stuff to bed. Practised her way out of body negativity, freed herself of the pressure to someday arrive, jubilant, at body positivity, and settled in nicely to body neutrality. The prospect of some brand-new neurosis flitting into her consciousness before she could strategise it back out – one rooted in some other aspect of her existence altogether . . . sure. Lizzy wouldn't have considered herself immune to that. But she'd really thought she was done with *this*.

Now, she thinks, it might not work that way. Maybe life doesn't give you a zillion different problems. Maybe it gives you a handful, and you have to solve them over and over.

Reaching some sort of acceptance of her own face and

body has been, for Lizzy, difficult enough when up against merely the normal vicissitudes of being a human woman. All of a sudden, with her eyes still fixed on a six-inch screen, despite the beautiful view in front of her, she can see very clearly that her chances in this new reality are not at all good.

'Hey, Lizzy?' she can hear Ciaran's voice calling, moments later. 'D'you have a sec? I just really *did* want to run this idea past you, you know I mentioned yester . . .'

He rounds the corner, trailing off when he sees her.

'You okay?' he asks.

Briefly, she considers attempting some sort of concealment, but she finds she doesn't have the energy for it. What she could do yesterday, and even this morning, she just can't seem to manage now. If that's weakness, then she's weak. She flashes her phone in Ciaran's direction.

'There's another article about us online. Pictures, from yesterday.'

He scowls. 'Seriously? Pictures of what?'

'Nothing really. Just us on the Croisette. Eating crepes.'

'Attractive,' he says dryly. 'Let's have a look?'

She hands over her phone, watches as he scrolls through.

'Well, *you* look cute,' he says, with a quick glance up at her before he turns back to the screen. He shakes his head a little, as if subconsciously.

'Still, though,' he murmurs. '*Fuckers.*'

He closes the gap between them, putting his arms around her.

'Sorry,' he mumbles, and she can tell he's aggravated. That's the difference, though. He's aggravated by this.

Frustrated – angry, even. He's not upset. Not the way that she is. He does not find this traumatising.

'You don't have to be sorry,' she replies, and she means it. She's seen no evidence of him even indirectly encouraging the attention, much less explicitly courting it. And there's a big part of her that is actually so pleased – so proud – that Ciaran has clearly landed right where he is meant to be, that he can carry even the heavier parts of his new life with relative ease.

'I don't think I . . . have the constitution for this, though,' she adds falteringly, once they've pulled apart, and he manages a little chuckle in response.

She swallows. 'I'm serious. I . . . really like you. So much. But if we keep doing . . . whatever this is that we're doing, there's only gonna be more articles. More photographs, more comments. And I just can see a situation where – eventually – that maybe, kind of, destroys me.'

Lizzy realises that's a pretty dramatic statement. She's tried to soften the edges of it a little in her delivery. But the stark reality *is* dramatic. It has no qualifiers, no punctuation. Any sustained version of what she has experienced in the past twenty-four hours or so seems like it would be extremely bad for her health and happiness. That's just the fact. Already, her cell phone seems to have become like a hip flask from which she snatches a furtive swig whenever she can. Already it is harder and harder to cling to the facts she's taught herself – *my appearance is average, average does not mean bad, some people find me attractive, there are so many more important things in life than looks; anyway, I look normal.*

Ciaran just studies her worriedly for a moment, and

she can almost see the second he decides to try and push past it – wind this conversation back a little.

'I get it,' he says earnestly, and she can tell that he really thinks that's true. 'But, look. A few more days and the festival will be done. I'm going to assume there's not a big paparazzi scene in Edinburgh. And I'm definitely not going to be suggesting we go to like, the Groucho Club or any of those places in London. Once we're out of the fishbowl, most of this shit will just . . . go away.'

It's not lost on Lizzy that this is the first time they've ever spoken about life after Cannes. She hadn't even been sure he wanted to have that conversation at all, and it definitely is not one she'd anticipated having right now. But maybe they couldn't have avoided it much longer, either.

'What if it doesn't, though?' she presses. 'What if, from here on out, you just get more famous? Creeps up on you, right?'

At this, Ciaran laughs, more than a little sourly. 'Ha! Not likely. My film just fucking bombed, or did you miss that? I'd say, if anything, I could be well on my way to being a lot less famous, Lizzy.'

Ouch. She's touched a sore spot there. And she knows he's been hurt by the critical response to *Wish You Were Here*. She knows he's tried to keep from her the true depth of his disappointment. She has empathy for that. But at the same time, right at this second, it's not exactly her primary focus. Nothing that has happened over the course of the festival appears to have dampened his fans' enthusiasm one single bit. And she hasn't seen any national newspapers drawing circles around parts of *his* body.

'I think you're gonna be *just fine*, Ciaran,' she finds herself biting back, more harshly than she'd intended.

After that, silence.

The longest seven seconds of silence that Lizzy can ever remember enduring.

'So, what are you saying?' he asks then. 'We leave here after the festival and just . . . that's it?'

His voice rises incredulously, and she feels put on the spot.

'I don't know! Okay? I don't know!'

Again, the silence settles between them, and she sighs, feeling the air go out of her. She gives a helpless little shrug.

'I mean, apart from anything else, we *do* live four hundred miles apart,' she says quietly. 'Yeah, I might be able to swing a few work trips to London here and there but . . . do you really think that could work?'

'Obviously *you* don't!'

'I ju—'

'It's fine!' he interrupts sharply. 'You're right!'

His eyes flash.

'You're right,' he repeats then, quieter this time. Something in him seems to have hardened, though. 'This is real life, isn't it? I'm not really Isaac, you're not really Claudia. We don't get to slap on a soundtrack and roll the credits here. We should probably just . . . I don't know. Call it quits, before we end up hating each other.'

He tosses the suggestion out like it's nothing, and Lizzy suddenly feels the threat of tears prickling behind her eyes. Her blood is pulsing urgently through her body, and she's not entirely sure of how they got here – and at such haste. In any event, it's where they've ended up.

'Yeah,' she replies, and she has enough pride left in her to try and match his delivery. 'I guess so.'

She watches as his mouth straightens into a line, the muscles in his jaw visibly tensing. 'Got it.'

He clears his throat, then, glancing down at his watch. 'I, uh . . . this is bad timing, but I actually have to go,' he says, and his voice sounds strange, strained. 'I have this work thing, and . . .'

Very evidently, this is bullshit – Ciaran hasn't done anything work related in days – but Lizzy gets the point. He wants to leave, and there doesn't, at this stage, seem to be anything to do but let him. How astounding, that after everything they've been through together, this is how it is ending.

'Sure,' she manages lightly. 'Of course. Go.'

And as she watches him turn around and stride away from her, no hint of hesitation, she presses the heels of her hands into her cheekbones. She gets to the tears so fast, it's like they never fell in the first place.

Almost.

Chapter Forty-One

The sun dips low in the sky as Ciaran finally hits motorway, and he puts his foot on the pedal. There's a sense of release in it – because of the speed, yes, but also because the process of getting here from the Hertz rental place has taken such a huge amount of concentration. Driving on the right-hand side is not easy, and so far, he's had traffic lights and round-abouts and jay-walkers to contend with. Now, it's just open road. All he really has to do is point the car.

He turns on the radio, and tries to stop Lizzy from sliding into the space that's been freed up inside his brain. It's easier said than done.

He's sure that plenty of people will ask him what he's learned from this whole experience, his first one of the Cannes Film Festival. Journalists seemed to love asking you what you'd learned from stuff. Ciaran doesn't have a clue what he'll say in response. The truth may require some cushioning.

What was it he had said to Lizzy, that day in the lobby, after they'd spoken to Alexandra? That it could be embarrassing, getting caught trying; having the best you could do still turn out to be a disappointment. He'd said that, back then, as though those days were over for him. Maybe, at some level, he'd thought that they *were*.

Quite clearly, however, they very much are not. And it turns out that Ciaran cares a lot more about what other people think of him than he'd believed he did. He has spent the last several days straight googling critics' reviews of his film like a madman. Thinking about his parents back home, about his father especially – so perplexed by him and then so proud of him and now . . . what? He'd tried to hide it from Lizzy as best he could – to avoid seeming neurotic or self-obsessed, to avoid being a downer. Maybe she'd seen it anyway, though. Or, maybe she hadn't seen it at all. Maybe he should have just told her straight up.

He doesn't know. The whole process has been humbling and terrifying, and . . . disorienting. Because the thing is that he still likes *Wish You Were Here*. He doesn't need to have it on a screen in order to see it – at this point, every frame is burned into his memory, and he's replayed the film over and over since the reviews were published. Part of him thinks it might be easier had he suddenly come to hate it, had he found a dozen things he wished he could change. But, in fact, he thinks he'd probably do it more or less the same again. He likes it. And Lizzy had liked it. Ciaran knows that for so many important people, for so many important reasons, that is nowhere near enough, but he is trying hard to make it enough for him. That's . . . a process.

What else?

He's probably learned, over the course of the last ten days, more about the film industry than he'd learned in the last ten years. Specifically, about his own position within the industry now.

A little over a decade ago, he'd come to London with zero connections and much more in student debt than in savings. It had been mind-boggling, the sheer extent of the poshness that had turned out to exist within the world of British filmmaking. People who could live with mummy and daddy, or in a flat funded by them, through endless unpaid internships. People who knew someone who'd been to Cambridge with someone who was now a superproducer. All that. All the time. Even to continue to speak fully in his own accent – to resist the urge to soften it, to round *out* his 'ou' sounds – had felt like it required of him a certain amount of fearlessness every single day.

In such a context – after so many years of cereal for dinner in shithole flats – Ciaran has never been inclined to view himself as being in any way among the privileged within this industry. But he is. He sees that now. A whole lot less privileged than so many other people, but privileged nonetheless.

He guesses he has Penny Ainsley to thank for that realisation, in a roundabout sort of way. At Figment Films, they just hadn't gotten a good vibe about her script. Wasn't that what Rupert had said? Something like that, at least. It wasn't a good fit, or it didn't grab them, or something.

And on the one hand, Ciaran thought that was a-okay. Surely everyone had the right, when presented with any creative endeavour, to just not *get* it, and no explanation required. He could say that, even with the natural sense of injustice that came with being un-*gotten* still all too fresh in his mind.

On the other hand, though.

On the other hand, when people like Rupert Brimble-Tollett were making the decisions, Ciaran has not been able to stop himself, over the last few days, wondering what exactly they were most likely to respond to. Spoiler: stories told by almost every other sort of person seemed to be bumped down the list, when a white-skinned straight man was around to do a similar-ish job. A famous man, at that.

Because, that's the other thing Ciaran has come to understand. He is famous. A whole lot less famous than so many other people, but famous nonetheless.

He hadn't ever thought of himself in those terms, before Cannes. He hadn't wanted Lizzy to be right, when she'd said it earlier – he'd felt somehow attacked by the suggestion. But the truth is that his life *is* different now, from how it used to be. And if he could turn back time, give it all up, he wouldn't.

He could probably stand to go with the flow a little less, though. To set stronger boundaries, to find better ways of harnessing the power he now appears to have. For too long, some part of him has stayed the fifth of six kids, the boy well used to the notion that in any given day there might be situations he did not create, dynamics at play he didn't fully understand, but that he nonetheless had to simply find a way to work with.

Over the past few years – the past year, especially – he'd sat in those big meeting rooms and he'd listened when people said *what can you do? That's the studio for you. That's the internet for you, that's the paparazzi for you.*

He'd accepted it when they'd told him *this is just how it works.*

Except, it wasn't really working for him anymore. And it sure hadn't worked for Lizzy. There was no denying the craziness that had, over the course of the festival, begun to spill over into her life. Maybe better, in the circumstances, for the two of them to cut bait. *Before we end up hating each other* – that's what he'd said to her. What he'd meant, of course, was *before you end up hating me.*

Friends, he tells himself now, is not so bad. An upgrade on the past twelve years, at least, and likely the more sustainable option. Of course, back there at the castle, neither of them had been rushing to exchange addresses. He certainly hadn't been his best self. But when they're each back home, and the dust has settled, Ciaran really hopes they can still manage to be friends.

As he makes a right-turn, though, watches the buildings begin to get bleaker and boxier, it does feel like very cold comfort. He hasn't had this feeling in a long time. Perhaps not since the day he knocked on the door at Rue Cabirol and found that Lizzy Munro was no longer in residence.

He'd walked over there – he remembers it as clearly as if it were yesterday – with the very worst hangover heebie-jeebies he'd ever experienced, and he hadn't even been sure what he planned to say to her, exactly. *I'm sorry* would certainly have featured. *I'm in love with you* might have featured. Both things would of course have depended on Lizzy, on how open she seemed to hearing them, on how likely she seemed to say them back.

In the end, of course, it was all moot. Caroline Gilhooly had ushered him inside the flat in such a way as to make him feel he might literally vomit, and even looking around at the space – at that same living room where they'd spent so many nights – Ciaran had been able to tell right away that something was different.

'Looks like Lizzy's thrown in the towel I'm afraid,' Caroline had said. 'There was just no talking to her.'

It was the first time Ciaran had ever felt heartbreak.

In the intervening years, work has been his number one priority, and by some considerable margin. He hasn't come close to loving any woman even half so much as he's loved his films. With Lizzy, though, it seems to be just . . . different. When he conjures her face in his mind – even now, after that horrible conversation earlier – the thing that he feels sits still inside him.

He knows that of everything he has learned in Cannes, the most precious facts are the ones he will never tell a soul. Her stories and secrets. The taste of her, the feeling of her limbs wrapped around him like vines, the ways to make her giggle, make her gasp.

Undeniably, it feels deeply, deeply grim, the prospect of the dirty dishwater of the Thames and no Lizzy.

He'll get used to it, though. Soon enough, he'll have no choice.

He pulls into a parking bay, slowing the car to a smooth stop. He's at the airport.

Chapter Forty-Two

The next day, as evening begins to fall, Lizzy surveys the castle. It has, by now, been just a little more than forty-eight hours since she first set foot up here. Some things, as it has turned out, have been relatively easy to handle. The caterers have agreed to re-route their little haggis appetizers, plus an array of other things that people may actually enjoy eating, to the new location. Word has been sent by email to all the invitees. Tables and chairs have been brought up from the Pavilion, and Brendan – dispensed to Nice to buy every fucking fairy light that Ikea was selling – has duly returned with a vast haul of decorative items, all to be placed with some attempt at artfulness tomorrow. Progress, in other words, has been made. Undeniably, though, the vibe at present is still a lot more 'backyard birthday party' than 'exclusive networking event.'

Shauna sidles up alongside Lizzy, wiping literal sweat from her brow. All afternoon, the place has been swarming with bodies, but they are the only two left up here now.

'I was kinda thinking,' she says. 'Aren't we going to need electricity? Like for mics and stuff?'

Lizzy winces, then exhales loudly. She deeply resents that Simon is not here, assisting with any of this. 'I trust your judgement implicitly, Lizzy,' he'd said calmly, when she'd explained the whole situation to him. 'Take Shauna, or Brendan or Jonathan. Any of the temps. Whoever you need. I'll keep things ticking over down at the Pavilion in the meantime. It's certainly not what we would have wanted, of course. And I'll be speaking to our lawyers about the breach of contract as soon as I get back to Edinburgh. But, for the moment, it seems we are where we are. If anyone can handle this, it's you.'

It had all been very nice. Supportive. And yet Lizzy couldn't help but feel a little like Simon had told her she was a great swimmer and then pushed her right off a cliff.

Today, more and more loudly, a voice has been whispering inside her that – contrary to her initial anxiety – this whole situation is not at all the product of her having been, somehow, so swept off her feet by romance that she'd dropped the ball professionally.

No. She'd actually met every single person she was supposed to during this festival, done absolutely everything she'd been asked to and plenty of things she hadn't. The odds were that she'd generated thousands of pounds' worth of business for the Scottish economy in the past eleven days, Ciaran or no Ciaran. And all the while, she'd kept Shauna on the right track, and coordinated with half a dozen local suppliers, managed a guest list of hundreds. . .

As to this entire debacle with Plage Raphael . . . well, she'd be inclined to place most of the blame squarely on them for a problem that was undeniably of their making, and that apparently predated the festival by several months. But, when all was said and done, *Simon* had signed the contract with the venue.

Simon had received, and missed, and failed even to really take responsibility for missing, an extremely comprehensive email from one of his direct reports entitled 'Please can you call Armand Henri at Plage Raphael asap.'

Simon had been nowhere to be seen any time Lizzy sought him out to discuss the matter, any time she might have had a legitimate expectation of his support.

She has, in short, come to think that perhaps this isn't really her mess. It certainly isn't *wholly* her mess. And yet here she is, cleaning it up.

'The bar, that's the other thing . . .' Shauna is continuing now, clicking her tongue against her teeth.

'Well, we were providing that anyway,' Lizzy says. 'Or, Edinburgh Gin are. And the temps from the Pavilion are going to serve. So, it's just a question of bringing all the stock here tomorrow instead of to Plage Raphael.'

'There's going to be beer and wine as well as the gin, though, right? And, like, tonic for the gin?'

Lizzy can see where Shauna is going with this. Refrigeration. The panic she's been doing her best to keep at bay threatens to rise within her again.

'Yeah,' she agrees faintly, and for another moment, the two women just stare hopelessly at their surroundings. Given the wheels that have already been set in motion, Lizzy no longer finds it hard to imagine that several hundred people, some of them fairly important, will be in this place in little more than twenty-four hours, attending a party. But she finds it increasingly pretty difficult to imagine that they'll be having an especially good time.

'Also, about the actual *ceilidh* element . . .' she begins then, and as she glances over at Shauna, she just can't quite seem to finish that sentence. For what feels like a long moment, her voice suspends in mid-air.

'. . . No Ciaran?' Shauna enquires then, quietly.

'No. No Ciaran.' Lizzy confirms, and she can hardly bear how final that sounds. She had thought, perhaps, that she might hear from him today. Even just to smooth things over, say goodbye properly. But, there'd been nothing.

For what feels like every waking hour since he left, people have been coming to her with a constant stream of questions, as though she has a master plan, some sort of grand aesthetic vision that extends to the placement of each solitary candlestick. She'd take that, she realises now, over *this*. Averting her eyes, she finds herself blinking rapidly, biting the inside of her mouth.

'We'll sort something else,' is all Shauna says in response. 'It'll be fine. Brendan did mention he knew how to call a ceilidh.'

Lizzy, as it happens, has had quite a bit of experience with the things Brendan said he could do. Results tended to be much thinner on the ground than the grand declarations that preceded them. Nonetheless, she just nods, finding herself almost unbearably grateful for her colleague's uncharacteristic tact. For her friendship.

'Does everybody know?' she ventures. 'About me and Ciaran?'

Shauna doesn't even hesitate. 'Oh yeah,' she says matter-of-factly. 'It's all anybody's talking about.'

And of course, once upon a time, that would have been Lizzy's nightmare – to have a whole bunch of people gossiping about her and Ciaran Flynn; about what on earth he saw in her, and what exactly they were up to together and – in the fullness of time – about what caused the break-up. As it is, she just barks out a laugh. She appreciates the honesty.

'You know what,' she says then, trying to get back to the matter at hand, new purpose in her voice. 'This is not our fault! The Hotel Raphael has gotta have a generator, right? A projector? Basically anything we need, it feels like they should be providing it.'

'Do you want me to go and ask?' Shauna offers. 'I could probably get down there before six.'

'Would you? That would be *amazing*,' Lizzy replies, and as the other woman takes off like a rocket, Lizzy can't help but smile. Monsieur Henri isn't going to know what's hit him. He could be about to become acquainted with the very particular tenor of a request made in the Glaswegian vernacular.

Left alone now, she looks around her, feeling a bit of a loss. There doesn't seem to be much more she can do here tonight. She does a loop of the space, straightening chairs that don't need to be straightened, and then gives it up, saying a silent prayer that Cannes won't experience any sort of overnight rainstorm.

Slowly, she begins to make her way down the hill from the castle, her feet heavy and throbbing underneath her. She misses Ciaran. Even if he, apparently, doesn't much miss her. She picks up a crepe for dinner and she misses him, and she passes by the Cinéma de la plage and she misses him. Eventually she flops down on the bed in her Airbnb. Missing him.

It's the most horrible, empty feeling. As if some sort of a light has gone off inside of her.

When she picks up her phone, there is an urge to check Twitter or the *Daily Mail* – it's frightening, really, how quickly a habit can begin to take root. She forces herself not to, though. What is the point in being without Ciaran, after all, if not to also begin the process of distancing herself from all that poison? She clicks some music on instead and lets it wrap itself around her, tries to re-set her perspective in the way that she usually does.

It kind of works.

Kind of.

It *is* helpful to count her blessings, which, of course, are numerous. It's true that she's survived, her family has survived, worse things than this.

But still, Lizzy finds she can't get anywhere close to feeling blasé about what happened yesterday – to convincing herself that this huge sense of loss is not a problem *at all*. The same way that she couldn't, honestly, quite get there when she was confronted with pictures of herself looking like a beached whale on the website of a national newspaper, or when strangers began mocking her on the internet, or when the event that had been the focus of the last six months of her professional life began to come apart at the seams.

The whole exercise, in short, has not been proving anywhere near as effective as usual. Not sweating the small stuff is a fine philosophy, but none of this feels like small stuff right now.

It's a funny thing, she thinks. It took so long – almost all of human history – for a woman to be allowed to say *I am happy and secure without a man. I am enough on my own.*

Lizzy happened to have been born inside the small handful of years that meant she'd always been able to say that easily. She's been saying it, and hearing it around her, for most of her life.

I would like to have a boyfriend, though. That's a hard one, for her.

Self-love does not always feel like an amazing alternative – an equivalent alternative – to romantic love.

How about that? It sucks so much that it seems to be true. Lizzy has been aware of it in various secret moments throughout her life, but never, ever more powerfully than right now, in this tiny room, without Ciaran.

Maybe when she gets back to Edinburgh, she thinks, she should start dating again. Make some effort, get on Hinge.

It seems, at once, like a good idea and an utterly terrible reality.

Aside from anything else, thus far in life, she doesn't seem to have picked up the knack for coupledom. She thinks back to that phone call with Ciaran the other day, when he'd tried to help her troubleshoot about the venue. Why had she been so snippy with him, she wonders now. Why had she been unable to quiet the voice in her head huffing *this is my problem, I'll deal with it*? She guesses maybe it is that she has worked hard to get good at being alone, to get capable of dealing with her own shit. Those skills haven't necessarily come naturally to her – and she does think they're skills. She's proud of them.

By contrast, she's not sure she is, or would be, much good at being stressed or sad or out of her depth, and having another person consistently there to witness and weigh in on all of it. That seems like maybe it requires its own sort of practice.

Maybe it is just as well, Lizzy tries to tell herself now, that she and Ciaran have gone their separate ways.

She wants to see him, though. That's the unfortunate, inconvenient part. It's been such a long day, and she really, really wants to see him.

The evening stretches out endlessly ahead of her, and it strikes her – suddenly and almost certainly very ill-advisedly – that there's one way she *could* see him. Or, kind of.

All the major films, in the days after their premiere, have several more screenings in Cannes. In smaller rooms around town, at odd hours of the day or night, they might play a dozen more times. And so it is that Lizzy's feet seem to walk themselves down the Croisette, into the Palais, and all the way up to the fifth floor. She's just in time for the 7.30 showing.

Of course, by now, most of those interested in seeing *Wish You Were Here* have already had a chance to see it. So, the audience is sparse – just a few other people dotted around – and Lizzy can only hope that none of them are active on Twitter. She slinks into a seat, glad of the darkness, and who knows? Maybe it's because she's alone. Maybe it's because she's already had an emotional few days, because she already feels a little raw and defenceless. But for whatever reason, as the first scene turns to the second turns to the tenth, the whole thing just hits her in a way it hasn't before. Not really.

That's her life up there.

A version of it, at least.

She sees it so, so clearly now, emotion rising in her like a tide, and by the time the credits roll, she's barely holding it together. She has to run to the bathroom, huge, pathetic sobs coming out in splutters as soon as she has the cubicle door closed. What a thing, Lizzy thinks, for Ciaran to have put two of them on screen like that forever.

What a thing, for him to have given them a happy ending.

Chapter Forty-Three

The following day goes by in a blur of activity. Monsieur Henri having proved extremely compliant, Plage Raphael sends up a variety of requested items, and Shauna mans the arrivals like a military general. For her part, Lizzy spends a lot of time on her hands and knees trying to establish how far extension cords will stretch, and a lot of time looking over her shoulder, as though the *gendarmerie* will be along to shut the whole enterprise down any minute.

She rushes home at five o'clock to change, and when she gets back to the castle by seven, it's a shock to see it with fresh eyes – to see how everything has sort of come together, even if she does say so herself. Some small miracle has been made out of heavy lifting and hoping for the best.

There are twinkling lights everywhere, and battery-operated candles, high-top tables and a little makeshift stage. The bar is stocked, the projector cued, and from somewhere, a large saltire flag has been procured and draped from the castle wall itself. The whole effect is nothing like as slick as Plage Raphael would have been – there's no getting away from that. There's something about the slightly home-made quality of things that Lizzy finds she kind of likes, though. And, maybe it's only right that an event celebrating Scotland should have a brand of enchantment that's a little more medieval than beachy.

Scanning the surroundings, she guesses there's a part of her that's able to be excited about all of this, able to be proud of it. She's definitely proud of Shauna and the rest of the staff. Overwhelmingly, though, what she wants now is mostly just for the night to pass, and for it to be tomorrow, and for her to be able to get on a plane.

Ceilidh Minogue is playing something rousing in the background as the guests arrive in clusters, and caterers begin to circulate with trays of canapés. For an hour or so, Lizzy meets and greets, and conducts the sort of silent, smiling troubleshooting that is familiar to all hosts. Then, eventually, it's time for the show to really get on the road. In a corner, Simon is studying cue cards that, presumably, contain the text of his welcome speech, and Lizzy's halfway over to him when she stops in her tracks. An actual gasp escapes her lips.

How many times would this make it now? That she has, during the course of these past twelve days, found herself just plain *astonished*? She's truly lost count. The source, on this occasion, is no different than it's been on most others. Over on the far side of the castle, looking a little winded from the walk up here, there he is. Ciaran.

His eyes are darting around searching for something – searching for her, it seems like, because once he spots her, his expression stills. He raises his hand in a silent wave, a sheepish hint of a smile on his face.

Lizzy finds herself returning the gesture, feeling momentarily frozen in place. She just can't seem to make herself move, and even if she could, she wouldn't have time to get to him – up beside the band, Simon is tapping into a microphone now. It is, Lizzy notes with some considerable relief, a working microphone. After that, though, she barely hears a word.

A hush descends as he trundles through the usual pleasantries, outlines the evening's basic shape. It goes on and on, until – *what's happening?* – Lizzy seems all of a sudden to be watching Ciaran stride up onto the stage. He's accepting the handshake Simon offers, and people are applauding enthusiastically. There must have been an introduction, but somehow it passed her by.

'Hi all,' Ciaran says, once he has the mic. 'So, as you might have noticed, not only am I not Douglas Maclaine, I'm also not even Scottish. But, look, close enough, right? In the Celtic family at least. On a good clear day, from the Inishowen Peninsula in Donegal, where I grew up, we could actually *see* Scotland, and I always knew my people were out there.'

The crowd chuckles, and Ciaran grins too, like there's some relief in having the first bit over, in discovering an audience that is with and not against him.

'Tonight, I want to encourage all of you to either embrace or invent some Scottish heritage,' he continues. 'Everybody up, come on! First dance is Strip the Willow and it's extremely easy! No stripping required but if you have high heels, this might be the time to ditch them, fellas.'

A bunch of people – almost all of them plants, friends whom Lizzy has prevailed upon in advance to promise that they would definitely take part – shuffle to the front, and as it's happening, Ciaran keeps chatting, all ease now, having apparently hit his stride.

'I'm actually here because of Lizzy Munro, who I know many of you know,' he says, and from her spot in the midst of the crowd, Lizzy feels her heartbeat quickening.

'Lizzy and I go way back, and I've been reliably informed that there might be some chatter on the inter-webs about whether she was the inspiration for a character in my most recent film.'

He pauses, a titter of laughter audible, and Lizzy begins to sense an array of nearby eyeballs on her. She feels her cheeks warming, feels something rise up and catch in her throat a little. How can this be happening? It seems so unreal, the sight of him up there.

'What I can tell you, here and now, exclusively, is that I wouldn't ever have made *anything* had it not been for Lizzy,' Ciaran continues, and as he says it, his eyes land on hers at last.

'I'd say a lot of us here tonight know what it's like to tell someone a crazy idea and have them just . . . *not laugh* at you. That's an incredible gift. My guess is that Lizzy – or one of the other amazing people at the Scottish Film Board – has given that to a lot of us. So, thanks, folks,' he says, and he raises his glass in an expansive, generalised sort of way, the crowd beginning to clap heartily. His eyes flicker back to her, though, and stay there. He smiles at her, a little shyly, such that Lizzy can be in no real doubt: absolutely none of this, for Ciaran, is actually about the Scottish Film Board. Certainly, in this moment, she herself could not possibly care less about the Scottish Film Board. It's all him – his accent and his perfect arms in that shirt and the warmth she feels every time he looks at her.

The last bit is important. It's the polar opposite, she suddenly realises, of the way she'd felt seeing those photographs of herself on the beach, or reading those comments online. That vicious stab of being not enough has never come from him. Under his gaze, his touch, she has only ever felt like *more than* enough.

Then, the last stragglers getting into position, Ciaran finally looks away from her.

'Alright! Let's get cracking!' he declares, shifting seamlessly into host mode once again.

Taking their cue, the band kicks in, and Lizzy clears her throat. She shakes her head quickly as though to try and snap herself out of a daze. There's movement all around her and she, too, needs to move. Time to circulate.

And, as it turns out, that's so much more fun than she'd thought it would be tonight. The music is lively and the breeze is balmy, and by this time tomorrow, most people – Lizzy included – will be a million miles away from all of this, free bars and sunset views a thing of the past for another year. Somehow, that collective knowledge makes for a nice vibe.

So many familiar faces are here – people she's worked with over the years, people she's never met but who are giants of the industry. There are her Oscar nominees! And James McAvoy! Lots of those who had RSVP'd but who she imagined might, when it came to it, get a better offer, have actually shown up. Time seems to fly as she weaves her way around the courtyard, with no need for any of her old networking tricks. It's just catch-ups and clinking glasses and browbeating everyone – in the nicest possible way – to go and join the dancing. Tonight, Lizzy realises, she feels every single bit as Scottish as she does American. Maybe more so.

'Lizzy! Honey! Everything looks fantastic,' comes a voice from behind her at some stage, and she turns around, her cheeks rosy with pleasure.

On a whim, she'd extended an invitation to Amy Solomon, and a bunch of others from the studio whom she'd met at Ciaran's premiere. Again, she's touched to see how many of them have come. It'll be a major gold star for her with Simon, too, having lured some more folks with real money. She wonders, though, if that really matters to her anymore. She has no doubt that Simon Muldoney would take every single ounce of energy she'd ever be willing to give him, for as long as she'd be willing to give it. However, perhaps even before this festival, and certainly during the course of it, he might have ceased to be a person she cares much about impressing.

Lizzy takes Amy's compliment, looking around her with a smile. 'Thanks, yeah. It all kind of came together in the end.'

'With a little help from our favourite Irishman, huh?'

From a distance, Lizzy can see Ciaran. He's in great spirits, or giving that appearance at least, as he laughingly calls out steps. He strides around the dance floor making jokes and, here and there, physically wrangling people back into position.

Things look to be going, overall, a lot better than Lizzy might have anticipated. Maybe it's the YouTube studying, or the memories from childhood, or maybe directing has helped develop in Ciaran some transferable skills when it comes to orchestrating the movements of large groups of people. Undoubtedly, there is still an element of chaos. But, that's okay. Firstly, there is, in Lizzy's view, almost *supposed* to be an element of chaos to a ceilidh. And secondly, the fact of the matter is that Ciaran is charming and good-looking and famous, which means that people don't really mind if he is sort of bad at something. They find it endearing.

She finds it endearing. For a second, she just watches him – watches him doing a ridiculous thing because she'd asked him to – and she feels such a rush of affection for him that she doesn't know what to call it. Or, maybe she does.

'Any change in status there?' Amy presses.

For a nanosecond, Lizzy hesitates. 'Nope,' she replies then, striving to infuse some sense of casualness, of chirpiness, into that one syllable.

Amy cocks her head. 'I gotta say, I'm surprised,' she replies. She reaches for another glass of rosé from a passing waiter, her expression brightening. 'So, you thought any more about coming out to La La Land?'

Lizzy exhales a chuckle. 'You don't give up, do you?'

'Hey,' Amy shrugs extravagantly. 'Far be it from me to be pushy. You do you, girl.'

Lizzy takes a second. For the first time, she lets herself really, truly consider the prospect of trying it for a year. Los Angeles. She glances around her with a little wince, because this does seem like a weird conversation to be having here, at an event hosted by her current employer.

'Look, Amy, I wouldn't say I'm overburdened with humility, okay? I think I have a lot of good qualities. I really do. But I'm not brave. I think going to Bordeaux might actually have been the only brave thing I've ever done.'

Even that, she thinks to herself, had been more a question of running from rather than toward something.

'And are you sorry you did it?'

Lizzy certainly *had* been sorry, at one point. During that long summer of schlepping between her parents' flats, watching *Deal or No Deal* and feeling constantly on the verge – just one photograph, one innocent question, one fucking *film* away from tears – she'd wished she'd never set foot in Bordeaux. But that had passed. Even before this festival, before she'd reunited with Ciaran, she ultimately had come to be grateful for the experience, despite the lows that matched the highs.

'No,' she replies. 'But I was twenty then. There's a certain latitude, isn't there? You take the good and the bad and the ugly, and all of it's at least cocktail party fodder. I think it's a little different in your thirties. The time you get given to make bad choices, I mostly pretty much wasted making good choices.'

Amy just looks at her, as though that's the stupidest thing she's ever heard.

'It's a risk, that's all I'm saying,' Lizzy protests. 'I don't even know what I'd want to do, exactly. I mean, let's say I did get a job in LA – which I might not even. There's just a million ways that could end up falling apart.'

'Well, sure! What do you think a risk is, girl? People use that word too much, if you ask me. For, like, bullshit pretend stuff that basically isn't going to go wrong. Or if it does go wrong, it doesn't much matter. That's not a risk. It's not really a risk unless you can *really* fail.'

Lizzy says nothing, just purses her lips, absorbs that for a moment.

For her part, Amy squints in the way that's become familiar, in the way that doesn't even slightly conceal her efforts to size up a situation. 'Let me ask you this, Lizzy,' she says then. 'What do you think Claudia would do?'

Lizzy thinks back to watching *Wish You Were Here* last night, to the sight of herself through Ciaran's eyes, and it's an easy answer.

'She would go.'

Chapter Forty-Four

By the time the ceilidh portion of the evening comes to an end, Lizzy hasn't managed to participate in a single dance. Maybe that's just how it goes. Her mom, forty years and one divorce later, still likes to mention, at any opportunity, the fact that she did not even get a slice of her own wedding cake.

As well as a singer, Ceilidh Minogue has live percussion, a finger-style guitarist, and an electric violinist. Together they're creating a sort of Celtic-pop fusion now, segueing out of traditional music and into classic crowd-pleasers. Over by the bar, the Scottish Culture Minister looks set to be sloshed before she even makes her speech.

Lizzy casts her eyes around for Ciaran. She can't deny that a part of her has been counting the seconds until he was done, until she could get to talk to him. When she can't immediately spot him, disappointment lodges in the pit of her stomach. Had he really made that swift an exit? Taken off just as fast as he could once his duties were done?

But, no. She sees him then. He's lingering at one of the high tables on the far side of the castle, having a well-deserved beer and deep in conversation with a dark-haired woman. She's maybe thirty-five, her hands moving animatedly as she talks, and there's something vaguely familiar-looking about her. Lizzy studies her for a minute. She's not jealous, she tells herself staunchly, she's merely . . . curious.

Before she is even conscious of it, she's making her way over towards them, as though propelled by some force outside of herself. Whatever it is doesn't quite take her all the way there, though. A few feet away from the pair, she finds herself holding back, lingering a little awkwardly. Ciaran turns his head, sensing, as people do, the presence of a hoverer and he raises his hand briefly in greeting.

She closes the rest of the distance between them. 'You came,' she says softly.

He gives her a little smile. 'Course I did.'

'I guess I just . . .' Lizzy pauses, extremely aware that they are not alone. 'I wasn't sure you'd be up for it anymore.'

'No, Jesus, I wouldn't back out. After the way you came through for me this festival?'

It's a perfectly nice thing to say, but somehow the inference – that his presence here is a matter of basic decency, of one good turn deserving another – makes Lizzy feel a little deflated. She manages a weak smile.

'I'm Lizzy,' she says then, extending her hand to his companion. 'I'm with the Scottish Film Board.'

'Of course!' the woman replies, in a broad Yorkshire accent. 'It's so lovely to meet you! Ciaran's told me all about you. I feel a bit of a gatecrasher at the party if I'm honest, I hope it's okay that I'm here.'

'I invited her,' Ciaran interjects. 'Lizzy, this is Penny Ainsley.'

Of all the names Lizzy might have been anticipating, that one would have been at the very bottom of her list.

'Oh!' she blurts out. She's sure she looks like a gold-fish. 'Penny. Great! Hi!'

Her eyes flicker back and forth from Penny to Ciaran a few times, perhaps not especially subtly, because Ciaran chuckles.

'Surprise,' he says bashfully. Penny, when Lizzy glances back over toward her, is the picture of placidity. Nothing about the situation adds up.

'Alright I'm just gonna ask: what's going on here?'

'I kept trying to tell you, but everything was just so chaotic with the ceilidh and all,' Ciaran says. 'So, you know how I was saying I'm kind of going through a dry spell, in terms of writing ideas?'

Lizzy nods.

'Well, I suppose I just got to thinking. I knew some-body – or knew *of* somebody, at least – who probably did have some ideas.'

Penny smiles. 'Guilty, yeah. I have, like, three scripts that I've just been desperately trying to get going for the past ten years. Ciaran's suggested maybe we could, sort of, team up, as it were. It's all been a bit of a whirlwind, actually. He asked to read my other work and the next thing I knew, he was picking me up at the airport!'

In Lizzy's brain, something slots into place. His swift departure on Saturday, pleading work obligations. Maybe he'd been telling the truth there, after all.

'Turns out we have pretty similar interests, in terms of themes,' Ciaran adds wryly. 'I thought maybe I could produce. Or exec produce, even. Just . . . I dunno. Use whatever clout I might have left to help make something happen. Penny would direct, obviously. We had a tonne of meetings today and yesterday, just to gauge interest, and hopefully we'll squeeze in another few tomorrow. Some people aren't flying out 'til night-time.'

'Wow,' Lizzy says. It's a lot to take in. And perhaps she's a less generous person than Ciaran – in fact, almost certainly she is – but suffice to say that her loyalties have shifted considerably in the past week or so. To the extent that she's finding it tricky to suddenly *un-shift* them. Some part of her looks at Penny now and can only see the woman who gave a borderline vicious interview to the press and who damn near ruined Ciaran's festival, to say nothing of his reputation in general.

'I guess I . . . didn't think you were exactly in the Ciaran Flynn fan club, Penny,' she ventures. She can think of no more polite way to put it.

The other woman's cheeks pinken a little. 'Guilty again, I suppose.'

'I think that whole thing was just a misunderstanding,' Ciaran jumps in. 'You know how those can happen,' he adds slyly.

Lizzy looks up at him, unblinking.

'I've heard,' she drawls, and his lips twitch a little in what might be amusement.

'I don't think it helped that Penny and I had never actually spoken,' he continues. 'The whole thing was lawyers and execs and then journalists. So, I ended up getting in touch a couple of days ago and we had a chat.

I can see how, all things considered, Penny could've thought there was something fishy going on. Who knows, maybe there *was*, somewhere along the line. I decided to just go ahead and send her a screener of *Wish You Were Here* – I don't think the lawyers wanted me to do that. In fact, I know they didn't. But it's like, how are we even going to have a conversation about this if we don't both have the same information?'

'And what'd you think?' Lizzy asks, turning to the other woman. The million-dollar question. She surprises herself, actually, with the nervousness that flutters up inside her when she asks it.

'I thought it was a really, really lovely film,' Penny replies. 'And there are similarities, for sure, but . . . it's not my film.'

At this, Lizzy looks over at Ciaran. She can tell, by the expression on his face, that it means something to him, hearing her say that. She thinks back to the *Variety* article, to the way it had made this woman seem so combative. She doesn't seem to be at all like that in real life. Even the photograph of her that had been used, gorgeous and all as it was, didn't quite match the reality. Lizzy finds she likes the real version better.

'I was just *so* sure, before . . . and I felt *so* powerless, and—'

'You don't have to explain,' Lizzy interrupts, because suddenly she realises that's true. She can only assume Penny has confided all the details to Ciaran already. Whatever was good enough for him is good enough for her.

'I think it's great you guys worked things out,' she continues, new warmth in her voice. 'I'm *so* happy you're here. Really. Have you gotten anything to eat? Or a drink? I know the bar doesn't look like much, but it's well stocked.'

Penny breathes out, visibly relaxing in front of Lizzy's eyes. 'I'll maybe go and get something now,' she says. 'Do either of you want anything?'

Lizzy and Ciaran each shake their heads, and Penny scans the surroundings for a moment, as if taking it all in. 'This place is just, like, *amazing*, isn't it?' she murmurs.

She turns to leave, and as she does, Lizzy looks over at Ciaran, feeling her breath hitch in her chest.

Alone at last.

It's all she's wanted, and yet she finds she hardly knows what to say to him.

Only the narrowest strip of orange is left in the sky now, the sun all but set, the mountains and the sea inky black in the distance. All around them there is light and life, but between the two of them, in their little bubble, it's quiet. It is very abundantly clear to Lizzy, in this moment, that she does not want to try and meet some random man on Hinge. Why on earth would she want such a thing?

'You are fucking incredible,' she tells him then, dead seriously. 'Do you even realise that?'

She doesn't think that he does. As she says it, Ciaran just exhales a laugh, casting a rueful hand across his jaw.

'I shouldn't have just left you here, the other day. That wasn't so incredible, was it? I did have to go and pick up Penny, and we've done literally back-to-back meetings since then, but mostly I was just . . . well. Gutted, basically.'

It's more honesty, faster, than Lizzy had been expecting, and she manages a tiny nod of agreement.

Not everything about the time she'd spent with Ciaran in Cannes had been easy. That was for damn sure. But the time she's spent without him has turned out to be so much harder.

'The thing is, I . . . I think maybe we did it again,' she says disjointedly, squinting over at him.

'What do you mean?'

'I think, the other day – maybe even before that – we just didn't exactly communicate, or . . . I don't know, I'm not good at this.'

She shifts her gaze, fidgeting with her hands a little, and she's reminded anew: *life doesn't give you a zillion different problems*. If this is one she has to solve over and over, she'd like it not to take her another twelve years. She forces her eyes back up to meet his.

'You're all I can think about, though, all the time – *again* – and I think I could look my whole life and never find anybody like you, Ciaran.'

Her heart is pounding as she says it, and she takes a deep breath in and out when she's done, giving him a helpless sort of shrug. That's all she has.

And, in the end, that's all it takes before his lips are on hers. It's a fierce sort of kiss, his hand pinned to the back of her head, and as heat flares between them, Lizzy moans a little into his mouth in a way she probably never imagined she'd do in the vicinity of so many people who need to respect her as a professional. She can't help it, though. She clutches at whatever parts of him she can reach and the feeling, more than anything, is one of sheer relief. Like the restoration of something right.

'Everything you said before, though . . .' Ciaran says, when they finally break apart, both a little breathless.

And of course, it doesn't take much, to recall the scrutiny that proximity to him appears to bring – the invasion of that, the damage it can do. Concurrently, the strange lure of the positive attention – the damage *it* might do. All of those are still very real, very frightening things, and Lizzy still does not think she's naturally all that well-equipped to deal with them. There's potential to get hurt and get overwhelmed and get tangled up in her own brain, and – maybe most scarily – to have to admit all of it to Ciaran out loud.

He still lives far away. He still has an inherently unstable job, involving vast emotional and practical fluctuations. He also could probably be annoying, in ways that were not necessarily apparent in the course of twelve days in Cannes. She couldn't, with the information available to her at present, absolutely rule out the prospect that he used the word 'doggo'.

And yet.

Lizzy thinks of how he'd shown up and somehow made this, a night she just wanted to end, seem suddenly alive with possibility. As though the light inside her was turned back on. She thinks of how smart he is and how funny and how unique, and how she just fucking loves the sight of his face.

'Yeah, well,' she says then. 'You get stuff and you give stuff away, right?'

He smiles, like he's surprised she remembers that.

'I know what I'd be getting,' she says quietly, and then she cocks an eyebrow. 'You sure you know what *you'd* be getting?'

She certainly doesn't think that she's a perfect picnic of a person – of a partner – by any means. She can well imagine the balancing exercise Ciaran might have to conduct in his mind too. He doesn't hesitate, though, doesn't fire back a joke as she'd been half expecting. He just dips his head, pulling her into him.

'I want everything,' he whispers, his breath warm against her ear, and then he's kissing her again, more softly this time, just lips on lips, gentle but sure. Lizzy shivers. This seems to have become another item on her list of things in the universe that are so much better than good. That are magical. Holy.

'And, look, the geography of it all, we definitely can work around,' he murmurs, some unknown amount of time later, pulling back from her a little. 'I could move up to Edinburgh, even. I hear they have great support for filmmakers in Scotland. Really go above and beyond, like.'

Lizzy's expression freezes. 'Yeah. About that,' she says slowly. 'How do you feel about LA?'

Epilogue

SIX MONTHS LATER

The first two months in LA have been much like the first two months in Bordeaux. Lizzy has loved it and thought she might never leave, and she has hated it and felt she'd likely need to leave immediately. *C'est la vie*. She's taking the rough with the smooth, or trying to.

Even in November, the weather is warm here, and Lizzy takes her coffee out to the rocking chair, feeling the seconds tick by at a snail's pace. This place – a little one-bedroom bungalow in Santa Monica – has an oasis of a garden, all sorts of colourful plants and trees that have been lovingly tended for years and that serve to entirely block the nearby road from view.

Lizzy appreciates the outside space – had produced the required rapture when the owner handed over the keys – but in truth, it's not the main attraction for her. She hasn't lived in an actual *house* since she left California as a teenager. For the first time in nearly twenty years, she doesn't have neighbours upstairs or downstairs or on either side of her. For the first time in nearly twenty years, she gets to sing at the top of her lungs, whenever she pleases. She has bought herself a keyboard on Craigslist.

Again, she looks at her watch. These days, even for something like the time, she tries to avoid her phone as much as possible – it's just too easy for a quick, innocuous task to morph into a lengthy, pernicious one. She hadn't been on Twitter in a long time now; never searches her own name or Ciaran's on the internet. Those just seem like smart strategies.

They're not a cure-all, though. Because, in fact – much as some part of Lizzy had perhaps suspected all along would be the case – so many of the little knots and knocks of the last six months have not had a whole lot to do with other people at all. Instead, they have simply been about the messy, imperfect process of trying to interweave two lives – about her and Ciaran having to throw their collective weirdness and vulnerability into the light and look at it all together.

She sips her coffee, and for another ten minutes, she just sits there in the afternoon sun, listening to the cicadas. It could have been very relaxing, were the whole experience not accompanied by the constant sense that she could just about burst out of her skin, until finally – finally – she sees him. Walking up the path towards her, looking better than any human being has the right to after twelve hours on a plane. Or perhaps it's in the eye of the beholder. That, Lizzy is finally coming to understand, really does account for a hell of a lot. They should teach that in schools or something.

He has a huge suitcase along with him, the sign that he's here to stay for a while, and she's up before she knows it, striding towards him, launching herself into his arms.

'You're here!' she cries, and he wraps her up in a fierce hug, squeezing her close to him. His mouth finds hers, and right away he's kissing her deeply – desperately – like he couldn't have waited another second to do it.

'I'm here,' he murmurs once they've parted, the words exhaled into the juncture of her neck and shoulder. He seems to breathe her in for a moment and when he pulls back to look at her properly, they're both grinning.

'This place is class,' he says then, his eyes darting around. 'I couldn't believe when the Uber stopped outside. You can practically see the sea from here!'

'Practically' being the operative word – but, it's no more than ten minutes' walk away. She'd thought he'd like that.

'The *ocean*,' she corrects. 'You're in *America* now, baby.'

He smirks. 'Jesus. Next thing, you'll be claiming this "ocean" water's warmer than about five degrees.'

She puts on a wince. 'See, again, I'm gonna need that in Fahrenheit.'

Ciaran laughs. 'I fucking missed you, Elizabeth,' he says emphatically.

For a second, she just looks at him, delight prickling at every inch of her skin.

'I fucking missed you too,' she replies, and as they walk towards the house, he puts his free arm around her shoulders, pulling her into him.

'How was the flight?' she asks.

'Grand, yeah. So many paps at the airport.'

Lizzy winces again, in all sincerity this time. 'Really?'

'Yeah. Seemingly there was, like, this YouTuber girl on the same plane, so they were all going mental. Plus, also – seriously – Tom Hanks.'

He squints over at her, all self-deprecation.

''Member in Cannes when we thought I was kinda famous? Turns out I'm pretty far down the totem pole here.'

Lizzy just laughs, and as soon as they're through the front door, his suitcase dragged in with a little clunk, she turns, looping her arms around Ciaran's neck.

'This might actually be the perfect town for us,' he continues, dipping his head to kiss her again. Their mouths move slow and sweet against one another's this time, and from the back of her throat, a hum of contentment escapes Lizzy.

Nine weeks have passed since she and Ciaran last saw each other, in London, and it's been good, in certain ways. She doesn't think a little bit of space, a little bit of a chance to miss one another, is necessarily any bad thing in a relationship, and she's needed to focus on work, on setting up the basic architecture of her own life here.

But nine weeks, she realises now, is really *too* long. She doesn't want to do nine weeks again if they can help it. She pulls back a little, nipping playfully at his bottom lip as she does.

'So I was thinking I might come with you tomorrow, after all,' she says.

Pleasure spreads across his features. 'Oh really? That would be great! I mean, you definitely don't have to, though.'

'No, I know. And I wouldn't do the carpet, obviously.' Offering herself up, quite literally on parade for the judgement of strangers, feels like another of the things that Lizzy would be wise to permanently avoid.

'But the actual ceremony,' she continues. 'Seemingly a tonne of people from Netflix are going too, so I thought maybe it would be fun. You know, bonding opportunity or whatever. And I could introduce you to everybody.'

'Amazing, yeah.'

'*Plus,*' she says, her voice lowering as she leans in toward him again, 'I want to see you win.'

Wish You Were Here has been nominated for three People's Choice Awards, among various other accolades. It has, so far, grossed nearly two hundred million dollars at the box office worldwide.

Not bad, Lizzy thinks, for a mere romantic comedy, for the film once labelled lightweight at Cannes.

To be light, as it turns out, is not necessarily to be flimsy.

Acknowledgements

At the outset, and in sincere solidarity, I suppose I'll make it easy for any prospective authors who have flicked to the acknowledgements solely in order to find out who my agent is. My agent is Sheila Crowley at Curtis Brown, ably assisted by Sabhbh Curran. I'm so grateful to both Sheila and Sabhbh for their wise counsel, and for their enthusiasm in championing my work.

I am hugely indebted, also, to Lynne Drew and Lucy Stewart, whose care and expertise has added so much to this novel. I feel incredibly lucky to be in such brilliant hands with them and the whole team at HarperFiction.

Thank you to everyone at Curtis Brown Creative – Jennifer Kerslake, Charlotte Mendelson, and all my classmates were a big support in the initial stages of drafting, and were so generous with their time. Special thanks to my early readers Susie Gordon, Katie Reed and Janelle Morris for their thoughtful feedback.

Thank you to any teachers who ever told me I was a good writer – they might not even have meant it that much, but I totally bought it. Sylvia Lester, Leona Peace and Nora Dobbins stand out in my memory for their dedication to all their students, and I was lucky to have their encouragement.

Thank you so much to my amazing family and friends, who have made the excitement surrounding this novel's publication all the more fun. Marie Taylor, in particular, has been in it for the long haul, and everyone should have a friend like her.

Thank you most especially, and more than I could ever write, to Caitriona, Mum and Dad, who, between them, are the source of every single good thing in my life.

Finally, I feel I might be remiss not to recognise, for their contribution, the very many romantic comedy films I have watched over the years, some of which have been extremely badly reviewed, many of which I have nonetheless enjoyed a lot. And, I perhaps should acknowledge, too, all those people I've encountered either at one film festival or another, or back in my own Erasmus days. I promise, this book is not about you. It really seriously isn't.

Credits

Together with the author, HarperFiction would like to thank the following staff and contributors for their involvement in making this book a reality.

Editorial
Lucy Stewart
Lynne Drew

Sales
Isabel Coburn
Sarah Munro
Alice Gomer
Hannah Avery
Tony Purdue
Jacqueline Murphy

Publicity
Emily Goulding
Elizabeth Dawson
Patricia McVeigh
Ciara Swift

Marketing
Lucy Upton
Sarah Shea

Audio
Charlotte Brown
Fionnuala Barrett

Design
Caroline Young
Claire Ward

Production
Grace Dent
Simon Moore
Sophie Waeland

Operations
Melissa Okusanya
Hannah Stamp

Copyedit
Charlotte Hayes-Clemens

Proofread
Penelope Isaac

Finance
Natassa Hadjinicolaou
Dooshima Gberbo
Katrina Troy

Legal
Arthur Heard